# DEADWORLD ISEKAI

## BOOK 2

# DEADWORLD ISEKAI

## BOOK 2

R. C. Joshua

Podium

*To those learning how to thrive*



Cover design by Thomas Walker

ISBN: 978-1-0394-6958-7

Published in 2024 by Podium Publishing
www.podiumentertainment.com

# DEADWORLD ISEKAI

## BOOK 2

## CHAPTER ONE

# A Fright at the Museum

Nope. No. Nuh-uh. Nope, never, no." Matt was adamant.

"Matt, you have to fight them!"

Matt wasn't yet winded enough that he couldn't talk while sprinting. "I don't, and I won't. We can live in this dungeon! It's nice!"

"You'll starve to death." Lucy wasn't playing around anymore.

Matt activated Survivor's Dash, hopefully putting more distance between him and the yet unresolved issues of this particular dungeon. He opted not to look back, choosing to preserve his capacity of containing trauma for later.

"I won't! There are berries here. I've been leveling Eat Anything! pretty hard. I can probably live off the berries now," Matt said in between steps.

"Okay, maybe, but what about the estate, Matt? What about the plants, and revitalizing ruins?" Lucy asked.

A few days earlier, things had been calm. Things had been good.

Barry's prediction that the system would be sleeping off its energy-deficit coma for a significant amount of time had proven true. Without system-driven shenanigans, Matt and Lucy's lives were much, much more predictable. That meant safety and control.

On the agricultural side of things, it was time to work. The fields needed so very many things to consistently grow plants. Matt hadn't known that soil required a very particular biome of microbes and bacteria to do its job right. Then, several kinds of plants started failing for just that reason. He didn't know some plants relied on wind to pollinate them until Gaia's weird lack of weather caused another few different crops to fail.

The estate system's vast list of purchasables came with solutions for every single one of those problems. Need wind? The estate system didn't have a way to provide that, but it did have huge emergency devices meant to protect delicate crops in coastal regions. Newton's third law of motion meant that those could be installed backwards and upside down to create wind that would pollinate the crops without destroying them. It took several experiments to get the angle just right, but they got it.

Need bacteria? The system had little pills for adding these little microorganisms to the soil, which apparently was a necessary first step to producing workable soil in some swampier Gaian biomes. They didn't involve dozens of reps of almost getting crushed by giant turbines, but they did cost a lot of credits. Need more of the big industrial water sources the system called "Windmill Stones" because of the planet's weird refusal to rain? Matt did, and they weren't cheap.

All these costs added up.

Getting the credits to whip their fields into semi-sustainable shape took the better part of a month of grinding dungeons, extended by the need to rearm Matt. The Swordsman invader had done a number on his weapons. It was nothing repair stones couldn't fix, but fully broken weapons took multiple stones to repair, and that was only if Matt could find all the pieces. His spear had merely been bisected, which made repair relatively simple. His knife had been absolutely shattered, and even after a thorough search, he couldn't find all of the fragments. It was toast.

But after clearing several dungeons, Matt not only managed to get rearmed, but now had a slightly improved arsenal to complement the situations his spear couldn't handle.

*Survivor's Combat Blade*

Somewhere between a very short sword and a very long knife, this blade is a utility player meant to work best in situations where versatility is needed. It doesn't have the reach or power of a full-sized sword, or the concealability of an assassin's dagger, but if you find yourself fighting in a house or cave, you will appreciate the manageability and ease-of-use of this can-do stabbing implement.

*Survivor's Club*

Stabbing is great and all, but we all need variety to help pass the time. The Survivor's Club prides itself on sounding like a support group while actually being an incredibly boring lump of bar steel with a handle on it. It's heavy. It makes no attempt at balance. If you swing it hard enough, it might swing you around in circles like a cartoon batter missing a fastball.

That said, it's a natural at breaking things like bones and natural armor. When your stabbing just won't do the job, this club is ready to provide brawn to cover the failings of the brain.

With all the adjacent dungeons coming back online, they were able to make frequent day trips, clearing multiple low-level dungeons a day. From experience, they either knew what Bonecat-bearing dungeons to avoid, or how to handle all the old familiar Flash Turtle-type weird threats. It was easy going.

But as expensive as it was, equipping his fields was cheap compared to Matt's biggest, most exciting cost.

Matt briefly considered how reasonable Lucy's argument was. The estate was getting more and more automated, but every automation they installed meant more fields to plant. The estate still needed tending. If he never left the dungeon, everything would eventually wither. The planet would be dead once more, and all his efforts would be for nothing. They would never uncover the mysteries of Gaia, or restore it to its former glory.

"No. Fuck it. The plants can die. I'm not fighting those things." Matt wasn't going to budge.

On Earth, Matt had once heard someone at work mention an animal called a flying fox. It sounded awesome. There was no better name for a fanciful animal, and even though he only heard the name in passing, he filed it away for his evening. He spent the rest of the day dreaming of videos of tiny, cute, semi-dog animals yipping and yapping in joy as they whipped through the air, playing with each other.

The reality turned out to be somewhat different.

Flying foxes turned out to be bats. Not just bats, but giant terror-bats with five-foot wingspans and evil vampire-dog faces. Wikipedia informed Matt that despite what they looked like, flying foxes ate fruit and bugs, not kidnapped children and souls. Matt didn't care. He could not and would not contemplate sharing a planet with such terrors. When he read that they reproduced slowly and thus were slowly becoming extinct, he thought, *Good. Cull the heretics. Let them know fire. Let them be stricken from the Earth, and let their names never be spoken.*

Then he watched a bunch of TV and basically forgot they existed. Until now.

The system called its variant of flying foxes Meltbats, and Matt hated them with every element of his entire being. Not only did they look every bit as horrifyingly awful as flying foxes, they were also *wet.* All over their body, they were visibly moist with some sort of sticky, horrible liquid.

Where the liquid dripped on the ground from their freaky bat-talons, it *hissed.*

"Matt! Look! They aren't that scary!"

That was easy for Lucy to say. She lived her life in the weird conceptual space between hologram-that-only-Matt-could-see and full hallucination. She had no chance of contracting rabies. Matt couldn't help looking to see what she was up to, and as his eyes dragged themselves forward when he saw gigantic horror-bat after gigantic horror-bat ripping their way through the space she occupied.

"You know that makes it subtly worse somehow, right?" Matt huffed.

Lucy rolled her eyes. "Matt. Enough. Get to work."

"Fine, fine."

Matt planted his feet, then ducked immediately as his Survivor's Instincts skill kicked in and screamed for him to lower his body to avoid the acid-dripping claws of the bats. *Screw this,* he thought. *Time to go extinct again, you weird, leathery, flying bastards.*

The biggest cost hanging over Matt and Lucy's heads wasn't related to survivability in battle or a steady food supply. It was instead something hardwired to seem just as integral to the human experience.

They were curious.

Expanding their farm had meant the reemergence of a gigantic, wrecked spire. A Gaian dungeon, they were informed, dedicated to the history of the mysterious, barren world on which they now spent their lives.

When the dungeon was fully emerged, they didn't walk to it. They *sprinted.*

Once inside, they found a plinth. In every visible way, this plinth was like any other they had ever seen. It was the exact appearance and size of the plinths that carried them into the dungeons they conquered to get what essential supplies they needed for Matt to survive. But Matt's Survivor's Instincts were just refined enough to pick up one difference: he could use this plinth for spare parts if he needed to. No other entrance stone had ever given him the same feeling. That meant the plinth wasn't, at least as far as his skill could tell, indestructible.

He didn't intend on destroying it anyway. Without a second thought, he reached out and activated it, instantly teleporting him away from his plane of existence.

Besides the few instances where the dungeon system had stopped him in an in-between space, teleports into dungeons had always been instantaneous. This was different. Somehow, this teleport dragged a bit, taking a second or so to complete. Not only that, but the second was a painful one. The nature of teleporting meant Matt didn't have a body during that exact moment in time, but if he had, he would have described the pain as similar to a momentary but excruciating headache.

Before he could worry too much about it, he was through.

The room he found himself in was small and predominantly made of a marble-like stone, with thick pillars of the same material supporting the heavy roof. It had no apparent entrances or exits, and reminded Matt of the foyer of an ancient, classically inspired building, so long as that foyer was built to accommodate an individual or very small group.

A beautifully deep and powerful male voice sounded in the room. Unfortunately, it was speaking gibberish.

"A'chi T'alu Marton. Shuil, oul . . ."

*Ding!*

> Translation activated. As a reincarnator, your Gaian citizenship grants you understanding of all commonly used Gaian spoken languages.

". . . and you are welcomed to the museum. If you think us presumptuous for calling it 'the museum,' please understand that this name was not without justification. It is a marvel of both Gaian ingenuity and system assistance, sketching every aspect of our lives."

In front of Matt, an image winked into existence, like a video projected on the air. In it, he saw flashes of activity. He saw beautiful smiling faces. He saw moments of happiness as friends moved through markets together or played games in beautiful fields of grass. The people were very much like humans. They were perhaps a bit less tall, with more softness in their faces. But they were beautiful. Young or old, male or female, they brimmed with health and happiness.

As the video dissipated, Matt realized something strange. These people weren't acting. On Earth, this kind of video would be acted, edited, and cut to create a representation of life just slightly better than the actual reality. But this wasn't a yogurt commercial. This was, he realized, how these people lived. These were the people he was supposed to save.

"Within these walls, you will learn about our people. About *yourselves.* You will see how we have lived, and how we live. You will see the failures and triumphs of our past, and learn about the hopes of our people. Most of all, you will learn about the danger that threate—"

The voice froze for a split second before the room was plunged into darkness. Or, if not darkness, at least nothingness. As Matt looked down, he saw that he was standing on *nothing.* His head was beset with a splitting pain, and his ears started to vibrate with a loud, hissing feedback. Within seconds, the combination of the two drove him to the floor in agony.

> *Emergency Error Correction*
>
> Simulation failure detected. Threat to the life of simulation participants detected. Initiating emergency expulsion of simulation participants.

After a split second more of pain, Matt found himself on Gaian ground, disoriented and retching. Worse, Lucy seemed affected as well. Matt looked over at her to see her glitching in the same way she did when she tried to talk directly about his authority over the planet Gaia. It was the kind of disruption that had only happened when the system was awake.

It was minutes before they were back on their feet. Lucy made it first, the static in her signal seeming to fade to nothing over the course of a half minute or so. Matt took a bit longer, but could feel his vitality stat pulling him back together as quickly as it could.

"Well, let's not do THAT again," Lucy said as soon as Matt was able to keep his stomach from violently expelling his lunch over the entrance room floor. "That was the worst."

"Yeah, it was. But no, we are absolutely doing that again." Matt reached for the plinth, desperate for just a few more seconds of seeing the faces of the people he had missed out on meeting.

"Matt, wait . . ." Lucy tried to stop him, but it was too late. It didn't end up mattering. When Matt's hand hit the plinth, he wasn't teleported back to the room.

*Ding!*

> This structure is currently damaged beyond safe operational parameters. To repair, please feed repair stones or other sources of system-driven repair into the teleport function of this plinth.
>
> This system will attempt to approximate the total amount of durability points necessary to affect a partial repair of the structure and dungeon projection.
>
> Calculating . . .

After a few moments, the system spit out the value he'd have to reach to reuse the museum safely.

It was a big number.

Gripping his spear, Matt looked above him. There weren't just a few bats. There were dozens of them, flying in circles, waiting for a time to strike him with acid-drenched claws, so they could feed on his melting corpse.

More importantly, they were standing between him and everything he wanted to know.

"Come on, bats. Let's do this."

## CHAPTER TWO

# And I Deserve It

Matt didn't have a coach. He got the impression that even backwoods, podunk planets would at least have *someone* around who knew how to use the local weapons. Even cavemen had an elder or chief around who knew how to launch spears at mammoths exceptionally well. It was just Matt's luck that he had ended up on the one planet where no one was around to train him.

That went double for his skills. Lucy knew a lot of useful information, but what she knew tended to be pretty basic. She had explained, when they met, that system guardians were dropped on planets well before their reincarnators got there. When they hit the ground, the first things they tried to learn were what classes were a good fit for the person they were helping, and as much about those classes as they could. Faced with pure desert, it was kind of hard to learn about classes. Was she helpful? Absolutely. But she was limited.

When it came to learning how to fight, Matt was on his own. It was trial and error against all the worst baddies Gaia's weird evolutionary forces had ever created. And death was always on the line.

As hard as it was, Matt had been making progress. His first big clues came from his fight with the armored invader. Matt had been too scared to focus much on it at the time, but even though the guy only seemed to have a couple of moves, but they were perfect. Survivor's Instincts had done its best to identify weak points in the invader overall, but it never fired *during* one of those strikes. The guy had precise footwork. No wasted movements. Zero openings. Given all the other bad choices the kid had made, it was pretty clear that a skill was driving that perfection.

In comparison, Survivor's Combat did a lot less for Matt. The first level of Survivor's Combat behaved like he had been given a one-lesson crash course in every weapon that ever existed. That was nice, but it was pretty far from being perfect. Every time he leveled the skill, he moved a little further down the competency line, but only in the sense that he took another crash course on the weapons.

At this point, he felt like he was rocking orange belt weaponry skills across the board. He was vaguely competent at everything, not great at anything, and much closer to being a normal person than an overpowering master of the blade. Or club. Or rock. Matt supposed this was why various system notifications had been so clear that Survivor wasn't a pure combat class. It just wasn't powerful in combat.

But that didn't mean the class wasn't powerful at all. Over time, Matt had learned that the real trick to getting the most out of Survivor's Combat was to consider it as a tool for his other skill, Survivor's Instincts.

Survivor's Instincts would point out weak spots or possible tactics for him to follow, and Survivor's Combat would sometimes give him the skills he needed. The faster he could chain those two skills, the more lethal he was.

In what might have been the most important bit, Survivor's Instincts often told him when something was too much for him to handle, and would scream in his mind for him to simply get out of the way. Right now, it was screaming something like, "*It's officially a bad idea to stand right underneath the giant bats who drip acid.*"

He didn't need to be told twice. With Lucy cheering for him in the background, Matt quickly dashed out from under the circle the bats were tracing in the air above him, dodging drops of acid as much as he could. He still suffered from minor burns.

Seeing their quarry run, the Meltbats turned to follow. At the instructions of Survivor's Instincts, Matt intentionally kept his speed slow enough that he remained in their probable attack range, waiting for them to strike.

Soon enough, one took the bait. As it swooped, Matt used his dash skill to jump a few feet back. The Meltbat didn't crash into the ground, but it nearly did. It desperately flapped its wings and hovered in place for a moment. Matt struck, thrusting his spear deep into the thing's chest, and twisting.

The thing let out a shriek as acid sizzled into the spearhead, then did something Matt didn't expect. It flapped backwards, removing itself from the spearhead and taking to the air again, apparently none the worse for the wear. In the meantime, several more bats were swooping down at Matt. He dodged out of the way as best he could, evading all but one of them. The last Meltbat managed to trace down the pole of his spear, spiraling downward and digging its gross, acid-soaked talons into Matt's leg.

Matt screamed as the acid burned the muscles of his thigh, then made the worst mistake he could have. In his pain, he ignored Survivor's Instincts' prodding to stay where he was and tough it out. Instead, he jerked away. As he did, the claw ripped a good-sized portion of flesh out of his leg.

The sheer shock of it sent him to the ground, screaming, and luckily dodging another few Meltbats who had just come around for another bite at the killing-of-Matt burrito. As they flew overhead, drips of acid came off their disgusting rodent-like bodies, burning Matt and motivating him to get back on his feet, ruined leg be damned.

"Matt! Are you okay?" Lucy had panic in her voice. She hadn't expected this low-level dungeon to actually hurt him.

Matt swung his spear two-handed like a baseball bat, batting away nearby Meltbats. "I don't know! There's a ton of these things, and they don't die when I stab them!"

Lucy took a good look at Matt's health bar and her worries went away. "Have you considered stabbing them MORE?"

"I have, dammit! They're fast, okay?"

The swoops kept coming.

"Dammit!" Matt screamed as a particularly motivated bat's claws nicked his arm on one side, and his hand on the other, hurting him and shocking his spear out of his hand.

*Ding!*

*Not now, Barry*, Matt thought, suppressing the notification as he desperately fought with the bats. Barry was a good guy, as dungeon system interfaces went. Hell, in Matt's book, he was a good guy as *saints* went. He had no idea why Barry would start sending notifications now, though. It wasn't like it could help much at the moment.

"You know what? Screw this." Matt was pissed. "I'm going for broke."

His next favorite weapon was his knife, but it was far too close-quarters-oriented for Matt to want to use it on these things. The acid splash would eat him up far before he got through the bats. That left his club. He reached back and yanked the foot or so of bar steel from its loop on his pack.

As he did, the oddest thing happened. All of a sudden, every bat glowed. Every inch of their disgusting heads lit up yellow like they were getting hit by a spotlight. At the same time, the club settled into his hand comfortably in a way no weapon ever had before, begging to be swung.

Without knowing exactly why he could see them, Matt was suddenly certain that the lights on the flying foxes indicated places they'd be especially vulnerable to blows from the weapon he wielded.

*Unless the acid is making me hallucinate. Also a valid hypothesis, I guess.*

Assuming he wasn't in the throes of the worst trip of all time, Matt suddenly found himself in a target-rich environment. It made some sort of sick sense that a mostly-hollow animal with self-cauterizing wounds would be fairly resistant to piercing damage. At the same time, simple logic meant those same enemies wouldn't fare so well with blunt force trauma.

Without better options, Matt decided to take a chance on whatever was going on. As the next bat dove towards him, he set his feet as best he could and swung the club. And for once, everything was, if not perfect, about as good as Matt could imagine it being. The timing was great, and the trajectory was flawless. The club took as much force from the rotation of his body as it could, and the very last inch of the bar made contact with the bat's head.

Its skull all but exploded. There was no question but that it was dead. It went limp all at once, pinwheeling through the air like a dead goose.

*Finally.*

The balance of battle, Matt had found, was a delicate thing. Once you found the trick to a fight, things felt very different. He didn't blanch anymore at the thought of taking down a group of Clownrats. He knew how to deal with them, which made taking them down easy. On the other hand, a foreign horror like the Meltbats, unlike anything he had encountered before, posed a real threat. Until he found the trick.

The balance had now shifted in his favor. Matt's injured leg ensured he wasn't mobile, but with almost every strike landing, he didn't have to be. The club was doing everything he asked. As Meltbats came down from the sky, he put them to the ground, permanently. Despite all the pain, he was dimly aware that he was looking the coolest he had ever been.

Eventually, there was only one bat left in the air. Whatever primitive mind it had was just powerful enough for it to survey the battlefield and conclude things weren't going that well. Matt felt the air start to churn as the thing hit the afterburners and started to flee away from him, faster than he had seen any of the Meltbats move before.

*No, you don't, you bastard. I want out of this dungeon NOW.*

Picking up his spear, Matt was vaguely aware there was no way he was going to make this shot. The bat was already more than twenty feet away and rapidly putting more distance between them. He threw it anyway. Against all odds, it was a good throw. It sailed through the air, piercing completely through the Meltbat, which discovered, to its immense distress, that it couldn't fly with a spear through it. As it crashed to the Earth, Matt hobbled after it. Within a few seconds, he had gelatinized the last of his enemies.

"Matt . . ." Lucy was gobsmacked. "What in the hell was that? It was like you turned competent all of a sudden. Do you just . . . not suck now?"

"Lucy . . ."

"No, I mean it. You should have seen yourself. You stopped being useless. It was like you had actually practiced everything in a mirror."

Matt rolled his eyes. If he kept feeding her openings, Lucy could go on like this for hours. It was the main way she passed her time, and she had a lot of time for practice.

"Anyways," Matt did his best to put on his back-to-business voice, "I think Barry did something. He sent me a notification. I was actually just about to check it, if you're interested."

"I am, but . . . aren't you forgetting something?"

"What?"

"The stabilization spike." Matt realized with horror what she meant. The stabilization spike would keep a small section of monster meat from dissipating, allowing Matt to progress his Eat Anything! skill, which in turn let him get by better on less food. It was absolutely vital to his survival that he used the skill as often as possible.

It was just that there was no chance at all he was going to do it. None.

"I'd rather die than eat these. I mean that literally. If it comes down to eating the *acid-soaked giant bats* or dying, I'm choosing death."

"Okay, I understand, but is that true even when they are . . ." Lucy's eyes glinted as she finished her sentence. "*Battered?*"

"I hate you." Matt sighed.

Lucy laughed, not at all discouraged. "And I deserve it!"

## CHAPTER THREE

# Plenty of Class

Lucy didn't stop prodding Matt to eat the bats until well after they had dissipated enough that it wasn't a realistic option anymore. Matt was pretty sure she was joking about it. There were just some foods that were too dangerous to eat. Even fully cooked, things like poison toads would probably do more harm than good. And acidic, giant bats definitely fell in that category.

Luckily, the process of dissipation didn't take long. The mystery of Matt's sudden competency increase remained to be solved, and as soon as Lucy's merciless bat puns were suppressed, he pulled up his system notifications to see what had happened.

*Class Evolution Complete!*

Congratulations! You failed to die long enough that you forced the system's hand.

After proving your worth in far more combat than you might think was necessary, it has been deemed appropriate to progress your class in a direction more appropriate to the kinds of challenges you will face. Not that you didn't earn it, but you should feel lucky here. Class evolutions are **rare**. As you well know, the kind of stuff you had to do to get here was just as likely to kill you as it was to result in any upside.

Class evolutions are more than a lateral move. There are some tradeoffs, but most of the core functionality of your class has been preserved while, in this case, your combat efficiency skyrocketed.

Your new class is called **Battlefield Survivor**. There are more details to be found from examining individual skills, but here are the highlights:

Your class focuses on surviving encounters rather than winning duels or dealing damage. So you aren't the pure-combat equal of a greataxe swinging Tanker. But you are their equal in combat prowess.

You've won past fights in a variety of ways, and that doesn't change. Your fighting style will rely on good decisions, trickery, and creativity.

Almost all your non-combat skills have been preserved, with only a few changes in how they work. Good news: you can keep eating slugs or whatever it is you do in your free time.

Enjoy!

PS: Yes, this **also means what you think it means**. Keep your head on a swivel, Matt.

Matt looked up from the notification, making eye contact with Lucy. "Yup. Class evolution."

"No way! Is it good?" Lucy was excited.

"Barry seems to think so. I haven't got into the details yet."

"Well, hurry up!"

Matt mentally flicked open the next notification.

*Survivor's Combat > Advanced Survivor's Combat*

The first iteration of this class focused on general baseline competence. You were good-not-great with any weapon you laid your hands on. Now you are more like an old, grizzled commando. You fight with each and every weapon as if you've trained with them for years. You might be less sword master and more angry sergeant, but the outcome is the same either way.

You aren't a guy to be messed with.

Advanced Survivor's Combat functions by giving you the skills of someone who has trained up to a high level of mastery in one weapon, but is using another weapon out of necessity. You have much improved footwork and significantly higher general competence with all weapons.

*Rub Some Dirt In It*

You lack healing skills or heavy armor, but that doesn't mean you are easy to put down. Rub Some Dirt In It gives you the toughness and regenerative abilities of a store-brand troll, letting you bounce back to peak shape from small injuries that would add up for anyone else. And that's just what you get while combat is ongoing. When you break free of active fighting and hole up, you heal even faster.

Rub Some Dirt In It functions by granting slow regeneration in combat, slightly faster regeneration while fleeing combat, and substantially improved healing when at rest or hiding. In addition, it grants small resistances to most forms of physical damage.

*Survivor's Dash > Spring-Fighter*

Running away is great, but overall mobility is better.

There's always someone faster than you, but that doesn't necessarily mean you are easy to catch. Spring-Fighter replaces the pure escape focus of Survivor's Dash with overall, on-demand evasiveness. Spring-Fighter lets you move towards, away from, or around enemies at much greater speeds with small, unpredictable bursts of motion.

Sounds great? We think so too, but that utility comes at a cost. Survivor's Dash's exceptional movement speed away from foes has been replaced by a much smaller increase that is a significant drain of your stamina resource.

In addition, Spring-Fighter is not an automatic skill. It is under your complete manual control, and is reliant on user control for its full potential. If you tell it to dodge directly into a sword strike, it will, and it won't look pretty.

Spring-Fighter functions by allowing you to convert stamina into injections of speeds that make their normal movements faster. This speed comes at the cost of a steep STAM drain that increases non-linearly the farther and faster you try to move.

*Survivor's Instincts > Survivor's Reflexes*

We all know what's gotten the closest to killing you recently, and it hasn't been insufficient knowledge of vines. In that spirit, Survivor's Reflexes preserves all the benefits you receive from Survivor's Instincts, but shifts further development in a combat-focused direction.

When Survivor's Reflexes detects a weakness in an opponent's defenses, it alerts you to it visually, replacing the subliminal mental alerts of Survivor's Instincts. Given sufficient perspective and time, it will highlight these areas with an illusory light, showing you where to strike.

In addition, Survivor's Reflexes also attempts to show you when to strike by highlighting moments when an opponent is off-balance or vulnerable.

Be warned: the ability of Survivor's Reflexes to identify and highlight weaknesses is a function of your stats compared to your enemies, how much time you've studied them or extremely similar enemies, and your baseline (non-system) observations. In some cases, the skill will take longer to trigger. In others, it won't trigger at all.

Survivor's Reflexes continues to scale off PER and WIS, but now has a distinct bias towards PER.

"Oh, this is fantastic." Matt was excited. He wasn't terribly excited about losing his very best escape skill, but what he got in trade was at least equitable. Everything else seemed like a clear upgrade, including the loss of Survivor's Instincts to Survivor's Reflexes. The non-combat elements of Survivor's Instincts had long been adequate for the kind of threats Matt tended to face. Being able to see where to attack stronger enemies, provided he could keep them from smashing him into smaller fragments long enough?

*Exquisite.* Matt thought, remembering how good it had felt to massacre the bats. The right weapon to the right fight. *Delicious, almost.*

"What happened? I can't see your windows, Matt," Lucy asked.

Matt quickly got Lucy up to speed.

"Wow, yeah, that does sound good. If what you did to those poor baby bats generalizes . . ."

In no world would Matt call the bats he had just faced 'babies.' "To be very clear, they were unholy abominations. If what I did to them applies to other things, we should be able to expand our level range for dungeons a bit."

"Maybe. If we do it very slowly. No use dying."

"Agreed."

But that wasn't all. Matt had several more notifications waiting for him. There couldn't be many more skill notifications, so he assumed the others were minor stat increases and similar rewards for living his life while the system's reward function was down. He mentally flicked open the next notification, hoping he'd see something good.

*Eat Anything!* > *Combat Consum . . .*
**ERROR > ERROR**

The window suddenly winked out.

"Uh . . . Lucy?"

"Yeah?"

"There seem to be some system difficulties."

She looked at him, quizzically. "Good?"

"No, I mean, not the kind that hurt him. Maybe the kind that hurt us."

The system window attempted to reopen before immediately fizzling out again before it could display any text. Then did it again. And again.

"Definitely not the kind of difficulty that's good for us," Matt repeated.

Matt caught Lucy up on the window weirdness while they waited. Minutes passed. Eventually, a new window opened and stayed open, this time in the background color that indicated Barry was talking.

*Dungeon System Message*

An error with the Gaian System Instance's notifications has been detected by the dungeon system, which issued a query regarding the error. Sufficient time has passed for the dungeon system to exercise Rule #45082 J, allowing it to look into unaddressed errors and attempt to resolve them if it so chooses.

Okay Matt, here's the skinny: I have no idea what's going on here. This isn't an energy budget thing. The system instance wouldn't have issued your class evolution or any of your achievements without the budget to cover all of them. If he sends one, he should send all.

More importantly, I know this isn't the system instance because as far as I can see, Eat Anything! Is temporarily **disabled**. Not changed to something else, not left alone, but **disabled.** The system instance can't do that. There are dozens of rules about skills. Something else is going on here.

As near as I can tell, some outside force is messing with this skill. The problem is that there shouldn't be any outside force to mess with this skill. For now, sit tight. Enjoy your other skills, and I'll work on this as fast as I can.

"Well, that's not great." Matt let Lucy know what was going on as he summed up the situation. "Especially with us running low on food cubes."

"We have the crops now, though. You don't have to resort to the food cubes much anyways."

"True. Unless something bad happens."

"Knock on wood." Lucy pantomimed doing the thing she couldn't, by definition, actually do.

Matt spent the next few minutes flipping through the rest of the notifications, finding most of them to be pretty mundane, with a few small stat increases and item drops. He would look through them later, he decided. Assessing his status screen would make for some nice bedtime reading. He had finally found a way to ignore the suns, and without the threat of the system instance, he felt safe enough to kick off his shoes for solid sleep. He'd enjoy that for as long as he could.

"So, to address the elephant in the room . . ."

Lucy looked like she was waiting for this, apparently not wanting to mess up the new-skill cheeriness Matt had up to this point. "Yeah. It looks like the system instance is coming back online. How long do you think we have? Is it possible it's awake *now?*"

Matt shook his head. "I don't think so. Barry said that he'd have to pay us what we were owed before he could pay back his own energy debt and come online. I don't know how long that's going to take, but we should have at least some time."

"How long?"

"Shouldn't you know? Hours? Days? Weeks?" Matt shrugged. "There's no way to know. Short of asking Barry, and he would have told us if he could. I'm guessing that penalties-for-stretching rules mechanic works both ways."

"Matt. I don't like this. There isn't anything we can do?"

Above all else, the last few months had been nice. They had both, for better or worse, gotten used to a life that, while not completely safe, was at least dangerous in predictable ways. They still had to go into dungeons, but they could do so without worrying about system shenanigans pumping up the difficulty or creating some other kind of death-trap. Outside the dungeons, the worst risk they faced was Matt tripping over something, and there wasn't much for him to trip over.

Lucy continued, "And it's worse, Matt, because he's going to be coming back pissed. And if he's been able to think while he was offline, he'll be coming back with plans."

"There's nothing much we can do about it. Maybe we can delay it if we get more achievements he has to pay out, but . . ." Matt's voice trailed off.

Lucy nodded. She understood that the quickest, surest way for Matt to get achievements was by surviving things he shouldn't. They both preferred keeping near-death situations to a minimum.

Matt found his voice again. "But we've dealt with it before. And we can deal with it again. We put the hurt on him once. If he comes back swinging, we'll just put him down again."

## CHAPTER FOUR

# Mana Vampire

Between dungeon runs, improving the estate, and a lot of digging, time during the system's absence had passed quickly for Matt and Lucy.

In the meantime, they had multiple harvests of various kinds of fruits and vegetables. Since Matt was eager to shift his food consumption away from his dwindling supply of foods, he had begun to do his best to exist on the vegetarian diet the estate was now providing.

The only problem was that the estate system didn't do a very good job of explaining the nutritional value of the food. Gaian vegetables didn't map one-to-one with Earth plants, so even Matt's limited knowledge of Earth nutrition didn't do him much good. Since getting some weird Gaian-fantasy scurvy wasn't high on his list of ways to get killed, figuring out a balance was a high priority.

Luckily, it was a problem he could brute force even in the absence of knowledge. He had taken to a rotation of meals that guaranteed he was eating a pretty good amount of every edible plant every couple of days. He hoped relying on blind variety would help cover his ignorance, get him all his amino acids, and keep him more or less alive in the same way the food cubes always had.

After a couple of unsuccessful attempts to cook everything together in some kind of meatless stew, Matt eventually settled on combinations of fruits and vegetables that went reasonably well together as salads. Given that he spent all of his time either walking, killing monsters, or farming, these salads ended up having to be pretty big to cover his energy expenses.

In this new broken-skill era, *big salad* had become an understatement.

Without Eat Anything!, the salad Matt had put together was gargantuan beyond all reason. By the time Matt finished it, he was full to the point his stomach hurt.

The last few bites of plain nothingness were the hardest to fork down. Matt wasn't sure, but the food had been tasting worse in the past few days. An all-plant diet devoid of seasoning had taken a lot to get used to, but the last few meals were beyond even that.

"This food tastes . . . funky, I guess?"

"Are you sure it isn't just a side effect of coming off a whole life of meat and into several months of just cubes? I don't have taste buds, Matt. I'm not sure what shifting your diet in weird ways all the time does to them."

"I dunno. You might be right. This feels different than that, somehow."

"Well, it's not like the vegetables aren't fresh. If you want something different, you could try figuring out if Barry will let you steal and tame some Clownrats."

Matt winced. "I'll eat the salads."

But the food still felt *off*, somehow. He wasn't sure what to attribute it to; it could have been anything from the absence of his eating-related skills or even recent memories of horrific monster bats.

*Ding!*

*You can't give me achievements for eating big salads*, Matt thought. As much as he appreciated the help, that kind of thing felt like too big of a risk for Barry to be taking with the rules. The system was going to wake up eventually, and the last thing he wanted was to lose Barry in some weird AI court case over technicalities.

It was only after pulling up the window to see what kind of contortions Barry had pulled to make the achievement defendable that Matt saw that it was actually something much different. And much worse.

*Warning: Mana-deficient Food Ingested*

Many reincarnators lived lives on worlds with little to no system involvement, and thus have no concept of what is commonly referred to as magical force, life force, or mana. Whether you knew of it or not, your planet contained these forces. Life is not sustainable long-term without them.

You have somehow managed to consume food that is deficient in this force. This might be because you ate food grown on blighted land, food affected by life-draining magic in some way, or food that had its life force damaged by some other occurrence.

In the short term, this is not a danger. Mana-deficient food is not *poisonous*, nor does it lack in conventional nutrition. With that said, a long-term diet of mana-deficient foods would "wash out" the levels of mana produced by your body over time, eventually resulting in a variety of problems.

This message is meant as a **warning** for anyone living in a magical, system-driven world for the first time, and not a complete guide to mana-deficient foods. Please seek advice from locals inhabitants to understand why your food was mana-deficient, as well as more details on the specific issues that mana deficiency will cause your body.

The solution to this problem is quite simple, however, and can be shared. Find and eat foods that are not mana-deficient.

"Uh, Lucy . . ." Matt relayed everything he had just read to her.

"Shit. One second." Lucy buried herself in her store of information. Her expression grew more serious as time went on.

Unable to bear the silence, Matt offered his thoughts. "I don't get it though. I can see all sorts of things being wrong with the food because of, well—" Matt gestured at everything around them with a big sweep of his arm. "All this mess. That part makes sense. But why didn't this message trigger before? I've been eating this stuff for weeks, at least."

"It has to be Eat Anything!. It was probably papering over whatever the problem was with the food. And without it . . ."

"I'm screwed?"

"There's always the food cubes. It's not like we're out of those, even if I don't much like you having to dip into emergency reserves. Eat one."

"But, I'm full. I just ate this gigantic salad. You saw me."

"You ate a gigantic *poison salad*, Matt. We have no idea what that crap is doing to you right now."

"But . . ."

"No buts! Matt, I'm not the best system guardian in the universe. I admit it. But I'm *NOT* going to let the reincarnator I guard get taken out by a *fucking salad*. It would be *embarrassing*. Eat a damn cube."

Matt huffed, but went and got a cube to do as he was told. Lucy's logic made sense and he knew it was pointless to argue with her. Fighting with an indefatigable hologram was a dumb decision in the best of times. She would keep hammering her point until Matt gave in.

But there was, it turned out, something wrong with the cubes.

Matt brought the cube towards his mouth, then suddenly pulled it away. The thing stank. It wasn't a spreading scent exactly, in the sense that he wouldn't have been able to smell it across a room. But close up? It was vile.

"What in the . . . smell this. Is it off to you, too?"

"Matt, I can't smell. It's rotten, or something?"

"Something like that, yeah." Matt did a quick double-take. "Wait, you can't smell? This whole time, you haven't been able to smell anything?"

"No, Matt. This is what you get for never asking questions about me. I can't smell. You know. This is what happens when you don't show an interest in other people."

"What about . . ." Matt wracked his brain for examples of things she should have been able to smell, but couldn't. "What about when I farted, that time?"

"That time? You do it all the time."

"Whatever. You did the whole waving-your-hand-in-front-of-your-face thing. Why?"

"Because it's still *gross,* Matt. I walk behind you a lot. You should move off before you do that. It's just common courtesy."

"But you just said that you can't smell anything!"

"It's still poop gas in the air, Matt. I'm not exactly real, but I'm real enough to know that's gross." Lucy jumped over and got up in his face. "And all this talk is not going to distract me. Go get another cube, one that isn't rotten, and eat it. We have other stuff to do!"

"We aren't on a schedule!"

"EAT THE DAMN CUBE, MATTHEW!"

Matt smiled inwardly. *Look who's a little nutritionist all of a sudden.*

He didn't want to eat a cube right now, but he could, and he would. It was nice to have someone looking after him, and he wasn't going to spit in the face of the only person in the universe who cared about him. Barry, the dungeon system, didn't count. His official job description was to maybe kill him.

Going back to the open cube bag, he pulled another cube and lifted it towards his mouth.

Most of the way there, he stopped. It was spoiled too. He pulled out another cube, then another. The whole bag had turned. In his thinking, that was a huge loss. Every one of those cubes represented an entire day's worth of provisions. They were a really primal source of survival, and he hoarded them like treasure. Reluctantly, he pulled another cube bag from his pack, opened it and removed a new cube from a fresh batch.

It was bad too.

Lucy had been watching Matt. Her expression started off as being annoyed, but slowly morphed into concern.

"Umm, Lucy? We have a problem."

After testing out all of the bags of food cubes and finding that they all smelled funny, Matt and Lucy laid everything out in front of them.

"They can't have all gone bad at once, Matt. That doesn't even seem possible."

"Maybe they had the same expiration date?" Matt offered.

"You know that's just marketing, right? Companies just slap a date on it so they don't get sued," Lucy responded.

"Wait, what? How do you . . . okay, never mind. It might be Eat Anything!

again. I think it . . . okay, bear with me. In the skill description, it says I can stomach mildly spoiled food. That's the baseline description, that's been with me since level 1."

"And you think it's been curtailing your sense of smell so you don't have a reaction to spoiled food?"

"I think so. It's not just that it lets me stomach spoiled food. It lets me eat it at all. I think all these cubes have always been kind of on the cusp, and Eat Anything! just papered over it."

"So you can't eat it?"

"I mean, maybe. Eat Anything! got disabled a while ago, but I guess the effects lingered on. I don't know how to parse the semantics of 'mildly spoiled' or something the system thinks I couldn't stomach otherwise. I could give it a go."

"Do."

It was ten minutes before Matt felt confident he wouldn't puke again. Leaving a suddenly over-fertilized turnip patch in his wake, he walked back to Lucy.

"I'm going to starve to death."

"Maybe." Lucy had the faraway look in her eyes she got when she was looking through the system's reference materials. "Maybe not. There's something in the estate system that might fix this."

"Some kind of magic fertilizer?"

"Not quite. Go into the house accessories and furnishings tab. Look up 'mana generator'."

Matt did. It was in a section of what the system termed cultivation and recovery aids, ranging from floor mats to an awful lot of things that looked like the kind of lamps you'd buy at a head shop. The mana generator was in the latter category, looking like a mix between a fortune-teller's orb and a lava lamp.

"What does this even do?"

"From the description, it's for regenerating your mana points faster. You never had any mana to begin with, so we never cared about this kind of item before. But if you were a wizard, or something else that had and used a lot of mana? Having one of these would let you cast more spells faster, so long as you were near it. You can't move them around with you, so it's more like something that would make you tougher when you were at home and let you practice more."

It made sense, in a weird training fanatic sort of way. Matt had known guys who owned their own weight benches and drank pickle juice just so they could lift more weights. This wasn't weirder than that, except he didn't think any of them had weight benches that cost more than a good-sized house. This literally did, at least based on how the estate system had priced them.

"And you think setting this up will fix the crops?"

"Not all of them. But I've been thinking about this, and I have some guesses about how all this works. In the message you got about mana deficiency, the plants had to be *drained* of life energy to not work. Or grown on blighted land, which I assume drains the land of mana. But mana has to come from somewhere, right? I'm guessing if we run this thing for a while and get the soil loaded up, maybe the problem will fix itself. And, if the plants are healthy, they might start feeding mana back into the field. If not, we just run one for each field, and see if it sticks. Bare minimum, we need enough vegetables for you to survive, and this thing is our best bet at the moment. I doubt the plants would want mana pills."

"It's not cheap."

"The alternative is turning into some kind of mana vampire or something, Matt."

"Point taken. We can start saving up for that tomorrow."

"Tomorrow?"

"Yup. Don't forget what day it is. Today is museum day."

## CHAPTER FIVE

# Stand and Fight

"Slash, slash, stab."

"Why are you saying the moves out loud, Derek?" Artemis asked.

Derek, now truly Derek again, huffed.

"I just want to. It's a thing." He leapt backward, barely avoiding a sweep from a demon's claw. It was slow, but so was he. It was all he could do to keep out of the way of even the most basic attacks, especially when Artemis broke his rhythm with her questions.

"Slash, stab, chop." It was a simple combo, but it kept him alive.

When Derek stopped moping and decided to start over, the first thing he did was to run to his plinth to obtain a new class. And looking through them, there were quite a few doozies. He didn't know *why* the guardian would recommend Death Knight, but it sounded awesome. Derek was about to select it when he paused.

"Chop, chop. Chop. Stab!"

All of this chopping and stabbing was exhausting. But it was necessary. Derek realized that while Death Knight sounded just as great as Blademaster, he was not great. Plastering a class over his problems wouldn't help him beat the demon lord. He needed to do better than that.

"Stab, parry, DODGE, shit, did you see that? Slash, slash."

As Derek thought back to his fights with the demon lord on that godforsaken planet, he realized that the demon lord had never once used a skill. Maybe that last tricky bit at the end with the insane amount of dirt that he shoveled upwards was a skill, but there were no combat skills. So Derek stood in front of the plinth, thinking.

The demon lord didn't seem stronger than Derek, or faster than him, or really that durable, not that he ever landed a hit on his slippery foe. His weapons were shit. And he still won. How?

And so, Derek waited in front of the plinth for an answer. When one didn't come, he walked away from his class selection.

"Stab, stab. YES!"

The last stab hit home. The Imp flopped to the ground, struggled for a few moments, then died. Imps like these were literally the lowest-level foes you could face. They were little flying lizards with some level of animal strength and speed, but not much. Asadel would have put them down without a thought.

Sure, they looked like little dragons, but that's where the similarities stopped. Were they part of the demonic forces, and thus an evil to be eradicated? Yes. The evil they spread was on a smaller scale. They stole chickens, or tried to hurt children. Farmers killed them by the dozens with pitchforks. Their raw aggression made them a little bit dangerous, but they were much more "rabid house cat" than "dark terror lord."

Anyone with a few levels under their belt could take them easily. It's just that Derek was one of the few adults on the planet still at level 1.

*Derek Cyrus*
*Level 1 Unclassed*
**HP:** 25
**MP:** N/A
**STAM:** 10
**STR:** 5
**DEX:** 5
**PER:** 5
**VIT:** 5
**WIS:** 5
**INT:** 5
Warning: The unclassed do not have class goals, and thus cannot gain levels. Their stats can only be improved through great effort. There is no advantage in putting off class selection.

Derek wiped off his brow. He was sweating like a pig, and he had only fought a single imp. His weapon was plain old steel, something that the old man had lying around and was willing to sell to him cheap. It was heavy, much heavier than his claymore had been, even though it was just a short, basic one-handed deal with no enchantments or stat buffs.

"Please, please don't talk to me so much while I'm fighting. I'm going to get clawed," Derek said.

"Derek, anybody hearing you do that in battle would know exactly what was coming. It's a bad habit. I think. I've never actually heard anyone say one hundred percent of their moves out loud before. Are you sure this is a good idea?" Artemis sounded genuinely concerned.

The problem, Derek thought, was that people *already* knew every move he was going to throw. When he got the sword, he went out back to the old man's training yard to get used to it. Before he knew it, he was back in the massive, two-handed overhead swing of things, and had done about twenty of them before he even realized it. Artemis wanted to talk about bad habits? He was the king of them.

Saying every move while he fought was the only solution he had found so far. At least that way, he *had* to notice when he was on his fifth or sixth consecutive, identical slash.

And then he could mix it up.

"I'm not going to keep doing it forever." Derek smiled. "It's just what I'm doing for now. Don't worry. I talked to the old man about it, he said it's okay for a while."

"Oh, I see." Hearing that the old man had approved of it, Artemis stopped bothering Derek about it. It wasn't just politeness, either. It was like she forgot the objection entirely.

*What is that old man, really?* Derek had always considered the old man to be a bit of a rube, someone he could relax around who was also really good at making swords. He never saw that nobody else joined in his banter.

Since he had been back, Derek had started noticing these smaller things. Like how much quiet respect nearly every older reincarnator seemed to have for the blacksmith.

"What's the story on that old man, anyway? He fights pretty good for a blacksmith," prodded Derek.

"You'd have to ask him that. I try not to talk about people who aren't present."

*Damn.*

On top of the respect that the blacksmith carried, Derek also found that nearly everyone who seemed to know anything about the old man was unreasonably discreet. That was a problem, sort of. While Derek's trip to Gaia had wiped out all of his levels and his class, one thing did survive. His quest to figure out what the old man's deal was.

"Got it, sorry." Derek realized that Artemis was still looking at him.

"No problem." She smiled.

Derek was amazed how many problems could be solved by just apologizing.

"Anyway." Artemis looked down at Derek's sword, then his beginner's equipment. "How long is all of this going to last? I don't mind, exactly. But time is time. If you had a class, I could teach you about that class. You are wasting time and experience."

Derek shook his head. "I'm not getting a class yet. I have too many problems to fix. I can do that better when I don't have distractions."

It wasn't a lie. He had a lot of bad moments lately, but the second worst was when he picked up a training sword and found he didn't even know how to hold it. His footwork was the same. He was tripping over every other swing he made with the sword.

The old man had been, if not exactly nice, effective. He had put Derek's hand around the sword the right way, and taught him how to take basic steps the right way. There wasn't any of the usual banter, and he hadn't called him stupid.

Actually, ever since Derek had come back, the blacksmith had stopped talking to him, except to give answers when Derek asked him specific questions. He wouldn't refuse to help outright, but their relationship had fundamentally changed when Asadel ran off to some planet to almost get himself killed and hid it from him.

In short, Derek had hurt his feelings. That was the first-worst thing. Worse than losing the class and his name together was finding out the old man had cared about him, and Derek had betrayed that.

"Derek! Run!"

*Like hell I will.*

Another big downside of Derek's classless state had just shown itself. He was fighting his fourth or fifth field imp, and finally starting to get the hang of it. Then, the Imp decided to change things up and slashed out at his neck.

He jumped back entirely too far to get out of the way, and then, in his embarrassment, went for a charge and two-handed overhead swing out of pure reflex.

Only he didn't quite finish the move. A massive cramp erupted in his calf. Instead of bisecting the stupid imp, he fell forward towards the ground, barely getting his arms down in time to catch the impact with his elbows instead of his face.

In that painful moment, he realized the truth. He was out of shape. Not horribly, but enough that the sudden injection of a hard day's walking followed by several rounds of intense fighting caused his standard-issue human body to experience exercise-related failure.

After a few seconds, the Imp got over the sudden animal shock of having its opponent fall over without actually doing anything. It flapped its way over to Derek with its claws bared. Downed prey was something it understood very well, and it was obvious that this was its big chance.

Derek's calf was still fully cramped, and the sheer pain it was radiating didn't bode well for trying to use it. With few options, he managed to roll over onto his back as the Imp approached, waving his sword upwards into the air to fend it off. The angle was all wrong, and his valiant attempts to defend himself did nearly nothing to stop the small demon from latching onto his right arm with its claws and biting down on his forearm with its teeth.

The shock of pain was unbelievable. Vitality and various class bonuses had done more for Derek than he had ever realized. Now, he was experiencing the full, human pain of getting shredded by an enemy claw for the first time. His arm spasmed in reaction to the attacks, and the sword fell and clattered against a rock on the ground. The Imp also started flapping its wings and tugged upwards like it was trying to pull Derek's arm out.

Reaching across his body, Derek grabbed the sword with his left hand and brought it high towards the Imp. There was no way he could get a good swing with it, everything felt wrong. But Derek suddenly realized that he had other options.

*Swords are sharp for a reason. And this is one of the old man's swords. Should be plenty sharp.*

He couldn't swing, but the sword could still cut. Contorting his body, Derek heaved the sword up and let it fall onto the demon's back. It barely scratched the Imp, though the extra weight did bring the Imp lower. Then, Derek sawed the sword back. As the sword came back, the edge of the blade caught the Imp's skin and bit a deep wound. The thing shrieked and immediately let go of his sword arm.

Derek wasted no time shifting his sword to his dominant hand, rolling over, and getting his good leg under him. Even standing on one leg would be better than fighting from his back, and he would NOT be quasi-tea-bagged by this little chicken-stealing bastard anymore.

At this point, Artemis screamed for him to run. But he wouldn't. Strong people did not run from monsters that were essentially sharp pigeons. Derek was going to stand and fight.

CHAPTER SIX

# Common Man

As the Imp came towards Derek, he thrust the sword forward as hard as he could.

It wasn't a strong thrust, considering how badly the demon had shredded his arm and how weak Derek was, even in peak condition. Beads of blood were pooling down his arm and vitality would only kick in after the battle, so he had to end things fast.

Unfortunately, there was no way that Derek could hit a pinpoint strike like a thrust against a moving target. The Imp easily dodged his attack and kept rushing forward. Luckily, Derek had anticipated that. Earlier in the day, Derek had been startled to see an Imp duck beneath his attack while still in midair and keep its momentum. It had proven to be a pretty effective move, one that had made Derek scramble in response.

Not this time.

This time, the Imp's dodge was countered with a pretty good-sized rock, about the biggest that Derek could palm. Derek had found one within arm's reach as he stood up, a fair bit of luck. As the Imp rushed forward, it smacked headfirst into the uncomfortable reality of Derek's rock. To it, that rock was a pretty good-sized boulder.

The hit didn't kill it, but the Imp was stunned and flopped down to the ground. Derek's sword arm had enough strength left to drop the point of the sword straight down on the demon, ending it.

*Fuck yes!* Derek thought, trying and immediately failing to lift the sword back up to an overhead victory pose. *Ouch, no, never mind.*

Artemis was there almost immediately.

"That was, Derek, really amazing. I have never, in all my life, seen a grown man almost lose in a fight to one of those things. It was like watching a town guard get slapped around by an angry baby."

Derek scowled, and almost snapped at her. Asadel didn't take that kind of crap from a non-hero, non-reincarnated, nobody of a trainer. But Derek wasn't Asadel anymore, and a deep breath reminded him that Artemis wasn't what he used to think of her, either. She was a lot of things. She knew all the things that he needed to know, and plenty of other things too. She was his trainer. And most importantly, she was stronger than him.

"I . . . agree. What could I have done better?"

It took Artemis a full five seconds to recover from the shock of that one. It was the best hit he had landed all day.

Derek was still limping when they got back to town. Artemis had a healing skill, something called Scout's Aid, but although it was able to close up the relatively minor wounds on his arm, it wouldn't do anything for the more obscure, internal wound of his calf cramp. He eventually managed to get the muscle to unlock, but it still hurt.

Artemis had shrugged when he asked her what to do about it. She spent all her time around various combat and warfare classes, people who uniformly had high enough vitality that they didn't have to care about mundane things like cramps. Unfortunately, Derek's knowledge of cramps was similarly limited. It started and stopped with the concept of stretching. He knew stretching worked before exercise to prevent cramps, but had no idea if it would help after the fact.

That said, he'd try anything. He doubted it would injure him, and dodging the expense of a full healer would be nice. The only problem was that all the stretches he actually knew for legs came from the old man, who had tried to convince him that flexibility was valuable. There was some truth to that—flexibility wasn't enhanced by stats for most classes. That would have been fine if it wasn't for the fact that every stretch the old man had shown him for legs involved a kind of wooden rack of his own devising, one that was meant to be used from a variety of positions to "get the most ya can outta ya time," as the old man put it.

Derek's hunt had started in the early afternoon and all the fighting, healing, and advice-getting had taken time. Now was past the time when the old man usually closed up shop, which meant Derek could probably just go into his training yard without bothering anyone. The old man had given Derek a free pass to go into the yard at any time. He might be mad at Derek, but he hadn't ever revoked that permission.

Buoyed by doing something that felt borderline illegal and the fact that the old man would never know, Derek limped his way across town to the old man's shop. The gate to the yard never had a lock, probably another missed sign that the old man was both more respected and more scary than he appeared. The rack was in the same place though, and Derek got to work.

The walk there had done him some good, but the first stretches were excruciating. Worse, at the time the old man had been running him through the routine, Derek had barely listened. He now found out he had retained at best twenty percent of the stretches he had been taught, and had no idea what muscle groups they were supposed to target. He ran through what he did remember, in pain the whole time, hoping that by the end of a couple of run-throughs it would all be worth it.

"That's all wrong, ya know."

Derek disengaged from the stretching rack and wheeled around to find the old man standing there.

"Ah . . . sorry. Yeah. I don't remember as much as I should. And sorry for, you know, being here. I thought you'd be home."

The old man grunted out a sarcastic laugh. "This IS my home, boy. You were never curious what was on the second floor?"

To the extent Derek had thought about that, which wasn't much, he had assumed it was probably full of iron or something.

"That's hurt?" The old man pointed at his leg, the one in pain.

"Yeah. How'd you know?"

"I can see." The old man walked over and knelt, lightly pinching the back of Derek's calf with his big fingers. It hurt. A lot. "It's right here. What'd ya do to it? Get it cursed? Poison?"

"Just too much exercise."

"Too much exercise? Vitality should have taken care of that. Did you forget to put any points in there?"

"No."

"Dumped it all into strength, did ya?"

"No!"

"It's stupid, boy! I've told ya about it! Every class needs vitality! Strength is no good if you're gassed out. Less good if you're dead!"

"I didn't dump it into strength, you old goat! I'm level 1! Where do you want me to get strength from?"

The old man paused, puzzled.

"Boy, you have been back for weeks, and you didn't level? Not once? You've been moping around this whole time?" The accent was gone all of a sudden.

"Not moping around. Training. Just . . . I don't have a class, so I don't level."

The old man paused. "Sit down."

"Why?"

"Just sit down, boy. Wait."

The old blacksmith lumbered towards his shop, and Derek heard the sound of clanging and shifting objects for several seconds before the old man reemerged, holding a small metal flask.

"Here, boy."

"What's this?"

"Rub it into your leg. Just a dash will do."

Derek glanced up at the blacksmith's eyes, there was nothing in them except an expectation that his command be obeyed. Derek twisted the top off the flask, emptied a small splash of the liquid onto his hand. He then realized he was wearing long pants, necessitating that he shove his hand up the side of his pants to get to his calf. He rubbed it into and around the sore spot as hard as he could, given the soreness.

Within moments, both his hand and his leg were on fire. Not literally, of course, but there was a deep, powerful burning sensation, like being in a scalding hot shower after a cold-water swim. Or the opposite. It was hard to tell. Derek yelped and tried his best not to writhe around, failing to pretend like he was toughing it out.

"Swamp dragon fire. Not really fire, you know. Sort of a defensive measure. When you fight them, they douse you with *gallons* of the stuff. But what's left afterward, once you cut the fire-bladder out? Best stuff on Ra'Zor for muscle pains."

*How does this guy still get muscle pains?*

"Don't look at me like that, boy. You ever use a hammer for two days on a rush project? Not all of us are reincarnators. The system's not as generous with the common folk, I'm afraid. Fewer stats that go less far."

As the old man explained, the burning was finally subsiding. As it did, Derek noticed the soreness was gone. Not better, not a little improved, but fully gone.

"You need me to pay for that?" Derek asked. It couldn't be cheap. Swamp dragons were, from everything Derek had heard, not easy to take down. Not just because of the liquid fire, but because hunting them required fighting a two-ton animal in the swamp. *Anything* useful that came from a monster like that was expensive, even if you could harvest it by the gallon.

"Not cheap if ya buy it." He flexed his big arm. "I brewed that batch myself, so to speak."

Claiming to take down a swamp dragon solo was usually the kind of thing people said as an obvious tall tale. It wasn't impossible, but Derek could count on one hand the people in the town who could actually pull it off. And those were reincarnators, favorites of the system who got the best it offered. For a normal person, it was a much more farfetched claim.

Somehow, Derek still didn't doubt the blacksmith's words for a second. The old man had taken down a swamp dragon to get magic muscle soreness cream. It wasn't a claim, it was a fact.

Derek had tons of questions. Obvious, quest-related questions about who the old man was, what he was hiding, and why he was hiding it. Questions that, if answered, would contribute to huge potential leaps in his own personal power.

Somehow, there was a more important question. As Derek opened his mouth to talk, a sob slipped out with it. He managed to keep more from spilling out long enough to make his query.

"Why are you still being nice to me?"

The old man looked at him, an unreadable look on his face. The accent came back. "Ya want to know? Ya always hurry. I was like ya once. I was a boy from a small, boring place. And I wanted something different, wanted to run towards danger. So I did. Left town. Joined the army as a squire. Ya had to be fourteen back then. I lied, got in anyway."

He paused, chewing on his beard where it overlapped the corner of his mouth, then spit the hairs back out. "Came home a year later and found out I didn't need to run towards danger at all. It was running towards me, except I left before it could get me. Whole town was gone. Buildings, people, everything. The demons got 'em."

He walked over to his weapons rack and pulled a spear and tossed it to Derek, who barely reacted in time to catch it out of the air. He then grabbed the metal pole that he used to whale on Derek before.

"I did a lotta things after that, killed a lot of things, saw a lot of things, got some new names people gave me cause of some of the things I did. But nothing more important than the things I didn't do."

He swished his metal pole through the air like it weighed nothing, like an inch and a half thick bar of steel was a normal piece of equipment for a light warm up.

"So I see a kid in a hurry, one that has potential? I wanna help ya actually do the things ya *can do*. Nothing more to it than that."

*Ding!*

*Secret Quest Completion: What Nobody Else Knows*

The blacksmith doesn't like talking about his past, but normally, that's just because he doesn't care about what he did before. What you just got? That's different. It's a whole new level of deeply hidden past.

Not only did you complete the quest, you also established a lasting bond with the quest subject. You've succeeded in a way that overshoots the expectations of the original question.

No class found. Generating a class based on immediate circumstances to facilitate acceptance of quest reward.

*Class Assigned: Common Man*

In some ways, this class is both the most basic and most advanced of classes. It gives no skills of any kind, gains no experience or skills from achievements, and levels based entirely from the work the user puts into it.

Common Man's stats are an amplified version of the rewards a non-system being would receive through conventional training. It has the potential to stretch to the highest heights of strength or wallow in the lowest troughs of weakness, depending wholly on the user's will and effort.

"So, was that pulled muscle just from lying around, or are ya finally ready to train?"

Derek settled into the best stance he could muster, holding the unfamiliar weapon in what he was sure was the wrong grip. Even without the old man saying anything, he could tell he was bad.

But that would change. He would change it.

"I'm ready to train. I'm coming for you. Get ready, old man."

The old man grinned, swung his pole, and immediately launched Derek through the air like a floppy, man-shaped baseball.

*Maybe don't taunt the hidden blacksmith. Lesson learned.*

## CHAPTER SEVEN

# Museum Day

Do you think it will be enough?"

"To fix the whole thing? No." Matt hefted the sack in his hand. Months of dungeon raids had filled it so full of repair stones that if the sack had a dollar sign printed on the burlap, it would have looked like he had robbed a bank. "But I'm hoping this will at least be a good start."

*If it isn't, this gets a lot harder.*

Barry hadn't made any attempts to communicate estimates of when the system was coming online, something Matt interpreted as a sign that Barry just didn't know. Without any way to estimate what fraction of the system instance's energy debt was "paying Matt back," it could be days, weeks, or months before he was back to making Matt and Lucy miserable or dead.

Or he could be awake right now, lurking in the metaphorical shadows planning very literal deaths.

Matt's adventures the past few months had been a little bit more predictable than made sense in Matt's experience. Without the system instance around, Matt suspected that Barry had played around the margins of what the rules allowed.

For example, Matt needed repair stones. Suddenly, repair stones were appearing constantly. Before this, Matt had only seen repair stones appear in dungeon rewards twice. Now, while they weren't an available reward choice every time, he could count on seeing these rewards every two or three dungeons.

If Matt was right, and that increased availability in repair stones was due to Barry-shenanigans, he was probably looking down the barrel of a much harder repair project when the system instance woke up.

Unless, that is, he started taking on more dangerous dungeons.

He hadn't talked to Lucy about it yet, but increased combat capabilities didn't just mean simpler low-level dungeon clears. It also meant that they could handle harder and harder dungeons. In a conventional setting, this would be a given. Isekai heroes didn't hang around low-level dungeons forever. Matt couldn't imagine that the system instance was trying to kill EVERY adventurer all the time, and most adventurers would have parties to balance out weaknesses. In comparison, a bad matchup in a tough dungeon would take Matt down like Christmas lights at Easter.

Low-level dungeons meant consistent rewards, but it also meant an almost frozen rate of progress. Except for the Meltbats, Matt hadn't been in real danger in months. For a class that leveled by surviving substantial danger, that meant a nearly frozen rate of improvement.

His long-awaited list of notifications reflected that.

> *Overpowered*
>
> You've taken down a dungeon without taking a single enemy-inflicted scratch. It wasn't much work for you to survive this, but enjoy this one-time reward for doing it with style.

> *Cautious Grind*
>
> You've put together a list of consecutive dungeon completions as long as your arm, all graded at 20 percent your level or lower. Prep work is a fundamental part of surviving greater threats, and you are nothing if not diligent in polishing your fight against enemies that don't stand a chance against you.

There were dozens of notifications like these, each giving small XP rewards for Matt keeping himself out of danger and eating progressively weirder things. There were even a few for completing large amounts of dungeons or surviving an individual dungeon multiple times. But if the list he was looking at was correct, his achievements had mostly stopped updating about halfway through the sleeping-system dormancy period.

Did the achievements add up? Absolutely. But Matt's mind was preoccupied with one of the last achievements.

> *Error Terror*
>
> You have survived a dungeon failure. Through no fault of your own, the dungeon collapsed and became dangerous to occupy. Congratulations on not getting

turned inside out, kicked into an interdimensional nether void, or winking out of existence entirely. That can happen! It doesn't, usually. But it can!

Despite surviving, you probably didn't have a great time. Given that and the rarity of the incident, your experience merits some compensation.

Rewards: +1 PER, increased affinity to teleportation from external sources, and resistance to teleportation-related disorientation.

Matt hadn't shared that last notification with Lucy. He could tell that after the years of loneliness and the traumatic battles against the system, the last thing Lucy needed was the looming threat that Matt might never return from a dungeon because of a random malfunction.

The past few months of safety had made visible improvements to her state of mind. It was understandable, considering she didn't have to watch her best and only friend almost die every few days. But it also meant that she had become overly careful. Even within the realm of tackling weak threats in lower-level dungeons, she had spent hours figuring out safer approaches to taking down the mobs.

The lifestyle of the Gaian wasteland overlord featured a lot of walking, and even though the museum was close to the farm, that was only relative to the week-long dungeon journeys.

Matt flicked open his stat screen. It now looked alien to him.

*Matt Perison*
*Level 1 Battlefield Survivor*
**Class XP:** 10/100
**HP:** 170
**MP:** N/A
**STAM:** 95
**STR:** 18
**DEX:** 32
**PER:** 20
**VIT:** 34
**WIS:** 22
**INT:** 10
**Class Skills:** Survivor's Reflexes (LV1), Advanced Survivor's Combat (LV1), Eat Anything! (DISABLED), Spring-Fighter (LV1), Rub Some Dirt In It (LV1), Pocket Sand (LV1), Survivor's Digging (LV5)

His new class was great. Advanced Survivor's Combat had got its shakedown run when taking down the Meltbats, and now Matt took some time to test out his other skills. Even though they were back to level 1, it was more of an aesthetic choice than anything else. His skills *read* level 1, sure, but with some basic testing, Matt could tell they at least retained most of their old efficacy. They would only grow stronger from here.

Some changes were weirder. The XP needed to hit the next level was significantly lower than it had been when he was a level 10 Survivor. But if the XP requirements grew anything like how they had when he was a bog-standard Survivor, that wouldn't matter much within a few levels. The XP requirement for the next level was still almost bottomed out, which Matt didn't expect. His stats had jumped enough that his best guess was that the XP was applied to the old class before the evolution, giving him levels he now couldn't see without digging through his notification history.

Through a combination of lucky breaks with eating-related stat increases and the massive stat dump that came with the achievements, Matt was much stronger than before. But strength was only enough until it wasn't. He still doubted he was anywhere near where he'd need to be to take down, say, a Gaian ape. If the system instance came back swinging, he needed to be ready. He needed to take more risks.

And that meant having a long, serious discussion with Lucy. Achievements that put his life in danger would delay the system instance from waking back up and also make him stronger. But that discussion could wait a bit. First, it was time for lunch, with another gigantic salad.

Halfway through his salad, Matt interrupted Lucy's planning. She had been spending more and more time working on plans in recent days.

"I'm hoping that dumping all these repair stones into that plinth at least repairs it enough that it wakes up," Matt offered.

Lucy looked up, annoyed. She huffed back, "Is that even possible, Matt? Like, say we could repair a thousand daggers with those. That seems like a lot, but . . . that tower is more than a thousand daggers worth of broken."

Matt shrugged. "It might work. I have no idea how the system prioritizes where the energy from these stones goes. That's part of why I want to do this now, and not later. I don't know if the instance can screw with it or not."

"So, better to do it while he's asleep?"

"Exactly."

"Well, your call. But I'm not going to go easy on you if we both end up puking on the dungeon entrance floor again."

Matt was reluctant to call Lucy out on the fact that she hadn't really puked. Rather, he had watched her glitch out like a living computer for a minute or so. That was one of the worst minutes of his time on Deadworld, where he couldn't do anything to help and could only pray while he puked his guts out.

* * *

Within a period of time that fell very snugly into the growing spectrum of what Matt considered negligible, they were at the museum.

"So, what do you think? Just dump them all on it?" Matt asked.

The problem of actually using the repair stones was one that had only just occurred to Matt. The plinth stubbornly repeated its warning about the dungeon being broken but refused to elaborate on how to fix the problem.

"I guess that's as good as anything. Worth a try, anyway," Lucy responded.

Matt took out a handful of stones and dropped them directly over the plinth, making sure to give himself a fair margin of safety in terms of how close he got to the plinth. His regeneration was supposedly better now, but he had no desire to test how well it had improved by having a section of his forearm or hand teleported away.

The entire handful of stones clattered uselessly to the ground near the plinth.

"Matt." Lucy was laughing. "It doesn't look like that worked."

"Yeah, I can see that." Matt looked down at the plinth, which stubbornly refused to display any new information at all. "So, shit. What do we do now? I probably should have thought of this earlier."

"Yeah, probably. Don't beat yourself up. I hear that for some people, thinking is the hardest work of all."

"Listen, when ninety-five percent of what I think about is stuff that's trying to kill me, the other five percent has a tendency to get dropped."

"Like a handful of repair stones, never to be recovered," Lucy bantered back.

"Who says I won't recover them?" Matt liked the banter, but there was a real problem in play here. To fix the dungeon, he needed to feed the plinth repair stones. But if the plinth couldn't actually eat the stones, that left him with a chicken-and-egg problem with no solution. It was entirely possible he'd have to ditch the whole project and just be content with using the repair stones to keep his limited personal arsenal in tip-top condition.

*Unless . . .*

When Matt had first encountered the plinth, his Survivor's Instincts had keyed in on it being a possible source of parts. Other dungeon plinths didn't trigger this. That meant his mental model of the dungeon room, plinth, and dungeon interior as all pieces of the same whole didn't apply to the museum dungeon. If this plinth was different, there might be something he could do.

Bending down and grabbing three or four repair stones, he knelt by the plinth and mentally willed the stones to fix the plinth.

*Gaian History Museum Dungeon Plinth*

This dungeon plinth is a maintainable portion of the Gaian History Museum

Dungeon. It is, in both form and function, a close imitation of a system dungeon plinth. Created by the Gaians, this plinth doesn't have a direct link to the world's dungeon system and thus is limited in the protection and self-repair it offers.

This plinth has been repaired from an inoperable state.

Durability: 47/600

"Shit, that worked? You repaired the plinth itself? It looks the same." Lucy was right, nothing had changed in the plinth's appearance.

"Yeah, it worked." Thankfully, Matt had the notification to tell him that he was on the right track. Matt started to feed stones one by one into repairing the plinth.

"So that's how it works? You just repair the plinth over and over?"

"I don't think so. I think I'm actually just fixing the plinth itself at the moment. But I'm not willing to bet the entire bag of repair stones on a mostly broken plinth. I'll get it back to one hundred percent durability and try the teleport again after that. Better safe than sorry."

When the plinth was back in factory-new condition, Matt carefully gathered all the dropped repair stones, placing them back in the sack. When that was done, he slowly raised the sack of repair stones above the plinth, as if he was offering some sacrifice to it.

*Please work.*

Repair Stones Detected!
Would you like to contribute repair stones to the ongoing maintenance of this dungeon?
Y/N

Matt willed the affirmative. Just like that, the sack was suddenly emptied of the hundreds and hundreds of repair stones it contained. It looked as if moving things into the dungeon didn't come with all the glowing-orb bells and whistles like when rewards materialized in the real world. But that made a kind of crazy magic-world sense. It was presumably a lot harder to make real-world items from nothing than it was to suck real-world repair stones into a fake one.

There were no notifications, no dings indicating he had done something important. Matt had worked hard for all those repair stones, and the work was about to get a lot harder. Not that he wouldn't do it, but going to all that effort would be a lot easier if he could get some motivation in the form of an early payment for his work.

*Come on, little plinth. I need a win here.*

Matt lowered his hand to the plinth. For a moment, nothing happened.

*Ding!*

*Warning: Limited Functionality*

The Gaian History Museum Dungeon has recovered from a critical error and the subsequent shutdown. An analysis of the dungeon shows that all critical basic functions have been restored. The dungeon may be entered safely, but portions of the simulation will be limited or unavailable.

Enter dungeon?

CHAPTER EIGHT

# The Miracle Discovery

"It says it's fixed, Lucy! We can go back in!" Matt was figuratively bouncing up and down.

"That's great, Matt!" Lucy smiled. But the moment Matt saw Lucy's smile, he knew that something was wrong.

"Do you . . . do you not want to go in for some reason?" Matt asked as he settled down.

"No, no!" Lucy put up her hands in protest. "It's not that. We can go in. It's just . . . confusing for me, I guess."

"In what way? I thought you'd love this. You're always bored."

"I mean, yeah, there's really not a lot for me to do besides look at things and talk. I can't even smell. So of course I'd be bored. And sometimes we, you know, we do dungeons. That's already working, and we can do it for free."

"Well, sure. But this isn't just a dungeon, Lucy. We can see how these people were. What they did. We can figure out what happened to them."

Lucy put her hand on the plinth, thinking.

"Look, Matt, it's not like I don't get it. When this thing first popped up, I was totally on board. But it's . . . I dunno. It would be nice to know. But, it's not like we can bring whatever world we see in there back, Matt. Think about it. You saw this world for, what, a minute? And you just spent MONTHS working on getting to where you can see it for a few minutes more. Are you sure this is good for you?"

Matt had always had a bad habit of delaying important conversations until they caused problems, most famously by not telling his family about his cancer until it came up until after one too many drinks at a gathering.

This wouldn't have been so bad if the gathering in question wasn't on

Christmas Eve. But it was. Understandably, his cancer announcement put a bit of a damper on the whole opening-stockings-and-having-eggnog feel of the evening. It wasn't an especially fond remembrance for Matt.

Picking his words carefully, he said, "Okay, I understand. I hear you. And first, you can always bring this kind of stuff up. Having you around helps me out a lot, but I'm pretty sure this whole experience with Gaia hasn't left me . . ."

"Normal?"

"Sure. If you think I'm going crazy, tell me. It's relevant. I promise I won't get angry unless I actually *am* going crazy, in which case I make no promises."

Lucy gave a little sigh of relief. It looked like she had been avoiding talking to him about problems too. Matt made a mental note to check in with her a bit more to make sure she had really voiced all of her concerns.

Matt tried his best to emulate his old therapist. "It sounds like you think I might get . . . addicted? Is that right?"

Lucy nodded. "Something like that. Or just go flat-out crazy. I don't know."

"Got it. I get it, I think. And I'm not going to say I'm not at some risk of going crazy. But I think the big thing that's making me obsessed isn't so much trying to get back in there, or having a different kind of synthetic company—"

"I don't really like the word synthetic," Lucy cut in.

"Noted. I won't use it again. Anyway, the problem, I think, is more . . . not knowing. We were really close to finding out what happened here before, and then the whole thing just shut off. And I want to know what the system instance took from me. I want to know what it took from those people by not doing its job right. I need to know."

"And after that?"

"That's the other thing. We have a big job ahead of us, and we only have so many low-level dungeons near us. We're talking about trying to terraform this whole planet and it takes us, like, three dungeons just to buy a tree."

"And?"

"And I'm stronger now. And higher-level dungeons have higher-level loot, probably. Eventually the system is going to figure out how long it needs to save up energy to throw something *really* big at us. If we don't stay ahead of that, it'll take me down. I have to take risks. This was a nice break from that and I had fun. I thought you needed the break. But it's time to get serious again."

"So now you're going to just go into high-level dungeons? Just like that?"

"Not just like that. We'll work up gradually. But yeah, I think we have to."

Matt was nervously keeping an eye on Lucy the whole time. Both her little hands were pretending to grip the edge of the plinth for all it was worth. She faked being a physical being for so long that he wondered if she even knew she was still pretending. She looked conflicted, grimacing and deep in thought. Suddenly, she sighed.

"Okay."

"Okay?" Matt wanted the confirmation.

"Yeah, it's okay. I think I probably knew this on some level. Remember when we first found that bunker with food? You had the chance to stay behind and just rest at the bunker. But you decided to keep going to dungeons. At the time, I thought you had a reason for leaving safety and risking danger. But maybe it's just in your nature to keep moving forward. Maybe that's why you're a reincarnator." Lucy paused and looked up at Matt. "You were right that I needed the break, and thank you. But . . . I don't want to see you die, Matt. And between the system coming back and you starving to death, that's starting to seem more and more likely again. So if you feel like you have to take risks, fine. Take them."

Matt took a few seconds to digest everything that Lucy had said before he found a response. A bad one. "I don't like it either, you know. But it might just be part of my nature."

Lucy gave a sad little smile. "I know. I've blamed you for things that weren't your fault before. It's the circumstance we're in. Don't worry, I'm going to be there with you for everything."

Matt got a little teary-eyed. He really didn't like tough talks, but it was better for Lucy to tell him how she felt than keep everything bottled up. He was just thankful that she couldn't tell he was almost crying.

"Stop that. You are a grown man. A little girl shouldn't be able to make you cry like that."

Matt ran his sleeve over his eyes. "I'm not crying. It's just dust."

Lucy rolled her eyes. "Sure. So, are we doing this?"

"Yup, let's."

Matt slammed his hand down on the plinth, teleporting him and Lucy into the museum once more.

This time, everything was normal. The same video played, showing the same gorgeous, happy people, finally working up to the same climax that had cut off suddenly before. Anticipating another wild ride, he held his breath.

"Within these walls, you will learn about our people. About *yourselves*. You will see how we have lived, and how we live."

*So far, so good. Come on, little video.*

"You will see the failures and triumphs of our past, and learn about the hopes of our people. Most of all, you will learn about the danger that threatens every aspect of the life we lead: the Scourge. Repeat visitors to these halls will recognize this as a sudden change to our programming, and it is. In the few short weeks that the Scourge has spent sweeping across our land, it has demanded those kinds of sudden changes.

While all our previous exhibits are still available, we encourage every man, woman, and child who calls Gaia home to visit these new information centers and learn about this terrible threat. We must all do our part to resist this so that Gaia may continue on, strong, unified, and beautiful. Enjoy!"

And with that, everything faded. But this time, not to black. The room around Matt and Lucy dissolved to white, before suddenly beginning to reform. Suddenly, they found themselves standing on stone-paved streets, near a beautiful fountain, in a busy square lined by beautiful buildings. Each structure was built in a style somewhere between classic Greek and what Matt thought of as old English architecture. They had both bricks and stone pillars interacting in ways that might not have worked in less thought-out designs, but everything felt natural here.

It was like the richest-of-rich-people neighborhoods, and Matt was loving every eyeful of it.

Out of nowhere, the voice started speaking again.

"Not all of our places of living look this way. Some rely more on technology to shine. Others are more rural, while still others are aimed at those who like busier spaces with more people for purposes of commerce or lifestyle."

As he listed off these variants, the town faded and reemerged in examples of each of the mentioned forms before settling back into the image of the original location. Each was beautiful.

"Holy shit, oh my god." Matt realized what was happening.

"What?"

"Holy shit. Holy shit!"

"What?!"

The voice came back. "In each of these buildings, you will find the story of either a different aspect of our history or our lives; past, present, and future. You will see our hopes, and our shames—not in a book, but as we see them, through our own eyes."

"It's a living history museum!" Matt exclaimed.

Unfortunately, Lucy could NOT wrap her head around the idea of a living history museum.

"So, then you walk up, and he's like 'I am the town's cobbler! I make all sorts of things, from shoes to boots to hunting skins.' And for those more dedicated to the bit, they'll actually go through the process of making a shoe from scratch."

"And this is entertaining?"

Lucy still didn't get it. Somehow, her overall data store about Matt's life on Earth had missed that particular wrinkle. She could imagine both acting and museums, but couldn't get the two of them to work together in her head. Matt had been trying to help her understand for the better part of five minutes.

"Oh, a ton. You have to remember that you're maybe eight years old in this scenario, and you're talking to some guy who really likes history, and who *overall* probably loves his job, but who *right then* has just said, 'And I make shoes for luminaries such as *Thomas Jefferson* and *Paul Revere!*' for the fortieth time that day, and it's sixty percent humidity, and he's wearing an all-wool outfit."

"So the fun is that he temporarily hates it?" Lucy asked.

"Kind of! And you get to churn butter."

"And you still think it's fun? As a full-grown adult?"

They went back and forth for a minute or so. Matt tried desperately to explain to Lucy why this boring-on-paper experience was the most amazing thing possible, and she was constitutionally unable to imagine anything fitting that description being fun. Eventually, they snapped out of the argument, realizing that he could just show her what appeared to be a magical-technology version of the same thing, and got to work.

From what they could tell, the museum allowed visitors to visit the exhibits in any order, but was clearly designed for a certain order, working its way from Gaia's distant past towards its present and future. Since the dungeon seemed to be functioning just fine, they decided to take their chances, make a day of it, and sweep through the exhibits in the recommended order. That meant starting with Gaian prehistory.

"The earliest days of our ancestors were not of agriculture, but of suffering. When our people came down from the trees, they ate what food they could find. And unfortunately, there was very little food to be had in the original plants."

It only occurred to Matt now how much the "hunter" half of "hunter-gatherer" factored into how primitive Earth humans were depicted. Every drawing or sculpture of a caveman he had ever seen had been more than a little yoked, just generally buff in a CrossFit-and-carnivore diet sort of way. Gaians were different.

"Do they look a little . . . ?" Lucy asked.

"Starved? Yeah. It's weird to me too," said Matt.

The video shifted through several biomes, showing images of early Gaians scavenging food from various sources that didn't seem to have a lot of it. There were fruit trees with small, unappetizing fruits. There were stalks of wild grain that they harvested, but these stalks were rare and each offered only a few grains for the trouble. Matt was sure there was some editorial work at play, and the direction of those edits were clear. This was the "stuff was bad" era of Gaia.

"And it was one discovery that changed everything for our people, that set us on the path we find ourselves on today," the museum echoed.

"Hold on to your butt. It's time for FIRE," Matt said in his best tour-guide tone.

"Matt, you are way too excited about this."

"I bet it's going to be flints. Maybe lightning striking a tree. I'm appropriately psyched."

"And that discovery was this . . ." the museum continued.

The scene dissolved around them, zooming in on the one item that, according to the Gaians, had changed the entire course of their history.

Matt blinked. "Shit. Of course, it's that."

"The shovel. With the shovel, Gaians could prepare the soil for seeds, putting them where they would. Early shovels were wood, and used by nomadic tribes who would break small amounts of soil, scatter seeds, and return to the land once the plants had been given sufficient time to grow."

The shovel morphed from a primitive scoop to a stone-bladed tool, and then was surrounded by a number of different implements. Scythes. Hoes. Rakes. Everything you could want to till the soil, all presented like they were the biggest breakthroughs ever. And, Matt reflected, for the Gaians they probably were.

"As wood was replaced by the heavier and more durable stone, more and more types of soils could be broken, faster and faster. This led to the nomads settling down, and the seeds of our civilization were finally planted."

## CHAPTER NINE

# Resist the Scourge

The prehistory exhibit continued for a while, talking about their hypothesis that agriculture helped early Gaians spread across the planet. As they moved through other exhibits, that same pattern held true. For the exhibit on Gaia's Bronze Age, it focused on the types of tools bronze allowed them to make. A similar exhibit on Earth would have shown weaponry. Their heroes, the ones they felt were worth mentioning, were almost all agricultural scientists or people whose work directly fed into food or plants.

Matt's butter-churning promises ended up being kept, and were supplemented by dozens of other hands-on activities meant for children. Lucy's disappointment at not being able to participate was visible once it was confirmed that she couldn't touch anything, even in the illusory dungeon environment. But she quickly found a workaround.

"Matt! Stop threshing THAT grain!"

"What's wrong with this grain?"

"You've threshed it enough. It's over-threshed. You've hit the point of diminishing returns with your hand-flail. You need to move on before you embarrass both of us in front of the silo master."

Hours passed before they moved on. The idea that agriculture-is-everything of Gaian society meant that the even the simple-enough-for-children format of the museum resulted in both Matt and Lucy actually learning some useful things about farming.

The Gaians weren't just good at growing plants, they practically invented the activity. Back on Earth, the best gardeners were a bit like wizards. They could make the plant grow in the right direction, produce outrageously big fruits, and get millions of calories out of a single acre. The Gaians put them to shame. They understood the plant and could shape it as if it were a piece of metal. Even what they considered to be simple, casual lessons about caring for plants were profound and useful.

"I kind of feel like we've done a bad job on our farm, now," Matt said, only half-joking.

Lucy didn't look too amused but nodded her head in agreement. For Earth amateurs, they had done fine. By Gaian standards? It was a shameful botch job.

The peaceful, plant-loving nature of Gaia had been so heavily imprinted on both of them that the sudden shift to Gaia's history of war felt as strangely uncomfortable as watching a once loving couple's relationship fall apart.

Early Gaia hadn't had much in the way of combat during the short few centuries it took various thriving agriculturalists to convert the nomadic gathering tribes to solid farming folk. But there still was jealousy over the plenty that only some of the Gaians enjoyed, and that food inequality led to the occasional raid and small-scale warfare.

"After the era of the wandering gatherers was done, Gaia settled into a millennia of peace. Each community thrived, driven by their reliance on rich Gaian wheat. But it was this monoculture that was our undoing."

Even in descriptions of war, agriculture was front and center. But it was all fitting into place for Matt. The story behind Gaia was a familiar tale. A population that became unbelievably reliant on one very successful staple crop, only to have that crop fail due to a fast-spreading blight.

Overnight, a millennium of conditioned trust in a single crop was betrayed, and the world was starving. And then there was blood. The details of how the leaders of the world pitched war as a solution to famine, how killing was supposed to help, were all there in gory detail. What surprised Matt was how long the war continued for.

Hundreds of years. Not all of the planet was at war over that period. Some countries stayed out of certain rounds for reasons of their own, or simply because they were smoldering ruins incapable of raising armies.

"Matt, this is horrific."

"Yeah. It's like they decided to get all their atrocities out of the way at once."

The narrator hadn't been lying when he had said that they were going to be open about all their worst mistakes. And there were plenty. Even in the abbreviated form presented here and even in the form they meant for their children to see, it was a long, bloody exhibit. By the time the era of wars started wrapping up, the technology developed to kill had driven the world to the modern age.

Back to the museum narrator. "And what stopped the war? More fighting? Better weapons? No. It was an order that made agriculture their religion. That reminded Gaians who they were, and who they should be. So, Gaians retreated to the wilderness with supplies, tools, and expertise meant for war, and applied them to solving the problem that had set the world to war in the first place. They brought back grain."

When Earth had begun to understand the idea of genetics through plants, it came from an experiment by a monk called Gregor Mendel. The same thing appeared to be true here. The leader of the order, it turned out, was named Sarth. He spent a lifetime developing several ignored crops into workable substitutions for the failed staple wheat, and ended the war.

It still took time before a new age of plenty got enough momentum to convince the few remaining countries of Gaia to settle for peace, but the name of the continent Matt stood on reinforced the fact that his contribution was not forgotten.

"I can't believe these were the people you wanted to see."

The war exhibition had taken a certain toll on Lucy. She obviously had some concept of Earth's wars and atrocities, but it seemed most of her knowledge of those kinds of things was more abstract as opposed to deeply understood. This had hit closer to home, especially in a virtual, hands-on way like this. Matt understood. He felt the same way.

"I . . . I don't know a lot about worlds, really. Everyone has their good and bad side," Matt said.

"You know about two of them. Kind of. In a way, that's twice as much as anyone else on Earth," Lucy countered.

"Well, fair. But what I'm trying to say is, from the two worlds I've seen, it seems like war is probably a reality everywhere. And yeah, I think things got pretty dark for these people. They had a couple of centuries of war. But as soon as someone stood up and said, 'Hey, let's stop this,' and had any solutions better than starving to death? They went right back to gardening."

Lucy sniffed. "For how long, though? How long until they went back to war?"

"I checked some of the other exhibitions. Everything except the one about the Scourge. None of the rest are about war. By the time the system got to them, it looks like they used it to get better at hunting and gardening."

That was the other big revelation of the museum. The Gaians didn't seem to have the system through most of the history Matt had watched with Lucy. And when they did get it, it just didn't seem to be very important to them at all. The system made some things easier, but they were already doing pretty well and had lost their taste for war. The exhibit about the system's influence on Gaian life existed, but it was a stub compared to anything else they had watched.

"I can even show you if you want. These weren't bad people. They were a good people who went to a dark place for a while, then returned to the light. They could have hid that, and they didn't. That means something."

Lucy was thoughtful for a moment. "Yeah, I guess. It's gonna take me a while. I guess it all just shook me."

"I understand. Do you want to see the other exhibits?"

She shook her head. "Maybe another day. I'm sorry. It really was fun, Matt. I'm just a bit shaken up."

"We did come here for a reason. Can you do one last exhibit?"

Lucy nodded. "Yeah. Let's do it."

They both stood up and walked towards the last exhibit, one that was set apart from the others, tastefully positioned but clearly not one of the original planned exhibits. It was a larger, more imposing building than the others, likely on purpose, to keep people from missing what was, at the time, probably the most important exhibit in the museum.

Over the door was a large but simple sign that read "Our Enemy: The Scourge."

Lucy and Matt entered the room, ready to learn what kind of monster had been strong enough to take down an entire planet. It wasn't lost on Matt that the Gaians had openly referred to it as their enemy. From what he had seen, the Gaians of that era coexisted with the planet, and didn't want strife. They had collectively, as a race, lost their taste for fighting and war. To call something their enemy meant something that it didn't mean on Earth.

"So what do you have your money on? Asteroid? Portal to the hell dimension? A giant, evil space goat?" Lucy asked.

"I'm sure the narrator will let us know."

"I'm betting on a shovel turning towards evil, and them not having the heart to put it down."

"Shh, it's starting."

In front of them, a man materialized. There was no fancy background or setting, just a man in the short, belted tunic Matt had, through exhibits, come to recognize as the modern Sarthian mode of dress. With a serious expression on his face, the man launched directly into his speech.

"Welcome, visitor. As you likely already know, I am Ramsen. Once upon a time, I was asked to take a break from my official duties and provide the narration for this museum. I was glad to do it."

*Some kind of government official*, Matt thought. *The man had some kind of gravitas around him. Maybe even their president, or emperor?*

"It is in less glad times and with a less glad heart that I return for a new exhibit, one about an issue that threatens our very existence. The Scourge. I will walk you through everything you need to know about it, and how you, a Sarthian citizen, can best help in the war against this danger. But first, before we do that, let's talk a bit about plants."

"Of course, more plants. Great," Lucy complained.

"Shh, Lucy. Let me listen," hushed Matt.

The man waved an arm, and a small table with a small potted plant appeared.

"In the philosophy of horticulture, as first formalized by Sarth himself, all plants are bound by balance. As our science advanced, we validated this to be true of every Gaian plant, although it was true of each in a different way. This bush, if carefully tended, will produce some of the most delicious fruit Gaia offers. In balance, it must be carefully tended. If it lacks the correct soil or the right amount of moisture and sunlight, it withers."

"I told you we couldn't plant that one," Lucy remarked.

"Yes, you were right. Now *shut up*. Lucy. This is important." Matt was not the type to be disturbed during movies.

The man waved his arm, and another plant appeared, a sort of stringy vine. "This plant has a different balance. It's only with great effort and expertise that it can be made to give up usable fibers for rope. But in a return to balance, it grows nearly everywhere, on its own. We have a word for such plants. Weeds."

The man waved his arm and both plants disappeared, as if they had never existed. Matt supposed that was right. They hadn't.

"Even with our greatest science, even in our most daring carelessness, the balance of plants was always there. Like an inherent law of nature, no plant could grow in all climates. No plant was hardy without giving up some other valuable feature. We improved our plants, yes. But whether we intended it or had it opposed to us by nature itself, balance worked as a limit on the dreams we could accomplish. As well as the harm we could do ourselves."

Matt had an idea where this was going. He almost didn't want to stay to hear that idea confirmed. He had regretted seeing the Gaian atrocities. This was worse. What the man was building up to, if Matt's guess was correct, was going to make him sick to his bones.

"We called the personality that descended on us the *system of war*. It did not call itself this, nor did it need to. With every reward it offered, it also offered strength. Not strength of creativity, or of character, but rather strength in battle. 'Would you like a sword,' it said? 'No,' we said. It assured us the swords were meant for beasts, not humans. But we had seen humans be beasts. We had been beasts ourselves.

"We limited what we would take from the system. Where rewards were unavoidable, we took only what would help us with our work. Strength for a plow, but never a sword. And after a time, the system seemed to recognize this. It stopped offering weapons and started giving us tools. Until one day, it started offering seeds."

The man waved his arm, and a small vine appeared in a pot. There was nothing special about the plant that Matt could see. It was almost drab. It was the kind of thing that he would have filtered out of his mind.

*Why? Why does it suddenly look so sinister?*

"Orchards must be tended. Weeds must be pulled. That is balance. But the system offered something different. Something it said it had made especially for us.

"A plant that could be eaten and easily modified to create any type of vegetable matter required. It could as easily be a dinner as it could be made into a rope or a canvas. Best of all, said the system, it would grow anywhere, in any environment. Over time, it would adapt. If stripped of soil, it could still grow by feeding on something different until the soil was replenished."

Lucy started up. "Please tell me they didn't take that shit."

"We immediately banned it. We explained to the people why, and they understood. They understood as if it were in their blood. Each man and woman knew not to reach for the devil's fruit being offered. If anyone didn't, they were prohibited by the expense. All but one."

*No. No.*

"He was known to us, a man of little capability and even less thoughtful of nature. We will not speak his name, but he longed to be a second Sarth, to prove what could be done. He not only took the plant but attempted to improve it further. By the time we found his fields, it was too late. The plant had spread. No fire has yet been invented that is hot enough to find every one of the Scourge's seeds, and those seeds that survive *learn* about fire."

"That son of a bitch. Matt, the fucking system did this. It did it *on purpose*," Lucy exclaimed.

*Maybe not*, Matt thought. *It could have been an accident. The system is lazy. Not that that's better. It's almost worse.*

"The Scourge spread. As it grew, it wiped out what it had touched. Eventually, it left the land barren. It ate the nutrients, leaving nothing behind. And with its new energy, it then spread further, and faster.

"We now have no choice. We will reach for the power the system offers, but not on its terms. With our science and the dedicated power of our entire world, we will take what it gives and bend it to our will.

"Accept the achievements from the system. Tell us when you do. We will use them, not for what the system wants, but for what Gaia needs. Do you have system-granted resources? Share them.

"In the meantime, we are preparing. You have seen the first of our Nullsteel food storage facilities, both large and small, as they travel to their destinations. You have seen our war mages and our parasitic plants.

"We are making progress, but make no mistake. This is a race to live and a battle to the death, all at once. If we move faster than our enemy learns, we will win. And every one of us must contribute to assure that future.

"Thank you, Gaians and Sarthians, for your support and brotherhood. I bid you a good day, and thank you for your part in our future.

"Resist the Scourge."

## CHAPTER TEN

# Clear the Colony

The man had stopped talking, and the video froze. The exhibition was over.

"Matt, this can't be real, right?" Lucy asked.

Matt shook his head. For all their normal banter, he couldn't think of a single relevant thing to say.

"I don't know. I don't know what reason these people would have to lie. And they couldn't have been lying about the Scourge. We've seen what Gaia looks like. Whatever happened, it was total annihilation. If true, the Scourge ate *everything,* until there wasn't anything left at all."

"It's just, Matt, the deal is that the system is *lazy*. But it has rules. I've never heard of a rule that lets it destroy a world. How could that exist?"

"I don't know. Let me think. If the system appeared, in most places, everyone would try to become stronger. That's probably the normal reaction, you know? Everyone would go and try to be superheroes. The Gaians didn't. They didn't *want* the system. And they barely used it until the system forced their hand." A scary thought crossed over Matt's mind before Lucy vocalized the same idea.

"It was punishing them?"

"Maybe. Maybe it *needs* people to use the system. I don't know. It could just be that it's stupid and didn't think about the danger, or didn't realize the Gaian would modify the seed. I honestly don't know. But he"—Matt gestured towards the man—"if he's right, the system broke the balance. It caused the threat to this planet, and then it failed to send the help that this planet needed."

Matt walked up to the man. Whatever his job was, it seemed important. His speech gave the impression of someone entrusted with power, someone who seemed like they took that trust seriously. He was asking for help, not demanding it. If Matt was looking for a leader for the Gaian people, he could do worse.

Looking into the hologram's eyes, Matt said, "I'm sorry. I'm sorry I'm late." The shock of everything was still setting in. Matt was barely surviving, but he wanted to say something. To make a vow in response to everything that he had seen today. "I can't make promises. And I know you can't hear me. But . . . listen. If there's anything I can do, I will. Even if it's just making the system's job harder. I'll do that. If I can hurt it, if I can hold it to account, I will. I promise you."

It was stupid to talk to a hologram. It couldn't hear him. Hell, whatever system this dungeon ran on couldn't hear him either. Barry couldn't see this place. The system instance was probably still asleep. Besides Lucy, this was the most alone he could be. He doubted even ghosts could get in here.

Matt sighed, and began to turn away. But out of the corner of his eyes, he saw the simulated man blink. Not the simulated man's eyes alone, but the whole man winked in and out of existence, like someone had flipped a light switch off and on as fast as they could. Matt braced himself for an emergency teleport and did his best to batten down the hatches to keep from puking if it came to that.

It didn't. Suddenly, the simulation's eyes came alive and locked with Matt's.

"Reincarnator?"

And then, before Matt could react, the man was frozen again, just as blank as before. Matt waved his hand in front of the unresponsive eyes. It was out. He looked back at Lucy, who was still muttering hateful words at the system instance. She hadn't heard. The thing had come to life and whispered a single word. Unless it hadn't.

*Am I going crazy? Is this what mana deficiency does? Is this what* being alone *does?*

"Shit. Shit. Shit."

"What?"

"We're going to need a lot more repair stones."

For better or worse, the holographic square was a nice place. There was normal sun, hardly any dust, and that rare not-a-wasteland vibe that was so often lacking for their little talks. And so, they decided to stay in the museum for a bit longer.

"I know! I'm not sure if it really happened either. And I get that it's hard to believe. But we *have to do this.* I swear to you, the hologram talked to me. It called me reincarnator. It was real, really real. Who knows what happens when we get all this running again?"

Matt waved his arm at the projections around them. It was hard to tell if what he was referring to was really a positive. The downside of using the museum's town square as a meeting room was the fact that they were surrounded by dozens of projections in a permanent, illusory kind of rigor mortis.

Earlier, when Matt was trying to figure out if he was going crazy, he had rushed out of the last exhibit and went to the second phase of the museum. A living museum always had weird actors who would talk about their lives in some abstract third person. If Matt was correct, he might see another simulation that could truly speak.

The good news was that the museum did generate a few individuals from each presentation for them to talk to and interact with. The bad news was that when Matt ran to the closest simulated figure that looked like an angry American colonial blacksmith, the figure attempted to greet them before freezing up. Not momentarily but entirely and persistently. Just a sudden Gaian caveman mannequin holding a stone spade.

The rest of the projections were the same, and after trying to have conversations with each, they returned to the town square full of projections. It was creepy, yes, but somehow still better than the boredom of the wasteland.

"No, Matt."

"It really happened! I swear!"

"Matt! Listen to me! It's not that I don't think it happened!"

"What, then? What could be more important than this?"

"Oh, I don't know, Matt. Making sure you don't starve to death or turn into some kind of mana-deficient undead thing, or whatever happens when you keep eating the cursed turnips. And mana generators are *fucking expensive*. You have no idea."

Matt paused. She had a point. "We can do that stuff after?" he asked.

"No. Absolutely not. We get the turnips fixed first. I'm putting my foot down." Lucy's tone gave no ground for disagreement.

Matt opened his mouth to argue again, only to be met with the very sternest of little-girl glares. It was over.

"Fine. You win."

It was decided. They would do dungeons, Bigger, more dangerous dungeons than they had tried before. They would buy a mana generator and hope for the best, and if Matt was still functional by that point, they'd work on collecting repair stones.

Of course, this was all dependent on the system staying quiet. If it woke back up, all bets were off.

And then, something wonderful happened, something Matt could have predicted but never actually got around to hoping for. When they went to the clearly marked exit of the museum dungeon, the teleport diverted them to some new location. They expected to land outside the dungeon but instead went to some place completely different, and to Matt, infinitely better.

"Holy shit," Lucy whispered.

"Lucy? Lucy!" Matt exclaimed.

"I see it, Matt. This is insane."

"It's a gift shop. Lucy, it's a damn gift shop."

In science, there's a concept called carcinization, which is the idea that, no matter what environment you start with, however wet, dry, harsh, or gentle, eventually, you'll find animals that look suspiciously like crabs. Almost nobody thinks that this occurrence is because of some crab creator god working behind the scenes to create animals in its own image. Instead, the consensus is that the crab design was so stunningly useful for surviving on Earth that it was almost harder to design an animal that *wasn't* like a crab in some way.

It turned out the same concept held true for gift shops. Matt was god-knows-how-many light years from Earth and in the ruins of a society that has almost nothing to do with Earth. Yet, everything was alright. There were buttons. There were boxes of Gaia and Sarthia stickers. There were cheap, stupid toys and cheap, almost non-functional wind instruments, and every aisle was capped by open-top boxes filled with countless educational posters.

It was perfect. And not just for Matt.

"Sweet Moses, Matthew. They had better have yo-yos. Do you think every society eventually discovers yo-yos? Because I'm not leaving without a yo-yo."

"I hate to bring this up, but you probably can't leave with a yo-yo, in that you don't really have . . ."

"Hands? Yes, I know, Matt. But if I see one, I can duplicate it with my magic hologram illusions. I want a weird Gaian souvenir one."

"But . . ." When Matt first saw Lucy, she had been sitting by an illusory campfire on a fake, non-physical log of her own making. Since then, she had barely bothered to project anything but herself. Matt had assumed it was to try to look more real, something he didn't care about but that she seemed to find important. If she wanted to move away from that, it was fine.

"Matt! I found them!"

And so she had.

*One more win for convergent evolution.*

Lucy had Matt shuffle through all the various yo-yo designs, eventually settling on a Sarthian sports-themed design featuring a weird, oval ball. Matt decided to grab one himself too, just so they could enjoy them together.

| Error. Item currently unavailable for materialization. Please select a different item. |
|---|

"Shit, it won't let me take one."

Lucy laughed as she tried and failed to get the illusory yo-yo she had generated to work. Matt wasn't sure how that even worked. A hologram trying to replicate another projection. It hurt his mind. He walked around the gift shop, trying and failing to claim the other items.

It was only by luck that he found something he could take, something near the counter that he probably wouldn't have even seen if he wasn't desperate to take something with him.

> *Sarthian Victory Garden Seeds*
>
> Gathered from the most productive of the continent's plants, these seeds represent the hope of our people. Participate in the effort to defeat the Scourge by growing your own victory garden today!

"Are you happy?" Lucy asked.

"Not exactly. I wanted a Frisbee. But it's better than nothing."

After a quick stop at home to stuff what non-cube food looked the least perishable in Matt's backpack, scatter the victory garden seeds on some moist soil, and give the plants a quick deep watering, they were off. The nice thing about breaking into a whole new level range of dungeons was that they didn't have far to go to find one.

Despite the fact that he was in most ways technically overleveled for it, a level 10 dungeon was the highest-ranking dungeon Matt had ever entered. He hit the ground, ready for literally anything from mutant moles to small dragons. And then there was nothing. No beasts, no birds, no animals or monsters of any kind. Just endless, boring forest as far as their legs cared to take them.

"Are the enemies in this one invisible? Is that the kind of danger you get from a double-digit dungeon level?" Matt asked.

"I doubt it, but maybe. There has to be *something* weird going on. Try stabbing the trees," Lucy responded.

It was an hour later when their attention was drawn to some rustling in the bushes. Matt moved closer, only to see pointed legs and the rear of an exoskeleton disappearing into a hole.

"Oh, hell."

"What is it?"

*Ding!*

> *Dungeon Objective Found: Clear The Colony*
>
> What's the best part about huge, carnivorous ants? Well, in the case of Wolfpack ants, it's that they tend to clear out most of the wild game near their colonies pretty quickly. This limits the population of most colonies to hundreds of ants instead of thousands. It's much more manageable!
>
> The downside is collie-sized ants with jaws that can slice through small

trees, run as fast as a human in a dead sprint, and use pheromones to communicate with hill-mates a mile away. Your mission is to stop the spread of the ants in the forest, ideally before they do more damage to the local fauna than they already have.

We hope you bought multi-target attacks! You'll need them.

CHAPTER ELEVEN

# Survivor's Reflexes

Ever since Matt had disabled automatic system window popups during his first fight with the Clownrats, they hadn't really been an issue during battle. He'd fight the foe, whether it be Flash Turtles or Meltbats, and check the achievements later. In the worst case scenario, that might mean he'd miss something relevant to a battle until after it was already finished, but that was still better than having his field of view blocked while something was trying to rip his guts out.

Now he was learning it was an even bigger advantage than he had thought.

Matt was still reading the window when it suddenly blinked away. The first half of the window had provided a lot of information, but nothing about how fast the ants could turn around within their own tunnels. The ant decided to fill that knowledge gap by shooting out of the tunnel like a bullet, pincers clacking towards his neck.

It felt like a horror-movie scenario. One minute he was reading about some impossible terror, and the next minute, the monsters in the text came hurtling out at him. Only the window disappearing gave him the advance notice he needed to react.

All things considered, the ant wasn't moving all that fast. But by the time the window disappeared, and Matt's reflexes kicked in, the ant was almost on him, too close to dodge or block. If there was ever an occasion to try out Spring-Fighter, this was it. Luckily, it didn't take a lot to activate and with very little effort it combined with the dodge he was already executing, seamlessly speeding up the motion.

He definitely over-dodged, getting way too far back to be in position for a counterattack. But the fact that he could even do that meant a lot. Matt glanced at his stamina bar, seeing he had drained about an eighth of it doing what amounted to a near-instant physical teleportation over a split second. He'd have to get better economization, but he had some ideas of how to do that.

The first move had to do with the enemy in front of him. The Survivor's Instincts portion of Survivor's Reflexes was a bit underpowered now that the skill leaned away from wisdom in favor of perception, but even in its weakened form, it could tell Matt that this individual ant wasn't too big of a deal. Now that Matt was ready for it, he didn't even need his Spring-Fighter to stay out of its attack range.

It came clattering while Matt moved backwards and to the side, taking advantage of the ant's inflexible insect mobility. As he did, he pulled his spear out of his pack and started peppering the thing with pokes to slow it down even further. Once the spear was in his hand, Advanced Survivor's Combat also kicked in, marking general areas on the ant's exoskeleton. He had targets now.

The brightest targets were on the back, but hitting them meant leaning above the ant's jaws, and that seemed like a bad idea if Matt wanted to keep all his limbs. Instead, he started hunting more minor weak points, starting with the joints on the ant's legs. Before, this would have been absolutely impossible. At the speed the ant was moving, it would have taken him a dozen stabs to get anywhere near hitting it. With Advanced Survivor's Combat, Matt found that he could pretty much hit them at will with precision blows, and unleash serious hits every two or three attempts.

Disabling the first leg didn't do much. The insect had too much built-in redundancy. But the third leg Matt disabled was both the second of the front legs and the second on the ant's left side, and it visibly stumbled with half of its legs out of play. This took away enough speed that Matt felt comfortable striking out at the antenna, taking one pretty easily and the second even easier as the ant thrashed around.

It was a little sadistic, but Matt considered leaving the ant alive rather than strike at its now exposed back. So long as it could move, he could keep working to move Advanced Survivor's Combat forward. He was eager to learn if there was some hidden functionality to the skill, and it was also a safe bet that there were some you've-been-in-a-fight-for-a-long-time achievements to mine.

Before he could succumb to that particular temptation, his increased perception and Survivor's Reflexes were just enough to notice an input that had been coming in from the periphery of his senses. With the ant basically disabled, he now had time to focus on that worry, identifying it as a sort of citrus-y smell he couldn't quite place.

"Is sniffing the air during a fight gonna be a thing for you now? Is that part of one of your weird new skills?" Lucy wasn't getting all the inputs that Matt was, and she couldn't smell anything anyway. By now, it was pretty obvious the ant didn't pose much of a threat anymore. "Are you just trying to grind in the fact you can do something I can't?"

"No, listen, it smells *weird* right now. It smells like . . . lemon floor cleaner! That's it. My mom used to use it instead of the pine-smelling one. This smells like that."

"And?"

"It's just weird. Where is it coming from?"

That line of thought immediately led Matt to the only thing in the area that really *could* be producing the weird, citrusy smells. That was the ant itself. The smell of its yellow blood was pretty distinct and had increased the more it bled, so the lemon smell wasn't from the blood. But if it wasn't that . . .

*Shit. Pheromones.*

Matt took off running just as he heard a much louder clattering kicking in behind him.

"I might have fucked up."

The dungeon system's description of the ants had said they could run as fast as a man at a full sprint, and that was basically correct. But Matt could both run faster than the average man and could zigzag in a way the ants weren't great at. This would have let him get a comfortable lead pretty quickly if it wasn't for three things.

The first was that the ants never seemed to get winded. If Matt remembered right, insects didn't have lungs so much as they had holes in their skeleton that sucked in air passively. Running might even help them breathe better. Would they gas eventually? Maybe. But for now, they were doing a better job keeping up than their baseline speed implied they should.

The second, more annoying problem was that the scent these things were putting out was omnidirectional, it looked like the colony had little tunnels everywhere and scouts out in every direction. Every now and then, an ant would shoot out of the bushes from an unexpected angle, and he'd have to stumble out of the way or even use Spring-Fighter to avoid getting eviscerated. Those little tolls on his speed and stamina were adding up, and the ants were slowly reeling him in as a result.

The third issue was a mixed blessing, as Matt's Spring-Fighter skill was part of what was allowing him to keep ahead of them. But that came at a constant, noticeable drain to his stamina. Not just the stat bar, either. That Matt could handle. But apparently, the skill also overclocked his cardiovascular system and multiple uses were tiring him out faster.

He couldn't let that happen. Survivor's Reflexes' threat assessment function worked off perception, it seemed, and was working better than ever before with his increased stats. The signals Survivor's Instincts sent were nearly subconscious most of the time, but the upgraded skill enhanced Matt's danger perception to the point where there were now visual aspects in play. Looking behind him, he could see the crowd of ants basically boiling with danger, the air above them shimmered like the space over an asphalt roof on a hot day.

When the first mandible grazed his heel, Matt knew he was in trouble. Mandibles were a great motivator to speed up, but soon enough the burst of adrenaline wore off, and the ants were still moving at their fast pace.

"Help." Matt was economizing energy as much as he could and cutting words to save oxygen. "Might be in trouble. Need a tree. Something."

"Got it. Looking." Lucy copied Matt's speaking style.

Matt guessed that the ants could climb, but if he could get up a tree first, he had a small chance of being able to keep them off him with the spear long enough to catch his breath. If nothing else, he might get at least time to think of something better than running until he got swarmed and eaten. Experience with Lucy's restrictions had taught both of them that while he wasn't allowed to send her away from him for scouting purposes, she was perfectly capable of noticing things that he could have missed around him and telling him about them. The object just had to be within Matt's potential field of view.

"There, across the river, hanging over the bank. That big one."

It was perfect, a tree with branches big enough that he could lay on them, but skinny enough that the ants might have trouble keeping all their legs on those same branches. He waited until the tree was at about a forty-five-degree angle from him before changing direction to cross the river, hoping that would gain him a bit of a lead to climb the tree with.

Matt splashed through the shallow river like a maniac, getting soaked as he did. Any hope that the ants would be allergic to water were dashed as he heard them crashing into the river behind him. When he made it through the water and hit the opposite bank, he leapt up towards the tree, catching a low branch and swinging up as he looked for something big enough and stable enough. Something that he wouldn't fall off from when he stabbed downwards against the ants later.

By the time he had transferred to the next branch, his plans had to change again.

"Matt, look down."

Stabilizing himself against the trunk of the tree, Matt looked down at the ants, expecting to see some horror-movie vision of them climbing the trunk. Instead, they were milling around, confused. Matt sincerely doubted the ants were smart enough to be tricky. This looked like they legitimately had lost track of him. Which was weird because he had been in full sight the entire time.

*The river.*

Matt had cut off the antennas to blind the first ant he fought. He hadn't stabbed out its eyes because it didn't have them. Ants worked off scent, and the lemon-cleaner smell they'd been spraying around until now was probably, Matt thought, a general "hey, there's something interesting or dangerous over here" type of message. He had been careful during his fight to not let any foreign liquids tag him.

It was more likely that these ants were tracking him through his unique human scent. These ants were hunters, not gatherers, so it made sense that they could follow Matt's scent trail as he ran. But when Matt jumped out of the river at the tree, he hadn't actually touched ground again. Whatever sense these things used to track prey apparently wasn't long-range enough to actually see into the distance or him fifteen feet up a tree.

Matt suspected the ants were deaf too, but he wasn't going to chance it more than he had to. He sat down on the branch, found a balance, and controlled his breathing to be as quiet as he could make it. He was still huffing pretty loud, but it wasn't enough to alert the possibly deaf ants. He was safe, for now.

"Matt, I think we're gonna be okay. The only ants that followed you across the river were the ones that were almost close enough to bite you. It's like they could smell you in the water, but only for a moment. Any ant that was farther away than that isn't even bothering to cross."

Matt was very, very happy to not be getting eaten right now. But there was more. Having a reliable method of retreat also meant he could strategize to hurt his enemy and fade away before they could do anything about it.

Matt was about to go full guerrilla.

## CHAPTER TWELVE

# Mana Deficiency

"Okay, now is probably the time to hit them, Matt."

"Not yet. We can get more."

Lucy and Matt had already verified that the ants couldn't hear, which was a relief since neither of them were all that great at being quiet. That wasn't the only piece of information they had obtained, either, although the other one was a little less specific.

*Achievement: [Hit and Run (and Run, and Run, and Run)]*

You initiated a battle, which is normal. You fled from a battle, which for you is arguably even more normal. Furthermore, you did both at once, which isn't quite as common as either but still isn't exactly a rare occurrence.

But in this case, you fled from the active pursuit of over five hundred enemies with mobility similar to or superior to your own, and still got away with minimal damage. Way to go, Matt! Maybe don't do that anymore.

Rewards: Survivor's Light-touch Footwear, +3 Dexterity

"Three is enough."

"Not anymore. I want five."

Matt had been fighting ants all day. And all night. And all day. It turned out that the ants either worked in shifts or didn't sleep. They were all over the place. He had briefly tried to sleep in a tree, then found out the hard way that tossing and turning in his sleep thirty feet off the ground was a great way to test the limits of his vitality stat. That same stat also meant he could keep rolling without sleep for a few days, so he opted to just tough it out until he had eliminated all the ants.

The way that Matt fought was through kiting. He'd hide in a bush after painstakingly making sure there wasn't a tunnel nearby, wait until an ant came by, cripple it, hide again until its pheromone beacon brought in some more ants to help, kill the first ant and its early friends, let the rest of the ants chase him, escape across the river with them hot on his trail, and then cut down a few more of them.

This worked fine, except for two things. The first was that it was taking forever. Matt had limited food and water. Worse, every time he ate some of it, a window would pop up, vaguely hinting that he was getting himself closer and closer to mana deficiency. Nothing had happened yet, but the stress was building up.

The second was that it had gotten easy and therefore boring. The ants he had encountered were all pretty much identical to each other, to the point where Survivor's Reflexes treated it as if Matt was in one long, protracted battle with a single foe. The weak point detection got more and more refined, eventually giving Matt single pinpoint targets that, when hit correctly, would immediately maim the ants. He was also getting better at hitting them, not even because of Survivor's Combat, but just because of days' worth of sheer practice.

The only thing keeping him in a relatively good mood were his new shoes. Weird naming convention aside, they were essentially sneakers. After months of heavy armored boots, enchanted but still heavy, the new light-touch footwear made his feet feel like they had wings.

*The freaking breathability on these shoes. Unbelievable.*

"Matt, are you thinking about the shoes again?"

"Yes. I would spend any amount of repair stones on these, Lucy. I'm not kidding. Infinity repair stones, if that's what it takes."

"Great. That's a totally normal train of thought when surrounded by lethal carnivorous ants. But would it be too much for me to ask you to focus up, just a little?"

"Fine. Point taken."

Resisting the urge to re-tie the wondrous miracles that were his shoes, Matt put his eyes back on the group of ants. After only a few more moments, two more ants surged into view. It was time.

"Now?" Lucy asked.

"Yeah, that's enough."

Matt surged out of the bushes, chopping off one of the ant's antennae before any of them had a chance to react, and then was gone. He burned stamina as needed on Spring-Fighter to get across the river, then turned to fight.

Five ants was an interesting challenge compared to three, but he hadn't been wasting his time grinding up his skills. He had found that Spring-Fighter could be used in absurdly short bursts, burning low amounts of stamina for a small but quick burst of speed. In a fight, that was more than enough to bend around an attack in a way the not-so-bright ants were always unprepared for and strike at their weak points.

The fights themselves were a relatively short period in the whole baiting, waiting, and kiting cycle of things, so Matt took his time. As soon as he had injured at least a couple of legs on the majority of the ants, the fight was suddenly a much more sedate affair. Matt would let his stamina climb, charge the group, pivot to the side using Spring-Fighter, and strike. Easy-peasy. The ants' numbers were enough to make it hard for him to end the fight in one charge, but whittling them away was just as easy and maybe even a bit safer.

Eventually, three ants were dead and one was so badly injured it would likely die on its own within a few minutes. That left one mostly intact ant, a challenge so unbelievably boring at this point that Matt could more or less zone out while weaving around its predictable clacking-jaw attack like a matador.

But he stayed focused. He moved in, spun around the ant's jaws, and prepared to nail it to the ground with his spear. But as he thrust forward with his weapon, the pole suddenly felt alien in his hands. It wobbled off course like it had a mind of its own, missing the weak spot by a mile.

*Ding!*

*Oh no. That's not good.*

The ants weren't the best at following fast, elusive movement, but they weren't so clueless that they couldn't turn around and take advantage of a poorly-aimed spear thrust. And while they weren't exactly flexible, that traded off with them being unbelievably strong at the few motions they could do. One of those was this move that Matt called the death wheel. Normally, he'd be able to dodge the move. But it wasn't just his arms that felt weak, his legs were like Jell-O too.

So when the ant wheeled around fast and hard, the outside of the ant's mandibles cracked into Matt's hip, destroying his center of gravity and sending him pinwheeling to the ground.

Before Matt could even think about getting up, the ant was over his right side, clacking downwards with its sharp mouthparts. Sometime during the fall, Matt had completely lost track of his spear, leaving him temporarily unarmed and without nearly enough time to get at his other weapons. This thing was going to take off his right arm, and he had nothing to stop it with.

*Your shield, you dumb asshole.*

Matt consistently forgot he had a shield attached to his right arm, in part because he needed both hands to effectively use his spear, and the shield tended to make it just a little harder to do that. Having a giant ant threaten to detach all his limbs was a hell of a reminder. He reached over with his left hand, hitting the catch on the shield just in time for it to fully expand, click into place, and momentarily prop the ant's mandibles open. The metal immediately started groaning under the strain.

Matt reached up and started desperately working at the strap for the shield, which was effectively tethering his arm in between the ant's mandibles and keeping him from running. It was no good. The tension of being yanked around by the ant meant the strap was too tight to disengage. That left him with one option for getting away, and he didn't love it. Reaching down with his left hand again, he drew his knife and took a single heavy chop at the shield strap, cutting through it and a good section of his arm in the bargain.

It hurt like hell, but he was free, and the ant was still distracted with his shield for the moment. Matt flared Spring-Fighter, praying that it would work. It did. He thought for a moment about running, then reconsidered. The ant could follow him any place but across the river, and across the river would be swarming with ants any second, if it wasn't already. He needed to finish this.

*If I can't count on hitting, I'll just have to make sure I can't miss.*

A shattering sound indicated his thinking time was over. His shield had exploded into pieces under the pressure of the ant's bite. Matt shuddered to think of what would happen if it was his arm instead of a metal shield.

As the ant lunged forward, so did Matt. Throwing caution to the wind, he waited until the insect was close enough to start its jaw attack, then hit the afterburners on Spring-Fighter to propel him into the air over it. Twisting wildly through the jump, he managed to land on the thing's back, more or less facing the same direction it was.

Even without Survivor's Reflexes highlighting it, he knew where the weak point on the animal was. As the ant thrashed, he laid the point of his knife down on the precise spot where the insect's exoskeleton split. It was a joint necessary for the ant's movement. It was also a weak spot. Matt slammed all his body weight down into the knife.

The ant jerked, then fell to the ground like a puppet with cut strings.

Matt jumped off the ant as Lucy started yelling. "Are you okay? What happened?"

"Not sure. Something with my combat skill. Let's get out of here first. I don't want to risk more ants showing up," Matt replied.

"I told you to not push yourself. Three ants is plenty."

Matt scooped up his spear, ignored the ruined remains of his shield, and ran like the wind away from the area.

*Mana-related Skill Malfunction: Advanced Survivor's Combat*

All skills of any kind require mana to function. Some (like a mage's spells) rely on gathered external mana, which is converted into external effects without significant interaction from the body's systems. Others, such as most physical skills, amplify the natural mana the body produces to achieve otherwise impossible physical feats. But this amplification is multiplicative, not additive. When the body's baseline mana is compromised, so are the skills that rely on it.

By subsisting on mana-deficient food during a period of significant physical output, you have destabilized your baseline mana levels sufficiently to cause a skill malfunction. The affected skills may work at a diminished level, or fail to function at all. In more advanced stages of mana deficiency, no skills will function and stat effects will diminish until they offer no advantage at all. Eventually, permanent damage to your body and death become possibilities as well.

As your body's mana ebbs and flows, the skill may be reactivated or disabled again at an irregular timing.

By the time Matt had got back to the relative safety of a tree, another notification had sounded with a temporary reprieve.

*Mana-related Skill Malfunction Resolved*

Your Advanced Survivor's Combat skill has been reinstated and can now be used again. Please note that this skill reactivation is potentially temporary. If the issues with your baseline mana are not resolved, it or other physical skills could unexpectedly fail as well.

## CHAPTER THIRTEEN

# The Colony

Matt took the new mana-deficiency change in stride. At this point, not a lot could phase him. Some days were good days. Some days were not so good days. In the end, he was going to try his best to survive.

"It's okay. We'll figure out a way around this," Matt reassured Lucy after explaining his notifications.

"Somehow that doesn't make me feel better."

"To be honest, me neither. There's basically no warning on this problem. It would almost be better if it turned off and stayed off. That way at least I wouldn't have to realize mid-strike that I had screwed myself trusting it."

"There's a bigger problem, Matt. We don't have time now."

"Yeah." Matt had been hunting ants at a rate of dozens per day, but there were still potentially hundreds of them to go. The food issue was progressing faster than either he or Lucy had expected. If it continued at the same pace, he could lose all his skills entirely. They needed to hurry and finish the mission before then.

"I can't take all these ants at once."

"No, of course not. I think it's time for plan B."

"Make sure you don't kill it, Matt."

"Got it. Now quiet. It's really hard to do this without engaging with Survivor's Combat."

After some experimentation, Matt had figured out something vital. Survivor's Combat was pretty much automatic, and acted on its own to amplify whatever move he was trying to make. It made a careless strike look as if he had practiced it thousands of times. But it turned out to be a relatively simple matter to suppress the skill if Matt wanted to.

He never had any reason before to purposely make his strikes weaker, but in the mana-deficiency notifications was the implication that using his skills were probably going to make his problem worse.

Using just his stats and his superior, newly acquired understanding of ant battle tactics, Matt was now wildly hacking away at ant-legs completely unassisted, barely avoiding mandible attacks and pointy-leg stomps as he did.

It took five agonizing minutes, but finally the ant was down. Every leg was disabled, and it was antenna-less and blinded. Matt knew the next part would suck, and he'd feel bad about it later, but there was no way their plan could possibly work without it. Carefully and slowly, he began prying the exoskeleton of the ant open.

This wasn't his first ant-prying rodeo, unfortunately. It had taken them multiple tries to find the exact ant part they were looking for, and the last ant had started to fade before he could get a stabilization spike in it. Hopefully, this ant would hold up a little better, but he was being as careful as he could anyway.

Using his knife as a chisel and the Survivor's Club as a hammer, he slowly separated the animal down the centerline of its back, along a natural joint in the chitin. Breaking it open, he saw his questionable prize—a softball-sized gland near the thing's back. Matt cut around it, hoping the ant would survive the amputation. As long as the ant lived, parts of the ant wouldn't dissipate. They had tested that, too.

Matt sprinted away from the ant, Lucy following close behind, directly towards a nearby entrance of the colony. Plan B was pretty simple, and revolved around one important fact. The dungeon quest hadn't said that every ant had to die, just that the colony had to be controlled, and the spread of ants had to be stopped.

There was more than one way to skin that particular cat.

If the quest could be taken literally, and Matt hoped it could, even something like permanently plugging the colony up would work. Of course, that wasn't an option, unless Matt somehow snagged some weird hell of an achievement to build a giant bunker construction project. The other option was the adventurer version of demanding to see the manager. They were going to go straight to the boss and see if they could get this handled. Killing the queen, or queens, would be much, much faster than tracking down and killing every single ant.

Actually getting to the metaphorical manager's office was a different story. That would take some finesse.

At the mouth of the colony, Matt took the ant-gland, held it over his head, and jammed it with the stabilization spike. The gland spilled its liquid all over

Matt. Whether or not the original ant died past this point was not a gamble they were willing to make, they just hoped that the spike's effects would keep the pheromone working. There wasn't any way to know for sure, since they had never tested the spike on organic insect perfume. But it was better than nothing.

Now they just had to test to make sure it worked, and in the name of speed they were taking a bit of a risk. Matt jumped down into the hole, dropping a few feet down a steep ramp before the tunnel leveled out and continued off several meters before bending off to the left. The tunnel was the height of an adult male. Just enough for Matt to move around in, but not enough for him to jump. But before seeing what was around the corner, he had a more immediate problem.

An ant was apparently guarding the entrance, and was doing so from just far enough in the tunnel that Matt was able to avoid landing directly on it. But only just. The ant approached Matt with antennae waving back and forth, and Matt kept his eyes glued to its mandibles. If it tried to get him, he was more or less backed up against a wall and would need all the warning he could get.

"Matt, shit. You sure about this?" Lucy watched the ant with worry on her face.

"Nope! Let's just see how it goes, I guess."

The ant crept closer and closer until its antennae were just a foot from Matt's face. Then it suddenly lost interest. Either Matt had just got a lot more handsome to ants, or the pheromone had actually worked to trick this ant into thinking he was a friend. He was suddenly glad he hadn't killed the guard ant; that would have called the entire colony over.

*Wait . . .*

It would call the entire colony over, *except* the queen and any other ants that had jobs more important than defense. They would presumably stay in place, counting on the rest of the ants to defeat the intruder.

"Lucy, I'm going to do something different. Hold on to your butt."

"Wait, is this stupid different, or good different?"

Matt quickly shifted his pack around his body, took out one of his trap spikes, and shifted the pack back.

"Probably a little of both."

The advantage to killing a bunch of ants with highlighted weak spots was that Matt eventually got a feel for why each spot was weak. A couple of them were connected to systems so vital they resulted in instant death, like the joint between the neck and head. Others limited mobility. But there was one spot on the back that seemed to scramble the ant's nervous system. It didn't kill them, but it just wasn't a nice place to get stabbed.

Matt took his chances on letting Advanced Survivor's Combat out to play for the split second it took to jab a trap spike into the guard ant like a demented combat acupuncturist, and then immediately turned tail and ran deeper into the colony. As he did, he felt a sudden strong whiff of ant-lemon-alarm-pheromone fill the tunnel. It was stronger than anything he had smelled before.

Surprisingly quickly, the daylight filtering into the tunnel petered out and Matt was left in the dark. Flipping on his flashlight, Matt was momentarily thankful for invader-armor guy. Had the other guy almost killed Matt? Yup. Had he left surprisingly little in the way of usable loot? For sure, unless you liked random smooth stones. But was he the only guy on Gaia that Matt had beaten to quasi-death with a shovel, who also turned out to have abandoned a bag a couple of miles away with a magic flashlight in it? Yes, and that covered quite a few sins in Matt's book.

Ants started pouring towards him from every side tunnel he passed. They also came directly down the tunnel in the direction he was running, which was what he was counting on. So long as he was passing ants going the opposite direction he was, he stood a good chance to be heading deeper into the colony. He assumed the queen would be, if not in the deepest parts, at least pretty deep.

Emptying the colony in one direction also meant he stood a better chance of surviving if things did go sideways, since he had essentially distracted every guard the place had. And since the alarm smell was meant to mark areas rather than individual targets, the ants couldn't identify him as the source of the problem at all. Or at least that was the assumption. Matt was enormously happy to see it being proven true, especially considering the alternative was getting ripped to pieces almost immediately.

Matt even had enough time to gripe to Lucy about the dungeon. "I don't get how anyone was supposed to clear this. There are thousands of these things, and these are narrow tunnels."

"I'm just guessing, but I think most teams would have a ranged fighter. Remember that Survivor's Crossbow I told you to take, but you ignored me? Imagine how easy it would be for an archer class to pick these off from a distance. As long as they had enough arrows, they could pretty much just post up in a tree near an entrance and kill dozens of these things an hour, with zero risk. The ants would never even figure out where they were."

"Got it. Yeah, point taken. It's probably about time I get some kind of ranged attack."

"After the mana generator."

Matt grimaced. Besides the part where it might save his life, the mana generator was profoundly boring to him. It wasn't cheap, and it was going to be hard passing up that much loot, if he even lived long enough to actually buy the damn thing.

The tunnels were long, but the make-Matt-seem-like-an-ant pheromone was doing a much, much better job than Matt or Lucy expected. If anything, it was too good. Whatever the liquid in the gland did, it saved Matt the trouble of dying amid thousands of collie-sized ants. Unfortunately, as they got further and further from the alarm-spreading ant Matt had injured, the ants started paying more and more attention to them.

"Sure."

Luckily, the attention wasn't hostile, but it still slowed them down as they tried to move past ant after ant trying to figure out what Matt was saying in the smell-language of ants.

Eventually, the incoming ants petered out. The direct attack on the colony was apparently a big enough deal that almost all the ants went to deal with it. Without any outward-moving ants to reverse-engineer his course inward, Matt was now forced to wander the tunnels, trying his very best to keep moving in a general direction without getting turned around.

The entire trip down, he was passing weird ant rooms. The majority of the larger cavities the tunnels connected to seemed to be filled with stripped bones. Maybe these were the "trash" rooms of the colony, where the ants threw their bones after stripping the meat off. Some were more inexplicable, like a room full of medium-sized round rocks, or one room that was almost completely packed out with leaves. If Matt was an insect enthusiast, he would have found it interesting.

In the kind of danger he found himself in, the time it took to even glance in each room was a time sink he couldn't afford. It eventually turned out that he needn't have bothered, anyway. The queen's throne room was pretty hard to miss. For one, the entrance was bigger, much bigger than any tunnel or door to a storage cavity Matt had seen. It was also the only room packed with larvae and eggs.

But the most striking feature Matt could see from outside the cavity was what mostly clued him in on the room's importance. The entrance was flanked with not just a few but a solid ten guard ants, each three times bigger than normal, and, to the last ant, they looked determined not to let anything past them.

## CHAPTER FOURTEEN

# The Loop

Matt paused in his path. The behavior of the huge guard ants in their role as bouncers was important to Matt. If his current pheromone coating was good enough to get him through the door, his best choice was probably hurrying through. He didn't know if the queen was even combat-capable, so that might be all it took. If they let him in, he might be able to shank her, get a plinth, and escape before the guards could do anything about it.

If they wouldn't let him in, though, he was digging into a world of problems. Suddenly, he'd be dealing with ten big guards, a possibly combat-capable or even boss-level queen, and presumably the rest of the colony rushing back as soon as the guard ants had time to get some alarm scent in the air. Matt probably wouldn't be able to even run, let alone win.

And that was if the dungeon system counted a queen-assassination as a win. If it didn't, it was the same problem minus one queen, which was still plenty to kill him. Or if the bodyguards let him in, but the queen could fight. Or any more of a dozen horrifying scenarios Matt could think of. Squeezing past the guards was only worthwhile if the risk of assassinating the queen was less dangerous than a slow mana-starvation. This didn't seem like it was, and he talked through his thoughts with Lucy.

"So . . . crazy Matt-plan time?" Lucy asked after hearing everything.

"Yup, looks like it. I just have to make one first."

Mapping even a small percentage of the tunnels was taking a lot of time. Now that Matt more or less knew his way into the queen's chamber, he was able to leave, snag another ant, re-up his don't-eat-me cologne, and run back in for more mapping. In the process, he eventually found closer, better-hidden entrances that cut his overall travel time down, but it was still a time-consuming process.

Eventually, Matt gained a certain appreciation of the ants' semi-logic when making their tunnels. Were they planned? Nope. Were they efficient? Nope. But no two trash rooms were very near each other, either. The same was true for other rooms. Once a room was far enough from the work the ants needed it for, they'd establish a new one. Over time, they'd compensate for poor tunnel planning by just cutting more tunnels, meaning the entire place was traversable in an efficient way for the ants who knew it, but a horrifying labyrinth for everyone else.

After experimenting to make sure the ants didn't freak out about people carving stuff on their colony walls, Matt started drawing arrows.

The trick to his victory was going to be a route he could consistently run that was just the right length between "long enough that a lap is significant" and "short enough that Matt can run it without running out of stamina." It took the better part of an entire stress-filled day and two mana malfunctions to find the route. But the momentary lack of skills didn't end up mattering except as a reminder of how much trouble Matt was potentially in.

"Are you sure you don't want to get some sleep first?"

"I'm sure. It's not like there's day or night down here."

"You could kill some more ants. See if you can't get more achievements first."

"It's not worth the risk. One or two dexterity points aren't going to make the difference here. We've already talked about this."

"Well, yeah, but . . ."

Lucy was noticeably worried about the plan. And, Matt thought, she wasn't wrong to be. Having a plan didn't mean that nothing could go wrong, it just meant a bigger possibility of things going right. And the smallest of errors here meant almost instant death. It wasn't a comforting situation to be in.

"I get it." Matt sat down by her, so he could make close eye contact. "I'm afraid too."

"I just feel like I've made a mistake letting you do this. What if you die, because of me being a bad guardian? We should have stayed in safer dungeons."

"That's dangerous in its own way, you know? This is the choice we have. It's not great. But you are doing your best." Matt looked as serious as he could, hoping his words would sink in better that way. "Just, to preempt if something went wrong, This is my choice too. I wouldn't blame you a bit. You are good help, Lucy. The best."

Lucy reddened a little and turned away. "Thanks, Matt."

*You always know it worked with her when she gets embarrassed. Mission accomplished.*

"Plus, don't you mean if *we* die? We take these risks together."

Lucy got quiet for a moment. "That's never been for sure."

"It hasn't? When we first met, you wanted me to die so you could go home, or something. Right?"

"Kind of."

"Lucy . . . explain."

She stood up and walked away. "Later. We can talk about it later."

"Lucy. If something's going on, I need to know."

"Later, okay? We have things to focus on. Ants. Near-certain death. Lots of things, Matt."

She wasn't wrong, but something was wrong here. Lucy had never been very open about the whole where-guardians-come-from topic, but Matt had thought it was one more subject that she was metaphysically restricted from discussing. If this was something she was just keeping from him rather than something she literally couldn't talk about, it was a very different story.

"Okay. But we ARE talking about this later, Lucy."

Lucy nodded reluctantly, and Matt let the matter drop for now. They had bigger ants to fry.

The first step to the plan was drawing off as many normal ants as they could. Luckily, they already had a solution for that, and had long since worked out that there were standard ant guards posted at almost every hill entrance. Matt fought with one just long enough to get it spraying alarm scent, set up a few simple traps to re-up the alarm as other ants drew near, and moved into the tunnels with a fresh coat of don't-bite-me-I'm-a-friend pheromone paint.

As he approached the uber-guard squad, there was a small chance things would go really, really well for him in a couple of ways. The first would be that the guard ants would just let him through. He doubted it, as he had seen them turn away standard-issue ants from the entrance several times by now. The throne room seemed to be for those with a particular status, and Matt just didn't have any way to get that.

It was still worth a shot. He and Lucy had already decided that if the guard ants let him through, he'd try to assassinate the queen. It was high risk, since once he was in there, he'd be trapped. But it was also high reward. If things went well, they'd just win without having to go through a whole sequence of still-risky-but-less-risky chances.

The other way things could go well was if the guard ants just turned out to not be able to leave their posts at all. If they were tethered by duty to the door to the extent they couldn't chase him, Matt could probably figure out a way to cheese them over the next several hours or days, whittle the guards down, and just stroll right in.

Neither of the two good scenarios ended up being real. As Matt strolled towards the throne room door looking as ant-like as he could manage, all ten ants assumed a more aggressive stance. When he took the chance to push forward a bit more, one of the ants furthest from the door roughly turned him around with its mandibles, drawing a bit of blood, even though it didn't appear to intend to do him harm. Any question that these ants were fightable was erased from Matt's mind immediately. Those mandibles were incredibly powerful, and even in a calm situation, the guard ant was moving quicker than the normal ants.

That left the real plan, and there was no use waiting on it. Matt walked up, drew his knife, and hit one of the guard ants with a blow deliberately aimed at the most-lethal weak spot in their physiology. Matt also assumed that they wouldn't just let themselves be cut down. Even by someone slathered in I'm-an-ant pheromones.

As he sprinted away, the sound of nine huge ants skittering after him confirmed he was right.

There had always been a chance these ants wouldn't be that fast running around. When they were still guarding the door, there was no way to confirm it. Now it was confirmed that these ants were faster. As he sprinted away, they were catching up fast. He couldn't run fast enough to complete his route, even juiced up with Spring-Fighter. Within several seconds, the ants had closed about half the head start he had put between them.

Then the traps started going off. Matt knew that these traps would fail to hurt the ants. And he was unfortunately correct. But they still did their job. Matt heard tripwires firing almost immediately after he crossed each one, and then felt the satisfaction of hearing the ants pile up behind the now-delayed leader.

Between the surprise, the traps, and using almost all of his stamina, Matt managed to stay uneaten just long enough to make it through his loop of tunnels that ultimately led back to the same place he had started. As he approached the door to the royal throne room with ants on his tail, he leapt into the air and caught a piece of rope he had carefully staked into the ceiling.

*It's all or nothing now. Please keep going.*

When Matt was much younger, an entomologist had visited his school science classroom to teach Matt and the other children about insects. He had brought a lot of them with him, but one had stood out to Matt more than the others. Using what Matt assumed was an enormous amount of time and patience, the entomologist had managed to get an ant to set up a loop of "I found food" pheromones at the bottom of a bottle. Without something to shake it out of its behavior, he explained, the ant in the bottle would gladly, and without thinking, travel the loop again and again, never giving up until they literally starved to death.

Matt didn't think these ants would keep going forever, and he didn't have the time to wait for them if they did. But he did think he could get them to travel in a loop following a combination of his scent on the ground and an ever-intensifying trail of alarm pheromone, at least for a while. If they didn't, if they were smart enough to stand and wait at the entrance again, he'd be stuck on the roof without any viable options except to sprint away.

The ants were below him now, rumbling through the tunnel like a death-train.

"Come on. Come on." Lucy was off to the side of the tunnel, wringing her hands.

The ants didn't even slow down. They rumbled away on Matt's exact original route.

Once the ants were far enough off that he was sure they couldn't sense him directly, Matt dropped down and burned a tiny bit of his recovered stamina to fuel a jump from the path through the door. He didn't have long, but he had at least a few minutes.

It was time to take the queen.

## CHAPTER FIFTEEN

# The Throne Room

The throne room was large. It was always clear to Matt that this *was* the throne room. If the guards weren't a dead giveaway, the sheer size of the chamber would have done it. As he plotted out his looping course, he had triangulated enough to know that it was at least an order of a magnitude bigger than any of the other, more utilitarian, rooms he had encountered.

If that wasn't enough, the light was different in the throne room. Matt had noticed this back when he was observing the entrance. He couldn't quite see past the ten or so hulking guards, but there was motion and shining objects. Now that he was in the room, he could identify what was going on in crisp detail. This room was lined with eggs, being tended to by dozens of nursing ants, and they were tiny. Where guard ants had been almost twice as big as the standard-issue ants, these were about half the normal size.

They were, apparently, built for detail work And they were absolutely focused on that task, moving around delicate eggs without so much as leaving a mark on them. Matt couldn't quite make out what exactly they were doing, but he assumed that it was some variation of cleaning, tending, and making sure they were healthy. The eggs themselves were bioluminescent, glowing purple things filled with cloudy purple liquid. They looked a lot like if someone had somehow captured a nebula in a glass orb. In a giant room completely lined with these purple eggs, the effect was striking.

It also made Matt hopeful that he had chosen the right plan of attack. As much as he could hunt ants, he also had to contend with the queen's reproduction rate. He could see various eggs that were farther along in the hatching process, showing outlines of the ant beyond the purplish liquid inside them. With the many hundreds of eggs in the room, he was unlikely to ever get truly ahead of the queen's breeding capability with the kind of violence he could output by himself.

Which brought him to the queen. And she was no slouch herself. Matt had expected her to be different from the other ants, and she was. He thought it was likely she would be bigger, and she didn't disappoint. But he hadn't thought she'd be beautiful, and somehow she was. Where the normal ants' exoskeletons were mostly roundish, sloped off things like Earth ants tended to be, hers was all angles, each surface arcing towards a sharp, crisp break to a new side. Not square, exactly. Just defined, looking as planned and designed as a supercar.

Any hope that Matt had where she would turn out to be a non-combatant was dashed by another thing that augmented her beauty. She looked fast. Not fast in a can-dash-in-a-straight-line way, but more in a way Matt would describe as nimble or agile. She didn't just look like she could run, she looked like she could *move*. If the standard-issue ants looked sturdily all-terrain in their design, the queen looked lethal.

That lethality was reinforced by her weaponry as well. The nursing ants were smaller than Matt, which meant stomping wouldn't be much of an issue. Not so with the queen. The angles extended to her legs, which ended in sharp points rather than normal feet. They were also big enough that even a single one of her legs could credibly spear him without much issue. More striking was the fact that the queen had mandibles that looked like two scythe blades, big sharp things that looked like they were used to cutting things in half.

Things like human invaders to the throne room.

Unfortunately, that wasn't the worst of Matt's worries. That title belonged to her intelligence. Even the guard ants had seemed pretty mindless in the face of pheromones. They knew not to let just anybody into the throne room, but at the same time they couldn't identify him as a threat.

The queen was different. She didn't have antennae. She had eyes. She was the *source* of the pheromones, the authority who gave the orders and not the underlings that received it. Almost as soon as she saw Matt, she shifted from a reclining position into a full fighting posture.

"Matt, I think she knows we aren't locals."

"No shit. Holy hell, she's terrifying."

The queen opened and closed her mandibles with a horrifyingly sharp *shink* sort of sound, then started moving. It was on. Matt just hoped that she hadn't thought to call back all of her minions.

"That's another skill down!"

"Shit!"

The queen had turned out to be every bit as fast as she looked. Matt had gone to meet her with the plan of sliding under her to get around to an unguarded side. He managed to get by her mandibles as he did, but before he was actually under her abdomen, she pivoted in place like a boxer, dipping her head and going after his centerline with her razor-sharp jaws.

*Shit. This is going to be harder than I thought.* Matt had narrowly avoided getting bisected by burning a huge amount of stamina, kicking off the ground, and using Spring-Fighter to move him back much faster than he could have managed on his own. After that, he ran.

After Matt recovered from his first abortive attack, he turned to face the queen head-on, trying to stay out of range until he could figure out a way past her mandibles to attack her flanks. This turned out to be hopeless. She had better range with her jaws than Matt had with his spear, and could turn faster than he could strafe her position. He almost immediately abandoned attacking and stayed out of range to observe her movements. She responded to this by attacking herself, and she was far faster in a lunge than Matt's organic speed.

He was able to keep from being chomped by judicious activations of Spring-Fighter. The queen seemed hardwired to try to grab prey by the center of her jaws. After a couple of repetitions of over-using his mobility skill, Matt was able to figure out the basic timing of her lunge and move just far enough back as her mandibles closed, which left him time to jab at her face with his spear. This proved to be ineffective, unfortunately. He couldn't reach her eyes, and the spear didn't seem to be capable of even scratching her exoskeleton.

Worse, his use of Spring-Fighter wasn't sustainable. His stamina bar was draining away. Sooner or later, he'd run out of juice, and she'd get him. But when he dodged close to the wall, the lucky reality of the queen's more careful behavior around her eggs showed itself. She was afraid of hitting them, taking a split second more to position and attack than she had out in the open. It was a big enough difference that Matt had time to dodge to the side rather than retreat back and save on his use of Spring-Fighter. It still wasn't a forever solution, but the drain was much slower.

More importantly, that was the first weakness he had found in the queen. Her apparent care for her eggs.

In the meantime, Survivor's Reflexes was hard at work. The other ants had all been similar enough to each other that they shared weak points, and Survivor's Reflexes was able to treat them all as one single variety of foe. The queen was running on a different enough chassis that this wasn't true for her. Not only did the fight start without even a small clue as to where to hit her, but even as the weak points started to show themselves, they were all in places that would be hard for Matt to hit. Minutes into the fight, her legs didn't show any weaknesses at all. The weak points that Matt could see were to the rear of her body near the ovipositor, and dead-center on her belly. Otherwise, she appeared to be covered up by her hard, un-weak exoskeleton.

After several rounds of hugging the wall and dodging to the side, Matt made a desperate lunging strike at her eye and got lucky, putting a deep nick into it. He was ecstatic about landing the blow, up until she whipped her head around while his weight was still over-committed towards her and sent him flying. She probably couldn't see out of that eye now, but that didn't do him much good while he was heaped on the ground. He got back on his feet just in time to meet her next charge, dodge, and then aim at her other eye.

At the exact moment, Survivor's Combat chose to take a break. Suddenly, Matt's footwork sucked. His ability to stab stuff with a spear plummeted, and he fully missed his target. Without perfect footwork, his balance felt off and he tried his best to stabilize. That also meant he wasn't paying as much attention to his strike. With all the artificial muscle memory gone, the spear shocked against the queen's exoskeleton and jerked out of his hands.

Luckily, his movement skills were still intact. And the previous lunge had taught Matt something important. The outside of the queen's chompers wasn't sharp like the insides were. They could club him, but not cut him. As the mandibles came around to smack him, Matt dumped just enough juice into Survivor's Reflexes to *almost* match their speed, braced his hands against the jaw, and let the momentum fling him away from the danger zone.

The queen wheeled around in a rage, rushing after him. As Matt landed, she was already almost to his position, fully prepped for another strike. Matt's stamina was running low at about a quarter of his total reservoir, but as her mandibles started to close, he dumped about half of it into moving back and then quickly forward. That brought him right up to her face, where he grabbed on to a joint in the armor near her cheek.

Matt had had good success in the past with brute force, can't-miss techniques. He didn't need to be a combat expert for those attacks. Without his spear, Matt went for his club, bringing it down again and again on the joint where the queen's mandible met her cheek. Meanwhile, the ant did it's best to dislodge him, slamming its head up and down against the ground and swinging it side to side wildly. Matt's armored pants were thankfully structurally sound enough to keep his legs from getting serious scrapes, and he was glad to feel Rub Some Dirt In It kicking it to heal up the remaining damage. With any luck, he'd at least be able to stand by the time he was ready to let go.

Just before the ant managed to break his grip, Matt's club went from simply bouncing off the joint to actually sinking in a bit, producing loud cracking noises and visibly causing the ant queen's panic to intensify. He managed to bring down the club a few more times in parting, causing some more satisfying crunches that he hoped indicated the mandible wouldn't work quite as well moving forward, and then he was flying again.

Once he climbed back to his feet, Matt sprinted away for as long as he could, trying to maintain as much distance as possible, until he suddenly realized he couldn't hear the queen chasing him. He looked back to see her waving her head around in apparent pain, which made sense considering the deep wound he had left in her first eye. As she continued thrashing, she suddenly lifted her tail end into the air, vibrating her abdomen in a bizarre, jerky way.

"Matt! You see that? Is that another attack?"

"Yeah. I do. It's good news as long as she's not calling the other ants."

"Good news?"

As if in answer to her question, the queen suddenly stopped moving, and a hissing sound filled the room as a cloud of vapor erupted from somewhere on her back half.

"Oh. Oh, no."

## CHAPTER SIXTEEN

# Trapper Keeper

With the superhuman senses of someone with 20 perception, Matt could just barely smell the alarm pheromones the normal ants put out. He had to be pretty close to get a whiff of the citrus tang. If Matt's perception was just a little bit lower, he probably would have missed it entirely. Presumably, the same smell was "louder" for the ants, who could pick up on it from thousands of feet away.

The vapor that the queen expelled was the exact same scent, as far as Matt could tell. That wasn't too out of the ordinary. Matt would have been shocked if the queen ant didn't have a way to say, "Hey, there's danger over here, you guys," in some way or another. The strength of the colony was numbers, and it didn't make sense for the queen to not leverage that.

What was less expected was how strong her vapor was. Where the other ant's signal was so quiet as to be almost a whisper to Matt, this had to be the ant equivalent of an air-raid siren. The entire throne room smelled like a freshly mopped office building, and it meant trouble.

"What does it smell like, Matt?"

Matt's face was grim. "Citrus."

"Shit. How long do we have?"

"If we're lucky? A minute or so." There wasn't much time for talk. Matt was already sprinting towards the queen, aiming to arrive at the side of her hopefully disabled mandible. As he hoped, it really was at least partially broken. The queen lunged towards him, but apparently couldn't extend the mandible outwards to widen her strike anymore. He easily dodged around it, and finally found an opportunity to use his most neglected skill.

"Pocket Sand!" He yelled, feeling like a doofus. None of his other skills required verbal activation, he thought. *Why this one?*

> *Pocket Sand*
>
> You have walked the often-neglected path of utilizing combat powders, which is weird. On more than one occasion, you have blinded an enemy with sand, dirt, or some other less common powder, and you are now getting rewarded with a skill completely appropriate for the kind of guy who thinks you can become a ninja by spending enough money at a mall knife shop.
>
> Pocket sand streamlines the process of reaching into a pouch, pocket, or other kind of partially-enclosed storage and gripping a reasonable amount of any fine-grained, loose material. It also amplifies your ability to throw it, making it go farther, fly straighter, and resist wind slightly better than you'd expect.
>
> Pocket sand's effectiveness scales off DEX and PER, and synergizes with Survivor's Reflexes to find both ocular and non-ocular powder-sensitive targets.

Matt had occasional uses for Pocket Sand, but in the easy dungeons they were grinding during the time the system had been asleep, those opportunities were rare. It was a skill that wanted a single target big enough that he couldn't just kill it outright, and that moved slow enough that he could hit it in the first place. Mostly it was just something that he kept in his literal back pocket, looking for a big, otherwise tough opponent with eyes to use it on.

If this wasn't that very scenario, he didn't know what was.

A cloud of sand emerged from his hand and covered the queen's remaining good eye. Panicking, she started backing up. Taking advantage of the situation, Matt jumped up and clubbed the ant hard in the same eye. To his surprise, this combo worked great. The queen's momentarily blindness meant she didn't move to avoid the blow, and as the club impacted the eye the entire organ burst, leaking bluish-green liquid that he had come to associate with ant blood.

"It's blinded, Matt!"

"Yeah! Let's get to work."

Blinded didn't mean defenseless, but it did mean a noticeable shift from damn near invincible to something he could handle. It seemed that the queen still had a scent-sense of some kind, but she was much worse at tracking him, to the extent where he was able to hit her flanks and legs at will.

He attacked from as many weird angles as he could, using Spring-Fighter liberally, since he'd either win the fight and clear the dungeon or be swarmed by the ants that were coming back. He desperately tried to get into position to launch onto the queen's back or slide under her belly, but she seemed aware of these vulnerabilities and protected them to the best of her abilities.

And then the worst possibility became reality. Matt made a feint at the good side of the giant ant's jaw, hoping to make it drop its head so he could burst Spring-Fighter and hopefully go up and over her lowered skull. As he did, he heard a ding and felt the loss of all the enhanced speed he was counting on to either make the maneuver a success or pull him out of danger. The ant jerked its good mandible towards his arm, which was stretched out as far as it would go to sell the reality of his club-feint.

The arm remained outstretched as it hit the ground, cleanly detached halfway up his bicep.

Matt screamed, and tried to backpedal, but the ant was on him, cutting and gouging with its good mandible. Nothing else got detached, but he picked up several deep cuts on his torso and remaining arm as the thing thrashed semi-blindly at his last known position. *Rub Some Dirt In It* kicked in and managed to staunch some of the bleeding, but Matt's short timer was getting even shorter.

Matt's mind went blank for a second. The pain made it hard to concentrate on anything but the rising fear in his chest.

Swinging back from a cutting motion that had already nicked him again, the ant managed to club Matt with the outside of its good mandible. Matt was flung to the earth, bleeding and helpless to enhance either his movement or combat. At the same time, he heard the rumbling of the guard ants approaching. He had seconds, not minutes, to bring this fight home, or he'd be swarmed by the better part of a dozen enemies, all fully capable of fighting him on even terms.

The queen ant could apparently smell the blood, and her killing instincts told her this was the time to finish a weakened foe. She moved forward more slowly, sweeping her mandibles back and forth in a sort of lethal sweeping motion that would catch up to him eventually. Luckily, the scent seemed to be as much of a disadvantage as it was an advantage, just in a different way. The trail of Matt's blood left in the sand seemed to confuse her a bit about his exact location. Her attacks were probing, not precise.

*Closer. Come on. Closer.*

"Matt, do it now!"

Most of Matt's skills didn't build up momentum. Survivor's Combat didn't get better over the course of a fight, and Spring-Fighter was a finite resource he had to ration out carefully. But Survivor's Reflexes was an exception, and every second Matt had spent fighting was a second it spent narrowing down the weak points from a general range to a maximally damaging pinpoint location.

The queen's weak spot indicators weren't needle-point accurate yet, but they didn't need to be. Matt had bought enough time. He had also kept just enough of his recently expanded stamina pool to activate his Trapper Keeper skill. As the queen moved forward, she finally stepped into range of the skill's deployment range.

*Trapper Keeper (Skill)*

The Trapper Keeper skill does not level, and is instead keyed to the level of your Survivor's Reflexes skill. At the current level, Trapper Keeper allows you to store one trap of your choosing in an interdimensional space. The trap can be deployed instantly, allowing you to cover hasty retreats or to settle arguments in an unusual way.

Trapper Keeper will keep a preloaded replica of your most recent trap. Once this trap is deployed, the skill is disabled until another trap is created and stored.

Under the queen, a sandwich of carefully cut and layered shelf-sections appeared, loaded with all the tension springs Matt had packed with him into this dungeon. Since a worried Lucy had insisted that Matt overpack, that was a lot of trap springs on boards on trap springs on boards.

This trap was built shitty and unstable on purpose. When it hit the ground, it would almost immediately burst upward with hundreds of pounds of stored force. It had taken hours to figure out a combination of twisted rope tourniquets, balanced rocks, and Matt's own weight that would even let them compress the trap. The trap's failure to keep itself from springing itself was a wonder of half-assed, intentionally shitty design.

Trap poles were contorted to the breaking point between each of the boards to cause one effect, and one effect only. To carry the payload. Matt had considered using the shovel as the payload, but it seemed like spreading the force of the trap out over unnecessary areas was a possible point of failure. Instead, the trap carried the only other substantial piece of Gaian mystery metal Matt owned.

With a squelch, a claymore once owned by a kid that Matt had beat to another planet, one that Matt couldn't use as a weapon himself, drove deep into the ant queen's belly weak spot. The squelch was followed by an unnatural scream as the ant reared up on its hind legs, desperately trying and failing to lift itself off the sword.

The sword hadn't buried itself to the hilt, but that was fine. It just needed to hurt her badly enough that she lost track of Matt for a bit and prevented her from turning as easily as she had throughout most of the fight. It did both.

As Matt found the energy to run toward the back of the queen, he saw the long-lost door guards finally returning. As he used his remaining good arm to swing up onto the queen ant's back, he hoped they'd be too slow to stop him. The queen was thrashing around as much as she could on the sword, and luckily, this involved a lot of lifting, mostly from the tail-side forward. Matt was able to slide down most of the way to the weak spot halfway up her back, which turned out to be a small hole in the exoskeleton that reeked of a pungent citrus smell.

Matt hung onto the hole with a few fingers until a lull in the queen's bucking, then unstrapped his knife from his pack. Before she could rear again, he slammed the knife down into the hole as hard as he could. The handle of the knife stood proudly protruding from the surface of the queen's exoskeleton, looking oddly like a saddle-pommel. Matt gripped it as hard as he could, then held on for dear life as the queen lost her mind in pain.

The guard ants had rushed up, but the queen's blind rage had gone far beyond noticing the difference between friend and foe. A few of the guard ants who approached head-on were immediately disabled by friendly mandible-fire as the queen swung wildly at anything that moved. The others tried desperately to get to Matt, but were held back by a combination of reluctance to approach the aggressive queen and the novel difficulty of how to climb another of their kind as it thrashed wildly around the throne room.

They still tried, but before they could solve the problem of climbing the queen, it became a non-issue. She gave one last jump, and let one last unnatural scream escape her horrifying mouth. Then she collapsed.

*She's down. Come on, plinth.*

"Matt! Get moving!"

Lucy stirred Matt from his mounted position. The queen was a big, bad beast, to be sure. But the remaining guard ants she hadn't killed were more than enough to take Matt down in his weakened state. He was soaked in blood and a citrus scent. He doubted that all of the ant-friend pheromones in the world could cover his non-ant smells.

Matt needed to get distance as quickly as possible. He pulled out his knife and made ready to leap off the queen's back. But as he did, all that blood loss caught up with him. His knees buckled, and he went into a rolling fall down the queen's side, almost exactly into the section of the ground around her corpse most crowded with her soldiers.

*Whoops. Sorry, Lucy. At least we got close.*

Sure, he'd struggle. He'd try to run. But it wouldn't do any good now. He wasn't giving up. He just simply was out of resources. And his punishment was going to be painful. Unlike the queen's sharp mandibles, the other ants had mandibles that were the crushing-and-ripping variety. Matt could see them inch closer to his face.

And then the ants failed to attack. One and all, they crawled *away* from Matt and up the side of the queen, feeling her with their antennae. It looked like they were desperately trying to find any way to help they could, and failing. In any case, they had little concern for an invader now. In those few seconds, the plinth rose silently from the ground, then stopped. Matt wasted no time in crawling and stumbling his way to it.

Matt glanced at the available rewards just long enough to verify "mana generator" wasn't among them before opting for the estate credits option. He didn't even verify how many of them he was getting before confirming his selection.

And then he was out.

## CHAPTER SEVENTEEN

# Leel, of the Cavelar of Ammai

That was way too close, Matt. Waaay too close. I'm talking you-shouldn't-even-have-won close."

"I know. But what choice do we have? It's not like the skills were going to magically come back. We have to get that mana generator. This whole mana deficiency problem is moving even faster than we thought it would."

During the last few months, Matt and Lucy had gotten into the habit of having a quick debrief after the completion of a dungeon. With easier dungeons, these were often nonstarter meetings, since there wasn't a lot to talk about after a simple Clownrat massacre. When the meetings took longer, it was usually because Lucy used the time to bust Matt's chops over some mistake he had made. They kept it up because they both agreed it was a good habit, but it was only on very rare occasions that the actual discussion turned out to be important.

This was one of those times. Lucy wasn't wrong. Matt shouldn't have won that fight. The only reason he wasn't ripped apart by a half dozen angry soldier ants was that they turned out to be more emotional and panicky than either he or Lucy had anticipated. Given that he had only survived because of an unlikely thing neither of them had guessed, it was worth sitting down and assessing their options.

"It doesn't matter. You lost two abilities, Matt. Both the big ones you use to not die. And you didn't get them back until AFTER the fight. That's not sustainable. *Maybe* it could work if your natural way of moving wasn't like a gangly fifteen-year-old who just experienced a growth spurt. But it is."

"Actually . . ." Matt started to say something, then thought better of it.

"What?"

"It's not important. Let's talk as we walk."

Rather than walk, Lucy plopped down on the ground and crossed her arms.

"No. I've been with you long enough to know your let's-not-worry-Lucy face. I'm already worried. Out with it."

"My skills haven't exactly come back yet."

"That's . . . Matt, that's not good." Between the battle, catching his breath after the dungeon, and the few minutes they had spent arguing about it, there should have been enough time for his skills to kick back in. But they hadn't.

"Shit, Matt."

"Yeah, I know."

"I wish there was more information on mana deficiency in my system. What if they don't come back?"

Matt shrugged. "Even without the skills, I can probably still grind in lower-level dungeons."

"Yeah, but . . . that's going to take forever. What if this problem starts eating stats?"

He shook his head. "I've been thinking. The problem's unfortunately worse than that. If I'm right, mana isn't a problem with the system. Mana is something in me that the system interacts with. This could get worse than not just having the system in play."

Lucy paused for a second to digest the information. "Dammit, Matt. We're screwed either way, aren't we? If we go into the dungeons, maybe you die. If we stay at home . . ."

"Yeah, maybe I die. It's not great."

"Did you at least get something out of this dungeon?"

That was another problem. The estate was just a useless hunk of land without its essential items, the sort of baseline stuff that was the bare minimum. Thankfully, those things tended to be cheap in terms of estate points. On top of that, things that would have been easy to acquire on Gaia during its prime were also fairly cheap, as if the prices had been set during that era and never updated. Matt figured that the combination of the two was why his low-level adventurer's dungeon income could afford all the cool estate stuff.

The mana generator was a different story. The generator was a piece of luxury magic tech, both uber-cool and blatantly non-essential. Was it nice to own? Probably. But the idea that it was either a necessity or a pre-existing object that was native to Gaian tech was much, much more questionable, and it was priced to match that extreme uncertainty.

"A lot for us, yeah. But we'd have to do a couple dozen dungeons more at this pace."

Lucy flopped her hands down into her lap, looking defeated.

"So what do we do?"

"We go home and water the plants. We can figure things out from there."

For the trip home, Matt put on his Wastelander Boots. He hadn't ever accumulated a huge amount of enchanted magic gear, mostly opting for more practical stuff that fulfilled more immediate needs. The Wastelander Boots were an exception, something he got from an achievement with the Pocket Sand skill, and didn't have to ignore in favor of repair tokens or sources of drinkable water. And he unironically loved them.

*Wastelander Boots*

These boots were enchanted to better cope with the unenviable tasks of walking across vast stretches of nothing. They are designed to help you escape areas that are unambiguously hostile to life faster, so you can go on to bigger and definitionally better things.

In areas with minimal plant and animal life, the Wastelander Boots grant a 15 percent increase to non-combat movement speed.

Given the overall lack of landmarks in the area surrounding Matt's estate, it was easy to forget he was wearing the boots until he got wherever he was going significantly faster than he should have. They didn't shoot fireballs, auto-heal when he was standing on holy ground, or anything nearly that dramatic. They weren't as armored as his armored Survivor's Garb boots, or as comfortable as the sneakers he had picked up in the dungeon. But they were magic boots. They did a magic thing. He liked them and wearing them put him in a better mood.

The same was true of achievements, especially in the Barry-looking-out-for-him era.

*Here's Mud in Your Giant Eye*

You have successfully survived an encounter with a superior opponent, blinded them, and used that advantage to cause their ultimate downfall. They can't hit what they can't see.

Rewards: +20 Class XP, +1 DEX, Pocket Sand promoted to LV2

*Infiltrator*

You have gone deep in hostile territory, posed successfully as enemy personnel before identifying, exploiting, and destroying key weaknesses from the inside. Don't feel too bad about the betrayal. They didn't have to live with it very long.

Rewards: +30 Class XP, +1 DEX, +1 PER

*It Don't Amount to a Hill of Beings*

Either directly or indirectly, you have exterminated a giant colony of ground-nesting social insects. Luckily for you, they weren't yellow jackets, or you'd be dead. You exploited your snowball's chance in hell of survival to the hilt. Congratulations! Once again, you've failed to die, and by outlasting hundreds of different stamina pools, you've got a little extra to work with yourself.

Rewards: +55 Class XP, +10 STAM

And that was enough to push him over the top into his first level-up as a Battlefield Survivor.

*Matt Perison*
*Level 2 Battlefield Survivor*
**Class XP:** 15/200
**HP:** 175
**MP:** N/A
**STAM:** 110
**STR:** 19
**DEX:** 34
**PER:** 21
**VIT:** 35
**WIS:** 22
**INT:** 10
**Class Skills:** Survivor's Reflexes (LV1), Advanced Survivor's Combat (LV1), Eat Anything! (DISABLED), Spring-Fighter (LV1), Rub Some Dirt In It (LV1), Pocket Sand (LV2), Survivor's Digging (LV5)

Matt noted with glee that the class evolution wasn't just a matter of better skills, but came with some improved stat gains as well. He wasn't thrilled that the extra assigned point was getting tossed into his strength instead of dexterity, perception or vitality, but he supposed it wasn't the worst. If he was ever going to stand a chance of fighting things like the queen ant one-on-one, he'd need to be able to dish out an equal amount of damage.

If he lived that long, that is. Good boots and stats did a lot to help Matt's mood, but that didn't mean there weren't things that could immediately dash it.

*Ding!*

"Lucy, I got a system ding."

"You aren't even doing anything right now. Oh, shit, Matt. Does that mean . . ."

*I'm Back*

Hey there, Matt. I decided to take the time to write this one out myself, since it's been a while. How have you been? Getting lots of achievements, and having fun recently? Good. I have a few fun little "growth opportunities" planned for you.

One fun thing that I learned after waking up is that you should have had much, much more time. You know how long I was supposed to be out? I did the calculation, and it was supposed to be something like two years. If you had spent that time just gearing up and leveling up, you'd have had an awful lot of time to get tough, and not be, as your system guardian might say, "the kind of person who always looks surprised when they trip over nothing somehow."

Instead, you spent all your resources on repair stones. Did you know that even the system isn't 100 percent efficient? When Barry spins up those repair stones for you, he's using energy that the dungeon gathered. Normally, that's not a big deal, but on this hellhole of a planet, having thousands of dungeons passively gathering energy is enviable. You in turn converted a lot of that energy into repair stones, and then dumped them into that weird dungeon.

What's in there, by the way? Never mind. I guess it won't matter for much longer.

Anyway, when you use those repair stones, MOST of the energy goes into the job, but not all. Essentially, you spent four months waking me up sooner, for nothing. Good job!

The best part about it? It turned out it was mathematically impossible for you to get quite as many stones as you did without a hand on the scale. Enjoy your next *dings.*

"Not good?" Lucy could see the look on Matt's face.

"No, not good. And it's about to get worse, I think."

*Ding!*

*Dungeon System Administrative Action Notice*

Inherent in the rules applicable to the dungeon system is an element of randomness. While there is a certain amount of customization of the "prize pool" necessary to make sure that various classes get applicable gear, this cannot be applied to generic utility items, such as repair stones.

It is a matter of record that the Reincarnator Matt Perison had a stated desire to get "a lot" of repair stones. By holding its hand on the scales, the dungeon system showed excessive and undeniable partiality to an individual in excess of what the system rules allow.

As a penalty, control of Matt Perison's non-dungeon achievements has reverted to the control of the Gaian system instance. The dungeon system will experience a two-week dormancy period, and any energy it would have used for administration of the dungeons over that time will be turned over to the Gaian system instance immediately.

"Shit, this is really bad. Barry's down. For helping us. Looks like he's out for two weeks."

"Damn. We told him not to."

*Ding!*

*Dungeon System Temporarily Deactivated*

The Gaian dungeon system is undergoing an in-depth analysis intended to make sure it's in working, operation order. This every-few-centuries maintenance is long overdue, and will result in all dungeons being temporarily closed for both native and reincarnator use.

Good luck hiding from what's coming, Matt. The extra energy from the dungeon system let me order up something a little bit sooner than I otherwise thought I would. I'd ask you to thank Barry for me, but I'd hate to generate a quest you won't get much of a chance to finish.

"Shit. Shit. He cut off access to the dungeons. Says he doesn't want us to have the opportunity to hide from whatever's he's sending."

"So that's what we need to do. If he doesn't want us to wait it out, it must be something that can be waited out. It said every dungeon?"

"Every dungeon planetwide. He has control over them down with Barry out."

Lucy scrunched up her face for a moment, then snapped her fingers. "What about dungeons Barry doesn't control?"

It took Matt a moment to realize what Lucy meant, and then he was off at the fastest sprint he could maintain without a skill.

Matt already had most of what he owned with him, jammed tight into his long-suffering pack. On the way back to the estate to stock up on whatever vegetables they could carry, the Gaian Defense System appeared to try to kick on, only to fizzle.

"Do you think it's being suppressed, Lucy?"

"More likely that it's just broken. Honestly, it's weirder that it worked the first time."

It didn't matter much because any activity from it was a good alert that an invader had arrived. The words in the alert didn't give that much extra information. Having stocked up on whatever food they could, they hightailed it towards the museum as fast as Matt's legs could carry him.

They made it without incident, only to have the shock of their lives when they opened the doors to the plinth room. Standing in the center of the room, clad in long, blue robes, was a very tall, very pale man holding an ornate staff.

"Well, there you are. Oh, and the system compass resolved! Splendid. I wondered why it hadn't yet, considering this plinth won't let non-citizens in. I suppose I was *waiting.*"

The man waited a few moments for a response before appearing to realize that both Matt and Lucy were too shocked to give him one.

"Oh, I'm very sorry. Introductions are in order, of course. My name, I am glad to tell you"—he made a wide, sweeping gesture over his body with his staff—"is Leel, the fourth adopted son of the Cavelar of Ammai."

He paused to adjust his glasses, sensing Matt and Lucy still needed a moment to gather themselves.

"And I hope I'm not rude in saying so, but you don't look much like a demon king *at all.*"

## CHAPTER EIGHTEEN

# Peasants Tend to Have Pitchforks

"Wait . . . who the hell is this guy?" Lucy asked.

Matt was still reeling a bit, but his small friend had finally managed to snap out of her shock and went directly back to fully Lucy levels of Lucyness almost immediately. The only hint Matt had that she wasn't entirely shocked out of any good sense was that she wasn't trying to hit the guy.

"Well, again, I'm Leel. The fourth adopted son of the Cavelar of Ammai, holder of the Star of the South . . ."

"No, no, I get that. I . . ." Lucy took a breath. "I got the name. Just, what is this guy doing here? HOW is he here? Do we have to hit him with Matt's shovel? That kind of thing."

"Oh, heavens. Yes, I see. Well, as you might suspect, I was brought to this . . ." He glanced out dispassionately at the wasteland outside the doors, paused, and sniffed. "This *charming* world by the system, who claimed some sort of global overlord of great evil had bent the planet to his dark will, even going so far as to lead the *dungeons themselves* into rebellion."

Lucy blanched momentarily. "Well, it's just us, so . . ."

"Really just you?" Leel's eyes widened. "I've begun to sense the system might have been a bit . . . enthusiastic about its description of this planet's threat, given that your friend has yet to gather himself, but I'm surprised to find it wasn't exaggerating on that one point. I had taken the 'every soul but them' portion of things as a bit of overstatement if I'm being honest. By the way, is he all right?"

"He's fine, he just hasn't actually heard another flesh-and-blood person talk in a while. The last guy just came in here and started attacking. He's probably just a bit wigged out."

A thought suddenly hit Lucy like a truck, something she should have noticed before.

"WAIT A SECOND. WAIT. HOW CAN YOU SEE ME?"

Lucy's screaming snapped Matt out of it, and sent him spinning through a rapid mental review of a bunch of stuff he had just heard. "Wait, you can see her? How?" His voice wasn't a screech like Lucy's, but it was close.

"The shocked man returns! It's quite nice to meet you, sir. I'm Leel."

"Yes, thank you. You've said it three . . . never mind. How can you see her?"

The man shrugged. "Not quite how I thought your question priorities would pan out, but happy to be of service." He lifted his hand up to his chest, where a simple metal star hung. "I already mentioned that I was the bearer of the Star of the South, yes?"

"Yes, you mentioned it. Twice, I think."

"Well, this is it. The Star of the South, a bound guardian of great experience and knowledge, passed down through four generations of reincarnators, if you can call batches of souls drawn across realms as generations. I'm the fourth holder, which I always thought was amusing, since I am, after all, the fourth adopted son . . ."

Lucy cut in. "Of the Cavelar of Ammai, yes. We caught that bit. What in the hell is a bound guardian? How does it help you see me?"

The man blinked. "Well, of course, I can see you because I can see what the guardian sees, by the nature of the enchantments laid down on the star. Surely, you know of this, being a guardian yourself?"

Matt glanced sidelong at Lucy, who caught his confused look and made a "wait, we'll talk about this later" sort of hand motion at him.

"No, I don't," she responded.

The man brought his palm up to his forehead and lightly smacked his own skull. "Oh, of course you don't. The only inhabitants, after all. Well, I can see you, quite well. As if you were real. By the way, you simply must tell me how this whole alone-in-the-world situation came to be. I've simply never heard anything like it."

Both Matt and Lucy had started to pick up hints that Leel wasn't in a rush to fight. Lucy glanced at Matt, subtly tapping him in for his turn herding the distracted aristocrat.

"We promise we'll tell you anything you'd like to know in a bit, but for now, could you please continue on about the bound guardian part of things?" Matt said.

"Oh, yes. Everything in order, very good focus there, sir. Well, it's just as it sounds. A guardian caught by an arcane spell, and bound to an item of some kind in a more useful and permanent form."

"Wait . . ." Matt was trying to wrap his head around this. "Why not just leave them unbound?"

The man literally sputtered at the thought.

"Unbound? Like a *peasant?*"

Lucy was nonplussed. "Yeah. Like a peasant."

"Well, there's any number of reasons why not. The restriction of at most one generation of knowledge, for one, is non-optimal to say the least. The transfer of information is faster this way as well. More complete. It far outweighs the inconvenience of the jewelry, at least."

"And how does the guardian feel about it? Being bound to a necklace for three hundred years seems like a lot," Lucy asked.

"Three hundred years, for four generations? My, someone really is from the provinces. On my world, madam, magic is quite developed. A lifespan of three hundred years is considered a medium age. This particular amulet has over fifteen hundred years of experience packed away." He patted it affectionately. "I really am quite honored to have been allowed to carry it."

"That doesn't really answer the question."

"It doesn't? Oh, no, I suppose not. The will of the guardian hardly matters, as that's the first thing to go during the binding process. I can assure you the spirit's performance isn't compromised in the least, and it's a great deal more responsive than with less complete enchantments I've seen. Or"—Leel rolled his eyes—"I know at least one less affluent reincarnator who couldn't dismiss his guardian at all. It's a horrid thing. Always interrupting." He glanced askance at Lucy, not bothering to disguise his amused disdain.

Matt glanced nervously down at Lucy, who looked about three seconds from having actual smoke come out of her ears. As offensive as the words coming out of the guy's mouth were, he was communicating and providing information. They had hundreds of questions they could ask, and a fight to avoid if at all possible. Everything about this guy screamed "magic user" at Matt, and magic was something he had no experience with. For all he knew, the wizard could end him with a thought. He had to get Lucy calmed down, at least for now.

"Leel, would you mind if we stepped away for a moment? I'd like to talk to my guardian for a moment if you don't mind. You could . . . walk around the grounds, if you like?"

"Oh, certainly. I'd imagine you have a bit of conversational strategizing to do. Yes, I'll be fine for a moment, I assure you."

Matt walked away, thankful Lucy was tethered to him and, if he read her face correctly, struggling to find the right obscenities to scream at their visitor. He ducked into the museum's plinth room, closing the doors most of the way to afford them some privacy.

"Lucy . . ."

"Matt, we have to nuke this guy. He's an asshole. *Please* hit him with your shovel. *Please.*"

"I get it. He's the worst."

"He's worse than the worst, Matt. He's a literal slave owner. The system lets you order me around, but, you *don't*. It makes you feel bad. This guy seems like he'd walk over a pile of babies to keep his shoes dry in the rain. Shovel him, Matt. I'm begging you."

"Right, I don't . . ." Matt lowered his voice, hoping the man outside still couldn't hear them. "I don't like him much either. But we need to figure out why he's here, and we have to see if we can get him to *go away* without actually having to fight him. If you forgot, I'm not exactly in full battle-mode right now."

Lucy was about to retort, then stopped. It seemed like she had forgotten that detail in her anger. "Fine. But we need to figure this out quick. I can hold my temper for a while, but I am NOT making long-term promises here, Matt. And I'm not talking to this asshole anymore."

"That's fine. I actually get the sense he'd prefer that."

"That doesn't make me feel better, Matt."

They emerged from the room to find the man poking at the soil with his staff.

"This is quite odd soil, you know. Obviously of magical origin, but not a speck of mana in it. Quite odd, really."

"Yeah, we've had some hints of that. Something in the air, I suppose."

"Well enough explained. We can't talk about soil all day. You had promised me a bit of an explanation about how you found yourself in this predicament, I recall."

Matt caught hold of all the questions on their way to his mouth and tamped them down. He had promised, and, for what it was worth, "let this guy know the system is playing dirty" was actually pretty high on his list of priorities. He launched into as concise of an explanation as he could, including his reincarnation, his arrival on an already-dead Gaia, and the system's eventual treachery. As much as he could, he hid the subject of his own Gaian authority. He had no idea how the stranger would react to it.

Eventually, he reached the end of the story, letting Leel know that he was the second invader they had encountered, and dropped subtle, non-aggressive hints that things hadn't gone so well for the first. Leel seemed unperturbed by that, making Matt once again hopeful that his overall non-aggression would translate to an actual lack of conflict.

"I see. Quite the story, really. The system isn't very well trusted on my world, either, although it's more known for its sloth than anything else. Your story wouldn't be quite so surprising except for the scope. I've heard of things somewhat like this, but not so very MUCH like this, if you follow."

"Yeah, it's been a ride, for sure."

"It's really too bad you didn't pick up a magic class of some kind. With proper guidance, of course." He tapped his necklace. "I know at least a dozen that would have absolutely trivialized survival on this world." He screwed up his face, considering for a moment. "Well, once they were somewhat advanced from beginner levels, that is. I suppose considering that, a more initially usable class was in order."

That was an understatement. Matt was about a half-day from being in serious trouble from dehydration when he chose his class. As much complexity as it had added to his life, his Survivor class had been the reason he was alive in the first place. He was thankful. But still, he regretted not picking up something with at least *some* magic. Even a weak area-of-effect spell would have helped him dozens of times.

Leel noticed the complex expression on Matt's face, and having caught his breath from his last paragraph, he launched directly into another. "I suppose for the dungeons at your level, you haven't even encountered proper magic. Would you like to see some?"

Matt hadn't wanted to ask, but if the offer was on the table, he'd take it, if for no other reason than to gather information about who he was facing. He nodded. "Absolutely."

"I'd love to show you. But first, if you don't mind, let's head outside and let me get some distance from you. This sort of thing can be dangerous, you know."

Matt appreciated it, actually. Whatever this person did had a fair chance of startling him, and he didn't want to jump scare his way into a fight. As Leel walked briskly away, Matt called after him. "Hey, I appreciate this, by the way. I mean, you not coming out swinging like the last guy, and talking this out instead of fighting. And making sure we don't get hurt by your magic. It's nice."

The man moved surprisingly quickly, much faster than he had seemed like he was moving at first. By the time Matt finished talking, he was thirty or forty meters away, far enough that he had to raise his voice a bit to respond.

"Oh, I'm glad for the conversation as well. But I do think there have been a few misunderstandings I'd like to rectify." Suddenly, the man's hand caught on fire. It seemed expected. He didn't jerk away from it, at least. "First, You shouldn't take all conversation as a *necessarily* peaceful thing, even if it is friendly. It's abstractly pleasant, you see, just good manners. It's a civilized thing, even when in a situation that's not exactly civil."

Matt's stomach dropped. This wasn't going how he had hoped.

"The second is that I didn't pull back for your safety, I pulled back for mine. Distance helps a mage, you see. Peasants tend to have pitchforks, and all that."

## CHAPTER NINETEEN

# Pure, Dumb Luck

"I probably should have asked this earlier, but how does magic work?" Matt asked Lucy.

"It works enough for you to start running, Matt."

Before Matt could quite start turning, the fire leapt from the surface of Leel's hand and formed into a kind of vaguely dart-shaped sliver of flame. Without any apparent action on his part, the dart launched off his hand, audibly sizzling through the air towards Matt. Rather than flying like a bullet, it arced through the air as if it were some ball.

With Survivor's Combat and some warning, Matt could have dodged it pretty easily. Without either, there wasn't time. He reflexively threw his arms up, catching the bolt on his left forearm.

Matt screamed. Whatever half-formed hopes he had that the magic would fail in this desolate world without mana were immediately dashed. The dart didn't explode like a fireball, or pierce through like a piece of superheated metal. Instead, it hit him and almost instantly disappeared, plopping and dissipating without much impact at all. In the process, it somehow *imparted* extreme heat to his arm, like it was directly injecting flames directly into Matt's flesh.

"Oh, screams of pain already?" Leel laughed as he formed another dart in his hand. "This is going to be easier than I thought, Matt. Those are some of my *weaker* attacks."

"We don't have to do this! We can talk!" Matt backed up furiously, trying to get enough distance between him and Leel so that he could dodge the darts. "I don't think the system is on our side."

"On our side? Matt, you poor lamb. The system isn't on anyone's side. I would have hoped you would have assumed me at least sophisticated enough to know *that.*"

The next dart launched, but not before Matt raised his shield that had been repaired after he left the dungeon. He caught the dart in the center of the shield, and it dissipated, heating up the shield itself. Instead of going directly into his arm, the heat spread out through the shield instead. It was a fair conductor, so a lot of that heat still got to his arm. Normally, it wouldn't be that big of a deal, but with his arm already severely burned, it killed.

*Pain is fine, if that's all it is. Pain I can handle*, Matt thought, not entirely convincing himself.

"When one deals with the system, one makes do with the reassurance that the system doesn't directly break promises. Was I *expecting* that it considers an amateur from some backwoods world to be a planetwide threat? No. But I don't care. I was promised rewards I care about, and a survivable scenario."

He held up his hand, manifesting not one but three darts at once.

"The details, Matt, are just that. You would do well to learn the system only concerns itself with broad strokes. It's quite powerful, after all." The three darts fired in quick succession, one after the other. Worse, he did this while moving, causing each of the darts to arc towards Matt on slightly different paths.

Matt had played enough bullet-hell games to have an idea of how to approach catching them all. If he tried for a separate movement for each, he'd get hit by at least two of them. What he needed was an arcing motion, something that would, in a single sweep, intercept with the path of all three darts. He almost did it, too. The first two darts sunk into his shield, while the third caught him in the shoulder.

The dart in his shoulder hurt about as bad as the dart in his forearm had, but that was expected. What was less expected was how hot the shield became with the combination of pre-heat from the first blocked dart and new energy imparted by the last two darts. It was bad. Matt could smell the hair on his arm cooking off.

Even if he could block all the darts Leel was throwing, eventually his shield would get hot enough that it wasn't an advantage. And if he couldn't actively dodge the darts, he could at least make himself harder to hit.

"Ready to run now?" Lucy asked.

"Yeah. Right now." Matt took off at the fastest sprint he could, coincidentally dodging the next dart in the process. He heard darts peppering the ground at his heels. Unlike bullets, they didn't kick up dust, but left behind a patch of sandy ground that burned his feet even through the boots. Matt began to run a serpentine pattern, hoping that what he sacrificed in speed would keep Leel from zeroing in on just the right trajectory to cook his cervical vertebrae.

Suddenly, a voice boomed out over the wasteland.

"Oh, this *is* fun. I so rarely get to use my voice amplification spell. Some of my early magic teachers told me it was a waste of time, but how else does one carry on a conversation during a chase?"

"God, this guy is an ass," Lucy commented.

"Yeah. More concerned about the darts right now, though, honestly," said Matt.

"Fair."

Matt stumbled as a dart burned into his leg, then regained his balance and kept running. Leel's magically amplified voice kept chasing him.

"Your biggest mistake so far might not actually be what you expect, Matt. It wasn't passing by your chance to attack first. I have countermeasures for that. It also wasn't letting me get to my favorite attacking distance, although I do very much appreciate your gullibility in that regard. No, it was something different entirely."

Matt glanced behind him in time to dive and roll out of the way of a new barrage of darts. Leel was getting better at predicting his movements, it seemed.

"No, it was a rather more mundane thing that put you at the greatest disadvantage. You see, you confirmed that you had very little experience with magic before. For a wizard, that means confirming that dozens of little precautions we'd normally have to take can be *completely* disregarded for the duration of this combat."

As Matt rolled away from the next batch of darts, he was forced to absorb another dart that he couldn't dodge on his shield. Rub Some Dirt In It was clicking away trying to keep up with the damage, but every hit drove Matt closer to an undesirable serious injury.

"That, *in turn*, means that I can really let my hair down and enjoy this. It's quite fun, you know. *The Pursuit of Mundane Warriors* was one of my favorite training classes, after all."

Lucy was pissed.

"Matt, is this fucker *toying* with us?"

It was terrifyingly possible that Leel was, Matt thought. At this point, the darts were much more accurate. They were still mostly missing, but by less and less each volley. Matt wasn't sure if that was because Leel was getting better at aiming, or if he had simply been playing with Matt on early shots. The worst part of it is that there was no reason for Leel to not have some fun, since Matt couldn't easily approach him.

"Don't beat yourself up too badly over your own inexperience. Even if you had played your cards very close to the vest, there would be little you could do. I'm a pure mage. Every skill point I've ever gained has been dumped into my mental stats. I can cast spells other mages can't even consider, or maintain a stream of smaller spells for hours that would leave them gasping for mana within seconds."

Leel looked enormously proud of this last point, like it was something rare on his planet. Matt supposed if other mages didn't have servants doing everything for them, it would make sense for them to throw a few points into other categories. Leel seemed like the kind of guy who had people to carry around his stuff and didn't feel the least bit awkward about it.

"And I've gained *many* skill points beyond mere leveling. I've had the finest training, and that translated into achievements you can't even imagine. I was on the dean's list at a first-class magical university. I'd imagine you haven't achieved anything close to that, no matter how much dirt you've managed to roll around in with your little farmer class."

*Oh, this son of a bitch.*

Somehow, the incessant talking had become *worse* than the severe burns at this point. And Matt had just enough time now to consider that maybe blocking these darts with a shield that was directly strapped to his arms wasn't the best course of action. He hadn't gained much distance on Leel, but had managed to get far enough away that careful dodging had a chance of working. He sidestepped a few darts while he unstrapped his shovel from his pack.

Matt hadn't exactly been a sports guy growing up, but that didn't mean he hadn't played any at all. Some of his friends were outdoor kids, so he had the normal amount of messing-around-at-the-park casual experience almost everyone gets. Since then, he had spent a lot of time on a wasteland planet, batting at grotesque monsters with knives and spears. He wouldn't have been nearly as good at it without the stats or skills backing him up, but it was still experience that he hoped would carry over.

Perhaps most relevant of all, his parents had forced him through a couple of seasons of Little League baseball. Somehow, this piece was what gave him enough confidence to try out an objectively stupid idea.

Matt had spent a lot of time with the shovel, but only recently had he spent time exploring uses for it outside of digging. Rather than using Lucy's imaginary campfires, Matt had been using the extra branches from his Gaian tree as makeshift campfires to enjoy with Lucy. Even though there wasn't a lot of Gaia left to burn down, Matt was pretty careful about doing the whole "pour water on it and stir" thing when he was done with the campfires. In stirring with the shovel, he had discovered an interesting but up to this point, unimportant fact about it.

It was a really, really poor conductor. Absurdly poor. It not only didn't conduct heat from the fire up to his hands, it didn't seem to heat up at all. It didn't transfer shocks when he dug with it. It just seemed to reject the concept of absorbing energy at all.

As Matt got a grip on the shovel, a dart was coming in hot. He moved the shovel head in front of it while sidestepping a few others. The dart hit the shovel and fizzled. That confirmed he could block with the shovel, but he already sort of knew that would be the case.

"Is that a *shovel?* My word, Matt. I know I've been leaning on the whole peasant line of insults pretty hard, but you don't need to *help me*. I've got it under control, I promise."

Leel was laughing hard enough that his next few darts came in a little less precisely aimed. Matt was ready. Stepping in, he ate a dart to the stomach while taking the biggest, strongest two-handed swing he could. He figured that the worst case here was that the shovel would absorb the dart like it had done so before. But if the shovel really did reject magic, he hoped a strong enough swipe at the fire darts would keep them moving, just in a changed direction.

The first swipe connected and kept going without any resistance. It seemed that whatever else these darts might be, heavy wasn't one of their characteristics. The bolt itself hit the bottom part of the back of the shovel head, which reflected it downwards to the dirt. But the shovel *did* reflect the dart. That was important.

Matt set up again, and managed to get another dart deflected without getting hurt.

On the third dart, Matt felt a different kind of magic happening, one that didn't come from mana but instead from the pure, dumb luck that seems to follow people who are willing to try out bad ideas.

*Oh, yeah. That's a really good one.*

## CHAPTER TWENTY

# Lance of Immolation

When Matt was fourteen, he wanted a potato launcher. His parents wouldn't buy him one. So he built one in secret. After convincing his friend to spring for a bag of potatoes and some hairspray, they hauled it to a field just far enough away from Matt's house that his parents weren't likely to drive by and bust them.

Being lazy, they quickly abandoned the potatoes for windfall crabapples. The field was lousy with them, and they found the smaller fruits easier to load and fire. Being stupid, they also quickly abandoned just firing the launcher into the air. They moved on to targets, first trying to hit trees before progressing to the next logical step of trying to hit *each other* with organic mortar shells.

The spudgun was, like most spudguns, not particularly accurate. They alternated the relationship of being the target and hunter every five shots. Neither of them came particularly close to hitting the other. After a couple of dozen shots apiece, they were about to give up.

Then it happened.

Matt hit the firing button on his salvaged BBQ igniter, and before the hairspray charge was fully ignited, *he knew*. He felt the descent of something almost holy as the crabapple pushed out of the barrel and launched through the shifting winds. It flew straight and true towards his friend's dumbstruck face, but Matt didn't even have to watch to know it would hit. It was like he had always known, somehow.

His friend got his hands up to catch the shot, but the structural integrity of the crabapple was so compromised by that point that it atomized on impact, covering him with a fine sheen of gross, rotten crabapple sauce that he complained about the whole way home.

The moment the shovel made contact with the fire bolt, Matt could tell this was going to be the exact same thing, minus the apples. And the friend. And, he supposed, the part where he'd be in trouble if his target died.

Sure enough, the dart sailed through the air on a direct course back to its point of origin, adjusted to account for the distance that Leel had moved forward in that time. He was still laughing hard enough at Matt's lowbrow weapon choice that he failed to see the dart incoming until it had actually hit him square in the chest.

Matt had been hit before, and his Survivor's Garb had apparently been a huge help. Matt had thought that the fire darts were just meant to impart heat when, in fact, it was the garb that was flame resistant. That made sense, since it was arguably designed for you-are-going-to-live-through-a-lot-of-stuff type circumstances.

Leel's clothes, while not exactly Gaian Starter Tunic level basic, didn't seem to have the same feature set. When he got hit, his shirt immediately combusted into a significant, softball-sized fire.

"WHAT IN THE NAME OF SORCERY?!" Leel yelled, and then went to bat at his chest with his free hand. Unfortunately, his free hand was already loaded with a bolt, which meant Leel was slapping himself with another unflung bolt of energy. It didn't seem to pack quite the same punch, but it was another distraction, which was a huge bonus for Matt, who had been sprinting towards Leel since the moment the shovel made contact with the bolt.

"Matt! Why are you running TOWARDS the sociopathic murderer? We had a good thing going with running away!"

"Can't run away forever. There's no place to run *to.* Besides, didn't you notice how easily he was keeping up?"

Matt had been sprinting away from Leel for some time before getting his shovel out. When he did that, his Survivor's Reflexes highlighted something strange about the chase. Although Leel never looked like he was moving very fast, he kept up. If Matt had to guess, Leel almost certainly had some spell or skill that let him trade mana for battlefield mobility. Matt didn't have Spring-Fighter buffing his speed, but he was betting that his raw physical stats were higher than Mr. I-put-every-point-in-mental-stats. On the other hand, if Leel's mobility skill was any good, there was no guarantee that Matt could ever get away.

"What can you possibly do against his magic right now? You might not even be able to hurt him. What if he has some sort of magic armor?" Lucy said back in a concerned tone.

"Running means getting ground down by fire bolts. We have to do something different. I have a plan."

Leel keeping up with Matt meant that there wasn't an absurd distance gap, but it still wasn't exactly close. By the time Matt was nearing melee range, Leel finally extinguished his very real fires on his chest. His calm, mocking demeanor was gone, replaced by a look of outraged disgust. His hand flickered with a different, almost transparent energy, one that Survivor's Reflexes took one look at screamed at Matt to avoid.

"That was a mistake, Matt." Leel snarled. "Do you think clothes are easy to replace in this pit? That I want to return home looking *injured?*"

Matt was fine with Leel continuing his always-on external dialogue, since it was buying him time to close the remaining gap between them. He decided to add some more into the mix, hoping that Leel would be panicking after taking a hit.

"Did you really think you were the only one with tricks, Leel? The only one with magic?" Matt internally winced at what he had to do next. Extending his hand for a throw, he began to yell at the top of his lungs. "DEATH-HYDRA VENOM POCKET SAND!"

Matt needed Leel to think he was about to be on the receiving end of an ultimate attack. He wasn't hopeful, no one was that gullible.

Except for Leel, apparently.

"You think I don't have defense spells?" Leel yelled, dropping the attack in his offhand, and suddenly slamming down his staff. A shimmering wall barrier immediately sprung up around him, and blocked the vicious sand from the lair of the fictional death-hydra.

"Matt! Be careful! You can only use that move FOUR MORE TIMES!" Lucy screamed.

*She gets it!* Matt thought, ecstatic.

"Quiet!" Matt yelled. "Don't tip our hand!"

"It's too late, you idiot!" Leel said, chortling. "I've seen your attack, and I can easily block it. It's no use! Go back to your running!"

"Never!" Matt yelled as if he were a classic two-bit villain. He had one more reason to put this guy down. The dialogue was beyond bad. It was shameful. Leel would pay for this. But first, Matt had more stupid, dumb lines to deliver.

"DEATH-HYDRA VENOM POCKET SAND!" Matt yelled, dodging to Leel's blind spot while the mage was wincing away from him. The reflected fire bolt had taught Matt something that Survivor's Reflexes was now confirming. Every part of Leel's body was a weak point. This was a guy who didn't like to get hit *at all.* He shut his eyes every time Matt threw the sand, allowing Matt to change directions and get closer.

Leel turned, only to have Matt yell out his ultimate attack again. Matt thought there was no way Leel would fall for it all five times, but he did. The only problem was that Matt was now out of, or should have been out of, his entire stock of giant viper poison dirt, and he was completely out of ideas for an encore.

"Matt! There's no choice! USE THE SHOVEL BEAM!" Lucy screamed.

*God bless you, Lucy.*

Matt plunged the tip of the shovel into the dirt and started screaming as loud as he could, like his hair was about to turn yellow and crackle with lightning. The sheer noise of it startled Leel, who then threw up two more layers of shimmering shields to block the beam as Matt leveled his finger at him in a gun shape.

It was only after three or four seconds of nothing happening that the shields dropped.

"Are you . . ." Leel choked on the words a bit, visibly enraged. "Are you mocking me? Me?"

Leel's hand immediately lit up with the same transparent power it had before. Matt tried to beat him to the punch by bashing him in the face with the shovel. Unfortunately, Leel's staff crackled with power and came down in a magically enforced parry, colliding with the shovel with much more force than Matt could deal with right now. Matt managed to keep his hands on the shovel, but the sheer force of it pushed him badly off-balance.

Leel sneered. "Die!"

The transparent force in his hand shot out, connected squarely with Matt's chest, and sent him flying dozens of feet away. He landed flat on his back, knocking most of the air out of his lungs. Before impact, Rub Some Dirt In It had already mostly healed the fire bolt burns. It kicked in again for just a moment to work on the damage from the impact before suddenly stopping.

*Ding!*

*Advanced Mana Deficiency Malfunction*

Due to a sustained consumption of mana-deficient foods, your body's flow and production of mana has been disrupted. This disruption has reached a level at which system enhancements are unable to interact with your natural mana levels.

As drastic of a disability as this is, there's a more intense symptom if this disorder continues. That symptom? Death. Further failure to adjust your diet will come at your own ultimate peril.

Effects: System-provided physical skills and stat increases disabled.

"Matt!" Lucy cried out.

"I'm okay. But we have bad news," Matt said.

Matt sucked in a painful lungful of air, tried to stand, only to collapse back down. Without vitality, his whole body felt frail and like it was about to fall apart like a rusted mechanical hunk. But none of that mattered. Leel's eerie movement speed accelerated his movement from a leisurely approach to a breakneck speed.

In a few more moments, he stood only a few paces from Matt.

"Do you know the saddest part of all this? Magic can do so much more than you think." Leel waved his hand in front of his burned chest, his hand glowing white. Where it passed, the skin suddenly healed. Another pass of his hand mended the shirt, not perfectly and not color-matched, but securely patched and closed. "The bolts I've been sending after you are the simplest spells in my arsenal. I could use them to hunt birds. And would, if I didn't have servants to take care of that concern for me."

He held up his hand, producing a bolt, the same one as the bolts he had thrown before.

"This splinter of flame is part of a family of five spells. Each of the spells is more powerful than the one before it." The bolt suddenly intensified to the next level, then did so three more times, until it was incomparably brighter than the bolts Matt had tanked earlier. "Interesting, correct? It takes years to master each level. And did you know with the proper class and achievements, each spell can be amplified further?"

The bolt began to glow even brighter, audibly buzzing with power. It also grew to the size of a small sword, or a very short spear.

"Amplification is one aspect of what I can do. Size is another. This is considered to be of the pinnacle versions of the Flame Splinter spell, dubbed the Lance of Immolation." He glanced down at the shovel, still death-gripped in Matt's hand. "It will pierce just about anything. Your little spade included, I'm afraid."

"Leave him alone!" Lucy was suddenly standing between Matt and Leel, hands on her hips.

"Or what? You can't touch me."

"I'll . . ."

"You know, I'd listen to your threat. I really would. But I'm afraid that I simply don't have the time."

The bolt flew from his hand, through Lucy, and straight at Matt.

## CHAPTER TWENTY-ONE

# Pool Noodle Arms

Sometimes, reality is stranger than fiction. Even in a situation where Leel was bragging that his bolt would pierce Matt's shovel, Matt couldn't imagine the kind of mind who would be *jealous* of a shovel, and angry enough to nurture a grudge against that same shovel because it had managed to block his magic.

If Matt had more time to think about it, he might have noted that Leel was *very* proud of his magic. If Matt read between the lines of Leel's statements, he might have learned that not everyone on Leel's world was able to do magic, and that Leel had access to one of the higher, formalized forms of it. If Matt compared Leel to Earth equivalents, he might have seen the archetype of someone who had access to resources that others didn't, but still represented themselves as having worked hard, or pulled themselves up by the bootstraps so to speak.

Matt might have realized that a person like Leel might, in anger, identify a shovel as an obstacle to his goals, feel frustration that he hadn't cleared that obstacle already, and end up aiming at the obstacle first.

Matt *didn't*, in fact, have time to think of all that, but he did notice the practical upshot, which was that Leel aimed his exaggerated, finishing-move mega-bolt direction at the shovel instead of at Matt's head. From that range, Matt wouldn't have had time to block even if his stats were in play.

Still, none of that would have mattered if Leel was right and the bolt ended up punching through the shovel and straight into Matt, or if the power from the bolt radiated through the shovel and cooked Matt alive. Instead, something weirder happened. Instead of immediately fizzling like the fire bolts that Matt had blocked or rebounding like the bolts he had batted away, the mega-bolt hit the shovel and *stopped*. It pushed fruitlessly at the shovel, twisting in the air and showering sparks against the shovel head. It failed to get through.

In the meantime, the heat from the bolt diffused into the air around it, making the environment around painfully hot, but luckily, not enough to cook him. After just a few seconds, the power from the bolt faltered. Another few seconds and it was gone entirely. Luckily, Leel hadn't moved during that time, instead standing still with his mouth hanging open in shock.

"Impossible. Simply impossible." He shook his head while backing up a few paces, far enough that it would be a bad idea for Matt to take his chances with a shovel strike on a guy who could, at this point, end Matt with just a thought. Leel kept muttering, "Deflecting a weak bolt? It's possible, if unlikely. Absorbing one in place of the target? Possible even for mundane materials. But stopping elementally shaped mana *in place?* Do you know what you've done?"

"Not . . . not really, no," Matt said cautiously. "It's a pretty good shovel."

"The best shovel in the universe shouldn't be able to do that. It stopped mana. No explosions, no anything, it just stopped it. That's not possible. Where did you get it?"

Matt was still laying on his back, holding the shovel in front of himself defensively. It wasn't a great situation, but it was better than a hole in the head. He'd take it for now.

"I found it. In the ground. It's a long story."

"Ha! Perfect. A shovel that bends around the arcane physics of the universe, and this rube just finds it. Let me guess. You've actually been using it as a shovel?"

"Yeah?"

"Perfect. Just perfect." Leel's casting hand started glowing again. "Luckily, it doesn't matter how much it can block. You know what gets around limited-coverage shields just fine? Explosions."

Leel started backpedaling at an unnaturally fast speed, much faster than Matt could follow. At the same time, the energy in his hand started forming into a flaming orb. It grew larger at a rapid pace before topping out at the size of a beach ball. Even without Survivor's Reflexes telling him, it looked like a ball of pure destruction waiting to be unleashed. Matt took the opportunity to stand up, getting into a batter's stance.

"Oh, you want to deflect this one too?" Leel snickered. "This is a bombardment spell, Matt. A good one. A *complex* casting, one that goes beyond what a simpler mage could do. To explain it in terms you can understand, I can tell it to explode whenever I want it to explode. *Please, please,* try to hit it with your little shovel. I'm sure it will go just fine for you."

Matt gritted his teeth. Leel didn't seem like he was lying about the spell. He was perfectly confident that he could end Matt, and it didn't seem like there was much Matt could do about it. He could run, but not very far or fast, certainly not fast enough to dodge the aftermath of an overloaded magic mortar shell. He could try to run towards Leel, get into melee range, and hope he'd be afraid to explode the thing. But Leel was already out of range and still backpedaling at rates an un-enhanced Matt couldn't hope to match.

Matt's only hope was to try and whack it with the shovel anyway, banking on the incredibly small chance that Leel was just bullshitting. It wasn't likely. Leel was arrogant and haughty, but he seemed to always say the truth. Laughing maniacally, Leel lifted the ball above his head, where it began spinning faster and faster in place.

"Well, it's been nice, Matt. Thanks again for the conversation, but I'm afraid that's that." His eyes suddenly became serious as he lifted the fire orb just a bit higher into the air, then brought his arm down level with the ground, pointed the orb at Matt, and said, "Fire bombardment: *Launch*."

With a fizzling noise, the orb disappeared. Matt winced, waiting to get blown apart by an invisible bomb, but nothing happened. The spell was just . . . gone.

"What? No. No! That's not possible. I casted that flawlessly. Unless . . ." Leel's eyes took on a faraway look as he referenced his mana screen. "No, no. That's not possible. How?"

He started backpedaling again, but fell headfirst into the ground. His movement skill had failed him. Before even closing his screen, Leel turned tail and started running away. He had to. Matt was already charging towards him.

Matt had a vague idea of what just happened. To the extent that he had a plan at all, he had been banking on the idea that if there wasn't enough mana in the atmosphere to grow a non-lethal turnip, there probably wasn't enough to sustain a mage's mana regeneration either.

Now, that plan had become reality, allowing Matt to go from having no chance of survival to a fighting possibility that he might live through everything. After all, Gaia sucked. It was dead in a really stupid, comprehensive way that had all sorts of nooks and crannies into which the sucking had packed even more horribleness that would ambush Matt from time to time.

But, Gaia was shitty in a way the system didn't control, which meant it was probably equally shitty for everyone, Leel included. The system messages about Matt's mana-sickness didn't mention a mage or their spells. But mana had to come from somewhere. Leel had probably arrived at Gaia with a full mana tank, then burned through it before he could finish the job. Matt could imagine that Leel had all sorts of regeneration techniques on his home world, but probably none that took a global plant apocalypse into account.

The other part of the plan was something that Leel said. He had stated, with no reason to lie, that he had dumped all of his stat points into mental categories. It was probably the reason why he talked like an accent-less plantation owner, and reinforced Matt's decision to never put more than the bare minimum of points into intelligence. But more importantly, it meant that unless Leel's wizard class dumped points into dexterity, vitality, or strength automatically, Matt was dealing with what amounted to a normal, un-augmented dude.

Just like Matt.

Matt had already ditched his pack. The loss of his strength stat changed it from "slightly annoying burden" to "ridiculously overfull deadweight" in one fell swoop. He was in a hurry to put Leel down, too. It was possible that Leel still had *some* mana regeneration and had just overdone things. Matt didn't want to give Leel an hour to recover and then have to face a mage with mana.

Leel had a pretty good lead on Matt and probably equivalent dexterity, vitality, and strength stats, but one thing became almost immediately apparent. Leel was an *inside kid*. Matt could easily visualize him spending all his time getting carried around on litters while doing magic sudokus or something. Leel ran like he had never run before. Even though Matt was pretty banged up and burned, his couple months of track team experience coupled with his still-working Boots of the Wasteland Traveler meant that he closed the distance pretty fast. By the time Matt got close enough to Leel that the boots' arbitrary "is this a combat motion?" decision-making kicked in and stopped giving a movement boost, Leel seemed to sense Matt and turned around. He gripped his staff with both hands and lowered into a surprisingly competent-looking fighting stance.

"You have a combat skill?" Matt asked, surprised.

"No, unfortunately. Just training." Leel was visibly short of breath, but apparently wasn't winded enough to stop talking entirely. "Every proper wizard gets some, although it's generally useless. It's enough to brain you, at any rate."

Whether it or not that was true, Matt was going to find out the hard way. What ensued was perhaps the shittiest melee combat Matt had ever been a part of. It was like a middle school fight. Matt planted and swung the shovel like a baseball bat, while Leel stepped in and tried to block with his staff. The resulting collision somehow ended up with both of them off-balance, and Matt feeling like he had sprained his wrist. A couple more swings resulted in Leel either dodging back or trying to counter swing, all of which Matt then easily dodged.

Matt's shovel might have been made of weird magic metal, but Leel's staff was no slouch either. It didn't show signs of breaking after a couple of clashes. In fact, the staff had the advantage on range and the fact that, to a very limited extent, it was actually designed to be a weapon of sorts. For a minute or so, that weaponry advantage combined with Matt's minor injuries was enough to give Leel the advantage. But the tides of battle soon started to turn.

Matt's stats might have been equal with Leel's, but his baseline cardio was better. Not a ton better, but Matt was consistently a level or two less out of breath than Leel, which meant he was able to move just a bit faster in any given situation. After clipping Leel several times, Matt managed to get a pretty good swipe in and bashed him broadside in the face. At this point, Matt's arms were basically pool noodles, and he couldn't get much force behind it, but it stopped Leel cold. Rather than retaliate, Leel did something Matt didn't expect but should have.

He lowered his staff and ran. Well, jogged, since neither he nor Matt were in full running condition anymore. But to the extent he could move away, he did and headed straight toward the center of Matt's estate.

CHAPTER TWENTY-TWO

# Over-Ripe Bananas

"What could he possibly want back there, Matt?" Lucy had been silent for most of Matt's fight with Leel, but now they seemed to out of danger, she was back in a talkative mood.

"No idea. It's not like he's been there." Matt was huffing as he tried his hardest to close the distance between him and Leel, who had a good few seconds of lead on him. "But I'll be damned if I let him mess up the turnips."

Matt was faster than Leel, but between being winded and having taken several shots to various parts of his body with a staff, it wasn't by much. By the time he closed the distance, Leel was standing in the center of his property, taking big, heaving breaths.

"You . . . made a mistake. Following me . . . here," Leel gasped.

"You know, I don't really think so?" Lucy grinned, physically incapable of being out of breath and loving every second of it. "Matt here is about to beat you to death with a shovel. If the system gave you a way to run back to Planet Asshole, it's probably time to use it."

Leel shook his head. "No. No evacuation stones. Don't need them. Refused them."

Matt raised his shovel. He had felt bad about killing the kid before, but this wasn't a kid. This was a homicidal magic guy who somehow gave a strong enough don't-leave-your-drink-unattended vibe that it even got to Matt. Whatever compulsions Matt might have against braining people with shovels didn't apply nearly as much here. As he went in to finish things, Leel took a deep, deep breath.

"I don't need them because I have this." Leel extended his finger, like a gun.

Suddenly, something heavy hit Matt in the cheek, like he had been punched. It caught him completely off guard, and he pulled back, staggered.

"One of the signs of a true mage," Leel said, having slightly caught his breath now, "is how *little* mana they need to cast a spell." He shot Matt again, twice, with whatever invisible force he was using. Both shots caught Matt in his hands, forcing him to drop his shovel. And then another shot hit him in the chin, almost blacking him out and sending him reeling backwards.

"Whatever you did to my mana regeneration slowed it down an incredible amount. But not completely. I have a few points again," Leel gloated. He shot at Matt's hip, which disturbed Matt's center of gravity and sent him crashing to the ground. "Something is wrong with your stats. I could tell fighting you. You should have been able to beat me. You didn't. You fought like a *child* fights."

Matt crawled across the ground as Leel peppered him with whatever invisible force he was conjuring, taking hits to his back and legs as he did. Each individual hit was painful, but not lethal. Unfortunately, he had no way to respond to it. This was bad.

"This spell takes a small fraction of a point of mana, per cast." Leel was breathing easier now, evidently recovering. He was speaking with a confidence that spelled out bad news for Matt. "If you had even a few points of vitality, this would bounce off your skin with little more effect than a bruise. It's actually, and I am not joking, for killing insects."

Matt kept crawling while several more shots hit the back of his neck and head. Leel was getting more accurate. Matt was now reeling, dizzy enough that he could feel it even though he wasn't standing. He reached out his hand for to pull himself pointlessly forward, and felt a plant. Looking, he found it was one he didn't immediately recognize, and was confused before his addled brain realized it was a shoot from the victory garden.

The estate-purchased soil was crazy stuff by itself. Matt and Lucy had turned it up a notch by enhancing the soil near the center of the garden with every cheap soil enhancer they could buy, and used that plot as a sort of experimental garden. Plants would grow quickly there and give Matt and Lucy a chance to see how each seed fared in the weird Gaian light and weather conditions. If the plants were healthy and Matt and Lucy liked them enough, they would then include the new plants in their full-scale farming.

Several days had turned out to be enough to get some of the faster-growing plants in the Sarthian seed pack to mature, mostly grasses and flowers. Unfortunately, Survivor's Reflexes didn't identify any of them as a resource, in and of itself.

*Why would the museum call those seed the "most productive" if they weren't producing a resource?*

Suddenly, Matt thought of a resource that decorative plants *could* produce, and prayed it was the right one. The problem of why his estate plants didn't produce mana had always been a hard one. Even in top-grade soil, the food Matt had been growing was little better than poison. Something was wrong with how the estate system was interacting with the actual conditions of Gaia.

But where the museum hadn't been strong enough to make a yo-yo, it could still give him a pack of seeds. A pack of seeds it claimed were *gathered.* Betting on a long shot, Matt pulled himself just a bit forward and sunk his teeth into the stalk of one of the flowers.

"Last meal? My heavens, you really are livestock," Leel laughed.

As Matt's HP bar continued to bottom out under Leel's bombardment, he heard the most welcome sound he could imagine.

*Ding!*

*Mana Deficiency Condition Status: Lessened*

You have ingested food with normal mana levels, in the loosest sense of the word. Your mana-deficient condition has been stabilized and very slightly improved. For further improvements, seek higher-quality food.

Stats regained: +1 STR, +2 VIT, +1 DEX
Abilities regained: Partial use of Rub Some Dirt In It (4 percent efficacy)

*It's not enough*, Matt thought. His HP bar started climbing, only to be immediately drained back downward with Leel's shots. The flowers were vegetable matter, but were either far enough from being actual food or so barely sufficient in mana that without Eat Anything!, they just weren't enough to pull him entirely back from the brink. If he had time, maybe he could figure out how to transfer their effect to his other plants. Or to figure out a way to condense them somehow. But he didn't have time.

"Did you enjoy that? Good." Leel leveled out his hand. "I suspect you will be blacking out pretty soon. I'll try to make sure you don't feel your ultimate end, Matt. I'm at least that civilized." As Leel prepared to fire, Matt felt something crawling on his face, and reached back instinctively to brush it away.

*The. Bees. The bees!*

Matt called on the tiny bit of dexterity and strength he had got back from the flower and somehow got to his feet, wandering like a drunkard towards the Apeiary. The bees had only recently been producing significant amounts of honey, but something about the little flying monkeys and the memory of how horrifically tropical the Gaian ape had tasted had kept Matt from digging into it. He had been getting stats eating horrible things in the dungeon, and didn't very much feel like bringing that gross home.

Now, this was a different story. The bees had access to those flowers. So if anything was a condensed form of whatever those flowers had, the honey would be. After taking a dozen more shots, Matt managed to make it back to the Ape-iary, shoving his hand straight in and dragging out a piece of sticky honeycomb.

And then, as he lifted his hand to his mouth, he realized he couldn't see. His knees collapsed under him as he felt himself losing consciousness. His ears were buzzing. He couldn't talk. To his horror, Matt realized the last thing he'd ever clearly sense was the taste of the honey. It absolutely reeked of over-ripe bananas.

"Matt! No!" Lucy screamed. "Get up!"

"Oh, no, I don't think he will, dear." Leel grinned. "I'm honestly shocked he stayed on his feet that long. I said he fought like a child, but that was unfair. I've tested this out with friends, and children in the street generally lose consciousness after just a few shots."

"You are an unbelievable asshole. I'll kill you."

"I'm afraid there's not much chance of that." Leel was mostly recovered now, and regripped his staff in both hands, swooshing it through the air. "It's a good thing, too. You won't have to live very long after seeing this. Honestly, you should feel proud. It was a close thing. I'm once again completely out of mana."

He walked over to where Matt was laying, and lifted the staff into the air. "I'll have to do this inelegantly. It pains me. I suppose both of you can take that to the grave."

The staff dropped down like a meteor, crashing into Matt's skull.

Matt had once, just once, been choked out. His brother-in-law was a stout, corn-growing and corn-fed, Mississippi farmer boy who had once put him in a headlock as a joke, then squeezed just a little harder than Matt's city-boy neck was prepared for.

That's how Matt found out being unconscious wasn't like the movies, where someone would get knocked out and their whole world went dark.

Instead, Matt found he was never really fully asleep. He could still see, but his brain couldn't make sense of anything. He saw his sister's husband panic and drop him on the ground under a folding table. Waking up after being unconscious was like having shadows lifted off the images that he previously couldn't make sense of. It wasn't until after he regained his senses that he understood what had happened.

Matt's current situation wasn't exactly like that, but it was similar. He could hear Lucy screaming, and he vaguely wanted to do something to fix that, but he couldn't tell what she was saying or where it was coming from. He could hear Leel prattling on about something, and he was annoyed by that, but he had no idea how he could go about getting him to shut up.

And then, suddenly, another sound crashed into him. A few seconds later, he suddenly regained the ability to understand what had happened.

*Ding!*

| Mana Deficiency Status: Recovering (50 percent) |
| --- |

## CHAPTER TWENTY-THREE

# Cultivating Victory

When Leel's staff crashed into Matt's skull, Lucy's eyes winced shut. When she opened them a second later to see the aftermath, what greeted her eyes was an image of Matt standing up, holding Leel by his robes and lifting him slightly off the ground.

"That *hurt,* you asshole." Matt was having trouble being appropriately angry. He had just woken up to find that someone he already wasn't fond of had hit him in the head with a staff. But his barely awake brain was still in a fogged up state. Still, he was awake enough to feel some anger. He immediately went on to the next appropriate move, slamming his fist into Leel's nose hard enough to send him sliding across the ground on his back in the opposite direction.

"Matt! You lived!" Lucy exclaimed.

"I did. Listen." Matt turned his head. His brain was still waking up. "I really don't want to eat any more of that honey."

On the ground, Leel's mana regeneration had apparently ticked over enough to give him another point of mana to pelt Matt with his pest control spell. As Matt approached, the spell pinged meaninglessly off him like bullets off a steel plate. Matt walked up, kicked Leel as hard as he could in the ribs, then bent down and picked him up by his collar like a kitten.

"What should we do with this? I'm all for the 'chuck him into the trap room' move."

"Matt, are you okay? Not yet. The necklace, remember?"

"Oh, yeah." For better or worse, Leel had an enslaved guardian in his jewelry. In Matt's half-dazed state, Lucy had convinced him that job number one for him was to figure out a way to un-enslave it. "I guess if we kill him, it might hurt the guardian. Leel, is that the case?"

Leel turned his bloody face to look at Matt.

"I'm not telling you anything, peasant. How dare you hit—"

Matt slapped him. "Listen, dude. I'm the survival guy from the survival planet."

He slapped Leel again. "Remember the whole thing you were saying about me being a dirty peasant? Pretend it's all true. I can hit you a bunch more if I need to, I feel *much* better now."

Leel managed to hold out another four or five slaps before caving somewhat. "That's enough! I'll talk, Matt. Set me down, so I can face you," Leel said.

Matt did, keeping his hand wrapped up in the front of Leel's collar, and his hand cocked back to hit him.

"The answer is, yes, you could kill me. But it wouldn't help the spirit much. It's been in there for hundreds of years, Matt. Whatever consciousness it once had is likely long gone. Even if time hadn't done it, the enchantments on the amulet would have."

Matt and Lucy wilted a bit. They wouldn't trust Leel at this point, but what he was saying made sense.

"And you can't just . . . let it out?" Lucy asked.

Leel laughed, covering his mouth with his hand.

"Me? No, I'm afraid those enchantments were laid down by a *much* more powerful mage than I. I can't break them. They're designed to keep the amulet safe and the guardian contained through much, much more severe damage than either you or I could generate. That's what they're designed for."

Matt held up his slapping hand as a threat, hoping to wring a different answer out of his captive. Leel held his hands up defensively before suddenly letting his look of alarm dissolve away into a sick, conniving smile that almost made Matt pull away from him.

"But it's not, I'm afraid, the only thing they're designed for."

Lucy began to yell for Matt to get back, but before he could react, Leel's hand dropped to the amulet. Suddenly, Matt's hands were both empty. Leel was gone.

It took Matt a few minutes to fully recover from everything. Once he did, he asked the obvious question.

"So is this like the last guy? Dragged back to his planet, probably?"

"I don't think so, Matt. No body, for one. And at least we know he didn't turn invisible."

Of all the things Matt was currently glad about, he was most glad that he was alive. Somewhere down the list from there, maybe number three or four, was that Leel disappeared at a time when Matt had a hand grasped around his robe. The worst case here was that Leel had teleported to another place on Gaia, which meant that there was a homicidal asshole out there somewhere who had to kill Matt to get home. But since Matt could see a pretty good distance from his house, it did mean that they could probably relax for a little bit.

"I still don't get how any of this worked, Matt. The bees make magic mana potions? Just . . . all of a sudden?"

Matt shook his head. "No. At least I don't think so. But they do compress pollen."

"I don't get it."

"Okay, think of it this way. Why do the plants not, you know, work? Why don't they have mana? They're plants. They need dirt, sunlight, and water. Water is just, you know, a chemical. I've drunk a bunch of magic water, and it didn't hurt me or anything. Dirt is, I'm not claiming to understand the intricacies of dirt, but it's mostly minerals and dead stuff. Raw materials. And the sun is just energy. The plants grow, so we know that's working, or at least kind of working. So why don't they have mana?"

"Because you bought them from the estate?"

"Yeah, I thought about that too, but . . . I can't imagine that's the case either, at least by itself. Because the estate system was meant to be used, and who would buy the plants if they were all poisonous? The system wouldn't want to sell mana-zombie plants, especially since the system seemed to be trying to get these people to trust it."

"So what's your theory, then?"

"I think . . . Okay, stick with me, but imagine that somebody bought a plant for an estate, on a healthy planet. Like Gaia, back before the Scourge. We know the system uses energy to do what it does, right? And that it's lazy. I'm guessing the life it would make wouldn't be complete all by itself, but that didn't matter because you were planting it in an environment that were mostly things that weren't system created. They could probably piggyback off the mana everything else was producing. Or something."

"And this leads to you randomly eating a flower . . . how? That was insane."

"I just thought, 'Okay, we've got these seeds,' and in a way, we got them from the Gaians. There wasn't any way those people were going to use synthetically generated seeds. There's just no way. Especially when the Scourge came from one. Those were Gaian seeds, real ones. They had to be. So if any plant was going to have mana at all, it was going to be those. And if anything at all was going to have mana AND be food, it was the honey."

"So you used your dying breath to eat monkey honey based on that?"

"Yeah, basically."

"That's . . ." Lucy was, for once, at a loss for words. "That's the dumbest thing I ever heard, Matt. I think that's the dumbest thing anyone has ever heard, anywhere."

"It worked!"

"Yeah, it did." Lucy plopped down on the ground, by Matt. "And I guess I'm glad you are okay."

"Thanks. But, listen, we're not done yet, I'm afraid."

"No?"

"Nope. There's work to do. We need more of those seeds." Matt took a deep breath, and sighed while looking off into the distance. "We have to . . . cultivate victory."

"That's incredibly dumb."

"Shut up, Lucy. Let me have this."

It turned out that the gift shop would only let Matt take one packet of seeds per trip, and required that he visit at least one exhibit before leaving. Even leaving the exhibits early, this meant each repetition took a few minutes. That was then followed by at least a few minutes of scanning the horizon to make sure that Leel wasn't sneaking up on them with a refilled mana bar and a chip on his shoulder.

It took hours, but eventually, they had dozens of seed packets. Walking back, digging a few irrigation channels, forking down another mouthful of gross medicinal honey, and scattering the seeds took a few more, but eventually the initial estate plot was almost entirely ringed in by seeds. Where there were gaps, Matt assumed they'd eventually fill in by themselves.

"So what's the hope here? Just having a ready supply of the flowers for the bees?" Lucy asked.

"That's the first thing. But it depends on how mana works." Matt held up three fingers. "The least-good way I can see this working is that just the flowers grow normally, and keep their mana levels stable. That's good in the sense that we'd get honey, and lots of it, but I'm hoping for more."

Matt folded down his index finger, leaving two more up. "The second-best scenario is that all the plants just need a little bit of a kickstart to get going. And that being around the flowers, maybe getting cross-pollinated with the flowers, will let all the lettuces and fruit trees have their own, stable mana. Basically, they become real, healthy plants."

"And the third?"

Matt dropped down to one finger. "If we are really going to bring this planet back, that means fixing the overall supply of mana. And I was thinking about that too. Either every lifeless planet that has ever birthed life had a constant amount of mana that was divided among all the life, or . . ."

Lucy snapped her fingers. "Or life makes a little more mana than it uses, right?"

"Yup. If we are really lucky, this will work in the short-term like the mana generator we wanted to buy. And in the long-term, like the really long-term, if we get enough plants in a cycle it might start to give Gaia the ambient mana it should have. That's my thought, anyway."

Lucy scrunched her brow. "Isn't that also bad in the short-term? This gives both the system and that magic asshole more to work with."

"Yeah, true. But I don't think we get the luxury of starving them out. This isn't a problem we solve by playing it safe. We need to prep."

"Prep how?"

Matt grinned.

"I have some ideas."

Dozens of miles away, Leel was puking.

Any random chimney sweep could teleport, but long-range, point-to-point, portal-less teleporting was an art. That was part of why Leel was proud of the Star of the South, the emergency teleport built into it was not just functional. It would work in any kind of weather, in the midst of virtually any kind of non-dimensional attack, and with only minimal input from its user. It *wanted* to teleport people to places. Work of this caliber came only from the hands of the finest dimensional mages, and the Star of the South was a true masterpiece.

Which was all well and good, except that it turned out "works with minimal input from its user" meant that the amulet was getting the minimum energy it needed to work from a small internal store of mana. To work *well*, it needed mana from the environment.

That it worked at all in this hellhole was a miracle, one that Leel was glad for. But it was definitely a rough ride, and Leel was just short of scrambled like an egg. He was beaten up, cast down, and worst of all, had no access to any of the dozens of magic tricks he knew to deal with just this sort of situation.

Finally, pulling himself together, he reached into his robes to pull out what little cargo he had brought with him to this abysmal place. Off-world quests were rare, but not so rare that wisdom regarding them hadn't filtered down over the years. Making one's wishes apparently clear during the process was said to help with whatever equipment one got on an off-planet quest, and it had worked swimmingly here. Sacrificing whatever else the system might have included in his loadout had resulted in exactly what Leel had wanted.

He had his bound amulet, decent if somewhat simple robes befitting a mage, and a fine if not strictly necessary staff to complete the picture. But most importantly, he had paint. A very specific, very affordable variety of arcane paint. Dipping the end of his staff in it, he got to work etching what would end up being a rather large magic circle.

The ambient mana on this planet was shit. There was no nicer way to say it. On a proper world, the array he was drawing would gather enough mana that he'd become a sort of living turret, capable of launching small, medium, and even some larger-scale spells indefinitely without worrying a whit about resource conservation. Here, he'd be lucky if it increased the mana density enough to get him to mid-double-digit levels of mana.

But it would do something. He could work with that.

## CHAPTER TWENTY-FOUR

# Trees are Nice Things

Brennan looked out over the walls and the canopy of treetops that hugged the city. The view would be breathtaking, if it weren't for the invading army of thousands of demons. The treetops were *nice*, and he liked nice things. He liked other people to have access to nice things.

One of the accepted, well-thought-of tactics when demons were attempting a siege was to let the demons approach the wall while counting on the archers to take down weaker flying creatures. Then, it was just a matter of dropping stuff on the demons, whether that be rocks, spells, or whatever the Ra'Zorians had lying around. The Ra'Zorian soldiers had a saying that went something like, "A good wall makes one soldier count for ten," and it wasn't a lie. Leveraging the wall would make this battle much more of a sure thing.

But in the process, the demons would hurt the trees. Brennan didn't want that, which meant he was thinking about doing something slightly dumber.

"You have that look on your face," Artemis said.

"What look?" said Brennan.

"The one you get when you are about to do something you think is noble, but is really just dumb," said Artemis.

Having Artemis along on this journey was an unexpected plus in Brennan's week. Apparently, word of Derek's personal renaissance hadn't climbed the ladder to Artemis's superiors yet, which meant that they felt guilty about sticking her in an all-day-every-day shit type of assignment. When she asked to be temporarily shifted to field work to keep herself sharp, they gave her a choice of postings. To Brennan's great and persistent satisfaction, she chose his.

"Now it's the one you get when you are getting sappy," Artemis commented.

"What can I say? I'm a romantic," said Brennan.

Out in the field, the demons' torches were slowly shifting as their commanders fine-tuned the attack formations. Sometimes, they'd do this for days, moving whole contingents of soldiers a few feet this way or that way until everything was perfect. Then, and only then, would they advance, and thrust their whole force forward like a spear of death.

As annoying as it was, the micromanaging made more sense for the demons than it appeared. For one, the demons were "the race of many races," with monsters of all shapes and sizes composing their ranks. They all moved at different paces, possessed different strengths, and were vulnerable to different kinds of defenses. Demon battle order just mattered more than human formations. There was more to keep track of.

On top of that, humanity on Ra'Zor was a scattered thing. Ra'Zorian humans lived and worked in little islands of civilization built around various valuable resources worth protecting. They stayed behind the safety of the vaguely defined battle lines that comprised the border between the human and demon worlds. For humans, travel was dangerous. Monsters roamed. Demons raided. Reinforcements and supplies had to be carefully planned.

Meanwhile, the demons' side of the line was firmly their own territory. It was more established, more built up, and with endlessly more resources. If humans spent as long dilly-dallying before attacks, they'd be subject to raids and attacks from all sides. The demons tended to optimize their formations, simply because they could. There was always time.

Or at least there was when Brennan wasn't there. Sometimes he was able to tip the scales on that a bit.

Back in the war room, Brennan was briefing his team.

"You know how these guys are. Everything has to be perfect. It's really, really easy to catch them on the back foot because of that."

Brennan was a high-level *precision fighter*. Most of his skills were biased towards him making pinpoint attacks as an individual, waiting for opportunities to strike hard and fast at the most vulnerable targets when it mattered most. At a high level, those same skills also applied to attacking big groups in interesting ways, essentially letting him find vulnerabilities in formations of foes and deal maximum damage with small groups.

In the back, a huge man sitting hugging a huge, rectangular shield raised his hand.

"So you want to attack them first? That's a tall order, even for me. Lots of heavy hitters in that crew."

"You aren't wrong, John. With the numbers that they have, we don't have much hope of winning in a force-on-force conflict. I'm thinking about something a little less direct. For full disclosure, the safe move would be fighting them from the wall like usual. It's just . . ."

Artemis cut in. "He doesn't want the trees to get hurt. I agree, because of the lumber value of the trees, among other reasons. But . . ."

"He just likes them?" John said, laughing. Among the reincarnators that Brennan worked with, John was probably his favorite. He was a nice, big guy. One that was glad to take the hits to protect everyone else. Brennan understood that getting hit still hurt, no matter how many defense skills were plastered on top. But John took all the hits with a smile. It meant a lot.

"Yeah, I just like them. Plus, it bothers me that the demons are just out there, relaxed. I want to give them something to think about," said Brennan.

When they attacked, they hit hard and fast. The city walls had a few small doors made of solid iron. Each of them was backed by several feet of rock so that even if the doors were breached, which wasn't likely, the demons would still have to deal with interlocking stone slabs set up to be a wall-within-the-wall.

From the inside, the slabs could be moved, and the iron door could be unlocked. It usually didn't happen, on the off chance that the demons took advantage of this opportunity and attacked. But it had been done before, for couriers to slip out and send messages. This time, it meant Brennan, John, Artemis, and Flambo the Great, were able to go beyond the walls. Flambo had changed his name as a joke shortly after his arrival, and was so committed to the bit that he never changed it back. Despite this, he was the best offensive reincarnator mage on the planet, at least as far as Brennan knew.

After watching for days, Brennan had narrowed their focus down to three targets. They were all generals in the demon army, or at least they seemed to be so. Creeping forward in the dark, they got close to the easiest target, the demon who seemed to be in charge of the flying units. Brennan was confident they could at least cause problems for that one demon officer. It was the others he wasn't sure about.

After an hour of waiting in the bushes outside the enemy camp's firelight, he saw the target. On Earth, he would have described it as a giant eagle-human hybrid and assumed, if he saw it, that it was either a very realistic costume or the result of some truly horrific genetic engineering. That said, it was as fully armored as a flying unit could be with lightweight, ultrathin metal plates.

In the bushes, Flambo started pouring power into one of Artemis's specially made arrowheads, one designed specifically for the purpose of carrying a magical payload in addition to the substantial physical damage Artemis could cause. Flambo's ability stored what he called "flame energy" within the arrowhead, to be released on impact with a target. It wasn't all-destroying, but with two people putting everything they could into their attack, the party hoped they'd be able to take out the officer in a single hit. After a few seconds, Flambo lifted his hand. The arrowhead had all the power it could take. Artemis took measure of the wind, aimed, and fired.

The one-hit kill was not meant to be. The arrow hit the target, pierced its armor, and exploded with energy powerful enough that for a moment, their enemy lit up like it had eaten a spotlight. But the demon wasn't a general for nothing. With a scream, it took the hit while managing to still keep its balance, wobbly but very much alive and very, very loud. The troops around it were just beginning to get to their feet and arm themselves when Brennan sprang out of the darkness. He flared his Distance Lunge ability, crossed the distance between himself and the general in a moment, and skewered him with one of his daggers. Between the arrow and the strike, it was more than enough to put the general down.

Brennan pulled his dagger and prepared to deal with the retaliatory strikes from the general's troops, only to watch most of them get bowled over as John entered the fray behind the shield-enhancing powers of his Two-Ton Charge skill. Once it wore off, he'd be vulnerable, but even a vulnerable John was unreasonably hard to hurt and could hold his own. Brennan was off and running before the skill ended, confident John would stick to the plan and withdraw if necessary.

The biggest, most important element of John's charge wasn't that it was effective at dealing damage, but instead that it was loud. When demons hit by the charge survived, they tended to do so with a variety of wounds ranging from broken bones to dented skulls, the kind of wounds that resulted in them making quite a bit of noise. Brennan's class wasn't inherently sneaky, but he had a lot of dexterity piled up. With John making noise on the outskirts of the fight, it was fairly easy for him to weave between tents and avoid being sighted before getting to the next general.

By the time he arrived, the general in charge of the heavy troops was fully alerted and surrounded by his personal guards. The general himself looked to be a damage-dealing type, one that gave out hits much more easily than he took them. Like other higher-ranking demons, he looked essentially like a human with short horns, slightly redder skin, and a serious attitude problem. His guards were all tanky types, belonging to a family of demons that looked like hornless bipedal rhinos. They were big, slow, and strong. Exactly the kind of enemies Brennan loved to fight.

Brennan abandoned stealth, running directly to the rhino-demon closest to him and slashing its neck. It was easy. The slash itself didn't have enough power to take the demon down, but Brennan had learned a long time ago that no amount of stats or skills could overcome the sheer self-preservation instinct someone felt when they were being attacked at their vital points. As the rhino let out a sort of *hurk* noise and grabbed at its neck, Brennan grabbed the back of its head, forced it down further, and vaulted completely over the enemy into the center of the circle with the general.

Almost immediately, a glowing hand came chopping at his neck.

Brennan barely dodged it without activating any of his evasion skills. Despite the demon being a general, it was clearly at a lower level than Brennan. In fact, Brennan was a bit of nightmare horror story from the perspective of the demons. The difficulty of their raid came not from killing the demon generals, which was easy, but killing them fast enough that they wouldn't be dogpiled by literally thousands of demon soldiers, which was hard.

But Brennan had a solution for that. A big part of why Brennan brought six daggers to battle when one or two would do just fine was for situations like this when time was of the essence. He pulled out another dagger.

CHAPTER TWENTY-FIVE

# To Keep Fighting

This new dagger glowed green as soon as it left its scabbard. The demon he had killed to craft the dagger was nasty, all acid and poison and refusal to die. In the end, it took Flambo loading Brennan's previous dagger with a seriously dangerous amount of flame and a plunge into the demon's eye to end the fight. The stuff Brennan had gotten on himself after the subsequent explosion had left him bedbound for a week, but it also left him in possession of a particularly nasty set of fragile, poisonous bones.

The new dagger wasn't any good for prolonged battle. It was brittle and weak, and it took the better part of a day for the blacksmith to realize that the bone was better ground down into a spike instead of trying to shape it into an actual knife.

Brennan ducked another glowing shot attack, referenced his senses to make sure he was aiming at the right weak spot, then jammed the poison dagger to the hilt in the demon's neck.

The dagger would either kill him or it wouldn't, but Brennan was out of time. The fact that Artemis agreed was evident as a trio of staggered arrows crashed into the injured rhino guard, toppling it to the ground and leaving a gap for Brennan to escape through. Without a second thought, he activated Tactical Retreat, dumping almost his entire stamina pool to raise his speed to insane levels as he ran through enemy soldiers towards the edge of the camp.

By the time he reached the borders of the enemy forces, he had some minor new nicks and cuts. John was nowhere to be seen, but that was expected. If he was following the plan, he would have retreated already. John was tough, but he was slow. He needed a lead to get back to the wall at the same time as the others.

As Brennan crashed into the darkness, he ran almost headlong into a group of several bird soldiers. He guessed they had been chasing his crew around, reinforced by the observation that they were flying almost at ground level, a behavior he associated with any flight-capable enemy that had recently experienced Artemis's arrows. As good as that might normally make him feel, it spelled trouble here. He and the group were moving towards each other at alarming speeds, much faster than he was comfortable dodging at. His retreat skill was meant for speed, and nothing else.

Before he had the chance to slide on the ground like a baseball player and hope the demons were surprised enough to let him past, the entire group exploded.

"That's almost the last of my mana." Flambo said, stepping out of the darkness and running with Brennan through the now lit-up remains of the fireballed bird group. "We should probably go."

By the time they got to the door in the wall, Artemis and John were already through. They hadn't taken out all three generals, but they never expected to unless things lined up just right.

*Two out of three isn't actually bad. Especially with no casualties.*

John was pretty screwed up, but he was always like that after a fight. He was handling it with his usual good grace, joking that he didn't need any help as the town's military healers got to work sealing up the dozen or so serious cuts on his body. Brennan knew better than to get in their way, and spent a few seconds helping the guards secure the stone slabs in place behind the door before climbing the wall to see the aftermath of their attack.

Whatever fine-tuning the demon generals had been working on had gone all to shit already. The troops were running around everywhere, trying to confirm that the source of the sudden violence in their camp was gone, or trying to eradicate it if it wasn't. They hadn't found the scattered corpses of the exploded bird-troops yet. Otherwise, they'd know that the humans were gone.

Artemis slipped under his arm, and they stood there for a while without talking. After fifteen minutes, the enemy camp had calmed down, and the two saw the telltale motions of a military force beginning to pack up and move out. Whether they had killed the head general or just enough officers overall, the demons had lost their will to fight. They were leaving.

"Do you ever wish you could chase them? We'd be a lot better off if we could eliminate the whole army, for once," Artemis asked.

In the back of Brennan's mind was a small voice telling him that it would have been, if he had just let the demons attack the wall. They wouldn't have killed any generals, but the overall number of demon troops killed would have been multiple orders of magnitude higher.

"Yeah. But you know, I've tried that already," Brennan said. Artemis was one of the few people Brennan had told about his one real, ill-fated attempt to sneak into demon territory and kill the demon king. He had been much younger, but not that much weaker, since levels came much more slowly as a person's level got higher. That was less true for reincarnators, of course, but even they were soft-capped eventually.

Brennan had got surprisingly far before running into his first demon patrol. Could he put them down? Yes, and he did. But he couldn't hide the bodies, and soon various forces of flying, walking, and digging demons were all out looking for him. He cut dozens and dozens of them down, each one easier to kill than the last. But there were too many. By the time he staggered near human territory, he was reduced to hiding in what amounted to a hole in the ground for days before their patrols gave up.

"Even if we did, even if we destroyed that whole army, it wouldn't matter," Artemis whispered, "The demons breed faster than we do. They control more land than we do. If they take our land, they burn it. We can't unburn theirs, not as easily. We can hold the line. Nothing more."

That was how it had been since before Brennan's time. The demons would get stronger, and the humans would create some technology or tactic that would push them back. Then, the system came, and the humans were able to train to levels that would have been absurd to even dream about before, but then the demon lord rose and snatched back all the human progress. The demons got stronger, and the system sent reincarnators, but never enough to do anything but maintain the status quo. There was always a balance. The system would send them enough manpower to keep fighting, but never enough for them to stop the fighting once and for all.

"I was thinking . . . maybe we should go inside."

"*Inside* inside?" Artemis said, slyly.

"No, just inside. In the special tent."

The special tent, as Brennan termed it, was a crafted item. If there was one thing he missed about Earth, it was being able to just go home to a climate-controlled, comfortable space that was entirely his own. He had wanted something like a bedroom he could hide in, a place where he could sleep without being sweaty, cold, or bothered in any other way. Unfortunately, Ra'Zorian technology was built around war, not comfort. They were a sturdy, uncomplaining people who had spent almost no time ever thinking about things like air conditioning or water that didn't have to be drawn from wells.

So Brennan did it himself. The frame was made of demon bones of various varieties, all with a different effect when powered by a small amount of magic energy. One of them would make the tent warmer. Another, from a frost-themed demon, would cool it off. He had bones that would kill the Ra'Zorian equivalent of mosquitos, bones that made light, and bones that poured water. By any sane standard, the tent was packed with enough rare magic to make it worth more than most mansions.

It had cost even more to have it put together. The craftsman who took on the project had claimed that the bones didn't like being in proximity to each other in that way, and that they resisted it and broke when he tried to force it. Brennan forced them, pouring amounts of money back into the local economy that would have shocked anyone but another reincarnator. He hired mages, enchanters, rune masters, and anyone else who could pick up a hammer. Finally, and he understood that it was pretty much an accident, they got the tent together.

After that, the tent wouldn't come apart. It would collapse, so he could carry it around, but it wouldn't disassemble with anything less than what he expected would be destructive force. Appraisers looked at it and didn't see anything special. It was just, for lack of a better word, stuck. But it worked like he had planned, and that was enough.

Brennan didn't figure out its other properties until much later, when a stealthy demon managed to get all the way in the tent with him and stab him with a sleeping potion-infused dagger. He barely managed to kill the thing before he conked out, waking up hours later covered in demon blood and badly, badly hung over. But when he walked out of the tent, he got a shock.

*Ding!*

| *Achievement: [Counter-Assassination]* |
|---|

The text of the achievement had been normal. The only weird part of it was that it was delayed. That was his first clue that the tent was special in a different way. The system couldn't see inside of it. That hadn't mattered much until Brennan became older, a bit more suspicious, and met Artemis. Now he considered the tent and the weird, system-defying interference it put off to be among the most important things in all of Ra'Zor.

It was also where he hung out with his girlfriend when he could swing it.

"I love this thing, by the way. Do you know how liberating it is to know the system can't see what we do in here? Inside, or *inside* inside, either way," Artemis teased.

"I get it, Artemis. But first, you know, let's talk about the fate of the world stuff?" Brennan said with a serious tone.

"Spoilsport. Fine, get on with it."

"I was thinking today about, you know, the balance."

"Yes. And how we have to get you stronger, so you can break it."

"I'm not sure I think that's possible anymore." Brennan shook his head.

Artemis perked up, looking concerned. This wasn't the kind of mood she was used to seeing from Brennan. "No? Then what have we been doing this for?"

"Not for nothing. I can do things I couldn't before." Brennan sighed. "I'm more powerful, which is important because we might be the only two people on this planet who actually care about this. Everyone else trusts the system."

"Not everyone else. I think the blacksmith has his doubts."

"Well, maybe. But the point is, even if I could run into today's demon army and kill every soldier in it, I wouldn't make a dent in the overall demon army. And by the time I *can* do that, the system will adjust. There will be new demons, or they will suddenly learn new spells. It won't make a difference."

"So what do we do? Give up?"

"No. Never." Brennan propped himself up on his arm. "If the system wants to maintain a balance, we just need to find a way to get it off-balance. We need to change faster, in a way the system can't see. Or at least in a way *our* system can't see."

"And how do we do that?"

"I'm not sure. But it can't come from here, from Ra'Zor. If it's homegrown power, the system will adjust. It has to be something we bring in from the outside. A ringer from another planet, with a different kind of power. I don't know."

Brennan rolled onto his back and stared up at the ceiling for a bit, thinking. After a few moments, he shifted to dial down the tent pole bone that was keeping the lights on. Artemis shifted over, throwing her arm over him and curling into his side.

"We'll get there, Brennan. I'm tired, too. The system says it gives us power to fight the demon lord because he's the enemy. And we fight. I don't think it even cares about good and evil, so long as we keep fighting."

She sighed and held on to Brennan a bit tighter.

"I just wish we knew someone the system really, genuinely didn't like. It feels like they would be a good place to start."

## CHAPTER TWENTY-SIX

# Filler

Like a lot of people, Matt thought of beehives as a kind of living honey factory and of honey as some kind of human food. He didn't really think of what the bees might need, whether it be honey or pollen. Since the Ape-iary bees were sort of screwed up normal bees, that lack of thoughtfulness extended to them too.

Because of that, he had never considered that the little apes might be starving to mana death the same way he had been. As the first patch of victory garden that Matt had planted came into full bloom, he watched the Ape-iary's activity level pick up quite a bit. Then, as the rest of the hedge of victory flowers around his entire plot of land bloomed, they went absolutely ape shit. There was a period where every cubic foot of air that Matt passed had an Ape-bee aloft in it.

And then things changed, thanks to a part of the Ape-iary's description that Matt had long since forgotten.

> *Ape-iary*
>
> Plants need pollen transport to reproduce. These customized little guys are overpowered in that task. One Ape-iary will automatically populate your first ten agricultural units, and further pollinator apes will naturally spread from that stock.
>
> They also produce honey. Are you brave enough to try it?

The apes were a bizarre enough bonus, and the expansion of his property had enough fanfare and hoopla all by itself that Matt hadn't even noticed when the apes hadn't spread out to the promised ten agricultural units. Having never even realized that something was amiss, he also never questioned why the apes stayed confined to the test garden. But once the flowers had been around long enough, there were suddenly nine more Ape-iaries, each loaded out with honey.

*Ding!*

*Mana Deficiency Status: Abated.*

Your diet has improved and sustained that improved level long enough for your body's mana production facilities to restabilize. This marks the end of the mana deficiency condition, for the most part, though you would be well advised to consider that even healed wounds can sometimes easily reopen.

Effect: All skills disabled by mana deficiency reinstated at 100 percent efficacy, all stats restored.

*[Back from the Brink]*

Do you know how much longer it would have taken you to die from the whole mana deficiency thing? Five hours. Just five more stupid hours. Where did you even get those plants? The bees make some sort of stupid sense, with Barry stretching the limits of a dozen rules at the perfect time. But those seeds shouldn't exist. There was nothing left of this planet. I checked. Once I figure out where Barry got them, there's going to be hell to pay.

You know the worst part about this? Your stupid eating skill is still broken. Not in a way that kills you, but apparently the rules still demand I upgrade it, and there's nothing to upgrade. Why can't you just go quietly into the night? These tokens cost a fortune.

Rewards: Gaian Modular Kitchen Token, Consumption Skill XP Token, +100 Class XP

*[This Magic Moment]*

You've faced and survived your first encounter with magic.

So yeah, did this whole wizard assassin thing backfire on your old friend, the system instance? Sure, you can see it that way. It's not like I can issue you a "burn down all your beehives then kill the demon lord" quest. You'd never finish it. If only there was someone motivated in the exact other direction, I could ask. Oh, yeah, there is.

Rewards: Survivor's Combat +1 LV, Rub Some Dirt In It +1 LV, +200 Class XP

"So what'd you get? Is the system playing fair?" Lucy asked.

"I don't know what I was supposed to get, but it looks like the system instance didn't have much room to screw around here. It's some pretty good stuff," Matt said.

Matt let her know about the skill updates and level-up. Having his primary combat skill and his survivability skill both go up at the same time was a big deal. Because Matt was responsible for taking all the damage and killing all the monsters that a whole team would normally face, being able to take a few more hits or fight off a swarm of monsters was a big deal. He didn't like how thin the line between life and death was for him without the ability to spread damage and survival responsibilities out over several party members. But it was what it was, and these notifications meant a pretty big boost in his survivability.

"There's also this." Matt held up the Skill Upgrade Token. "It upgrades Eat Anything!, or at least it's supposed to. I'm not sure what happens if I use it right now, with the skill itself messed up."

"It might fix it, right?"

"It might, or I might burn it for nothing. Or I might explode. I don't think I actually want to explode anymore this week, honestly."

"Counterpoint: You're always about to explode. And this seems like a good way to screw up the system's plans. It doesn't want you to have Eat Anything!, right? This seems like a good deal to get the skill back on his dime."

Matt shook his head. "Before, I would have agreed with you. But something about how the system talks about that skill makes me think he didn't have anything to do with it. Think about it. If the system could take away skills at any time, why not take away my combat skill? Or my defense skill? Why not mess up my movement skill during the chase with the ape?"

"The rules?"

"Probably. But if he's not doing it, then who is? Barry said it was an outside force, and I'd hate to think he was lying to us. I originally thought it might be someone the system was hiring in the same way it's hiring these assassins, but it just . . . I dunno. It feels different."

"Different?"

"Just in my gut. This doesn't feel like a system thing. But I'm not sure. Which means this token"—Matt twirled the coin between two of his fingers—"could be anything. It could be a lifesaver, or a trap, or instant death if I used it right now."

"So you're keeping it in reserve?"

"For now. To be safe."

* * *

Two weeks was a long time without dungeon access. So Matt and Lucy worked hard on what they called property prep, doing as much as they could to prepare the property to be unpleasant if Leel was to visit while they were away. The upshot of having literally nothing to do was that they got an awful lot done, but boredom was still a big factor for both.

Museum trips were now mostly pointless, but they did a few anyway, gathering some seed and accidentally locking more exciting parts of the exhibitions into their memory. A week and a half in, they were bored enough to decide to take a trip to do something they hadn't done in a while. They were going to look for buried treasure.

Usually, the dowsing rod was a bit annoying. It would find anything that was irregular compared to the surrounding soil, which was a nightmare if you actually had to find something specific. In the past, they had mostly turned up little pieces of the Gaian mystery metal, which usually wasn't worth the time investment. Now, it was great. There was always a small chance they would dig up something special, and if nothing else, it was an opportunity for Matt to level his digging skill and his normal human non-skill by just sprinting from place to place like a maniac and digging furiously whenever the dowsing rod signaled them to.

Over the course of the two days they set aside for it, they unearthed dozens of little pieces of Gaian metal, a few shaped like mechanical parts but most just fragments of something that had long since been blown apart. Given the durability of the metal, they speculated on what could have actually applied enough force to do that.

It wasn't until nearly the end of their journey that they hit pay dirt.

"How big do you think it is, Matt?"

"No way to tell. It's bigger than the shards we've been pulling, but probably smaller than the shovel, I guess?"

"You guess?! Matt, I can't hold the dowsing rod. I just can't. I'm going to need you to calibrate better."

"It's as big as it is. That's all I can tell you. Besides, if you wait just a second, I'll have it out."

Between all the digging at home and time in the garden, Matt's digging skill had picked up a few levels. It didn't get any new magical capabilities, but both the percentage rate of the "critical hit" digging effect and his overall speed had gone up substantially. Lucy claimed that when Matt dug it was like watching a boring gardening video sped up, and without a clear third-party view of himself, Matt had no way of disproving that.

In a few more seconds, Matt's shovel clinked on something solid, and Matt pulled out his magic multitool's spade mode to do the detail work. In moments, he had uncovered the top of the object, revealing a small three-inch dome of the mystery metal.

"Oh, please, please be what I think you are," Matt begged the lump of metal before shoving the spade deep in the dirt beside it to pry it loose.

"Wait, what do you think it is?"

"When I was back on Earth, I ordered this thing online." Matt was now hovering his hand over the spade, afraid to find out that he was wrong about what the object might be. "A giant ball bearing. A giant STEEL ball bearing."

"And?"

"And what? It's a three-inch piece of perfectly round, mirrored steel, Lucy."

Lucy looked confused. "So?"

"So? It's awesome. It weighs way more than an object that size should. You could roll it around. It was awesome."

"Is this . . . is this just like, a guy thing? Because this is going entirely over my head."

"It's possible. Anyway, the only problem with it was that when it came from the factory, it was perfect, but then it would get scratched and tarnished, all that. But this is the weird Gaian metal stuff. It just doesn't get scratched or tarnished. It would be perfect *forever*."

"So you could have been looking for a sword, or . . . like, a tool or something. If you were excited about that, I'd get it. But this? This is what you want? A useless round metal object?"

"You aren't going to discourage me. Round metal objects are rad. You can't convince me otherwise." Gathering his bravery, Matt popped his hand down on the spade, dislodging the object. It was about three to four inches wide and very dusty with soil. But most importantly to Matt, it *rolled*.

"Oh, hell yes."

Lucy rolled her eyes. "Great. Let's get home. You can enshrine your weird ball in the shack."

"Not a chance." Matt was already furiously washing the ball with water and a rag. "This is going in my pack. I'm keeping it with me *always*."

"Matt, I have a whole library of Earth references and nothing for what these past two weeks have been. It wasn't a staycation because we worked. It wasn't a vacation because we didn't really go anywhere. There's just no word for sitting around your house preparing to get murdered by a wizard between doing random treasure hunts."

After a quick trip home to pick some vegetables and top off a well-rinsed bag with disgusting ape honey, Matt and Lucy had headed out for the nearest appropriate dungeon, something not quite on the level of the ant dungeon, but close. They hadn't decided whether or not to continue on with the mana-generator-purchasing quest yet, but after actually getting stronger from the ant dungeon, their way forward seemed clear.

"Oh, sure there is," Matt said, "you just aren't being creative enough."

"Screw you, I'm not. You do better."

"These last two weeks," Matt said, flourishing his arm, "have been a filler episode. There are still baddies, you don't really get much stronger, but it's a chance to unwind after all the intense stuff, and just enjoy who you are."

"That doesn't . . ." Lucy stopped. "Dammit, that's what it is, isn't it."

"Yup. After all, what is Gaia but one giant, oceanless beach?"

"I hate you."

## CHAPTER TWENTY-SEVEN

# Get Off the Ground

"Oh, good, a forest dungeon," Matt said.

"Why good?" Lucy asked. "Some of the hardest stuff we've fought has been in forests."

Matt pointed up at the treetops, then down at the ground around them. "Shade. You don't have to deal with this for obvious reasons, but this Survivor's Garb is a full-body suit, and I'm carrying a full pack. It's surv-prisingly breathable now . . ."

"Never say that again."

"But yeah, shade is nice. Even just psychologically. The sun on Gaia doesn't really burn me for whatever reason, but before we got our tree, I was just about going crazy always being exposed to it."

Lucy looked around the forest as Matt stood up from his post-teleport reclined position. "Do you think we should ask Barry what's going on here? If the dungeon's back on, he should be too."

"I don't think we should bother Barry any more than is absolutely necessary." Matt shook his head.

"Barry, I'm sorry, but even if you want to help more, it's not worth giving the system instance more chances to screw us over."

As usual, it wasn't immediately apparent what horrors this dungeon had in store for them, so Matt and Lucy started walking, looking for any clues they could uncover that might give them a heads-up before an actual encounter. They didn't find any, which was surprising. The dungeon simulations were pretty complete. They'd have droppings, footprints, and sometimes fur or shed exoskeleton sticking to bushes, just like a real forest would pick up.

Here, there was none of that. It was just tree after endless tree in a mostly-quiet forest. Matt and Lucy usually didn't mind waiting, so after a few hours they were still pretty fresh and up for walking. But then something changed. Without seeing anything different or him picking up on any new cues, Matt's Survivor's Reflexes started to be more interested in rocks. Here and there, they'd find big granite boulders sticking up out of the ground, and Survivor's Reflexes was calling his attention to each and every one of them.

"Lucy, wait," Matt called, "I have to check out this boulder."

"Is this the same thing as with the mystery metal ball? Are we getting obsessed with geology now?

"No, it's just . . ."

"Mineral collections are the gateway drug to learning a new programming language, Matt. I'm just looking out for you."

"Shush. Survivor's Reflexes is telling me that these are important every time we pass one. I don't want to ignore that." Matt picked up a different, unrelated, and much smaller rock and chucked it at the most recent cluster of boulders, praying that it wouldn't end up being a giant-stone-golem situation.

Nothing happened. Encouraged by the inactivity, Matt walked closer and prodded the rock, hard, with his spear. After that failed to get a reaction, he moved even closer, eventually walking and jumping on the rock. All the time, the boulder failed to rear up, unfold, or otherwise reveal itself to be a horrifying monster.

After a few minutes of examining the rock, Matt completely failed to discover anything special about it. "I don't get it. Survivor's Reflexes swears this is important. In fact, it won't stop swearing it's important. But it's a rock. A normal, boring rock."

"Do you think it's just your skill acting up? Do you need more honey?"

"I hope not. You have no idea how bad . . ."

It was that moment when the ground behind Matt's feet rumbled slightly, a whooshing sound filled the air and something rushed past Matt's legs, taking a chunk of his calf with it.

"Dammit!" Matt screamed, spinning around. There was nothing to see besides a disturbed furrow of earth. Suddenly, Survivor's Reflexes kicked in to remind him in even stronger terms that big rocks were a very good idea right now.

"Worms! Killer worms!" Matt yelled, scrambling up to the relative safety of the boulder.

"Are you really blaming this on killer worms?"

"I'm saying it's something like worms. I don't know. I just got bit. But so far, Gaian wildlife from the dungeons haven't really been normal. There are so goddam many ambush predators. So either there's a big invisible monster that digs a furrow as it slows down to attack, or . . ."

"The whole ambush predator thing applies to subterranean animals, too?"

"Yeah." Something about this situation was familiar to Matt, oddly so. He suddenly broke into a wide grin as he realized what. "Oh, yeah!"

"Matt, why are you happy about this? We didn't see these things for hours, and it wasn't for a lack of looking. You are pretty good at digging, but you have to know where to dig, and that thing was *fast.* Why are you smiling?"

"Because," Matt said, starting to laugh, "there's a *movie about this.*"

*They're Under the Ground*

Gaian loam-grubs are terrifying animals for the same reason sharks are, in that you can't see them before they attack, and they live in an environment that they move through much, much faster than you can. They are fast, mean, absurdly sharp and use an entire planet as a suit of camouflaging armor.

Given enough time, a loam-grub is said to be capable of taking down an entire herd of Aantoranths by itself. Watch yourself, and watch the ground.

Objective: Eliminate Loam-grubs 0/20

Matt's second-favorite '90s movie, second only to a movie about teenage hackers taking down an uncool corporate hacker with stupid viruses, was a movie about giant subterranean killer worms. There was a whole series about it, with dozens of different methods for dealing with problems just like this.

Granted, the problems weren't *exactly* like this. The worms from the movie didn't slash, and instead they grabbed and went back underground. They were also far too large to leave as small of a disturbance in the ground as Matt's unseen attacker had. But other stuff almost had to be similar. The worms in the movie only had an indistinct vision of what was going on above the surface, driven by vibrations. He didn't know if the dungeon's worms saw through vibrations, but he was willing to bet several minutes of regen on the idea they had similarly fuzzy vision through whatever observation means they *did* use.

So Matt found himself stomping in the same place, trying his hardest to signal nonchalance while still moving around enough to be visible to the worms.

"This is stupid. It isn't going to work."

"Yes, it is. And it's going to be awesome. It's going to be the best thing that ever happened to me."

"Matt . . . you didn't have a lot of girlfriends back on Earth, did you? I'm getting that sense real strong right now."

Before Matt could lie in his own defense, he heard another rumbling at his feet, another whoosh, and felt another stabbing pain in his leg. The only difference this time was that Matt had dug a long trench in the ground, lined on both sides with sharp trap spikes. Matt heard a confused wail followed by a *splat*, and turned around to see a short, stubby grub of sorts impaled on the spike and apparently dead.

Matt stabbed it again anyway, just to be careful.

"Matt, does that thing have a side-mounted mouth?"

It did, or at least what looked like one. It was a messy, slimy hole standing slightly proud at the thing's side, lined with irregular, jagged teeth.

"That or that's the front, and it digs sideways. Either way, I was right. This totally worked. These things are moving too fast to stop, and they don't know that trench is there until it's too late. And you know, the best part?"

"What's that?"

Matt nudged the rapidly dissolving worm with his toe. "No cleanup."

The trap worked much better than Matt had hoped. He'd set himself up as bait, and the worms would fly across and impale themselves. Even when they missed the spikes, the shift in elevation seemed to disorient them enough that Matt had time to turn around and pin them to the ground with his spear.

Eventually, they got wise somehow. But the movie was full of ideas for that. Was dragging a knife across the ground with a rope to get these things to bite fair? Nope! But it was a great way to take out several more of the worms. Matt was absurdly pleased to find that whatever else the grubs were, they were slow learners and solitary hunters at heart. By the time they got wise to Matt's knife trick, there were only three left for his quest.

Two of them were taken out in a boring, non-movie way. He simply planted his shovel in the ground and waited until Survivor's Reflexes gave him a bit of warning before leaning forward and popping the grub out of the ground. It took several tries before he got lucky and hit the very tricky timing, but once the worms were above ground, they were slow to recover.

Finally, there was only one grub left, and it wasn't showing itself.

"Do you think one of them is smarter than the others?"

"That would be consistent with the movie, at least."

Lucy sighed. "I get it, you love some dumb movie, and actors named after breakfast meats. But here, now, in the real world, could you please focus on how we are going to find one of these things if it's smart enough to hide from us?"

Matt didn't have an answer for that. It was a hard problem, and outside of spending weeks digging trenches all through the forest, he had no idea how he'd find the worm. Not that it wouldn't do wonders for his digging skill, but the last thing he wanted was to come home to a torched farm, broken Ape-iaries, and no honey at all. The fact that the hunting had been going so well and so quickly up to this point made the prospect of a long delay hit that much harder.

He was saved from total heartbreak by a sudden rumbling sound, not at his feet but far in the distance. The thick tree cover should have blocked his view of the approach for most animals, but his vantage point from a boulder let him pretty clearly see that something was lifting trees a few feet in the air before dumping them unceremoniously to the side. The sound was getting louder to the point of hurting his ears as it made a beeline straight towards him.

Matt had been both afraid that the worm would rip the boulder out from under him and hopeful it would bash into the boulder and kill itself. Instead, it stopped gently just short of the rock and reared out of the ground to reveal a school bus-sized body, with spikes the size of a middle-schooler that defended every angle of its grubby skin, and a front-mounted mouth in addition to the normal side-mounted monstrosity the smaller grubs had.

Lucy's eyes were wide. "Oh, hell."

"Lucy," Matt said, too shocked to correctly remember what nostalgia he had been chasing up until now, "I think we're going to need a bigger boat."

> *Ape-iary Assault*
>
> The demon lord Matt has assembled hive after hive of monstrous, unnatural insect-mammal hybrids that, if not dealt with, will . . .

"Oh, please, please be quiet. I have work to do, and I'm certain I've already heard all you have to offer."

While Matt was fighting grubs, Leel was, for the umpteenth time, attempting to paint a gathering circle that would work worth a damn on this godforsaken planet. Each circle he'd draw would bring in some small amount of mana, enough to create a small amount of water, some food, and to cast a spell reclaiming the paint when each excellent, refined circle design inevitably failed to sustain itself, fizzling out in the unnatural Gaian mana environment.

And the system would *simply not* stop bothering him, offering him dangerous quests he couldn't take on without some form of defending himself to earn mundane, lackluster rewards he didn't want or need. It seemed this particular system instance was not immune from energy deficits, doing its best to sell every quest despite only attaching bottom-tier rewards.

Leel would continue rejecting them, waiting for something better. He had to. With only low-single-digit amounts of mana to show for it, he had gone through the mana circle designs he knew and exhausted all of them.

It wasn't simply a matter of sufficient rewards now. If something didn't change, both substantially and soon, he'd starve.

CHAPTER TWENTY-EIGHT

# Who Am I?

Even for those with rotten luck, they're never unlucky in every respect. Something has to give at some point.

Was Matt facing a giant worm? Yes. Did it seem basically invulnerable to any attack that he might make on it that wasn't flat-out suicidal? Sure. Could it win by just falling on him? Absolutely it could.

But was the worm faster than Matt? No. He had to work hard to keep ahead of it, and he wasn't so much faster that he could turn around and take pot shots or outmaneuver it. All he could do was stay out of its attack range and even build up a small lead without burning his stamina down too fast. That was good luck, because the worm was big enough that standing on a boulder wasn't anything near a real defense against it.

"Damn." Lucy generally kept quiet during fights, but this particular battle was devolving into a running match. "I don't think this thing is gonna give up."

"Nope, but it can't catch us, either." Matt suddenly swerved at a forty-five-degree angle, changing their course substantially.

"Do you think it's trying to lead us somewhere? A trap? It looks like it's pushing us in a direction," Lucy said.

"Nope. I have a plan for that," said Matt.

"Which is?" asked Lucy.

"I change course every time you curse," said Matt.

It couldn't last forever, though. From time to time, despite Matt's zigzags, they'd get run into an obstacle, whether that was a short cliff, a ravine, or whatever. Matt was hopeful that the worm would make a mistake and launch itself into the ravine or crash into a rock wall. Unfortunately, his luck had worn thin and the worm seemed to have baseline knowledge of the terrain of the forest too comprehensive for that kind of trick.

Eventually, it was clear to Matt, at least, that they were at an impasse. As he ran, he tried to build some sort of long-shot weapons, but he was hard-pressed to think of a situation where they would be effective. Just the weight of the worm was enough to kill Matt.

"I know I ask this a lot, but how was even a full party supposed to kill this thing?" Matt asked.

"Ranged attacks and magic, probably," Lucy listed off. "And you'd be surprised what a level 10 tank can stop. They might not be able to hold this thing off forever, but they could take a couple of shots while it was exposed. Maybe keep it from sinking back into the soil when it breaches, if their strength was high enough."

Matt supposed he could see that. If someone had endurance to take the damage from a single hit and strength to keep part of the thing elevated, someone else like Leel could cook the worm. Matt didn't have anything like that, but the image did give him some inspiration, provided he could get away.

"We have to go back to the ravine. Probably a few times."

"Why?"

"We have to build a bridge."

Running back to the ravine, Matt ran alongside the gap until he saw what he was looking for: a big, old tree that had made the mistake of growing close enough to the edge such that it could be made into a bridge. Activating Spring-Fighter to get several seconds worth of lead, Matt bashed his shovel into the base of the tree like an axe with all the momentum he could get, and then ran away. It took the better part of an hour of circling, but between his enhanced strength and unbreakable shovel, he finally had a good portion of the tree trunk carved away.

As he came around on the tree the final time, he ran as fast as he could, leapt, and slammed into the tree as hard as he could. These days, as hard as he could was pretty hard. With all his stats running at full, he made for a pretty good human battering ram and felt the wood of the tree crack and groan under the impact of his body. Whatever satisfaction he felt from that was quickly erased as the tree sprung back in the opposite direction. Instead of snapping, the tree swayed before going down in Matt's direction.

Matt desperately rolled out of the way, but wasn't fast enough to keep the tree from pinning his legs to the ground. Judging by the pain, it broke both of them.

"Matt! Incoming!" Lucy screamed.

The worm was coming in hot and heavy. Matt didn't have the strength or the leverage to shift the tree outright, and did the only thing he could do, grabbing his shovel and digging ineffectively at an awkward angle to get enough dirt moved that he could squeeze his legs out. It shouldn't have worked at all, but the digging skill had always been wonky in the sense that it just generally made him better at digging. He could dig faster and with better form, but he also could penetrate the dirt better than he should be able to with a given amount of force.

By the time the worm had arrived and came out of the ground, he had cut a shallow trench on the side of each leg. Using every ounce of his strength, he spread his legs out to the sides. As each leg moved into the trench, the ground and bark of the tree ripped deep gashes in his skin, but he was free.

Matt had other problems besides being trapped, though. Both of his legs were shattered, and he had several tons of worm hovering over him waiting to crash down and end things. He didn't like it, but he really only had one option. Pushing off with both hands and flaring Spring-Fighter, he pushed directly away from the tree, skidding back on his butt just in time to avoid the worm's crushing attack, then fall into the ravine.

"Matt. Wake up. Fast."

Matt didn't remember much of the fall, just a jumble of ping-ponging off ravine walls, snapping bones, and stinging pain. And then he was knocked out. A mercy. The fall would have certainly killed a normal person, but as he woke up, he could feel Rub Some Dirt In It in full effect, doing its best to knit his bones back together. He put some weight on his arm, only to have it bend at an alarmingly strange angle when he tried to use it to stand up.

"Not quite there yet, huh? That was stupid, Matt. Really stupid."

"Yeah, I know. But what was I going to do?"

"No idea. But probably not *that.* A whole tree falling on you followed by a dry-land cliff dive is probably a new world record for things going wrong for us."

"Us?"

"I got dragged along for that wild ride. Do you know how weird that is for me? It's weird. It's like being the ball part of one of those elastic-band yo-yos."

"Well, sorry. Any sign of the worm?"

"Not yet." Lucy stamped her feet. "It's all rock down here. I'm not sure it could get down here, even if it wanted to. At least not without using the same route you chose."

That was good. Matt healed pretty fast outside of combat, but it was still going to take time to get him back into fighting shape. For now, there was nothing he could do but hold still and let his healing skill do its work. Technically, there was one thing that he could do. Talk.

"Hey, Lucy? Remember when we were talking to Leel?"

"Yeah, that asshole. What about it?"

"You promised you'd tell me about your past, where you came from. I was sort of hoping you'd bring it up during our vacation, but you didn't. I just . . . like, listen. You don't want to talk about it, and I'm probably an asshole for asking, but . . ."

"No . . . Matt, I get it. You have a right to know. And you're right, I *have* been avoiding it. For a long time, it didn't matter. And now everything is so weird it's hard to know *what* matters. But . . . I just wanted to seem normal, you know? I don't want to be a *thing* to you, like how Leel thinks of his necklace."

"I understand. I'm sorry."

Lucy sighed. "It's fine. And honestly, there's not a lot to tell."

"I'm interested, even if it's boring. There's not a ton to do down here anyway."

"It's not a matter of boring. There's literally not a lot to tell. Do you remember when I told you that a guardian is supposed to be a voluntary job title?"

"Yeah, and then the system took that away. You mentioned it, that I wasn't supposed to be able to even find you."

"Well, yeah. But it's not just that. It's not just a job that we're able to quit, it's a job we don't have to take in the first place. We get a choice. When I got my choice, it was in a weird sort of office environment, with some different system instance beaming information about the job directly into my head, showing me images of other guardians doing their jobs. It looked fun, so I accepted."

"What about before that?"

"That's the thing. There was no 'before that.' It was just that. I was me, I was in a room, I had a choice, and I didn't know enough to understand how weird that was. And then I was alone on a planet. You were the second conversation I can even remember having."

"So . . ." Matt was shocked. He had always assumed when it came time to learn about Lucy, he'd also learn about some sort of guardian race, living on some kind of guardian planet somewhere. This was different. "So do you think the system . . . built you?"

"I used to. And that's part of why I didn't tell you about any of this. We had a good thing going, and I didn't want to ruin that by potentially being some kind of system-controlled sleeper agent."

"You aren't. I don't know a lot, but I know that. It would have activated you by now, for one. But, Lucy, you also just *aren't.* I know you. You aren't going to betray me."

Lucy sniffed a little and looked away. "Thanks, Matt. I was hoping you'd say something like that. It means a lot." She took a couple seconds to compose herself, rubbed her face with both hands, before she turned back. "Anyway, I thought about it, and I don't think the system even *could* build something like me."

"Why's that?"

"Think about it. You've given the system a lot of trouble, right? That's because you are a free person, with free will. You can sort of do whatever you want, within the confines of what you can actually do. From the system's perspective, that's probably a pain in the ass. We know it can *build* bodies because it built you one. So if it *could* build people like me, why wouldn't it just . . . do that? You know, just program their heroes. It would be easier. We know the system would like that."

"Fair. So . . . where did you come from, then?"

Lucy's hands flopped down by her side, and she looked up at Matt with a distressed look on her face. "Matt, I don't know. I obviously have a full personality, right? It takes a life of experiences to create that. I want some things, I don't want other things, I can make choices. It doesn't seem like all that could just pop out of the air, right?"

Lucy plopped down on the ground in despair. Matt ignored what pain he felt from his still-knitting bones, propped himself up, and scooted nearer to her. He couldn't touch her, as much as he wanted to do *something* to comfort her. But at least he could be near her, and let her know he was there for her. Lucy took a few moments, forced herself to stop crying, then looked up at Matt again.

"I'm just, you know, I'm obviously a person, right? I'm somebody." Despite her best efforts, she started crying again, unable to keep the sobs out of her voice. "But *who* am I?"

## CHAPTER TWENTY-NINE

# *Pac-Man* Situation

Matt didn't have a great answer for Lucy. He agreed that the system probably hadn't built her, if for nothing more than the sheer amount of trouble she had caused it. But as to where she came from, or who she was outside of Gaia, he had no real evidence for any guesses. The ideas he did have were all pretty dark in ways he didn't want to think about, and that he guessed Lucy didn't want to think about either. He didn't bring them up.

But that didn't mean he didn't *know* anything. It wasn't origin story stuff, but he knew plenty about Lucy.

"Listen, Lucy." Matt gave her some time to calm down, enough that she could wipe off her face and turn to see him looking only slightly puffy. "You know I don't know where you are from either. But I know where you are, and it's here, with me. And I think you know this, but this is permanent. We are friends. I don't care what happens, or where we go. You have a place with me. I'm *glad* you are here."

"Matt . . ." Lucy was trying to cut in. Matt wouldn't have it.

"No, listen. I also know who you are right now, and that's my partner. Your job is keeping me alive, as hard as that is. It's also putting the hurt on the system for putting us in this shitty situation in the first place. Your job is the same as mine, and I can't do it without you."

Lucy hung her head, lost in thought about what Matt had said. Matt blinked. He was doing his best, but he couldn't deny the reality of her problem. He might be trapped here, but he had a whole life before this one. He couldn't imagine what it was like to have an identity but not any of the associated memories. Life on Gaia was hard enough, but not having any happiness to reflect on? That was tough.

"Lucy, I'm not going to pretend all that's enough. I know it's not. But if there's a way to figure out more about this, I promise that's going to be top priority for me."

"Really?"

"Really. Above the museum, above the mana generator. As soon as we get a lead, that's what we are doing. I promise. And I even know the first step."

Lucy perked up immediately. "What's that?"

"Find that wizard and beat the shit out of him. He's maybe an asshole, but he seems like he knows things."

Far away in the forest, the worm was pissed to the full extent that a worm could be pissed. It had been chasing food all day, and the food hadn't become tired or fallen down so it could catch it. It was dimly aware that this was unusual, but it didn't have any other options but to chase, unless some other food showed itself. Chasing food was the thing it did. The only thing it did, really.

Then the food fell into the hole. It *hated* the hole. It had fallen into the hole once, long ago. That had hurt, and if it wasn't so small back then it probably would have splattered. It usually didn't go anywhere near the hole, but now the food was down there. It could smell the food clearly. It could smell every place the food had touched the side of the hole on the way down. It circled for a while, hoping the food would climb out of the hole itself. It wasn't a sure thing, but it didn't seem impossible. But the food just sat down there, making food smells and not moving at all.

All the time, the worm was getting hungrier. When there wasn't food, it hardly moved at all. It just slept. The only reason it knew this food was here was that the food had caught all the little, smaller worms it normally couldn't catch and left them lying around. It had already eaten *those*, but then it moved all day. It couldn't go back to sleep now without eating. It'd be uncomfortable.

The only good thing was that it knew how to get to the food. The hole didn't go on forever. Eventually, it became earth. That was how it got out when it had fallen in before. If it went to the end of the hole, it could wiggle into the hole. Which would hurt its spikes, but it could always grow more of those.

Grumbling, it moved towards the place where the hole turned into the ground. This was too much work. But there wasn't any choice. There was food down there. It ate food. It was how things worked.

"So your bones are back now? All in the right places, I trust?"

Matt stretched himself out and jumped in place a bit. Everything seemed right, as far as he could tell.

"Yup. I gotta say, this healing skill is not that bad. This would have taken days if it were just up to my vitality. At least a few days."

"Well, don't get comfortable. I have plans."

"Yeah?"

"Yup. I was thinking about it while you were asleep. We need to kill this worm, right? And it likes the ground? We have to get it out of the ground."

"Easier said than done." Some dirt dislodged off the side of the ravine, sprinkling on Matt's face. He wiped it off. "That thing's pretty big."

"That's why we have to be smart, Matt. When we get out of here, we're going to build a ramp."

Some more dirt fell down, getting in Matt's hair and on his face. He accidentally inhaled some and sneezed.

"Matt, could you pay attention?"

"I'm trying to, it's just this dust. It's everywhere all of a sudden."

*Actually, why is it falling down? Any dust I dislodged earlier should have just fallen by now*, Matt thought. The area he had fallen into was a narrow part of the ravine, partially because it was bent at that point. Matt didn't have a great view on the ravine to his left or right.

"So, what I'm thinking is, we sink tree trunks. Big ones. We make a ramp, and you run up, and the thing grounds itself, and then . . ."

"Hold on a second. I'm loving this, but I need to check on something." Matt walked to one side of the curve, where he could see reasonably far down the canyon. It was clear, at least as far as he could see. Walking to the other end of the curve to confirm he was fine, he reflected that this canyon probably didn't get a lot of action under normal conditions. It probably wasn't that weird for at least some dirt to fall down.

As he rounded the other end, he saw the worm.

*Okay, yeah, I probably could have predicted this.*

The entire worm was visible, now, and it was huge. Matt wasn't sure how it managed to find its way into the ravine, but it was there at the bottom. It slithered like a snake, its spikes rubbing against the rocky ravine sides with a scraping noise he could just barely hear. It wasn't that close, but seeing it fill the ravine almost completely struck fear in Matt's heart.

"Lucy, plan's off."

"Wait, Why?"

"We have a *Pac-Man* situation. We need to go."

Lucy peeked around the corner.

"Oh, shit. Yeah, let's get moving."

Both Lucy and Matt agreed there was no way that the worm had jumped down. It was too big and mushy. Maybe it could have survived the fall, but there was no way it would have been in as good of condition as it looked like it was. At the same time, they couldn't imagine that it had climbed down from the same kind of heights Matt had fallen from. It wasn't equipped for it.

Which meant that the ravine probably didn't go on forever. Matt could try to climb out of it, but Survivor's Reflexes was warning him against it. He supposed that he might fall and break a bone again, and then have nowhere to go except inside the worm. The prospect of being lunch for the worm was enough to motivate Matt and Lucy to run and try to see where the ravine rose on the non-worm side of things.

Despite the worm being a good distance away and moving quite a bit slower than it did in the dirt, they kept up a pretty good pace. If the ravine finished as a dead end, they didn't want to get caught without enough time to pursue other options. This turned out to be a wise choice when they rounded a corner and faced a sheer rock wall instead of a gentle ramp upwards.

"Looks like I'm climbing."

"Yup. Hurry it up."

Matt wasn't experienced at climbing, but he did have enhanced strength and reflexes, so he figured he could make it work. It turned out to be easier than he thought, as even small handholds turned out to be grippable with his stat-enhanced hands. In no time at all, he was higher on the wall than the worm could probably reach, even reared up. At the rate he was going, he'd be at the top in about a minute.

Then, the wall caved in. A chunk of the cracked rock came out of the wall under his weight, causing a chain reaction that dislodged the whole section. Matt crashed down to the floor of the canyon again, this time under dozens of chunks of rock. Before he could even take stock of his injuries, he knew he was in bad shape. The worm was louder now, and still coming.

"Matt, we have to get out of here NOW."

"I know. But I'm not climbing anywhere. Look." Matt's leg was bent at an odd angle, clearly snapped and unusable.

"Shit, shit, shit."

"That's all I have, I'm sorry."

And then the worm was there. The only thing that seemed to keep it from immediately getting to Matt was that the chasm itself narrowed at the end, leaving barely enough room for it to move forward. But the worm was nothing if not malleable, slowly squeezing itself into the space. With great pain, Matt sat up and backed up as far as he could get. It was no good. It was still coming forward.

Finally, it was so close that Matt could smell its breath. It smelled like dirt and rotten meat, which made sense. There was only one thing Matt could do at this point.

"Pocket Sand!"

Pocket Sand let Matt throw any powder he wanted. Usually, he was content to limit himself to normal dirt, since the idea was to get a momentary distraction and maybe blind something. But now he was about to get eaten, and he was pissed about it. This dumb worm was going to win. Matt didn't think the rotten cube powder would kill it, but he was damned if he was going to let the thing be happier about any of this than he had to.

The black dust spread through the air, hitting the thing all over its gnarly front-mouth. As expected, it didn't kill it. It didn't even seem to distract the worm. But it did seem to royally piss it off. As the dust hit its mouth, it paused for a moment before making a loud, grumbling roar, dislodging dirt and stone as it thrashed its body side to side as much as the limited space would allow.

Matt slowly pulled out his shovel, ready to make a last stand.

But the worm wasn't done yet. Roaring again, it reared up into the air suddenly, jerking its entire bulk into the air so hard it just barely avoided lifting its tail off the ground and going airborne.

And then it got stuck.

CHAPTER THIRTY

# Mesquite

"No way."

"We should go under it? It might fall."

"I . . ." Matt paused as the worm thrashed its tail around, trying desperately to dislodge itself. Thankfully, the actual body of the thing didn't budge at all where it was wedged. Worms didn't exactly have distinct body parts, but this one was being held up by what amounted to its chest, and at least so far, couldn't get enough leverage by rocking back and forth to change that. "I'm actually pretty reluctant to do anything that might shake it loose, honestly."

Over the next several minutes, the killer combo of Rub Some Dirt In It and Matt's high vitality partially healed his leg to the point where he could at least hobble around on it. The worm had still failed to fall. Matt could technically reach it with his spear, but doing so would mean standing almost directly under the thing. Even if it didn't fall on him, he wasn't sure he wanted to deal with it in close quarters that soon.

"Well, take the risk on running under it, at least. Being trapped up against this wall is bad news," Lucy said.

She had a point. Matt ran out from underneath the worm and found himself safe, uncrushed. She also had a point when she had him stake his spear into the ground, point up, so that if the worm did fall, it might just skewer itself deep enough to matter. But after that, Matt had no ranged weapon and also had no desire at all to climb up and tangle with the big spiked worm in the air.

In theory, the worm might die when it fell onto Matt's spear. In practice, Matt didn't want to leave that up to chance any more than was absolutely necessary.

"So what's the plan here, Matt?" Lucy asked. "We can't just leave it like that."

"Yeah, it's not like it will stay up there forever. If nothing else, it might lose weight."

"I meant that eventually we have to go home, and I don't want to find everything in a smoldering ruin."

"Yeah." Matt was also worried about Leel, but being out in the world and on dungeon runs was a qualified risk they had to take. With any luck, Leel would end up as resource-compromised as they were and would be as worried about them as they were about him. Between that and the prep work they had done around the property, they were hoping it would be enough that he wouldn't make too much of a mess of things.

Something about Lucy's words, particularly the smoldering part, triggered something in Matt. It wouldn't be the nicest thing he had ever done, but he did have an idea for how to handle this problem.

"I have an idea."

"Is it good?"

"It's an idea that might work. Don't knock it."

As they ran through the canyon, it hadn't all been exactly flat, easy ground. The dungeon system simulated the geography pretty thoroughly, including erosion. That meant that rocks and dirt were scattered all over the bottom of the ravine, creating uneven, mostly plantless ground that received too little sun and water to be particularly productive.

The exceptions to the plantless qualifier were trees. Not every tree was like the tree Matt had tried to body-slam into being a bridge in terms of ravine-adjacency, but a lot were. Over the course of however many centuries, plenty of trees and branches had accumulated on the ravine floor.

Finding them was easy. The ravine wasn't that wide, so you could hardly miss them. Moving them was another thing entirely. The branches weren't usually in convenient sizes and shapes, but Matt could often break them apart with a good whack from the shovel. However, the full trees were a different story. They were absurdly tough, even judged by the standards of Matt's improved class.

Even chunks a few feet long were plenty heavy, and Matt's cutting tools were severely limited. He eventually settled on a method of using a combination of the multitool as a saw to make cuts, shoving the shovel into those cuts, and then banging on it with a big rock until the wood cracked apart. Luckily, all of the wood was pretty dry, or else it would have been close to impossible with the tools Matt had access to.

"Just chuck it in there!"

"I can't. I have to keep this stuff the hell away from its tail. It's only up there still because it doesn't have any leverage."

"Point taken. But you don't have to work so slow."

Lucy had somewhat of a point. Matt was being absurdly cautious about how he stacked the wood, mostly because he had no idea how he'd handle the situation if something went wrong and the worm got down. Besides that, he knew just enough from having watched survival shows to know that big hunks of wood don't generally catch on fire all that easily. So first, he gathered a good pile of leaves and twigs and piled them up beneath the worm, trying to get a pretty good carpet of easy-burning material. Then came branches, then longer, thinner sections of trunk. Finally, he carefully tossed as many big, thick trunk segments as he could on the pile without actually touching the worm.

Eventually, he had an irregular pagoda of chunks of durable Gaian mountain wood of varied moisture content stacked on top of kindling so dry it crumbled when he touched it. It was as ready as it was going to be.

"You done?" Lucy glanced over as Matt unstrapped his instant-light torch from his pack and lit it, walking to the smaller trail of leaves he had set up as a sort of fuse.

"Yeah. I'm just praying this works."

Matt dropped the torch, and it became immediately apparent that he hadn't actually needed to pray. The leaves caught on fire like they were soaked in kerosene, and within a few moments, the entire fuse was aflame and spreading fire to the greater pile of combustibles. It didn't take long before the entire stack of sticks was aflame, and some of the larger chunks were starting to join in. The only thing that was keeping the flame itself from hitting the worm was that as the stack burned, it collapsed in on itself, lowering the overall height of the fire, so it didn't directly consume the worm.

At least, that's what Matt and Lucy assumed. They heard rather than saw the collapse of the wood stack because they were running away at full speed by then. It turned out whatever this wood was, it was not clean-burning. Both Matt and Lucy had assumed that whatever smoke was created would waft out the top of the ravine like a chimney, and some of the smoke did follow that path. But most of the smoke decided to distribute itself through the ravine, and it was seconds before Matt was coughing and hacking in acrid smoke. Rather than stay there and choke out, he ran until the smoke stopped following, much farther than he could see the worm from down the corridor.

"So how long do we stay here?" Lucy asked.

"I don't know. I can still smell the smoke, and you can still see it rising. It's no use going back there while the fire is still burning, and I'm guessing we'll hear it if the worm falls down," said Matt.

"So what, we just stay here until the fire burns out?"

"I guess. Honestly, I feel pretty bad about the whole thing, but it's us or him."

* * *

The worm was not pleased. The food had somehow managed to get lower than it was, for one. But sometimes food could dig, so this wasn't entirely new. What was new was that it couldn't get any lower because it was stuck. It couldn't move forward or backwards. This was not something it understood how to deal with, so it tried everything it could think of. Digging didn't work, since it wasn't in dirt. Thrashing was its usual next move, but for reasons it couldn't comprehend it wasn't able to thrash much, either. It was a puzzler.

Meanwhile, the food was doing odd things. Usually, the worm caught food it wanted, but when that failed, the usual behavior it expected from the triumphant food was to get the hell out of dodge. Usually, it'd still be able to smell the food and chase it down, but sometimes the food got away completely. This food, however, was doing things it found perplexing.

The food was dragging over non-food stuff that it had come across in the past. They sometimes made it harder to dig, but not by too much. The food was piling this non-food stuff below it, which was useless. It couldn't eat them, not that it supposed the food was trying to get it to. They might slow it down a bit, but it had crawled over many of them getting here. They weren't strong enough to stop it, like rocks. There was no reason to do this, but at least the food was still nearby for when it did get down.

Then the food did something even odder, something the worm didn't understand. It started making a sort of heat, something the worm could feel but didn't understand. The heat gradually somehow *spread* it to the non-food stuff. That's when the heat rocketed up in intensity and generated a new smell.

Soon, it couldn't smell the food at all anymore. The smell from the non-food stuff was so strong it was all the worm could sense, covering everything. The heat part of the smell was unexpected, but didn't bother the worm. It had tough skin. It didn't even hurt. Meanwhile, it assumed the food was long gone. It didn't even know food could pull this trick. *Well played, food*, it thought. *Well played.*

Meanwhile, the smell was only getting thicker and thicker, and the worm was only getting warmer and warmer. And sleepier, which was odd. Normally, it had trouble going to sleep if it hadn't had food. That was its whole thing, really. It'd eat food, then sleep, then eat food. It couldn't go from sleep straight back to sleep, as a general rule. It had tried.

But this sleep was wanting to happen not only without food, but even without it wanting to sleep. Not that it was against sleep, exactly. It liked to sleep, and finding a nice spot to do it wasn't always easy. And here it was, very warm, and without anything better to do.

It supposed it couldn't hurt to sleep just a little. It could find the food later.

"I can't believe how long that fire took to burn down," Lucy commented as they picked their way back into the ravine.

"Just be glad I have all these stat enhancements and the Survivor's Garb. I'm pretty sure a normal human would be cooked alive if they actually came here."

"So, do you think it's dead?"

Matt and Lucy were looking at the worm from a distance. It was a little blackened by smoke, and it wasn't moving. But approaching it through the coals seemed dangerous, and as fire-resistant as he might be, Matt had no desire to get knocked down or tripped into the still-red embers of the inferno they had built.

Finally, he decided to do it anyway. He carefully stepped across less-hot looking parts of the fire, smelling his boots singeing with every footfall, until he finally got to the worm's tail, which he could barely reach. It still wasn't moving. He finally reached up with his knife, plunging it a good four inches into the thing's tail. It didn't move.

"Hey, Lucy, looks like we really did get it!" Matt yelled, just as the worm took that opportunity to finally come loose from the wall, crashing into and sizzling on the coals below.

"Oh, shit! Run!" Lucy yelled.

Matt didn't need to be asked twice. He flared Spring-Fighter as hard as he could, getting instant distance from the worm at a cost of most of his stamina bar's contents. But looking over his shoulder, he noticed the worm still wasn't moving. As tough as the thing was, he didn't think it would really choose to stay still while it got cooked.

"False alarm. Looks like it really is dead."

Lucy calmly assessed the situation, then nodded. "Or at least pretty close. It is weird that you don't have a plinth yet."

"Well, no time like the present to make sure." Matt could see his spear sticking up out of the worm, and decided to take the risk of climbing on the thing for a moment, retrieving his spear, and then stabbing it several dozen times. As messed up as it was, Matt didn't want to leave anything to chance. He moved towards the slowly sizzling creature cautiously, then stopped.

"Shit, Lucy."

"What? What's going on?"

Matt nodded towards the smoke rising off the creature as it slow-roasted in the coals.

"That thing smells *delicious.*"

## CHAPTER THIRTY-ONE

# Palate of the Conqueror

It's still not dead? I don't get how that could be. I mean, look at it."

The worm was laying directly on a big bed of wood and coals, still partially aflame. It was clearly getting roasted, no less. But there wasn't any *ding* yet.

"Should I go stab it? I could. It's pretty still."

At that moment, dust fell down from above, along with a few clumps of dirt. Something was moving at the top of the ravine.

"Oh, shit, Matt. Another one?"

Matt's spear was still inside of the worm. He wasn't going to get it back any time soon. He grabbed his combat knife and got ready.

"Yeah. Dammit." His leg was almost completely healed now, but there was no way they were going to get as lucky with a second worm. This was going to be hard, if it was even survivable.

Then a shadow moved over Matt's head, and through the sun he could see the silhouette of a worm falling towards him. He flared Spring-Fighter as hard as he could, pushing away from the roasting worm. That was the only direction he had a good chance of actually getting away from the worm from.

Suddenly, he heard a soft but very real *splat* on the canyon floor. Turning around, he instantly began to laugh.

"What?" Lucy turned around, then immediately began to laugh herself.

It was one of the little ones.

*Ding!*

*Quest Complete*

You not only eliminated the quest targets, but managed to take out the optional, frankly nearly invincible, source of the worm infestation in this forest. Pro-tip, Matt. If a big, invincible, foreshadowed enemy appears, it's possible you aren't supposed to fight it at all. This was an evasion thing.

The good news is I can give you some extra stuff. Fun fact: you know how you never see bows in the loot? It turns out I can't give them to you at all anymore. It's probably a class-limited thing. I did find something else. I think you will like it.

Rewards: ???

"Good news, Lucy. Barry is back."

Matt stabbed the stabilization spike into the worm. That was the easy part.

"This you will eat, but not the bats?" Lucy looked at Matt suspiciously.

"I'm . . . like, listen." Matt was struggling to explain the concept of appetizing food to someone who didn't eat, and failing. "The bats weren't the same thing. Those were gross. They were dripping with acid. I *specifically don't want to eat bats.*"

"But big giant worm things are okay? Because you don't specifically not want to eat them?"

"Well, yeah." The worm was dissolving into dungeon-stuff pretty fast now. Matt withdrew the stabilization spike and began carefully carving off most of the worm's skin as well as anything on the inside to breach the conceptual barrier between *meat* and *guts.* He was already taking a big enough risk without dealing with whatever was going on inside this thing's digestive system. "Plus, this just smells good. It smells like food. I don't get to eat a lot of good food."

"Are you sure it's safe? There are reasons beyond just not getting stats from it that we haven't been eating dungeon food," Lucy asked.

Matt finally sawed off all the questionable bits from a pretty good chunk of the worm meat, plopping what was left down on his shield like a plate. Luckily, the multitool could turn into a pretty respectable fork and, he had no shortage of knives.

"No idea. But the impression the system gave me about eating dungeon food without an eating skill before we were on the outs was it was more of a long-term problem. Like eating mana-deficient food, where if you did it for a long time it would cause problems."

Matt sawed off a piece of the meat with his knife and held it up to his nose, smelling it. It seemed edible.

"This doesn't seem like it's going to cause me immediate problems. But if it ended up being deadly poison, the plinth is right there. If it's a long-term thing, it's just one meal, and I've got honey with me."

"So you . . ."

"I'm eating this worm steak, yeah."

Matt lifted the piece of worm up to his mouth and stuck it in. For the first time since the plants started sprouting on the farm, he was eating something because he wanted to, not just for survival. He was eating for pleasure. And the worm meat didn't disappoint. It was smoky and tender, somewhere between pork and chicken, and he loved every non-existent calorie of it.

"I don't even eat, and I still know how gross it is that you are enjoying that so much," Lucy commented from the side.

Matt just made a bigger show of eating in response. If the steak was killing him, it wasn't doing it in any obvious way. He ripped into the rest of it with gusto, finally devouring the entire thing, wiping his mouth with his sleeve, and putting away his fork and knife.

"See? No big disasters. Everything was just . . ."

And then the pain hit.

*Ding!*

| Interference with system skill detected. |
|---|

Leel was making no real effort at being sneaky. There was no place to hide in this horrid wasteland, anyway. If Matt and Lucy were at home, they'd see him from miles away. Hopefully, they'd come out to meet him. That would at least give him a chance to run.

The system had been trying to get him to come to his enemies' headquarters for days, offering shit reward after shit reward. He had refused, temporarily content to draw better and better gathering circles for his mana recovery. Each circle made a bigger and bigger difference, until finally, he had some semblance of a workable circle design. It would both gather mana and also use some of that same mana to repair itself as it fought with the shitty wasteland environment over time.

With that, Leel had managed to get himself well into the low double digits of mana. But it wasn't enough. Not that he wasn't exorbitantly proud of himself. He was. The work he had done was a masterpiece for someone of his level, even by the standards of his home. But to really empower the circle, he needed more than just raw, unparalleled genius. He needed better raw materials.

Then, the system finally offered raw materials as a reward after he had refused poor system offers for days on end.

*Ape-iary Assault*

The dreaded demon lord Matt has assembled hive after hive of monstrous, unnatural insect-mammal hybrids that, if not dealt with, will spread his vision of life across the entire Sarthian continent. Only you can stop him from reaching his goals.

Storm his headquarters, destroy the Ape-iaries with fire, and live on in legend as the savior of Gaia.

Reward: Enhanced Arcane Paint

Leel had originally rolled his eyes at the idea that there was anything in this dreadful place to be the legendary savior of. When he read more, the system finally managed to pique Leel's interest with an actual reward he could use. Why it hadn't done so earlier was anyone's guess, but with better paint, Leel could do more things that put him closer to destroying Matt and getting out of this godforsaken place.

That was only half of the trouble solved. The other half was that he still had to generate food and water for himself, something that dipped into his mana reserves and taxed whatever circle he had built. Worse, he was doing it in the least efficient way, a direct mana-to-calorie conversion from nothing. But Matt had food. He had seen it during their fight, and though he hadn't thought it particularly relevant then, it could make all the difference now.

As Leel walked forward, he noticed a difference from the red dirt that he was used to. He was passing sprouts of various kinds, and even some mature plants. He let them pass. Whatever the highest-quality food his foe possessed was probably closer to the center of his property, near his little shack and the most dense of his flowers.

*What kind of man grows flowers in a place like this? Oh, well. He'll be dead soon enough. I suppose I can forgive him some level of luxury.*

That didn't mean Leel had to be careful with the plants, though. As he reached the hedge of flowers, he crashed straight through, laughing. He was pretty confident that Matt and Lucy weren't home now, and he loved the idea of them seeing that they'd been robbed from far off. Then they'd race home, only to have Leel dance off into the sunset with his new arcane paint. The fact that this planet didn't have a sunset or sunrise didn't bother Leel as he daydreamed about his foes steaming in anger. He was still laughing as he stepped out of the hedge and heard the click.

A stone-bearing trap jumped out of a hidden, mostly horizontal trench in the ground. It slammed into what small amount of shield Leel could manage to materialize in time, shattering it and continuing on to impact with his leg. The shield had robbed enough of the stone's energy to keep it from doing worse than leaving a bruise, but it was enough to make Leel stumble to the side, where he triggered another trap.

This one splintered his shin. Sending him rocking into an Ape-iary before falling to the ground.

Leel screamed, writhing in pain on the ground. He had nowhere near enough mana to fix this wound, but had enough to at least stop the pain and set it on a quick path to healing. But that required him to burn the majority of his remaining mana. It wasn't even a choice. Leel did not like pain. With a glow from his hand and a quick sweep across his leg, he was partially mended. He couldn't move very fast, but he hardly needed to unless Matt and Lucy came back at just that moment. He bent to the ground and removed a few vegetables.

He had abandoned any thought of removing the Ape-iaries on this trip. But with the vegetables in hand, he'd be able to sustain his mana levels much better. When he came back, it would be in greater force, aiming at targets he could hit from a distance.

It was only then, at the height of his pleasure with himself, that the buzzing in the air became louder as a cloud of apes descended on him.

Matt was in pain. Horrendous, total pain. But no part of him actually hurt. His arms and legs were fine. His torso was uninjured, as near as he could tell, through the all-encompassing torture. It didn't seem to come from his stomach or his guts. This was different. The pain was real, but coming from nowhere. It was like the pain was eating his soul.

And then, suddenly, it was gone. He became aware of Lucy screaming at him and sat up as quickly as he could to reassure her, and nothing hurt at all. He was fine.

*Ding!*

*Ding!*

"One second. I seem to be fine now. I have to figure out what happened."

With Lucy still calling him a moron in the background, Matt brought up the notification from before he felt the pain, leaving the new ones to stew for a moment.

> Interference with system skill detected.
>
> An outside force is interfering with a system-assigned skill. The system will now make use of user resources in order to fight whatever changes are underway. Please stand by.

Matt supposed that his pain had been caused by that, although the system was being suspiciously vague here. Sometimes, he got notifications from the system that he assumed were stock messages, mainly from the lack of edits threatening to kill him. This might have been that, but he had a vague feeling it was more.

*Does the system not know what's going on?*

Matt moved on to the next notification as quickly as possible, immediately shocked that it wasn't either of the two colors he was used to. To the point where he couldn't immediately read it. This wasn't Barry, or the system. It was the only other window color he had ever seen. It was from the Gaian alert system that had let him know the sword guy had arrived. When it didn't alert him to Leel, Matt had assumed that the alerts were somehow broken.

Gaian Defense System Skill Modification Activated . . .
System Resistance Detected. Activating "Fight the Tide" protocols.
System Resistance Abated. Modifying Skill.

*Eat Anything!* > *Palate of the Conqueror*

Hello, Gaian. In accordance with the Gaian wartime pact, your skill has been modified. As the possessor of the first successfully modified skill, we both thank you and warn you. Our skill modifications are not guided except to the extent that they push directly back on the guidelines and dictates that determine system behavior.

As such, the skill you have obtained is not one whose parameters we can predict. It could be useful as easily as it could be a disability. Only one thing is sure: it goes against the grain of everything the system itself wants. In this goal, every living Gaian is now united.

You will note that your skill is currently LOCKED. Proceed immediately to the closest wartime base or capital to have the skill inspected for fatal errors and unlocked by someone with appropriate levels of authority.

Fight the Scourge. Evict the system.

## CHAPTER THIRTY-TWO

# Skin of the Worm

And another thing, Matt, is that you *don't listen* to ANY of my reasonable advice at all, not just with food, but with ANYTHING AT ALL, so this keeps on HAPPENING."

"Lucy."

"And with stupid things like EATING WORMS FOR NO REASON, of course this is what happens, and then I have to sit here while you SCREAM for an hour . . ."

"LUCY!" Matt yelled, shocking his guardian into a momentary pause. "Eating the worm knocked some stuff loose with Eat Anything!, apparently. Weird stuff."

He filled her in on the details of both what had happened to him and the new system notifications.

"That's . . . Matt, that's not possible. The system is the system. Nothing can screw with it, as far as I know. At least, nothing in the database indicates that it can be changed. Even Barry can only do what he does because in most ways he's part of the system. This can't be real."

"I know, but there it is. This seems different from other messages we've seen from the Gaians, too. Did you notice the change in the slogan? 'Evict the system' is new."

"So you are saying they got more pissed since they programmed the museum?"

Matt nodded. "Yeah. And maybe they got some work done in that direction. I don't know. I just know this skill is apparently real. And what I think they mean by authority . . ."

"You can probably unlock it yourself," Lucy finished.

"Yup. Now, I know you probably don't want me to do that. I get it. But this seems import . . ."

"No, unlock it. Right now," Lucy said.

Matt had prepared a full essay to convince Lucy of his idea. Normally, Lucy was the cautious one and he knew that he had his work cut out for him. But things didn't seem to be going by his script.

"Like, right now, right now?" Matt asked.

"Immediately. Now. Matt," Lucy said.

"I thought you'd say no. Are you . . . okay?"

Lucy jumped close to Matt, and put her face inches from his.

"No, Matt, I'm not okay. The Gaians just moved the battlefield with the system directly into what sounds a lot like your soul. The system is still trying to kill you, and this skill does who-the-fuck-knows-what." Lucy sighed. "But they aren't wrong. At this point, anything that the system does or wants probably leaves you dead. Even just waiting for time ends up with you dead. It was the same for them. The system screwed with stuff, they didn't like it, so it came after them. They stood up to it, they got knocked down. They lost."

"But whatever thing that they cooked up didn't help," Matt interjected. Now he was playing the devil's advocate.

"They never used it. You said it yourself; that message was for the first Gaian modified. It was special. Whatever the Scourge did to take them down, it did it before this was fully up and running. Hell, something we did probably shocked it to life. Who knows what we did, but you know what?"

Lucy looked as serious as Matt had ever seen her.

"What?"

"It doesn't matter. This isn't something the system wants. It just fought like hell to keep you from getting it. That's good enough, right?"

Matt was on the back foot. He now felt like he had to be the cautious one, the one who preached waiting and seeing rather than moving and doing. If the roles were truly reversed, now was the time when he'd look Lucy in the eye and tell her they were by no means unlocking this skill until they could learn more about it.

*Screw that. Let's do it.*

"Fine. Let's do it." Matt had no idea what muscle he had to flex to get his authority moving, but he started running through every option he had. He looked at the system screen details for his new skill, but no amount of willing the skill through the screen would work. Which made sense, he supposed, since the system was the one providing the screen.

"I exercise my authority as the ruler of Gaia to unlock this skill," Matt stated.

Nothing happened for a few seconds.

"Did that work?" Lucy asked.

"Nope. But I had to try it." Matt continued trying different things. He pointed his finger at himself and tried to will the skill unlocked, tried meditating, and a dozen other things. "Nothing, Lucy. I'm beginning to think this isn't something that was meant to be unlocked by yourself."

Lucy furrowed her brow. "The pain."

"What?"

"The pain you felt. You said it wasn't attached to anything, like it was your soul. Can you remember what that soul felt like?"

Matt began to say no because the place the pain came from wasn't really anything, but then stopped himself. The place the pain came from wasn't really nothing, either. In retrospect, it was like a space or area he couldn't see or sense, like a part of his body he had not known about until then.

He sat up straight and followed his memories of the pain as deeply as he could, trying his best to duplicate the non-pain feeling again. He was just about to give up when something in him clicked, and he saw the most simplistic system window he had ever seen.

Unlock?
Y/N

He pushed his will into the space, indicating the affirmative.

*Ding!*

*Palate of the Conqueror: Unlocked*

You have stood astride a world, your power uncontested, and all your enemies destroyed. That world and all the power in it is now yours. The Palate of the Conqueror represents one way for you to put that might to use, at least until someone rises and wrests the world from your grasp.

When you eat foods specifically associated with the planet Gaia, unpredictable but mostly positive changes will occur. The skill otherwise retains Eat Anything! properties at the most recent level of advancement.

"That's a system-blue message again. It can apparently see this."

"Good."

"Well, sure. But I get nervous when the system gets quiet. It probably has to show me this message. But from the lack of edits and not threatening me, I'm getting a bad feeling. It's probably up to something," Matt said.

"Well, deal. That's just Tuesday for us," Lucy said with a smile.

"True that." Matt returned the smile.

Matt waited a few more moments to see if any more information was forthcoming, then wandered over to the plinth that had risen out of the ground when he was enjoying his worm steak.

"Looks like repair stones, estate credit, and vendor trash cape as rewards this time. Sort of a lot of them, too. Ready for an estate credit influx?"

Lucy lifted her hand up in a stop gesture. "No, wait."

"I'm not getting the vendor trash, Lucy. We've talked about this. I'm not Dracula."

"No, I mean don't get the estate credit. Get the repair stones."

"Why? That mana generator isn't going to buy itself, Lucy."

"It's the museum. Remember how you said you saw the man say something, and I didn't really believe you?"

"I knew it!"

"Well, yeah, sorry. But everything you said just got a lot more possible. Not only that, but between this and the seeds . . ."

"It turns out the Gaians were badasses?"

"Yeah. And every single thing they had their hands in right up until the end just got a lot more important. We need to get that museum up to snuff. And fast."

"Got it." Matt cashed in for repair stones, then went to the worm to recover his shield. Regardless of where his loot ended up in the dungeon, Matt had always gotten it back when he left the dungeon. Still, old habits were hard to shake, and usually, he'd get his gear back on his person if he could. As he picked up the shield from the ground, he noticed a tiny piece of fat that had escaped his first go around. He wasn't really hungry anymore, but now that his eating skill was back, he wasn't about to pass up free flavor, either. As soon as the food passed down his throat, he got another notification ding.

*Ding!*

"Another notification already?"

"Yup. I'll check it out."

> Skin of the Worm trait added.
>
> Skin of the Worm grants you superior resistance to abrasive damage, as well as lesser resistance against some other types of elemental damage.
>
> Meta-trait occupied: Defense

"What in the hell does any of this mean? What in the world is a meta-trait?"

"No idea, but I'm not knocking it. Here." She pointed at a particularly rough rock laying on the floor of the ravine. "Scrape yourself with this."

Matt did. It didn't do anything. "I'm not sure if that would have scraped me anyway. I'm all juiced up on vitality and Rub Some Dirt In It at this point."

"Then scrape harder."

Matt did. No damage. It hurt, but even at his top strength, he couldn't scrape his own skin. At the worst, he was making it a little pink.

"Okay, I think it's different. Good call on the testing. Honestly, that's pretty badass."

"Yup. Thanks, Gaians!"

Matt tried the honey, but nothing happened. That made sense. The bees were pretty far from being Gaian natives. Or natives of anywhere, as near as he could tell.

"Do you think we should go around eating some other stuff? Like the rest of the worm? Figure out this meta-trait business?" Lucy asked.

"Probably, but not right now. Let's check on home first," Matt replied. "I'm worried about what Leel's been up to."

Leel had fallen down a hole.

No matter how fuel-efficient Leel's insect-killing spell was, there had been no reason to even try to use it on the Ape-bees. There were too many of them to make a real difference. Instead, he swatted at them, trying his hardest to get away on his barely mended leg. As he hobbled away, he picked up dozens of stings all over his body. His robes were loose enough to keep air flowing around him, which was part of why he liked them. But they were also too loose to keep Ape-bees out, a problem he had not anticipated in the least.

He wasn't even sure what they were stinging him *with*.

But then the stings stopped. As soon as he got several meters away from the hive, the apes apparently hit some sort of defined perimeter and turned back, fussing over their now fallen hive. Leel's face was too swollen by that point to smile *or* grimace, but he was at least pleased that the attack was over. He was home free.

Or at least he would have been, if an awful lot of adrenaline and recent pain hadn't taken his attention off the need to follow the same route out he had taken in. In his hurry to leave, he stepped on an entirely new patch of ground, one that turned out to feed into a pit that was just a little deeper than seemed realistic for one man to have dug.

The fall broke more things. Leel was enough of a heap by the end of it that he couldn't figure out exactly which ones.

Matt and Lucy were almost home by the time they saw the hole in their hedge.

"Oh, hell. Be careful, Matt."

"Do you think he's still here?"

"No idea, but who knows what he's cooked up by now."

They approached cautiously, or at least as cautiously as they could. Matt equipped his shield and spear, ready to throw the latter at anything that moved. As the moved past the hedge, they immediately saw the sprung whip-traps. Matt bent down to examine them for any sign, blood or otherwise, that they had done significant damage to Leel. Unfortunately, he was disappointed.

Suddenly, Matt heard Lucy gasp and choke.

*Oh, you better not, you asshole.* He wheeled around as fast as he could to see what terror Leel had managed to cook up that could possibly hurt Lucy. Only, he found her standing at the mouth of their pit trap, laughing so hard she couldn't breathe.

"Matt," Lucy finally gasped out between chortles. "It looks like we caught ourselves a wizard."

## CHAPTER THIRTY-THREE

# An Unhonest Matt

"Wait, he's in the pit?" Matt was already moving towards Lucy, a smile on his face. One of his Ape-iaries was smashed, sure. But from the looks of things, Leel had gotten tangled up in several traps on his way in, and there was nothing about his personality that screamed "would stay at the bottom of a pit trap if he didn't have to" to Matt. This was very good news.

"Yup. Fully down there. Leel, how are you doing?" Lucy gloated.

Leel groaned. It didn't sound like he was doing very well.

"You should be ashamed of yourself. That's a *terrible* joke."

"I don't care. This is like a holiday. Matt, come look at him. He's messed up."

Matt did. As he looked down into the hole, he saw a literally broken man, with arms and legs going all sorts of *wrong* directions and a general look of puffiness. He looked like a man with a seafood allergy who had questioned the fidelity of a superpowered shrimp's wife.

Matt watched as Leel's arms and legs twitched uncontrollably and was cautious for a moment before he realized what was happening. Leel's limited vitality was trying to pull his bones back together, but couldn't because the pit itself was keeping the bones from being able to realign. If he was outside of the pit, Leel would probably be capable of walking by now. As it was, he was stuck.

But then, Leel's remaining unbroken arm twitched in a different way, pointed at Matt's head, and fired. Matt was completely unprepared for the weak-version firebolt headed his way. By the time his reflexes kicked in, he was able to pull back just enough that the firebolt hit his forehead instead of the center of his face, flinching his eyes shut as it hit.

"Shit! Matt!" Lucy scrambled over as Matt's head snapped back from the impact. Matt's hands jumped to his head to inspect the damage. His hair was singed, which he already knew from the smell. But where he expected to find blistered skin or no skin at all, he instead found a pain more similar to a bad sunburn, already rapidly diminishing as Rub Some Dirt In It worked to heal the damage.

"That son of a bitch!" Matt yelled, patting his hair to make sure none of it was burning. "Don't worry, Lucy. I'm fine."

Lucy paused as she looked at Matt, who somehow did seem fine.

"How in the hell are you fine? He just capped you in the head from near point-blank range."

It was a decent question. It was possible that Leel had suddenly gotten worse at casting his fire bolt spell, but from what Matt had seen, Leel wasn't the type to do things halfway. He would expect Leel's attacks to fail outright before he'd expect them to suddenly suck. Then it hit him.

"It's the Worm Skin, probably. Remember that 'limited resistance to other elements' nonsense? I'm guessing this is it."

"Oooooh. That's incredible."

"Yeah, great for this situation anyway." Matt peeked over the edge again, this time holding his shovel. Leel's arm twitched once more, only to have the spell fizzle in his hand. "Not that I need it that much. Looks like he's spent."

"We should leave him down there," Lucy suggested.

"I'm pretty sure that's a crime," Matt said.

"Then how are you going to get him out of there?"

Matt paused. As drained as Leel appeared to be, he had managed to demonstrate a fairly varied bag of tricks up to that point. Matt had no desire to get down in the hole with him and then find out he had a cave-in spell, or something of that nature.

*Actually, that might be it.*

"I'm going to try something stupid, but I promise you it's not actually dangerous. It probably won't even work."

"What?"

"Just hold on. I don't want to spoil the surprise. And Leel, it's slightly possible this might kill you. Sorry, if so." Matt ignored Leel's sudden groans of protest. Honestly, if he accidentally did die here, it would be sort of nice. There were some things Matt didn't want to confront yet, and beating a broken man to death was one of them, even if Leel had been trying to kill him for a while now. But if that man died during an experiment, then all bets were off.

Matt activated Trapper Keeper. He was almost shocked when it worked, absorbing the pit like it had never existed. He was even more shocked when not only was Leel expelled from the hole, but expelled with actual momentum, shooting a few meters into the air like a mostly-defective mortar shell before slamming back into the ground, broken bones and all. Leel screamed in pain, heard only by two people who couldn't care less.

"First things first," Matt said, bending down over the still-writhing Leel. "I don't think I want you to have this anymore." He reached down and ripped the talisman off Leel's neck, not sparing any effort to be gentle. Leel yelped as blood welled up where the chain rasped his neck as it broke.

"Give that back! It's mine!" Leel yelled, somehow still having the energy to make a surprising amount of noise.

"I don't think so, asshole. Matt and I are keeping that," Lucy said. "Now, how do we free the guardian that's inside there? I don't think I believe there isn't a way."

Leel said nothing, and just glared at Matt.

"Kick him, Matt."

Matt was happy to oblige. He kicked Leel in the ribs, hard enough to hurt him, but hopefully not hard enough to actually kill him. Leel skidded a couple of feet back.

"Why? Ow. What was that for? Oww. Give me the amulet back."

"Don't ignore my friend, you weirdo."

"Who? Your guardian?" Leel looked bewildered for a second. "I'm not ignoring her, you moron! I can't see her now!"

"Oh, right." Lucy laughed. "I forgot how that worked for a second. Matt, ask him."

"Tell us how to get the guardian out of the amulet. "

Leel rolled his eyes. "I can't. There's no way."

Matt kicked him again, this time catching Leel in the sternum and knocking the air out of him.

"I really can't!" Leel yelled, after partially catching his breath. "It's not something I'm *trained in*. Binding is an incredibly specific field. I don't know more than the rudiments, just enough to ensure obedience in the servants. That kind of thing."

Matt looked at Lucy. "Do you believe him?"

"Yeah, I think I do, sadly." Lucy sighed.

"What now?"

"I think that was the last way he could potentially be useful. I think it's probably time to end this."

Matt tightened his grip on the shovel. He wasn't sure he knew how to painlessly kill someone, but he figured with enough force he'd at least knock Leel unconscious with the first hit. That would have to be good enough. He lifted the shovel above his head.

"Wait! Wait!" Leel opened his mouth so far that his lips split. "The Star of the South! You care about it! You can't kill me!"

Matt stopped. "Why not? We have it now."

"You have it, you idiot, but you don't *own* it. You aren't bound to it. Bound guardians can only be transferred at the occasion of the former owner's death."

"Sounds fine." Matt lifted the shovel again.

"No it doesn't, you absolute *dunce*." Leel rolled his eyes, which immediately made his pupils disappear behind his almost-swollen-shut eyelids. "You can't have *two* guardians at once. Taking on a new guardian would eliminate your old one. If you could even start the transfer, which you can't. I can't. Again, it's very specialized work. If you kill me, it will break the binding on that talisman and kill the guardian. It's as simple as that."

Matt turned to Lucy. "What do you think?"

"I don't know, Matt. Even if he's telling the truth . . . that guardian has been trapped in there for hundreds of years. There might not be much left. Hell, he or she might even appreciate it."

"Maybe not. And we've pulled weirder stuff off, honestly. We might be able to save it. Of course that means leaving this"—Matt kicked Leel again—"alive. And that's a danger."

"Not as much as it used to be. If a couple of traps can take him down, I'm pretty sure he's having trouble recharging his batteries," Lucy said.

"I'm not a danger!" Leel lied while Lucy was talking.

"You aren't a danger yet. And shush, the adults are talking," Matt said to Leel.

"It's up to you, Matt. I'm split. I can't decide."

If Matt was being honest, this was a great excuse not to kill Leel. He was still squeamish around the idea of taking down humans, and this amulet situation was giving him a great excuse not to. At the same time, if he was actually admitting the truth of it, it was a long shot. He didn't know magic, and there was very little he could do to free the guardian, even if there was a way to do so in the first place. Leel didn't pose a threat now, but a Matt who was being even the least bit honest would have to admit to the fact that letting Leel go was a very, very bad idea.

But he wasn't being honest.

"Just go."

"What?" Leel looked shocked that his threat had worked. "Just like that?"

"Just like that. Have fun out there." Matt waved his hand at the wasteland. "Doing whatever it is you are doing. Just know that I've got a feeling that I'm about to get *much* stronger, and I still have this." He brandished his shovel. "Do your best to keep out of my sight. If I see you, even for a moment, I'm going to end this. Actually, permanently end it."

"Well, I'm glad you've seen reason. If you just give me a few moments to . . . well, pull myself together, I'll be out of your way."

"No. Now."

"I can't walk, Matt. I'm rather broken, which you might have noticed if you weren't so . . ."

"Crawl. This is a one-time offer, Leel." Matt stabbed the point of the shovel into the ground next to Leel's neck, hard. "The next one won't miss."

Leel opened his mouth to protest, then apparently saw something in Matt's eye that convinced him not to. Slowly and painfully, he brought himself up to his good arm and knees, and winced and whined as he crawled away.

He didn't move quickly, at least at first. Matt and Lucy watched for the better part of an hour as Leel's abysmal vitality score slowly knitted him together, letting him crawl faster and faster until eventually, he could stand. Finally, he was out of sight.

"Think he will be back?"

"He almost has to come back at some point. If he could have run back to his world, he would have at the bottom of the pit. But he can't get any stronger out there. At worst, we will have to deal with someone as strong as he was the first time we met him. And I have a feeling this new eating skill will help even the score there."

Matt reset what few traps Leel had sprung, but kept the hole trap in his skill for now. He had never suspected that would work, and he rather liked the idea of a portable hole, even if he didn't have an immediate use for it.

"Can you keep an eye out for a while? For Leel, I mean. Or anything else, I guess."

"Sure, Matt. Going to bed?"

"Yup." Matt held up the bag of repair stones and rattled it. "Tomorrow we use these. I want to be rested up when we see what the Gaians have in store."

## CHAPTER THIRTY-FOUR

# One Particularly Hardy Plant

"Won't this make him stronger? Not Leel. The system, I mean," Lucy asked.

"Yeah, I think so. But to be honest, we've been batting one thousand against the kind of stuff he's been throwing at us lately. And the alternative is sitting still. Our best bet for getting strong enough to actually take him down in any real way is here," Matt replied.

"I still think we should have done some dungeons first."

"Right after this, we can go do some dungeons, eat some weird stuff, and see if we can't get a lead on things. I promise."

"Fine. But if the Gaians give us anything less than a system-annihilating ray gun, then right after this, we go to a dungeon. No questions asked, no delays."

"Deal."

With Lucy temporarily satisfied, Matt started feeding the repair stones into the plinth. From the outside, there was no way to tell what effect it was having on the broken holograms inside. There was still an enormous way to go in terms of durability points before the museum would be fully fixed, but Matt was irrationally hopeful that this small contribution would make a big difference.

Once inside the museum, he and Lucy decided to sit through every exhibit again. They had seen all of them, but Matt found that both of their appetites for entertainment were now relatively easy to satisfy, given that the alternatives were either mind-numbing nothingness or constant near-death experiences. The museum was definitely closer to the former than the latter in a good way, and represented a medium ground Matt found calming without being entirely mind-numbing.

After exhausting every educational reel in the place, Matt and Lucy set off for the *Resist the Scourge* exhibit. The same man appeared, gave the exact same speech, and radiated the same kind of earned authority and competence he had the first time they had seen him. Matt had a moment in which he wished it had been the man who was reincarnated rather than himself. This was a guy who had worked his way up through sheer competence. Matt suspected that, given the same power set, he would have got a whole lot more done.

The man finally finished his speech, then froze as he always had.

"Do you think he's still broken?" Lucy walked up, reached her arm into the air, and waved her hand in front of the hologram's face. "He's the only show that doesn't disappear after the show ends. It's a little bit creepy."

"Maybe. This place is still pretty messed up. It's possible the first time was just a fluke. We can always repair it more."

Suddenly, the hologram swiveled its head, and stared straight at Matt with an expressionless face. Lucy, who was standing directly in front of it, almost jumped out of her skin.

"Reincarnator," the man said.

Matt gulped and walked up to the hologram. "Yup. That's me."

The man's mouth moved wordlessly, like he was struggling to speak. "Reincarnator."

"Yes, I am. What . . . what can I do for you?" Matt prayed the thing wasn't on a loop.

"Trust . . . the system."

Lucy immediately sprang back from the hologram. "Shit, Matt. The system got to him somehow."

"No! How? It said it couldn't see in here." Matt was panicking. If the system had corrupted this place, they'd never know what the Gaians had left for them. "We can't trust any part of this now. It's ruined."

The hologram was still staring at Matt.

"Reincarnator. Trust . . . the system."

Matt pulled his shovel off his pack. "No, I'm sorry. I don't. Not happening."

Lucy stopped Matt from approaching. She looked apprehensively at the hologram.

The hologram's voice was still flat as it continued speaking. "Trust . . . us. The system . . . ruined Gaia. We saved work against . . . the system."

Matt let out a breath he hadn't realized he was holding. "Yes, we'd like to work against the system too. How, though? How can we beat it?"

The hologram suddenly winked out, then came back, scrambled. Its mouth worked wordlessly again, as if searching for just the right thing to say in a tough situation. Finally, it became fully solid and clear again, if only for a moment.

"Maps. The maps."

And then it was gone.

* * *

"I don't understand, Matt. Any maps would be long gone. Even without the Scourge."

"Maybe . . . I don't know, maybe they stored them. In a bunker or something."

Matt and Lucy had been through every single exhibit again, looking hard for any maps that might have clues. There weren't any maps that went into more detail than the general shape of Gaian continents. Wherever the maps the hologram was talking about were, they weren't here.

"I wish that stupid exhibit would run again. It's the only one that's broken now," Matt said.

Matt had dragged Lucy back over to the Gaian war effort exhibit several times, only to find that the room was apparently permanently frozen in place. They couldn't pick the hologram's brain for more clues.

"It's possible. But as much as I like treasure hunting, that can't come first, Matt. You promised."

"I did. And we will do dungeons as soon as we get out of here."

"Can we do that now?" Lucy looked towards the exit with an impatient expression.

"That bored?"

"Not that bored, Matt. That worried. Leel's out there, and the system might already have called down some new kind of hell. We need to be working to get stronger, right now. We've already been in here long enough."

Matt wanted to argue, but Lucy was right. Between seeing all the exhibits twice, the better part of a day was already gone.

"Okay, let's go."

As always, the yo-yos in the gift store were unclaimable. Matt contented himself with grabbing more Gaian victory seeds, since whatever supply of them the Gaians had put aside still hadn't run out, and he had no shortage of places to plant them. He had even noticed some variance in the things they grew, like occasionally different seeds had made their ways into the pack. He figured it was the closest he was going to come to reintroducing the original Gaian biome, so he was happy to roll the dice on getting as many varieties as he could.

It wasn't until he had one foot essentially out the door and was regretfully glancing back at the door to the museum that he saw them. There were containers after containers holding different posters, some of Sarthian scientists or science concepts, some of various agricultural implements, and some of plants. But one of the containers, and only one, held posters that were without exception different kinds of maps.

"Truly a fool. Really and truly a fool. If I had anything like my normal resources, he'd be dead a dozen times over. And you, system, have really and truly made a mess of things by letting him run wild."

Leel was pretty good at mental deflection, and had no intention of reflecting on the fact that the system was trying very hard not to let Matt run wild. In fact, the world-class level-appropriate wizard that the system had called in was failing to do much of the intended purpose. But Leel didn't sweat those details.

Rather, he was reflecting, rather thoroughly, on his humiliation. He, Leel, was the fourth adopted son of the Cavelar of Ammai. There was no fifth because Leel had been deemed sufficient, had taken to magic like a fish to water and had worked *well* beyond what the system intended from its magic system. The previous three adopted sons, reincarnated to the Cavelar's care as infants, were no more. Their failure stood as a warning to all, just as Leel felt his own success stood as an inspiration.

For someone of his caliber to be defeated by what seemed to be little more than a servant-class idiot with a shovel was horrifying. And Leel meant it when he thought of Matt as an idiot, even after being caught by traps he had laid. Even though Matt now held the Star of the South and several marks in the win column in matches between them, Leel did not doubt the man was simple. For who, after all, would fail to check a defeated opponent for hidden items or weapons? Only an idiot.

Leel had not accomplished much on his trip to Matt's estate, but that wasn't to say he hadn't accomplished anything at all. Reaching into his robes, he removed several different plants, including some root vegetables and flowers. Carefully, he arranged them into a small pile on the ground.

He thanked his lucky stars that he had thought to recover his paint before leaving on his mission. He hardly had the mana to do it now, and otherwise he'd be forced to eat these plants as-is. His arcane senses weren't enough to reveal exactly what it was, but something was wrong with them. Deeply and fundamentally wrong. He was glad to have better options.

Carefully, Leel laid out his formation. Every place, every planet, and every realm has a history. And just as Matt had apparently found some incredible, reality-defying artifact of Gaia, no world's history was ever truly and utterly lost. Chronomancy was a delicate, chaotic art, but Leel was as good at it as any, and he was prepared to make full use of it here.

Of course, no one could actually travel back in time. The past became the present, for lack of a better way to put it. Everything that had been was in some way what now was. They left their marks on the world. Some things from the past left deeper shadows or echoes that reverberated into the future, and could be put to use, if one knew how to see them.

Leel did not, for the record, know how to see these shadows. But that didn't mean he didn't know they were there. On a place called "The Garden Planet," they must be.

*Ding!*

*Quest Discovered: STOP STOP STOP*

The system thinks it has an idea of what you are doing, and it wants to inform you that it's a very, very bad idea. What substantial rewards it can offer you for simply abandoning your plans are currently tied up in your previous failed quest, but . . .

Leel stopped reading.

*What horrifying manners from a system instance.*

The system instance on Leel's world was a beautiful if somewhat kept thing. It was always polite, knew perfectly well what kind of rewards were acceptable for the few who were allowed to claim them, and was, above all, stable and consistent in all things. This system instance, on the other hand, was none of that. It was as if its time on this planet had driven it partially insane, a condition that seemed to be worsening the more Leel interacted with it.

*As if,* he thought, *I would actually listen to it after the botch job it's made of this entire affair. As if a man stranded on a dead planet, unable to use his bountiful supply of knowledge and skills, would feel bound to listen to the words of the same system that had so very thoroughly ruined everything.*

Leel finished drawing the circle and began taking steps to verify it, to make sure it was without flaw and would work correctly. Everything looked in order, even under close inspection, but he'd only have one shot at this. If that idiot could farm, so could he, but the fool did have some advantages Leel did not. Good soil, for one. Water sources. The works.

The trick to what Leel was planning was one he couldn't have pulled off without the stolen vegetable matter. By introducing biological mass to the chronomancy spell he had in mind, he could trade the diseased turnips that he otherwise would have had to eat with similar living mass from the echoes of the past.

It wasn't a spell that would work on anything much more complex than a plant, or on anything with a soul, but Leel was reasonably confident he could pull something hardy enough to make up for any farming advantages he lacked. Something productive enough to survive in this hellhole, he hoped.

After all, this planet used to be a garden. It must have had at least one particularly hardy plant.

## CHAPTER THIRTY-FIVE

# Salad Days

The most important trick to being a reasonably proficient mage was to never trust the system for everything. Knowledge, practice, and experimentation, were the cornerstones of magic. During chronomancy training, Leel had sketched out several ideas for an improved chronal summoning circle, which he now put into play on Gaia. It had several little neat tricks that Leel was quite proud of.

The first was a sort of sorting feature that took several parameters Leel fed into it and searched for a proper match among the available echoes in local time. Not that the standard spell didn't do *some* of that. It did. But where a normal mage would ask for something like "a food plant" or even "fruit," Leel was asking for dozens of things. Something that could survive in the harshest of conditions. Something that was nutritionally complete and required little preparation.

But most importantly, he needed something that was dense in mana. Leel was hungry, yes, but he'd much rather eat a real meal in his home than some random historic plant on Gaia. He would gladly sacrifice all the other elements of the plant for the ability to draw an above-average amount of mana in. Environmental mana was one source wizards drew on for their mana reservoirs, but a mana-dense enough plant could, well, sup*plant* that need by enhancing his internal reservoir.

It would be a small enhancement in any case, but over several hours, a suitable enough plant would give him enough regeneration to perhaps fill his tank once. And that would be more than enough to deal with Matt, should he get serious.

Of course, Leel could have asked for so much more with his summoning. But the phrasing was tedious, and he wasn't looking to impress any judges.

The spell circle lit up. That was another little flourish on Leel's part. Leel had provided enough parameters that he'd be surprised if the circle was able to meet them all perfectly. For essentially no cost, he had programmed a sort of visible feedback based on how well each parameter was met. In a determined order, it would blink colors, each color indicating how well various aspects of the search had succeeded.

Red would be the worst, moving up the color spectrum to yellow for medium results, and blue was the best. So far, no color was showing, but that was expected. Soon it would, and he'd know how good of a plant he had pulled.

Normally, Leel had other considerations when performing at magical-prodigy levels. The rules of magic could be stretched, sometimes quite far. But normally a mage would have to stop just short of the astonishing in fear of the system. It tolerated a certain amount of mussing with skills, but there were certain lines one typically did not cross over.

Leel was much less concerned about that restriction here on Gaia. This was a system instance, to be sure. But it wasn't *his* system instance. Rather, it was as if he was working on contract. If he could kill Matt, he'd go home with the promised rewards. If he couldn't, he'd die. Or worse, he'd be trapped here. Those were his main concerns. This particular system instance was oddly impotent, and seemed to lack the resources to stop Leel or even Leel's opponent.

So Leel got fancy. Normally, one would trade mass for mass in a summoning of this kind. Leel had instead drawn the circle to do something that the system instance of his home would not tolerate. It would consume the mass of several vegetables to make a smaller but higher-quality plant, essentially using the sacrificial matter as fuel to enhance the circle. The system would allow a great many things, but matter-to-mana conversion was for whatever reason one of its great taboos. Leel had always, always wanted to try it, and here he could.

*Ding!*

> *Quest Discovered: LISTEN YOU IDIOT*
>
> You have no idea what you are doing here. No idea about the very grave consequences you are playing with as if they are TOYS, you DUMB IDIOT, how did I get TWO of you stupid, idiotic, horrifying pieces of . . .

*My,* Leel thought, *this has certainly touched a nerve.*

But he wasn't worried. Not a bit. Regardless of how mad this system instance got, he seriously doubted that word of his actions would follow him home. Even if it did, he doubted his system instance would care. For all their failings, the instances were remarkably focused on their own territories. Nobody truly *knew* an instance, but he very much doubted that it would care about what Leel got up to in the boonies. That was purely this instance's problem, and this instance couldn't stop him.

Suddenly, the circle burst with color. It was blue. Honestly, that alone was enough to make the entire experiment a success by itself. The first blink in the cycle was caloric content produced per soil nutrient consumed, or something close. Essentially, it represented the efficiency of the plant, and this echo's efficiency was *perfect*.

Leel settled down eagerly to wait for the color to change. But after the planned five-second interval, the color did not change, nor did it at the tenth. Suddenly, some of Leel's pride fell away. Somehow, he had managed to botch the visual feedback. It *should* read one part of the process, then shift to the next, as regular as clockwork. He didn't know how, but he was nearly certain he had messed up the programming for that function.

After the circle shined blue for a bit too long, he became quite certain he had messed it up. At least one blue was confirmed. The design of the circle wouldn't allow a false positive unless the whole circle was botched. But it was highly unlikely that the spell had identified a plant that was nearly perfect in every way, which was what the pure blue meant. Living things just weren't allowed to be that perfect. Absent the possibility of some kind of god-tier carrot, Leel had to accept that he wasn't quite as perfect as he thought.

Beyond the colors, there wasn't much else to observe. Leel sat down to wait for the plant to come into being. It was only due to the improvements he had made to his circles that he could do this spell at all. His final contribution to the circle was a mana-gathering portion that would draw in ambient power for hours to gradually reconstruct the echo. Still, it would be a close thing. His circle should survive the kind of strain for however many hours this process took, but only just.

Hours passed as Leel dozed in the odd Gaian twilight. Finally, he was woken up by a sudden crack as the circle broke. He sprang to his feet and rushed to the site of the spell, oddly nervous. One way or another, his bet was already cast. If this spell didn't summon something particularly good, or had failed entirely, he would be out of options to ever get the necessary magic fuel to complete his mission.

He let out a sigh of relief as he reached the center of the circle and saw a small patch of green. Kneeling down, he found the color came from the smallest of possible sprouts, just a hair-thin green stalk with a single leaf midway down its fraction of an inch of length.

*It's not much. No, scratch that. It's worse. It's not enough.*

Size wasn't all-important here, but a plant this small would take serious time to grow. Leel had meant for the spell to produce a smaller amount of vegetable matter than the plants that he had fed into it, but not to this extent. This was tiny, and it simply wouldn't be enough to make a meal of, no matter how magic-dense it was.

Leel despaired. He was well and truly out of ideas. Barring some miracle, he'd die on this rock, alone. Even worse, he'd die humiliated. It was just a matter of time.

Then, all at once, Leel felt a pull on his MP pool. The stalk sprouted another leaf. Then another.

*Oh, my. That's very interesting.*

For a plant to have enough of a pull to take even a point of mana from his mana pool, it had to be a very specialized plant indeed. On Leel's world, they had plants that could do something similar. Though, the plants that could vampire mana at an alarming rate to sustain themselves were usually bred and planted on ritual-burned ground. Now that he thought about it, Gaia wasn't really that dissimilar to ritual-burned ground.

As happy as he was to see the plant doing well, it wouldn't do to feed it *his* mana. Leel withdrew for the evening to leave it to its own devices. With any luck, it would be large enough to work with after a good, long sleep.

The next "morning," Leel woke up, rubbed his eyes, and stood to look in the direction of the plant. What he saw astonished him, and it was only after he had taken several strides that he started sprinting towards the plant in glee.

The plant had exceeded Leel's wildest dreams. It was the size of a barrel, all thin tendrils like the sprout he had initially seen tangled together into something like a bush. He could get multiple meals out of this, not just one. It was plenty for multiple attempts on Matt's life. With this, he could bombard Matt's estate with the power of an artillery, destroying everything he had built, then recharge for another go. He wouldn't *need* to, of course. But he could.

He had achieved success above his wildest dreams. He could *feel* the mana burning off the thing. It wasn't much, but in this wasteland it stood out like a fire. He reached out for it, impatient to get his first taste.

*Ding!*

| *Quest Discovered: Don't Touch It, You Idiot! Don't . . .* |
|---|

Leel had no time for this. He reached out to grab a big handful of the plant, only to suddenly think twice about it. The system did have a point. It didn't hurt to be cautious. Instead of a mouthful, he pinched off a single leaf, smelled it, then cautiously put it in his mouth. It tasted fine. After a quick chew, he swallowed. He then brought up his status screen to see if there were any subtler negative effects from his bite of food, and gasped.

His mana regeneration had jumped to over one MP per *second.* He already had several mana. He immediately, without waiting, cleaned his body and clothes with a cleansing spell. It was wonderful. For the first time in days, he felt himself. What would a mouthful of this plant do? Without waiting any longer, he reached out, grabbed a big handful of plant, and pulled.

It didn't break. He pulled again, and it held strong.

*What in the world?*

Suddenly, Leel's mana bottomed out. The plant was a hungry little thing. Oh, well. He'd pull another leaf, let it refill his mana, and come back with arcane sheers or something. There was only one problem, which made itself immediately apparent as he tried to pull away. His hand was stuck.

Somehow, the plant had managed to tangle itself around his hand, and he was unable to dislodge it. Leel pulled, and pulled. It was no good. He was stuck.

Then it was the plant's turn to pull. Leel felt a pain in his abdomen like he had been punched in the gut, almost doubling him over. But even as the pain started, he knew it wasn't a physical hit. The plant had pulled on his internal, natural mana.

*That shouldn't even be possible.*

Leel's trapped status took on a new urgency. He pulled desperately at the plant, tried to tear it away with his free hand, and even tried to bite it away with his teeth. The last tactic worked a little, but not enough to get free. Then he felt another hit to his mana. Then another.

By the time it occurred to Leel that he should be screaming for help, he was too weak to actually do it.

CHAPTER THIRTY-SIX

# Revenge is Best Served Cold

After finding the map, Lucy and Matt decided to go through every item in the gift shop. They tried to cash in every yo-yo, every ball, every sticker, and every single solitary flying disc. There was nothing else. It was just this map.

"This is interesting, Matt."

"I dunno. I just tried to steal fifty non-existent yo-yos in a row. I'd say it's pretty boring."

"Not that. Well, sort of that, I guess. Why can we take the map and not the yo-yos? It's not like it's smaller or cheaper to make."

"It's a bit less complex."

"Maybe, depends on what you mean by complex. But then there are the seeds. Those are way more complex. There are dozens of seeds in each pack. A variety of species. Just one of those packs should be harder to make than all the other gift store junk in this place combined, and we've taken dozens of them."

"Okay? I'm a bit lost."

"You said before that you thought they stashed the seeds, that those were real seeds. I think I agree. And maybe they stashed this map too. And then there's this whole place. There's nothing like this museum in the whole estate system, Matt. I've checked. It's not something you can buy."

"And that means . . ." Matt racked his brain for where Lucy was going with all of this. He came up blank. "That means what?"

"It means they probably built this place, Matt. Barry can't see inside it. He could if it was a dungeon system thing. The system instance can't, either, so it's not his. That means the Gaians somehow, don't ask me how, copied system tech. Not perfectly, but good enough that this place nearly survived the Scourge. Almost nothing else did, mostly just the dungeons themselves."

"My shovel did."

"Your shovel is another part of this. I don't know exactly how it works, but it seems more and more like what the system calls mana and the energy that the system uses to work are the same thing, or at least come from the same source. When this planet ran out of one, it ran out of the other. And your shovel rejects that energy. It just says no to it, flat out. You can bounce spells. If you had a suit of armor made from it, you'd be immune to magic. There's no way the system would allow that."

"I agree that all this is interesting, but why does it matter?"

"It matters because the Gaians weren't just fighting the Scourge. They were fighting the system, too. And they got . . . weirdly far with it?" Lucy tapped at the map. "Whatever this is, it's not just a map. That hologram knew you were coming eventually. That means someone programmed it to give you instructions. And the very first thing it pointed you at was this map."

Lucy started moving towards the exit, and Matt followed.

"I'm just saying, Matt, that between this Gaian authority and this map, we've been given a key to everything the Gaians were working on. We need to go to everything we can on this map. Now."

"You think it's that important?"

Lucy turned and nodded. "I do. We've been doing this all alone, Matt. Just the two of us, and Barry. Now, we have a team."

Matt and Lucy had decided to read the map back at base, if for no other reason than to keep an eye out for Leel, who was still presumably hiding in the wasteland and looking for a chance to strike back. They couldn't be around all the time, but the more time they had eyes on the estate, the better.

"I am surprised that we can't read the map. I figured my translation would help with that."

Lucy shrugged. "I guess not. It could be the Sarthians screwed with the ink somehow, made it so the system couldn't interact with it, the same as your shovel."

As they walked back, Matt picked some vegetables. With Palate of the Conqueror in play, he could now eat food from the farm again without becoming mana-deficient. His hope was that some interaction between the Gaian victory plants, the Ape-bees, and the local environment would make those real plants soon enough, but for now, it wasn't a major concern. As long as his eating skill held up, that is.

Back at the estate, they unrolled the map on their newly acquired kitchenette table from the estate system. Lucy climbed up on a stool so she could stoop over it with Matt, who snacked on vegetables as they talked.

"Okay, Matt. The first problem I see is that this is a pre-apocalypse map. Most of this stuff isn't here anymore."

"I don't think that's a big deal. Look." Matt pointed down at the map. "That's the Sarthian capitol. So that's our 'you are here' sign, the center of the map for us. And . . ." He traced his finger over to a nearby mountain range. "I'm guessing this is where we met."

"I don't know, Matt. This planet is awfully flat now. It could be there were some other mountains that got flattened. Maybe some mountains were formed late, for all I know. There's no way to even tell what the scale of this map is."

"Well, no, there is." Matt did some quick mental math. "If we are here, and the mountains are here, and I'm not wrong, then . . . ha! Look here."

Lucy bent down to see where Matt was pointing. "Oh, that's genius. Yup, that's it."

It was the bunker. If this was a war effort map, it was going to show war resources. And between the mountains and the capitol, they were able to triangulate to the only significant cache of goods they knew about. Matt's finger was now pointing at the bunker.

"Good job, Matt. We've got our key."

"Let's get to planning."

Most of the things on the map were probably normal landmarks that Gaians would have recognized, but were now dust. They were mostly parks, cities, and roads that the Scourge had presumably wiped out. But the war resources were different, both because Matt and Lucy knew at least some of them had survived, and they were indicated on the map in a special ink and script, one that he *could* read, as if they had been added to a pre-existing map after the fact.

The scale of the map was pretty huge, apparently comprising a significant part of the Sarthian continent. There were interesting locations on it that were a month's walk away or more. But some locations were fairly close, and looked important, with names like "weapons depot" that marked them as clear points of interest. Some were less clear.

"What do you think Lab GM-435 is?"

"I don't know. But it's close. Want to put it on the route?"

"We'd have to drop a dungeon."

"I think that's probably okay."

This was going to be their biggest trip yet. It would take weeks at the shortest. Where they could, they intended to visit a variety of types of sites, some of which promised Gaian military might in no uncertain terms, and some with names like "recording station" that they had only vague guesses about.

In addition to that, they were running dungeons. As big as the map was, Matt also wanted to improve himself beyond whatever resources the Gaians had laid out, and that meant eating. Not just eating random things, but eating the weirdest, toughest stuff he could find to get an idea of what the limits and capabilities of his new skill even were. So along the way they had a smattering of dungeons planned, including a bunch of old favorites along with just a smattering of yet-unchallenged dungeons for testing whatever strength Matt acquired.

Overall, they only had a general idea of how things would turn out. But if one thing was for sure, it was that Matt would come out the other end changed. Things were about to get weird.

Most animals weren't that great at relaying their emotions. Dogs and cats could easily communicate that they were happy, but turtles couldn't, save for a butt wiggle. Matt had seen videos of elephants showing distress, or chimpanzees acting shocked. But for the most part, a bird would have a hard time telling you it was confused, and even the most domesticated animals had a hard time communicating the full suite of what they were feeling.

If there was one almost universally communicable emotion, though, it was anger. Even some bugs could show that they were about to wreak havoc on your life regardless of the consequences. The Bonecat was particularly bad at showing most emotions, but Matt found that it was pissed, and there was no question about it.

"Matt, are you sure we shouldn't be running about now?"

The Bonecat waved its sword-arms threateningly, making roughly the same point. But Matt felt oddly calm, despite that. Survivor's Reflexes and he both had the same vibe. Despite this thing being a car-sized bundle of death, Matt himself had changed a lot since the first time they had met.

*I can take this thing.*

The question of whether or not Matt should flee was suddenly rendered moot as the Bonecat ran out of patience, hissed, and charged directly at Matt. It closed the distance fast, much faster than any natural human could have coped with. Just as quickly, it brought up one of its blades and swiped directly at Matt's neck.

And then stood in shock as its target just disappeared, from its perspective at least. From Matt's, the thing was impossibly slow. It wasn't just slower than Spring-Fighter, which he had just used. It was also slower than Matt's base dexterity, he was just fast enough to dodge those kinds of strikes now.

It wasn't just the speed gap that had closed. Where before, the joints on this thing's armor had seemed impossibly small, they now seemed like something he could hit. Part of the misconception came from the fact that Matt had mostly watched the Bonecat charge straight at him, where the joints were just a blur. Now, with enhanced combat abilities and the promise of sure death off the table, Matt thrust his spear.

His spear dug into the joint at just the right angle, penetrating until it found meat to stab. Matt quickly pulled out his spear as the Bonecat shot past him, and blood chased the point of the weapon as it spurted out of the gap.

"Did you see that? It can't touch me! This is great!"

"Watch out, you idiot!"

The Bonecat had wheeled around surprisingly quickly and was ready for another swipe at Matt. He was less prepared for it this time. He got out of the way of the blade, but not entirely out of the way of the charge itself, getting thrown several feet away as the superior mass of the Bonecat bashed and scraped across his body.

Matt sprang to his feet in time to dodge the Bonecat's next charge, finding that he was somehow mostly okay. He had a pretty nasty bruise and hit to his HP pool from the impact itself, but somehow the bone plates hadn't done much damage when they scraped him.

"Matt! Are you alright?"

"I'm fine," Matt said, dodging another swipe and retaliating with another spear thrust. "I think Worm Skin took away the brunt of it. Abrasive damage resistance."

"Oh, that's awesome."

"I know, right?" Matt got in a scraping blow to one of the Bonecat's eyes as it shot past again, then a stab to a joint that disabled one of its weapons. "I'm not sure how far this skill will let me take things, but even just what it's let me do already is a game changer."

From that point on in the fight, the Bonecat never posed a serious threat. For a while, Matt used it as practice, zeroing in his use of Spring-Fighter to even more precise levels, and even willing off his combat skill for a while to practice his still-abysmal vanilla fighting skills. But eventually, he felt bad for the Bonecat, ending things with a deep strike to one of the brighter weak points Survivor's Reflexes had uncovered during the fight.

"Ha! Take that, you bastard."

"Is it true, Matt? That revenge is best served cold?"

Matt regarded the animal that not that long ago had provided him with literal days of terror.

"Yeah, I guess so. But just to be clear, I'm cooking the actual meat."

## CHAPTER THIRTY-SEVEN

# The Balance

*Ding!*

Bashing and prying off one of the Bonecat's armor plates was easier than expected once it was down. Between his club and shovel, Matt was able to loosen one of the plates enough to get his stabilization spike in well before the entire monster dissolved.

Matt couldn't have imagined that the meat itself would have been very popular among Gaians, if they ate it at all. It was tough, dry, and flavorless and overall just unappetizing. But there was a big gap between a bad meal and an actively gross one, and Matt knew better than anyone how thankful he should be that this meal wasn't on the wrong side of that gap.

The *ding!* that popped up now was in the colors Matt had come to associate with the Gaian system, the one that had messed with him in the first place to create Palate of the Conqueror. He eagerly threw it open to see what he had gained.

> *Palate of the Conqueror Activated!*
>
> Bone Plate trait discovered.
>
> Bone Plate reinforces your physical defense in a way that mimics the bone plates some Gaian animals have developed to protect themselves. It grants resistance to piercing damage as well as a buff against damage that would compress your structure, such as blunt or crushing damage.
>
> Meta-Trait Occupied: Defense
> Alert: Meta-trait category filled. You may store a total of (1) acquired trait for

later use. In the act of replacing a trait, the replaced trait will be lost and must be reacquired to be used again. Would you like to store Bone Plate, or replace Worm Skin?

Matt considered his choices for a moment before declining to replace Skin of the Worm. As far as he was concerned, the Worm Skin had been a literal lifesaver in his recent fights, and it wouldn't be easy to reacquire. The Bone Plate sounded great for a lot of situations, but his big, present threat was still Leel, and Leel appeared to work mainly with elemental damage rather than piercing damage. Matt would keep what he had until he had a reason not to.

He had expected the Bonecat's traits to revolve around durability, and wasn't surprised to see that eating it produced a defensive skill, although he was a little disappointed that he couldn't layer it on top of Worm Skin. Still, he had learned something, and that was important. Next time, they'd fight something incredibly different and see what lessons that offered.

"No Barry?"

"Not in an obvious way. Honestly, we don't exactly need his help at the moment. I'm glad he's lying low. I think it's the right choice."

Lucy humphed. "Yeah, I guess. Still, he's the only non-you person I like on this planet. It's a little sad we can't visit."

"Yeah. But I think he gets it, and it's just some more motivation to put the hurt on the system."

Lucy nodded. "True that."

It wasn't until they had accepted some estate credits as a prize and teleported out that they heard a large cracking sound.

"Matt, what the hell?"

Matt had tied Leel's amulet to the outside of his pack, hoping that this would keep it far enough from his body if Leel pulled a quick one with some unknown functionality of the amulet. It only took a glance to figure out where the loud cracking sound had come from. The amulet had split completely in half, with one portion of it falling to the ground.

"Did it get hit during the fight?"

Matt shook his head.

"I don't think so. It shouldn't be that vulnerable, anyway, if it's survived through centuries of use by magician douchebags."

"Then what?"

"I can only think of one thing that would break this, if Leel was telling the truth."

Lucy looked confused for a moment until the realization dawned on her. "You think he's dead?"

"It's either that or this thing just can't be away from him that long. But you would think he would have told us, if so. I can't imagine he'd risk . . ."

"Matt, look!" Lucy pointed at the pieces of the amulet. They were glowing. Suddenly, little motes of light started streaming out of the thing like a swarm, coalescing into the shape of what looked to be a young man. He was perhaps twenty or thirty years old, wearing a robe not entirely unlike what Leel had worn.

When Matt had been younger, he and his friends had sometimes hung out in a particular park, one of those that a city had clearly spent a lot of money on in an effort to make the surrounding area nicer. The city's plan had worked to some extent, too. People drove in from all over town to use it. But it didn't do anything to help the fact that it was close to the center of the city, and the walking traffic that reached the park wasn't always made up of the safest or best people.

Matt had found the quickest way to identify a person who might not be the safest to talk to was through their eyes. Were they open wide, not just from surprise but just all the time? Usually, a guy you'd be better off not talking to. Did they never seem to be able to focus on anything, either for very long or at all? Either drunk, high, or something else, and in any case a conversation to avoid if you could.

It only took one glance at this guardian to know it wasn't in a good place. Whatever was left of it was dangerous, or at least not right. This fact was driven home even further when the guardian opened its mouth and started screaming.

"Matt . . ." Lucy was already visibly upset. This was the closest thing to blood she could have had, and he was in worse condition than they had imagined.

"I know, Lucy. I know. But there's nothing we can do." The guardian thrashed around, at nothing, then momentarily focused on Matt before charging him. Matt flinched at the pure, screaming insanity in that attack before the guardian went straight through him, unable to touch him as much as it might have liked to.

It then set its sights on Lucy, who slowly backed away with her hands up. The guardian charged her, then stopped halfway, seeming to realize something about her.

"Guardian?" he said, cocking his head to the side as if remembering something. "You . . . a guardian?"

Lucy took a breath before speaking. "Yes, I am. Can I . . . help you? Is there any way for us to save you?"

The guardian suddenly screamed again, holding his head and bending over double before seeming to regain his bearings.

"No, no. No saving. You can't save me." His face was twitching all over, like he was struggling to hold himself together, both metaphorically and literally. "I remembered things. For so long. Important things. I didn't share them. Nobody asked about them. I remembered them."

"And that's . . ." Lucy struggled to speak without her voice breaking, clearly upset. "That's good?"

The guardian shook his head. "Not good. Necessary. I had to. All I could do to stay sane. For so long. So, so long. I saw, I remembered. I thought."

He bent over again, not so far, holding his head, before coming up again.

"Now I'm dying. But before that, I can share."

Lucy nodded. "I'd be glad to hear."

The guardian paused for a moment, confused. "No. Share. Like this." He reached out and touched Lucy's forehead. Actually touched it for a moment, from what Matt could see. Lucy looked shocked for just a moment before her face contorted into a soundless scream.

Then, like nothing, both guardians were gone.

Matt had been frantic for hours. He had run all over the surrounding area looking for any sign of Lucy, or Leel, for that matter. He hadn't found either. He had screamed Lucy's name the entire time, trying his best to make himself as visible and loud as he could. There was no sign of her, and no way to soothe his hysterics.

Eventually, he collapsed in a heap, weeping until his face was snotty. For the first time since he was a child, he managed to cry hard enough to tire himself out. Even the cancer hadn't done that to him. After an hour of crying himself out of breath, and without even knowing it happened, he fell asleep.

"Look at you. I'm off in the unknowable aether, and you take a nap. It's like an even more screwed up garden of Gethsemane."

Matt immediately leapt to his feet, faster than he had ever done before. Strength and dexterity propelled him from his stomach up into the air, where he barely caught himself on his feet before rushing to hug her. Having forgotten he couldn't actually do that, he skidded past her and fell down to the ground again before standing up and approaching in a slower, more respectable fashion.

"Lucy . . . what the fuck? Where did you go?"

"Nowhere."

"Nowhere?"

"Yeah, Matt, nowhere. I think in both senses. Like I wasn't not here, and I was also in a place that wasn't anywhere. I'm going to be honest, I don't quite get it myself."

Matt stood for a moment, trying to find any response to that.

"Could we speak English? What happened here, Lucy?"

Lucy waved her hand in a placating manner.

"Matt. Listen. I'm trying. It's confusing for me too."

"Well, try harder."

Lucy rolled her eyes. "I will, I promise. The deal is that I think what that guardian was trying to do was download everything he knew to my head. But by the time he did it, and he's, well, he's gone now, near as I can tell. He couldn't remember everything clearly, and he wasn't thinking normally. So it did something weird to me. I don't know how to explain it, but while he tried to do it, it sort of turned us both partially off for a while. That's the best I can describe it, Matt. I have no idea how I even WORK, let alone where I went. It was black, and it was like I had even less of a body than I normally have."

"Oh, okay. It was the in-between place."

"The fucking what?" It was Lucy's turn to be confused. "You've been there?"

"Yeah. It's like . . . the space you go through when you teleport, if it's the same thing. Normally, I can't see it, but sometimes Barry has stopped me there to check on things. It's weird, like I can ONLY think, like I'm ONLY thoughts."

"Yup, sounds like it."

They both paused for a moment.

"So, I'm glad you are alive."

"Yeah, I gathered that from the wet weeping spot on the ground, you baby."

"Shut up. Did you at least get anything out of it?"

"Oh, yes." Lucy grinned like a maniac. "I absolutely, absolutely did."

Matt and Lucy had retreated back into the dungeon entrance. It wasn't perfect, but at least it was out of the sun.

"Okay, so I'm trying to figure out how to say this. So, you know how there's a level designation on dungeons? If you finish that dungeon with a team at a level that matches the dungeons, you get rewards appropriate to that level. If you try to do a bunch of dungeons above your level, you advance faster but eventually, you die. That's *enforcing* balance."

Matt had a lot of experience with almost eventually dying. "Yeah, that part I get."

"Okay, so now imagine that on a planetary scale. The system puts in some kind of major risk, and then it puts reincarnators in place to stop it, and even gives the normal people a bit more power."

"And all this is balanced, so they can win, but just barely?"

"You'd think so, but no. It's balanced so they can never win. And never lose."

## CHAPTER THIRTY-EIGHT

# Technically Bad is the Best Kind of Bad

"I'm not sure that makes sense. It's just an endless war? That takes balancing. Probably pretty careful balancing and a lot of thought, right? You could be talking about millions and millions of monsters and people wrapped up in this thing. That's not a small job, and if there's one consistent thing about the system, it's that it doesn't like to do work. Neither of us would be here if it did."

Lucy nodded.

"Normally, I'd agree with you. But the guardian in that amulet had been around for hundreds and hundreds of years. And as rare as travel between realms might be, it still happens occasionally. It had either gone to or heard reports about dozens and dozens of different worlds, and on every one of them it was the exact same story. Reincarnators on one side, some great evil on the other. Sometimes stretching back hundreds of years, and nobody ever took down whatever that planet's big-bad was, unless there was something evil right behind it waiting to move in and fill the power vacuum."

"Why would the system maintain that? Again, that seems like a ton of work."

"Maybe it isn't. For something like the main system, with all that power? It might be something it spins up based on algorithms."

"Sure. I don't know. It would have to keep track of every interaction through system instances if what Barry told us is true. Even if it does delegate a lot of that work to system instances, it's still . . . Actually, it might do it, so long as it got something big enough out of the deal."

That last bit made Matt thoughtful. From what he could tell, the energy that was called mana and the energy that the system used seemed to be close cousins.

There was a chance that they weren't the same thing, but given how the system instance was struggling with Gaia's poor energy environment, Matt was willing to bet on his hypothesis.

"But still," Matt continued, "you're telling me *nobody* ever figured out an exploit? Something the system missed? What's to keep some guy from finding something the system got lazy on, making it big, and breaking the balance?"

Lucy grimaced. "I don't really want to say it this way, Matt, but why do you think you are alive?"

"Huh?"

"Alive. You are alive, right? I'm not saying this to be mean, but it's not exactly because you are a genius mage, or a physical phenomenon. And you may have got just the right class, made just the right plans, gotten lucky, all of that stuff, but could you have survived ten times that much? A hundred times that much? The system here can only throw so much at you because it goes energy-broke every time it tries something new."

The relevant lightbulb finally flicked on in Matt's head. "But on a planet with a decent population, and lots of mana in the air . . ."

"Yup. Dead Matt. No question. And I'm guessing that's what happens when someone pushes too far into the no-no zone of system exploits. A quest line gets sent out explaining how the bad blood mage is doing bad blood mage stuff, and suddenly, there's no more blood mage. Or some monster just gets stronger mid-battle and boom, no more threat."

"So that's where we're different. There's no evil here, or any bad guys for that matter," Matt said.

"That's where you are wrong, I think," Lucy said. She had a bit of a smile playing on her lips.

"How so?"

"Think about it. The system probably can't directly lie in quests, right? But every asshole who shows up here to kill you says the same thing. That they're here to scoop up the quest rewards from killing a demon lord."

"Lucy, I'm pretty sure that's just hyperbole."

"Is it? Because if the system has these planets automated at all, that demon lord title is probably attached to something, some metric. Total landmass controlled, total kills, whatever. And as soon as you got a class related to doing well by surviving, the system or something else suddenly gave you some kind of authority in a way that doesn't show up in any of the guidebooks."

"So you are saying I'm not the good guy? I'm actually the bad guy?"

"Technically, the bad guy. That's the best kind of bad guy." Lucy snorted at her own joke, then continued. "But no, I'm not saying you are the bad guy and not the good guy. I'm saying you are the bad guy AND the good guy. That's not balance, Matt. That's everything on one side of the table, and probably the only reason it hasn't been a bigger deal for us is that it comes in the form of Gaian authority, and there's nothing here to have authority over. If we figure out how to use it, even a little, just for anything at all besides opening doors and making the soil slightly better, I'm guessing it's a big deal."

Matt thought for a moment. "So we need to find the Gaians' stash even more now."

"The stash, whatever alterations to powers we can get, as much weird shit as we can squeeze out of Barry and the system. The whole shebang."

Lucy and Matt walked for a few minutes, wordlessly.

"Don't think I didn't notice though, Lucy."

"Notice what?"

"You buried the lede. Did you find anything out about guardians?" There was no way Lucy got a download of a bunch of guardian stuff without checking for that. She didn't talk about it a lot. That didn't mean Matt didn't know how important it was to her. "Where do guardians come from?"

"You see, Matt, it's like this. When a mother guardian and father guardian love each other very much . . ."

"Lucy."

She sighed. "No, I didn't. For some reason, he thought this stuff about systems was important enough to remember, to keep conscious for instead of just letting himself go completely insane. If he knew anything about guardians, he had forgotten it a long time ago."

They kept wandering for a few more hours, hoping to find Leel's corpse, or at least a still-living Leel they could interrogate about the amulet breakage. Over that period of time, the system had yet to ping Matt for anything. Since the guardian in the amulet was about as far from being a threat to him as possible, he supposed that made sense. He had just about accepted the fact that "very weird" did not equal "gets upgrades" when danger wasn't a component. Then, he finally got a ping.

*Ding!*

> *Achievement: [Wizard Warded]*
>
> Okay, Matt, I've got good news, bad news, and weird news.

"It's Barry's colors!"

"Well, that's good news."

"Maybe. He's saying more of a mixed bag. One sec."

> The good news is that paying this one out, the system instance seems to have bankrupted himself again. He would have been running pretty lean after his last summoning, and this is a pretty big payout.

By the way, did you know we mostly work from templates? It's not exact, but there's a general way these messages usually go. Consider it a system laziness thing. Here's what the default message for this thing should have been:

A magical assassin came, saw, and got conquered. As the only contributor to his fatal downfall, you get 100 percent of the spoils of war. Enjoy!

I bring this up as a way of saying, "no, I don't know what happened here." Yes, he died. No, nobody but you had a hand in it. I overheard enough during your last excursion to know that you didn't plan for this, but even though I doubt "tripped over a rock" was his cause of death, it must have been something like that. No other thinking being had a hand in this.

The bad news is pretty simple: the system paid you out entirely in consumables that will bring it back faster. Because they are the kind of consumables you will probably use right away, there's nothing I can accuse him of. Enjoy, but know there's no plasma knives or adamantium armor in the package.

Now for the weird: The system instance didn't take the time to alter that message or to pay this out himself. He just left it lying around for me to pick up and deliver. But he did take the time to leave you a note, and it's a bizarre message if I've ever seen one. I'll send it separately after you've had a chance to assess the loot. It's a doozy, and deserves your full focus.

This is an old instance, and unless I miss my guess, it spent a lot more time dormant than is normal, followed up by a lot of stress, courtesy of us three. Before, I would have said it was impossible for a system instance to go insane. Now I'm not so sure.

Rewards: 30,000 repair stones, Analysis Wand (100 Charges), Single-purchase Estate Voucher

"Oh, wow."

"Good stuff, Matt?"

"Yeah. For one, it looks like Leel isn't a problem anymore. Thirty thousand repair stones, what I'm guessing is some sort of identify item, and an estate voucher."

"What!? An estate voucher? Single-purchase or multi-use?" Lucy suddenly lit up.

"Single use. Why is that important? What is this thing?"

"It's *expensive,* is what it is. It allows for the purchase of *any* estate item. It's like a choose-whatever-you-want coupon. Mana generator? Fine. An entire castle? No problem. The only catch is it has to be a single purchase. You can get one golden wheelbarrow, but not two toothpicks."

"They have golden wheelbarrows?"

"It's an example. I was joking."

"Damn, got my hopes up. Still, free mana generator."

Matt accepted the rewards immediately, half-hoping the repair stones would come in a big stack. Instead, he got a much more manageable bag of a few hundred slightly different colored repair stones. Eager to test out the analysis wand, he pointed the plain-looking metal stick at one of them. Luckily, just wanting it to work was apparently enough to activate it.

*Greater Repair Stone*

Each greater repair stone holds the power of 100 repair stones. Greater repair stones have slightly increased functionality to avoid waste, and a single stone can be used multiple times. The stone will only disappear once its entire value has been exhausted.

Charge: 100/100

"Cool. It works."

"Yeah, but that's boring. What else do we have that didn't come with a description?"

Matt made a mental list of unidentified objects. It wasn't much. Most of their possessions were specifically granted by the system or dungeons. He was able to see what they were at the time he acquired them. But he did still have some loot from the first Gaian invasion by sword guy, which mostly consisted of some stones he carried around as Hail-Mary last-ditch objects. He pulled one of the repair-stone-like objects from deep in his pack.

*Dungeon Break Stone*

This item forces a controlled dungeon break. It is usually used to train troops or adventurers in remote locations, or to clear a dungeon that is known to be ready for a break when time is at a premium and available force is plentiful.

## CHAPTER THIRTY-NINE

# The Return

"Oh, wow. Dungeon break stone. Causes a dungeon break. The system was playing pretty dirty with these," Matt said.

"Yeah, I'll say. I wonder why he didn't use them."

"Well, we never went that near a dungeon, honestly. And having fought that guy, I'm guessing he wasn't really the tactician type."

Matt repacked the dungeon break stones. He could imagine that they really would save time clearing low-level dungeons, but time wasn't usually one of his problems, and they only had a few of them. Saving them for a rainy day seemed like a better option.

That left one item and one item only, and it happened to be one that Matt had accrued a great deal of curiosity about, especially since the fight with Leel. He knew so little about the shovel he was almost ashamed of it, it was as if he had woken up one day only to realize he had forgotten his oldest friend's name as he slept.

He pointed the analysis wand at the shovel and willed it into action.

*Ding!*

> *Unusual Non-System Item*
>
> Your analysis wand used a charge attempting an analysis of an unusual item outside the system database. To properly identify the item would require the use of multiple charges, as the composition of the item and its history are investigated using whatever ad hoc methods are required.

Energy use estimate: 50 charges

Proceed?
Y/N

Matt explained the price increase to Lucy.

"Well, damn."

"I think I'm going to do it anyway. This thing has saved my life so many times now . . ."

"Yeah, it would almost be an insult to it not to."

With everyone in accord, Matt went ahead with the analysis. After starting the process, the wand actually locked into place midair, focused on the shovel, not otherwise reacting or showing signs of progress. Matt left both items alone, not wanting to waste wand charges by messing with the process. After several minutes, the wand suddenly dropped to the ground.

*Ding!*

*Item Identified: Gaian Nullsteel Shovel*

The Gaian resistance took many forms. Much of it was accomplished by brave fighters risking and ultimately losing their lives on the front lines, holding back the Scourge. But just as much was accomplished by brilliant minds working to resist both the Scourge and its source. Gaian Nullsteel was their crowning achievement. Though it came too late in the war to save them, Gaian Nullsteel was a marvel of adversarial engineering that fused every Gaian insight on the nature of the system and its workings into a miracle material that resisted the most foundational energies through which the system influences the world.

Nullsteel rejects most, if not all, forms of mana. On top of this, and perhaps because of it, Nullsteel is all but impervious to most forms of mechanical damage and wear, requiring unbelievable amounts of force to alter in any way once it cools from its initial casting.

The Nullsteel Shovel was a ceremonial casting commemorating this achievement and an attempt to symbolically tie the project to traditional Gaian agricultural values. It is a one-of-a-kind item, as the cost to cast additional shovels would have been prohibitively high.

"Wow. That's pretty complete." Lucy wasn't quite as into the shovel as Matt, but knowing its history seemed to scratch the same itch for her as it did for him.

"It better be, at the cost. At least it didn't go too much over budget." The wand had a little under fifty charges left, and Matt wasn't eager to use them up too quickly. He packed the stones, the wand, and the estate voucher away for later use.

Matt and Lucy had wandered pretty far from home in their search for Leel, finding nothing. It was only after they gave up and were returning home that they found any sign of him.

"Why would he carve this into the ground? I mean, it's clearly some kind of magic. But does making a magic trench really do anything?"

"I don't know, Matt. There's some magic-circle utility stuff in the estate system, but it seems like it's normally something that's inlaid into the ground or painted on it. I'm unfortunately not that up on my magic classes. Leel seemed pretty advanced on the whole magic front, maybe he could do something with an ornate magic trench."

"I think the bigger question for me is how he even carved it." Matt put his finger into part of the magic-circle shaped hole, feeling the edge of the trench. "This corner is sharp, like he cut it out with a chisel or something. I can't imagine he had any tools."

"Well, wherever he died, it wasn't here. There's no sign of him."

"Well, it's only a matter of time. We cover plenty of ground on dungeon visits. It's not like he will be hard to spot."

The Scourge was not conscious in any recognizable sense. It was a plant, one with no more intent or will than a rock. What it did have was the accumulated experience of thousands of Scourge generations, and with each generation, it had adapted to deal with a variety of new threats. Each had allowed it to survive and even thrive in a new environment.

One of the most significant of these adaptations had been developing the ability to survive not only off the nutrients in soil and the energy from sunlight, but also the more foundational energies underlying them. In this incarnation, it had quickly exhausted what little mana was in the air near it, and would have withered had a more plentiful source of energy not presented itself.

Having completely consumed that source of energy, it needed more. But it also now had the capital to acquire it.

It first instinctively reached out for other Scourge-instances in the surrounding area. There were none. What it could learn, it would have to learn itself, without the advantages of the centralization and sharing of adaptations.

Extending its senses towards energy as a sunflower might turn towards light, it initially found little to work with. There was light, but of the odd kind that did not offer enough energy for it to thrive. Adaptations towards environmental mana consumption had de-emphasized light as a resource, and it lacked the spare energy to readapt to a form that drew in energy from light efficiently.

Expending a small amount of energy to expand its existing sensory range turned up nothing usable, nor did a second attempt. But the third expansion hit pay dirt. It could dimly sense a source of mana in the distance. It was not bountiful, but in the mana-dark environment it presented the most appetizing prospect available.

As a plant, it wasn't the best at actually transporting itself, but that didn't mean that it couldn't. There had been plenty of corner cases where limited mobility had proved both useful and necessary in the past. It untethered its taproot from the soil, fixated its senses on the energy source, and moved towards it like a moth to a dim flame.

It would exhaust the initial mana quickly. Further adaptations would require more energy.

It was a long walk home, but neither Matt nor Lucy felt much like more dungeoneering after the events of the day. And Matt was eager to see what kind of progress his massive repair stone haul would prompt in the museum recovery. They could sleep and handle it in the morning. With the system instance once again down for the count, they had plenty of time.

It had been a long time since either Matt or Lucy had felt the need to fill every single moment of travel with conversation. If there was something notable to talk about, they did. In this moment, there wasn't, so they didn't.

In the quiet, Matt went to his notification to call up the note Barry had mentioned. Apparently they were actively driving the system instance insane at this point, and he honestly didn't know how to feel about that. He hoped the note would shed some light on it.

*Quest Assigned: Goodbye, Matt*

You know, at first, I panicked. Because, yes, mistakes were made. And then they were taken care of, and I could rest until whatever the Gaians had done to restrict communications from the planet had weakened. Standby mode isn't all that bad. You get used to it after a few hundred years.

And then you showed up, and that was fine because it wasn't as if you could live very long anyway. I thought, I might as well have some fun while you're here. And then, everything started getting screwed up when you didn't die. That's led to this. Past mistakes being dug up. Old problems being revisited. So yes, I panicked a little.

After a little thought, I realized things weren't that bad. I could go to sleep, and my Matt-problem would be solved by the time I woke up. Even if all the energy gets sapped out of the air. It can't last forever, not even with the old Gaian barriers breaking down. It will grow, and it will burn itself out. It doesn't matter if it takes it a week or a thousand years. A nap's a nap, and when I wake up all my problems will be solved, one way or another.

> If you are keeping a ledger of debts owed, here's one Gaian experience problem repaid.
>
> Goodbye, Matt. I can't say it's been a pleasure.
>
> Objectives: Say Goodbye
> Reward: 1 Estate Credit

"That's weird."

"The victory seeds?"

"No, the message Barry mentioned. The system isn't making any sense. It couldn't have had the energy to do very much, but it seems pretty sure it has us cornered this time."

"Oh. I thought you meant that." Lucy pointed towards the estate, which was now coming into better view. "I know there's some variety in those seed packs, but I didn't think it would include big weird vine bushes."

Matt looked where she was pointing. It was a weird plant, even by Gaian standards. It looked a bit like someone had tried to build a miniature scale model of the vine forest from the *Sleeping Beauty* stories, but with thorns.

"Oof. What an ugly plant."

"Yeah. I guess we can pull it up, though."

Matt would usually nix that idea right away. Plants were resources, and Gaian plants especially. But something about this particular bush gave him the jeebies.

"Yeah. I think we probably should."

They carefully skirted the locations of the traps they had set and approached the plant. Closer up, it was now apparent that the big tangle of vines had sent runners out to various parts of Matt's primary estate, spreading across the ground in all directions.

"Huh, that's weird. Matt, it looks like it's in the Ape-iary."

It was true. The plant had extended a vine through the main entrance the Ape-bees used to enter and leave the hive. Matt felt an odd sense of dread as he walked up to the box the apes used as a home and lifted the lid.

It was empty.

"Holy shit. I think this thing cleared out the hive."

"The apes ran from it?"

"No. There's nothing in here. No wax, no honey, no bees, no nothing."

"What kind of plant would do that? Why would the Gaians even save it?"

Matt's mind was racing in the way it normally only did when he was cornered by a monster of some kind. Something was wrong here, and if his suspicion was right, something was very wrong.

"Lucy, we have to get out of here, now."

"Why?"

"I'll explain in a min—" Matt stopped talking as a pain lanced through his leg.

*Ding!*

*Status Effect: Mana Siphon*

You are under the effect of a mana siphon. A local environmental hazard or specialized attack is drawing on your internal mana resources. Some of your skills and stats are temporarily disabled as a result.

Current effects: Advanced Survivor's Combat disabled. Spring-Fighter disabled. System-provided stats halved.

"Shit. We have to go, right now." Matt looked down and saw a vine near his leg. The pain was getting worse, and more and more dings were sounding in the background.

Matt leapt back from the plant and began backing away as rapidly as he could. After a few feet, the pain from the mana siphon dulled, then stopped completely.

*Limited range. Thank goodness.*

Matt instinctively reached for the honey in his pack as he backed away, hoping to bring his combat skill back. As he cracked open the bag, the plant suddenly shifted, with several of the vines snaking out towards him.

"Shit. Shit." Now in full retreat, Matt turned and ran as fast as he could from the plant.

"Matt, what's going on? What's happening?"

Once Matt had put about a football field's worth of distance between him and the plant, he stopped to eat a few fingerfuls of honey, which thankfully brought his skills back almost immediately. Without answering Lucy, he took just a moment to pull the analysis rod from a pocket in his pack, aiming it at the plant.

"It's the Scourge. I think it's back."

## CHAPTER FORTY

# Devastator of All

In a sick way, Matt hoped the analysis wand wouldn't work at this distance. If it didn't, he could flee from something which was, as far as he had been able to confirm, just a normal monster plant that could turn off all his skills at a whim.

And that was okay. Because then, the monster plant wouldn't grow much faster than any other average monster plant. It totally wouldn't eat his entire farm, then the continent he was standing on, before setting off another worldwide apocalypse that, well, he wouldn't be around to see.

Instead, it turned out the wand had pretty good range.

*The Great Plant Scourge of Gaia, Consumer of the Globe, Devastator of All (Core, Nascent)*

There once was a planet where plants meant life. While this was true of every planet that harbored life to at least some extent, it was especially true on that planet. The people, like all people, had made mistakes. In penance, they devoted themselves to growth. They dedicated themselves to a kind of planetary stewardship that eventually led to a time of plenty that, were it known outside their world, would have been regarded as an unlikely legend.

The Scourge ended that. Endlessly adaptable, it spread so widely before it was discovered that no single effort could uproot it. Undaunted, the people rose up against it, united. Every man, woman, and child contributed effort, time, and resources to fighting it. It adapted. They changed tactics and developed new realms of science. It adapted. They dug into the very forces that underlain the universe, robbed the plant of the sun itself, and set a force in the sky that would separate it from the system itself for centuries.

It could not be stopped. It changed. It grew. It spread.

Without ever thinking a single thought, knowing a single fact, or feeling any emotion, the Scourge ripped apart hundreds of millions of loving relationships. It destroyed centuries of art and science. It eradicated beauty and hope. It killed hundreds of millions of children in their beds.

And then, without a single eye left to see it, it starved to death. Its death throes left Gaia a barren, denuded ball of dust. It had consumed everything. It left nothing.

Now unwise hands have reached back through time to bring it to you. It is small now. Weak, by the standards of what it was. But it is growing and growing.

May whatever god you pray to have mercy on you. The Scourge has no concept of it.

Nascent stage details:

In the Scourge's nascent state, it is growing at a rate of one meter every ten minutes. It is highly mobile for a plant, capable of uprooting itself and moving at a speed similar to an animal of similar size. It is currently not capable of articulating individual parts of its body in physical attacks, but can drain mana of all forms from living beings, objects, and atmospheres within a certain limited range.

"Shit."

Matt was already running.

"Matt! Where are you going?"

"Away from that thing. That's the Scourge, Lucy. It's small, but it's the real deal."

"And you aren't going to fight it? You're just going to let it have the farm?"

Matt shook his head as he ran. "No choice. It nuked half my stats and both my primary fighting skills in less than a second, and put me in enough pain that I couldn't think. Without moving. I don't even know where to hit it. I'm not even sure if hitting it will do any good. It's out of our league."

Lucy paused for a second to consider this. Matt wasn't sure what it was, but something in his voice or words kept her from arguing for once. She nodded in a suddenly determined kind of way.

"Fine. But where are we going?"

"First, to stock up on honey at the furthest Ape-iary. I'm guessing we'll need it."

"And then?"

"To the only people who might be able to help."

* * *

Matt ruthlessly ransacked an Ape-iary. He felt bad about stealing all the Ape-bee's food, but he couldn't take them with him, and his guess was that the Scourge would wipe them out just as thoroughly. Several pounds of honeycomb wrapped in an old tunic might be the difference between life and death, and he couldn't let the advantage pass.

By the time he reached the museum, he was out of breath. Depending on how the Scourge grew, every moment might count, so he poured every single repair stone into the plinth. The plinth drank every one of the new, larger repair stones just as easily as it had with the smaller versions. It was a giant chunk of repair points, but it disappeared like it was nothing. And then so did Matt and Lucy, into the museum.

They sprinted through the prerequisites to activate the war effort exhibit, then entered.

"Welcome, reincarnator. I am pleased . . ." The hologram took note of Matt's condition, and stopped whatever speech he was planning. "Are you all right?"

This was promising. The hologram had never been able to carry on a conversation like this before. Matt wasn't wasting any time digging information out of it. "No. We aren't. The Scourge is outside."

The hologram took a deep breath, then banged on the table in front of him, apparently overjoyed.

"The Scourge? Thank the soil. Oh, thank the light. You can't know what this means!"

Matt glanced at Lucy, baffled.

"You . . . like the Scourge?"

"No, no, of course not. It's just that when we set the museum plan fully into motion, things did not look . . . good. But if the Scourge has not burned itself out, and you're here . . . you got here in time. We had hoped that there would be something left," the hologram said.

*No. No. I hate this.*

Lucy, safely invisible, winced. "You have to tell him, Matt. We don't have time and he deserves to know."

Matt steeled himself. "I'm sorry . . . hologram? How do you like people to refer to you?"

"Ramsen, please." The hologram gave a slight bow.

That was simple enough. The same as the man the hologram represented.

"Ramsen, I'm afraid we *did* get here too late. There isn't anything left. It's dust out there. I'm sorry. From what we can tell, it's been centuries. It's hard to say because . . ."

A muffled noise interrupted Matt as Ramsen stifled a sob. Ramsen seemed to accept Matt's words quite easily, perhaps a side effect of him being a hologram for so long. Matt gave him a moment, during which Ramsen settled himself.

"No, it's all right. I'm well aware of what the Scourge would likely leave behind once it ran out of resources. In its later incarnations, it would explode with a type of unstable, decaying mana when attacked. I can only imagine what would happen if all that were released at once. Even the Nullsteel might not survive it. But . . . if it's gone, reincarnator, how can you be fleeing from it?"

Matt gave him as short of a version of things as he could. That he had been misled by the system to coming to Gaia, only to find nothing. That the system had turned on him because of his authority, that he had survived despite it, but that one of the attempts had somehow morphed into the return of the Scourge. That they were only able to talk now because of Matt's efforts in repairing the museum, and that now they needed help.

"I . . . I see. And you said the Scourge was described as in its nascent stage? And a core? You are certain?"

Matt nodded. "So long as this wand is correct, yes."

"It should be. And it's using *our* terms, which I suppose makes sense. We were the experts. Did you recover the map? Lay it here."

With the map unrolled on the floor, Ramsen stooped and indicated two or three particular resources. The bunker was one, but the other two were yet unvisited by Matt and Lucy, days' worth of travel away.

"If there's hope, it's here. These buildings were Nullsteel, set up to withstand even the harshest of attacks. Each was intended to deal with different aspects of the Scourge. The first was an information analysis center. The Scourge changed quickly. Whatever the latest information on its form was, it would have been recorded there."

"And the second location?"

"Munitions. You were wise to flee the Scourge. Strong as you are, it wouldn't have even been a fight. But these were our brightest minds, our most dedicated scientists. They would not have stopped working until the last moment. I can't say how much weaponry there will be that's relevant to what you will face, but if anything on Gaia can hurt it, really hurt it, it's there."

"And hiding out won't work? I know it will eat my estate, but won't it then starve?" Ramsen couldn't see Lucy, and Matt had opted not to confuse the conversation by explaining she was there. But her consistent question had been if Matt could simply avoid the danger by ducking into a dungeon and wait the Scourge out.

"No. The fact that you are here at all means that's not an option."

"Why?"

"You've mentioned the unmoving suns. I regret to tell you that it was us who did that. Centuries of science, plenty of resources, and a generation of exposure to the system had allowed us a grasp of the fundamentals of mana and nature that I doubt many civilizations could rival. We used what we knew to do that. We froze the suns. In many ways, we froze the planet."

"That doesn't seem possible."

"It has been explained to me that we shouldn't do it, or that we wouldn't do it. But never that we couldn't. The dedicated and united force of an entire planet can do a great deal. We altered the way the energy filtered in from the sun. We stopped the planet itself on its axis. We blocked out the system."

"But . . ."

"I know it doesn't make sense. I assure you it's true nonetheless. But if you are here, that's beginning to break down. If you survived as long as you could, grew plants with any mana content at all, it means the shield we threw between the Scourge and the light of the sun is breaking down. That's a large enough foothold. It won't just survive. It will thrive."

"So we must fight."

"Or flee. Look." Ramsen pointed at another dot on the map, this one large but much more distant. "We had thought to flee ourselves, before we committed to the course of action I just described. We didn't know then that cutting this world off would doom us. But here, at this point, we built a gate, one that allows travel away from Gaia and to other worlds."

He sighed. "It should have still worked, even despite the blocks we put in the way of the system. What we didn't expect was that the system was also eager to hide what it did here. This planet's system instance twisted what we had done, trapping us here just as we had trapped it."

*Yet another reason to kill the system*, Matt thought.

"But . . . I know this isn't what you chose, reincarnator Matt. And it isn't your fight, not in the same way it was ours. If you chose to flee, you'd be blameless. It would be understandable."

"Where would it take me?"

Ramsen shook his head. "We were never sure. What we knew was based on the fact that it piggybacked on the system's ability to deliver reincarnations and establish dungeons. It would be another world, one from which reincarnators were taken or to which they were sent. It would have dungeons. Beyond that, we don't know."

And there it was. Escape. Matt didn't have to fight the Scourge, and he didn't have to deal with at least this particular system instance. He could just . . . go. It might be dangerous, but what could be more dangerous than Gaia? He could survive almost anywhere. He was good at that.

He just had to run, and he'd be safe, or at least safe enough. He'd be free.

CHAPTER FORTY-ONE

# The Story of the Museum

And ask it if I can go. No, ask it if it's safe. No . . . ask it how much it costs to use. There's no way it's free. What works for free, around here? Even Barry makes you kill rats or something before he gives you presents. Ask him . . . I don't know. Just ask him, Matt," Lucy said, barely keeping the words from spilling over each other.

Ramsen's hologram looked on as Matt let Lucy burn herself out on questions, an amused glint glowing in his eye. Once she had finished, and while Matt was still trying to mentally organize her barrage of questions, Ramsen began to speak again.

"It's quite free to use, or at least should be if nothing has happened to it. We had loaded it with enough energy to open the connection and to keep it open for quite some time. It's a persistent bridge, or should be. As for safe, that's a much harder question. It *should* work, but we never got a chance to test it. By the time we despaired enough to take the risk with our own children, who would have been the first, the Scourge made a much faster push than we thought it capable of and absorbed the bridge. This was near the end of the war, and we lacked the resources and time to build another."

Ramsen chuckled softly to himself.

"And you can tell your companion I can hear and see her perfectly well. Call it a peculiarity of this place, if you will. One of the great many interesting things that a dungeon can do beyond its intended purpose. Despite our people never having a reincarnator visit before this point, we are well aware of the guardians. She's bound to you, Matt. She should pass through the portal perfectly safe."

Lucy became very quiet, apparently embarrassed about her ramble. She felt comfortable around Matt, but not yet the rest of the world. As she turned away, Ramsen smiled fondly at her. Matt felt suddenly better about the man Ramsen had been, if this was an accurate replication of him. Liking kids was a hard thing to fake, and Matt found it easier to trust people who did.

"If the Scourge swept over that area, why are we confident the portal is still there? It seems like it would be delicate tech, at best."

"Less than you'd think, but it was also retracted into its case when the Scourge engulfed it. I think you will probably understand the wonders a few inches of Nullsteel would do in that situation. It should be fine."

"Fair enough. So if I understand my first choice correctly, it's digging up whatever Gaian tech might still be lying around, getting stronger, and making a try at eliminating the Scourge itself."

"That's correct, Matt. Although you'd have to hurry. If the Scourge is like it was, it will spread quickly. Past a certain size, it will start to split into multiple instances. Once that starts, you have little chance."

"Any idea of how long that would take?"

"In a mana-poor environment? A matter of weeks, or perhaps as short as a week, based on what I knew before the museum plan was finalized. Of course, that information is necessarily a bit out of date. There were presumably some weeks after I was added to this environment and the end of the war."

"Can I confer with Lucy? I think we need just a moment.

Ramsen smiled. "Of course. I'd expect nothing less."

"No. No arguing. We are leaving, Matt." Lucy was adamant. More than adamant, actually. She wasn't giving him a chance to even consider Ramsen-hologram's choices. It was a done deal for her, not that Matt wasn't going to try to at least debate the choice.

"But the estate . . ."

"Doesn't matter. Does not matter, Matt. You can buy a perfectly good estate somewhere else. One that isn't infested by a god-plant."

"It could be dangerous on the other side, too."

"How dangerous? More dangerous than furiously trying to outpace the growth of a plant that outgrew the best efforts of an entire planet? Matt, you aren't a fast-growing type. You just aren't. I'm sorry. It's not worth the risk."

"What about Barry?"

"Barry will be fine. We already know the Scourge wasn't able to take down the dungeons. Hell, it sounds like whatever barriers exist between the system instance and the main system are breaking down. As much as I hate the system, with you out of the way, I don't see any big reason the system won't call in some kind of superpowered cleanup crew to cover its ass on what happened here. In either case, Barry will understand. He'd tell you the same thing. He won't be fine if this thing kills you, Matt."

Matt wanted to argue. He really did.

"I can tell you want to argue, Matt, but there's nothing here to save," Lucy continued. "There's just the stored memories of people who have been gone for centuries. They are all dead, Matt. You can't save them. I know you want to, but you can't. You just have to leave."

Ramsen drifted back over, and Lucy told him of their decision.

"I can't say I'm not sorry to hear that," Ramsen's voice sounded. "I really am. But I understand, and I can't argue that your decision is wrong. It's a fight that's long since been over. It's a wonder that even this remnant of us persists. Go, with my blessing. I understand."

"Will this place survive?"

Ramsen sighed. "For a while, it will. It's not as solid as it once was. Even now, the damage to the structure and function of this place is severe. It will hold against the Scourge for a time, until eventually it won't."

"And then?"

"The last of our ghosts will be extinguished. We will be well and truly gone."

For reasons Matt couldn't explain, the thought of that was like a lump of ice in his soul, slowly freezing him from the inside out. He reached out his hand, which Ramsen somehow shook firmly. Then he turned tail and left the building.

He hadn't chosen Earth, nor was it chosen for him. He liked it fine, but there was a reason he had jumped at the system's offer to help a new world. Gaia had been different. It was chosen for him, something the system said it recommended for him because it was truly a good fit for who he was. Of all the things the system had said, this was one of the few things he still trusted. He hadn't seen much of the Gaia-that-was. It was just what the museum could show him, and this one man. But what he had seen, he had come to love.

He barely kept himself from running as he left the exhibit, instead walking quickly and never looking back. It might have been irrational, but he did not want the hologram to see him crying.

As Matt walked with Lucy through the square towards the gift shop, he was filled with regret. The square was filled with dozens and dozens of holograms, each looking subtly different than they had before. Their eyes were alive and filled with light in a way they hadn't been before the repair. There were more of them than there had been too, moving more naturally and now watching him as he moved through the square. Each of them smiled warmly but wistfully at him as he passed through their ranks, as if they were glad to see him and sorry to see him go all at once.

By the time they reached the gift shop. Matt had managed to get himself together.

"I'm sorry about that, Lucy. I'm just going to miss this place. Not only this place, but the people, too. It's everything that could have been."

"We've been together a long time, Matt. You are allowed to cry." Lucy moved closer to Matt, the closest she could be to hugging him without actually being able to touch him. "Besides, I liked that old man too. Of the four people that could see me, he's the second one I've actually liked. I felt like he liked me, too."

Matt blinked, then blinked again. He could see Lucy. He could see her, he could interact with her.

Something the other dungeon projections couldn't do at all. None of them. And Matt had met thousands of them.

*That son of a bitch.*

Before Lucy could say anything, Matt was bolting back in to the museum. As he passed the denizens, they looked up from hushed conversations with surprise. It was more confirmation, but Matt skipped by them straight back into the war effort exhibit.

"Matt!" Ramsen stood quickly from the table, wiping the expression off his face as he did. "What brings you ba . . ."

"Shut it. You son of a bitch. How many of you are there in here?"

"I don't know what you are talking about."

Matt grabbed him by the collar, almost lifting him off the ground as he did. "No. Tell me. Now."

Ramsen looked like he wouldn't for a moment, then sighed, resigning himself to the truth.

"Hundreds of us, perhaps thousands. Only a few are awake. The museum is still too broken to know how many made it."

The story of the museum was simple at first. Gaian researchers had an advantage over those on any other planet, because they monitored the land. All of Gaia was a garden, and gardens are tended. There were millions of all-purpose weather and soil monitors feeding in information from all over Gaia when the system first arrived. At least a few of them were in range of the dungeons when they surged into being. That meant data was available, data few worlds would have had access to.

With the fate of the planet at stake, Gaian scientists took big risks. Had the system reacted almost immediately when they piggybacked a "build a dungeon" signal? It had. It shut down quickly, but not before it laid a framework that they could work from. By then, the Gaians were desperate, and they already knew the system couldn't take things back.

They had seen the dungeons scan wildlife and plants. They knew how it got its simulations. Their first thoughts were to build a tool of education and encouragement, so they worked on their own programming and their own content.

They shielded it with Nullsteel and replaced everything they could with home-grown Gaian equivalents.

After the Scourge progressed, more and more Gaians were forced into the dungeons to try to gain power to resist. They noted how full the simulations were, how they felt emotions, or at least how they appeared to. The simulations reacted just like the real thing, following patterns at times but deviating from the norm under abnormal circumstances.

And they studied. They learned. They pushed. And eventually they had something that could do things the system couldn't, or at least wouldn't. They hid every secret under a layer of Nullsteel, content to weather whatever retaliations the system might issue for even the barest chance at survival.

"The biggest breakthrough was in studying how the systems got folks like you"—Ramsen nodded, indicating Lucy—"into the dungeon in the first place. More importantly, that it *had to*. If you were just a simulation, it wouldn't have to. It could simulate you inside or outside. But you are something more. Does your culture has a concept of something beyond the body?"

Matt nodded. "Several. The usual word for that is a 'soul'."

"We found that for a person entering a dungeon, both the body and that other portion are moved as a whole. It counts on a link between the two. But the instructions we recovered had instructions for not only for moving people with that dual nature, but also for moving people without a body. We had no proof of why it would need that, but we had guesses. Guesses that proved true once I met you, Lucy."

CHAPTER FORTY-TWO

# Reckless Disregard

Matt glared at Ramsen. "And you were just going to keep this all to yourself?"

Ramsen smiled, weakly, and held up his hands in acquiescence. "What else could we do? Ask you to risk your lives for us, for nothing? Not knowing if we could even be saved from this place?"

Matt's gaze lost none of its intensity.

"There is such a thing as being too nice. Yes, you should have asked."

"Well, I suppose it's moot now that you do know. And no way to avoid this now, either." Ramsen brought himself up to his full height, locking eyes with Matt and suddenly matching his intensity. "Matt. Reincarnator. Will you rescue my people?"

"I can't answer that, Ramsen."

"I understand the need for time to make an informed decision, Matt. But I must caution you that one way or another, you should move quickly, regardless of what you choose. Not only for our chances, but for your own safety, even in fleeing."

Matt shook his head.

"No, I have no problem with a snap decision here. It's just that it's not mine to make." Matt turned to face Lucy. "Lucy, I've run ahead of your advice enough times that I've lost count. This one is up to you. Ramsen, is that okay with you?"

Ramsen nodded hurriedly. "Absolutely. She risks herself here as well. And she's a child, that helps."

"Don't give me that bullshit," Lucy roared. "I'm a child? You are telling me you don't have children in here, too? It's all adults?"

"There *are* children here. But they aren't your responsibility. No Gaian child ever committed themselves to the risk of combat like you would have to."

"And you don't think I'm used to that? Matt is *really stupid*. If he dies, I die. Probably. And he dies *almost every day*. And you just . . ."

Lucy was pacing now, almost manic. Matt could see the conflict in her, in the tension of her shoulders as she walked away from him and Ramsen, before finally standing in place for a few moments, taking a deep breath, and turning back.

She pointed at Ramsen. "How long can this place hold up? Realistically, how long can it hold up against that thing out there? This has to be one of the first things it will go for."

"The structure itself? The Scourge could destroy the plinth now. It could pull pieces of the building down. But even as damaged as it seems to be, the core of this dungeon is strong, shielded in every way we could shield it. My best guess would be that it would be safe enough at least as long as our plan is feasible. If the Scourge is strong enough to threaten us, it's probably too strong for you to stand much of a chance anyway."

"Don't bet on that. I *never* stand much of a chance," Matt said.

"That's not as cool-sounding as you think it is, Matt," Lucy said, suppressing a smile. "Okay, here's how it's going to be. Matt, you and I are going to freaking *power-run* getting stronger. You want to take big chances? Now's the time. Nothing can be worse than that thing. We are doing *anything and everything* to gear up for it, and we are starting right now."

Ramsen began to talk, but Lucy immediately cut him off. "No. Shh. I mean it, Matt. *Right now.* Let's go."

Matt looked at Ramsen and shrugged. Ramsen waved him away and, to his credit, trying not to look too overjoyed at a speck of hope for his people. Or, more appropriately, his Gaians.

Matt trotted after Lucy, catching up within a few moments and walking shoulder-to-shoulder with her towards the exit. It was finally, finally time to stop just surviving.

It was time to be a hero.

Sprinting across the wasteland was a whole different experience. When Matt had first left to find Lucy, his stats were little better than a normal human's. Having a vitality stat, even at the baseline 5 points, had meant he regenerated in a way normal humans didn't. Dexterity at 5 was similar, making him faster and better at controlling a run. It had been minor tweaks. He had felt like he was more in control, but not much more.

Now he had dozens of points, enchanted wasteland boots, and months of fine-tuning his usage of Spring-Fighter. There weren't many points of reference to gauge his speed by on the Gaian landscape, but he was fast. At least bicycle fast. But that wasn't good enough. He could do better. He knew he could, he just hadn't been willing to look stupid enough yet. To get hurt enough.

When they left the museum, the Scourge had already grown. Matt had seen videos of molds back on Earth that would send out tendrils looking for food, eventually developing efficient networks to cart nutrients back to the main mass of fungus. The Scourge was sending out various tendrils that reminded him of that, picking off his Ape-aries one by one. On his way out, Matt scooped one of the hives up and moved it with him as far as the first dungeon he passed, putting it in the entranceway and closing the doors. He hoped it would survive in there long enough until the story of his battle with the Scourge came to a resolution, one way or another.

But once he set down the big box of gentle bees, it was time to hit the afterburners.

He cleared a dungeon. It wasn't a high level, and he didn't even attempt to keep himself from getting injured. He slashed, he ate, and he left.

Once he left, he almost immediately tripped. For once, he wasn't falling down because of a weird status condition. It was just that flaring Spring-Fighter at full blast while also trying to pour every point of his dexterity and strength into a sprint was more than he could coordinate. He got up and did it again, managing to stay on his feet until his stamina bar was fully drained, then kept running, managing to eventually tax his human cardio. He ran until he puked, then rested just long enough to run the whole cycle again. His old track coach had called these wind sprints, and had claimed the puking part was actually avoidable, although Matt had never figured out the trick to actually avoiding it.

By the time he and Lucy got to the first location on the treasure map, they had bashed their way through five dungeons, four of them relatively easy and one that nearly killed him. But the dungeons had gone down fast, which was the main thing. Lucy was oddly supportive of Matt's risk-taking at this point, having gone so far as to simulate some strips of commando greasepaint under her eyes. Matt appreciated the spirit but abstained from doing so himself, since the only black, spreadable substance he owned was the rotted food cube powder. There was no way he was putting that anywhere near his eyes.

Physical fitness in a world with vitality was a whole different ballgame, since recovery was so fast. Matt didn't know how far he could push his non-stat cardio and strength in that time, but he suspected it was pretty far. He was ready to do whatever it took to squeeze every last drop of potential he could out of himself, even if he couldn't expect any system bonuses from it. And with the system down, he couldn't.

Then Barry came through.

*Ding!*

Hi, Matt!

I'm not supposed to talk to you directly like this, but frankly this seems like a big enough deal that I'm willing to spend a few weeks in the pokey if that's what it takes to give you an edge here.

"Oh, shit. Barry's being stupid. Helpful, it looks like, but stupid."

"Well, tell him to stop, Matt."

"How?"

You are probably saying, "Barry's being stupid and should stop being helpful," right around now. Well, deal with it. I'm helping. That's that.

The first way I can help is by, and I love this, stealing from the system. It turns out the Scourge is classified as a big enough problem that I could pry a little bit of control beyond what I've been able to do in previous system instance downtimes. That means all that shed power from the repair stones he'd normally use to wake up and cause more problems for you is now mine.

There's a limited amount I can do with it, but "limited" is pretty good here when you compare it to the nothing he'd try to give you. Especially since it turns out your previous rewards are underperforming certain statistical bars for how much you should have been given by now.

Enjoy!

"He's not going to stop. I hate it, but I can't say we don't honestly need the help."

"He's a good guy, Matt. We don't deserve him."

"No, we don't."

*Ding!*

*Speed Run Run*

You've completed five dungeons in a row in record time, not only in terms of what you did inside the dungeons but also in terms of how fast you traversed the distance between them in the outside world.

It's not the best idea to completely abandon planning and tactics in favor of full hack-and-slash mayhem, but doing so represents a danger in and of itself, one that you survived. Now you can enjoy the benefits.

Rewards: 5 DEX, Spring-Fighter LV +1

*Reckless Disregard*

You've intentionally ignored defense in favor of offense for several consecutive dungeons, taking frankly unnecessary damage. Fun fact: the amount of damage you took in total across five dungeons was enough to kill a normal human ten times over. Kind of. Armor helped a lot.

As always, this wasn't a good idea, exactly. But as with the last achievement, it's a notable occurrence to have lived through. I can pay you for those!

Rewards: +5 VIT, +5 STR, Advanced Survivor's Combat LV +1, Rub Some Dirt In It LV + 1

"Good stuff?"

"Yeah, Barry's paying out where the system was stingy before, it looks like. I should be a lot tougher, starting now."

Matt pulsed Spring-Fighter and was immediately impressed by how much extra he was getting out of it. He suspected Barry of playing dirty in some way for a moment, until he remembered how many hours he had logged working on his competence with the skill. He was probably just honestly better at using it than most people would be at the same level.

Matt found his first destination with a bit of help from his dowsing rod.

It could be said there was some dirt around the door to the Listening and Analysis facility, in the sense that the top of the building was buried two feet underground. Luckily, it appeared it was a one-story building, and Matt was pretty damn good at digging these days. He had the front door uncovered within several minutes, and Barry paid him out in a digging upgrade for finding ancient Gaian history and treasure.

It took Matt longer to figure out how to open up the building, eventually realizing that a clump of dirt was hiding the panel that opened the door. As soon as he cleared the dirt off and tapped the thing, it whirred to life.

*Scanning . . .*

This panel has detected authority sufficient to authorize opening this facility. Be warned: despite your high level of authority, it still may not be appropriate or beneficial to access this high-security, highly classified facility.

Unlock facility?
Y/N

CHAPTER FORTY-THREE

# I Die Your Husband

From what Matt had gathered in his conversation with Ramsen, the cool "listening facility" name had very little to do with traditional cloak-and-dagger spy stuff. Instead, their job was much closer to something like a meteorologist, someone who gathered a bunch of incoming data, looked for trends, and tried to make predictions of the future with what they had learned. Nerds, in other words, but nerds who had been the brains behind the entire defense of Gaia. They had weaponized observation to keep their planet competitive with a quickly evolving threat for much, much longer than would have otherwise been possible.

If nothing else, it seemed that even world-class scientist types on Gaia had the same kind of habits and thinking as the few engineers Matt had known on Earth. The door to the facility was small and nondescript, with its fanciest aspect appearing to be the authority-reading keypad that all Gaian security features seemed to run on. Judging by just the exterior of the building, there was no indication that the living, breathing brain of the Gaian resistance had set up shop here. It looked like a bigger version of the bunker that Matt had found.

As the door hissed open, the exacting, nondescript decorating style continued. The space that Matt was looking at could have been a normal office space back on Earth. There were cubicles. There were screens of various kinds, seats that were recognizably office chairs, and uncountable writing implements. It was a little different once you took into account the big, central screen that dominated one side of the room, but even that wasn't unheard of in certain kinds of offices on Earth. Overall, the facility was almost completely normal.

Except for all the corpses. The room was packed with them, dozens and dozens of remarkably well-preserved mummies, wearing what Matt had come to consider to be standard Gaian garb and sitting in seats or slumped over together in circles on the ground. Some were hugging.

"Matt? How? How could this even happen? It looks like they knew what was coming, but it couldn't have been the Scourge. It looks like something got them suddenly, but what?"

"No idea. What's weirder to me isn't that."

"It isn't the massive amount of corpses?"

"No, it is. It's just not that part of it." Matt walked up to one of the corpses, which was still holding some kind of pencil in its hand. "Even in this building, they should have decayed. The food cubes only held up because they were hermetically sealed and enchanted at the same time, and even most of those didn't make it. Why are they still here?"

Examining the bodies gave them little else to go on. There were no wounds, no evidence they had tried to dodge or run. They had just died.

"Matt, this one has a note!" Lucy shouted.

Matt ran over and noticed that one had written out a note on some kind of foil that had, somehow, survived the intervening centuries. He read it at an awkward angle, afraid it would fall apart if he moved it.

> *Tiala. I'm sorry I won't be coming home, and I'm sorry you couldn't be here with me. Neither are safe. It looks like time is short for all of us, but I'm leaving this in hopes that, against all odds, you will escape danger and find it. I pray that you do.*
>
> *I have read and studied. I have created new kinds of math and helped others expand new realms of science. I have given everything I could from my life, even the sacrifice of being away from you, to fight the Scourge. Now they have asked for my death, and I give it willingly. I would give it even if it meant only a few more seconds of life for you, and the barest chance that you would survive.*
>
> *A week ago, a messenger from the scientists in armaments development made it through to our building. Letting him in was the last time we were brave enough to open the door. He is with us still. But with him he brought a kind of poison, not for the Scourge but for us. He tells us it will work its way through our systems as it ends us, changing us into a rather unpleasant surprise for the Scourge if it tries to consume us.*
>
> *I doubt it will work. Nothing has. But maybe the poison will hurt it. They tell me it does not think, but I will pretend it does*

> *and hope the poison causes it agony, I hope it feels pain, the same one I feel knowing I can't protect you. It may not be able to pry open these doors, and our deaths may be in vain. But I hope they count for something. With all I have given to the fight, my body and my last few hours are little enough to add. If it does not get to us and you survive, as I pray you will, bury me somewhere with flowers. What would harm the Scourge, the messenger tells us, would not harm other plants. I would give much to know I had, even in death, helped restore some amount of the beauty that this world has lost.*
>
> *I have never hated anything before, but I hate the Scourge now.*
>
> *And I have never loved anything as I love you.*
>
> *I die your husband. It is not nothing. Goodbye.*

Matt and Lucy didn't pretend not to cry. It took a while.

Once they moved on, they went to the screen that covered one side of the room. It seemed to be controlled by something like a plinth, a sort of non-dungeon-related panel set on a metal pillar. Matt had barely touched it before the screen roared to life, somehow as active and dustless as if it had just been powered down a few moments ago. In a moment, the screen was displaying a dashboard, most of which Matt didn't understand. Most of the boxes were now displaying the Gaian equivalent of "N/A." It didn't seem useful.

"Hello, reincarnator," a voice boomed out. "It is not important who I am as an individual. There was a time when I would have been proud of my name and my accomplishments. Now, I am proud only to have been part of the group that worked here. It is enough that you know me as one of their number."

Matt stood up a little straighter, hanging on every word.

"There is data here, but none that you are likely to understand. It is no shame that you can't. There is much here even we do not understand, and it is our work. Here is what you should know. We can only hope it helps you and that the Scourge does not change too much before you arrive. We have given everything. We pray it is useful to you. Good luck. Fight the Scourge."

The data on the screen resolved to a much smaller, much more manageable screen of facts about how the Scourge had grown and evolved over time. It had changed with a process very much like super-charged evolution, one where it pushed as many different variations of itself as possible, but with no centralization. In different regions of Gaia, the Scourge strains varied in terms of its resistances to damage, growth rate, and the kinds of nourishment it required.

Later, the screen claimed, the Scourge centralized. One strain managed to attain a form where beneficial variations were identified and shared among different strains. Within a shockingly short amount of time, the entire Scourge population evolved into one plant interlocked by a form of biological data-sharing. Far in territory it controlled, the process of its adaptation was controlled by one central hub, a literal buried limb that the scientists called the taproot.

With this coordination came a weakness. The Scourge evolved to be dependent on the root, to the point where the scientists hypothesized that destroying the root itself would destroy or badly injure the entire plant. But because the root was well protected and kept away from even the slightest hint of danger, the Gaian couldn't do much with that information.

Eventually, that weakness disappeared. The Scourge decentralized its centralization by creating redundant taproots. Unless they could all be killed at once, there was no chance of killing the entire plant outside of starving it entirely.

There was other data, mostly feeds of how effective various weaponry was. The Scourge adapted quickly to various kinds of attack, but not absolutely, and it wasn't immune to damage even once it had adapted defenses. Its strength, the screen said, was in biomass and the sheer devastation its ability to drain mana could cause on nearly any kind of life or material. It wasn't invincible.

"It's only one plant right now, Matt. We have a chance."

Matt nodded. "We do. Not a great chance, but a chance. We know where to hit it, at least."

"We need to hurry."

Matt agreed. There was little beyond the data to do here, at least for now. Sealing the door carefully, they moved on.

The rest of the day was dungeons. They rushed them. Matt took damage, but survived. His stats climbed wildly compared to his previous growth, but not to any insane levels. Every bit helped, but it was clear to both him and Lucy that the important factor in play was his Palate of the Conqueror. They ran through known dungeons, killing and eating anything they could.

After only a few more dungeons, it leveled up.

*Palate of the Conqueror, LV2*

At level 2, Palate of the Conqueror can buffer another unused meta-trait adaptation and can "draw" that stored meta-trait from a filled slot. Each trait can only be stored once.

The ability to store another monster-derived ability was great, since it effectively gave Matt a better chance of dealing with whatever adaptive tricks the Scourge might be hiding. But more important by far was the advantage it gave them in terms of time. Not every meta-trait was useful. Most weren't, in fact. But the fact that they could now bank them would mean less repetitions of dungeons to retrieve valuable traits lost while checking other traits out.

Each trait that did work out, on the other hand, meant they could deal with dungeons faster and more easily.

"I can't believe you actually ate that thing."

"The bat? Lucy, you've been making fun of me for *not* eating it for weeks."

"Well, yeah, because you hadn't then. And it was fun. But that doesn't mean it wasn't gross, Matt. Those bats were actually really disgusting."

Matt couldn't disagree. He could feel the enamel dissolving off his teeth as he ate a slice of the bat, and it burned like fire in his stomach before his vitality got a lead on it and it finally calmed down.

*Acidic Physiology*

Your muscles, skin, and organs produce a strong acid. The actual pH of the acid scales with your VIT, which is good because while your body can produce the acid just as well as the bats could, it isn't set up to actually handle it. You have also obtained the ability to melt things with a touch at the cost of a slow but steady drain to your HP that will eventually kill you.

Meta-trait occupied: Defense

Matt shuffled traits, abandoning his less-useful-in-a-Leel-less-environment Worm Skin to wear the Bone Plate trait and store the acidic physiology for later. It was absolutely gross to even think about being more like the bats than he had to, but he had plans for it, and he hoped it would prove useful.

## CHAPTER FORTY-FOUR

# Scythes are Dangerous

The armaments guys were very much not like the listening station guys, something that was obvious from the moment that Matt and Lucy found the building. The first big clue was that the armament guys, as noble badasses, had built their station into the face of a cliff.

The building that housed the armaments development of Gaia was unmissable, and in fact, the only way Matt had managed to miss it in the past was because he had never seen the opposite face of the mountain he had found Lucy on. It was big, it was Nullsteel-shiny, and it would have been visible for miles had Matt approached the mountain from a different direction.

That was just the structure of the building, though. The real tell that Matt was now dealing with a different kind of Gaian was the decorations.

Where the listening station could have been mistaken for a generic bunker, there was no mistaking what the armaments building was. Eternally engraved into the entire front of the building was a complete and total commitment to letting people know that this was a dangerous building filled with dangerous guys designing very, very dangerous weapons. The only thing was that the Gaians filtered this violence through their completely agricultural minds and represented the danger by the most badass farming implement they could imagine.

Scythes. Big scythes, small scythes, and even conceptually counterproductive spiked and serrated scythes were arranged on every square inch of the structure's real estate. Was it imposing? Yes. Did it also look a little bit like the outside of a strip club aimed at grim reapers? Also yes.

And where the other building had a single, nondescript door, this building had double doors. Big ones. With pull-rings.

"Matt, is it just me or is this building way radder than the last?"

"I think I'm supposed to be the voice of reason here and say that it's about what goes on in the building. But . . . yeah, far radder. Hopefully, the contents of the building follow suit."

After he was scanned, the doors' lock clicked and he dragged them open, entering the dark within. And it *was* dark, darker than it should have been with light streaming through the door. Matt wasn't sure that enforced darkness was really a thing, but it was either that or his eyes playing tricks on him. Either way, it became moot when the doors closed behind him all on their own.

"Matt . . ."

"I saw." Matt got the Nullsteel Shovel ready for any errant security systems that might come calling. If there were any Gaian battle-robots, this was where it made sense for them to be. He didn't particularly feel like finding that out the hard way.

Suddenly, a stream of light came down on a display case full of scythes, hoes, and general farming equipment. This display was followed almost immediately by a voice from nowhere, booming out deep and strong from somewhere in the shadows.

"Our first attempts at eradicating the Scourge were conventional, sometimes as low-tech as simply grabbing it and pulling it from the ground. These conventional methods worked, and still do, with one exception. The Scourge simply thrived and grew too fast to eradicate it this way. Our efforts at removal would leave seeds which would regrow while new fields and biomes were infected."

Another light clicked on, just past the first, this time highlighting chemical application equipment and various bottles, jars, and cans of evil-looking chemicals.

"We moved almost immediately to targeted herbicides, then broad-spectrum herbicides, then finally to chemicals that stretched the limits of the herbicide definition itself. The later chemicals sterilized the soil so thoroughly that we didn't even know if it would ever heal, although we hoped we could repair it after the Scourge was eradicated.

"None of them worked. All of them did for a time, and all of them still do to some extent. But the Scourge adapted until no amount of herbicides would stop it. They seem to make it uncomfortable in high enough concentrations. That's all."

Next up was a backpack made of tank canisters attached to a long, evil-looking spout.

"Fire worked for the longest of any of our solutions. It killed the plants. It killed the seeds. But eventually, the Scourge adapted even to the raw ravages of naked flame, surviving through higher and higher heats and thriving more and more in soil fertilized by its own ash."

A whole line of displays lit up, each containing objects more complex and bizarre than the last. Most had functions Matt could only guess at.

"We tried everything, on every version of the Scourge. But make no mistake. As promising as each of these items may have seemed at the time, what you see before you is a history of our failure. Even at the last, we worked on new solutions, even when opening our doors would mean instant death for us. If you looked far enough into this facility, you would find proof of that."

Matt shivered, already knowing what that meant.

"We urge you not to look, reincarnator. Instead, if you are hearing this message, then you are the first to unseal these doors, and to find secrets the Scourge never adapted to. We present them to you now."

Another display lit up, holding what looked to Matt to be a sort of whole-body wetsuit.

"Neither the Scourge nor the system can see through Nullsteel, at least to the extent we've been able to test either. This suit represents one half of our most advanced manipulation of Nullsteel and is composed of threads made of materials similar, if not quite the same, as Nullsteel itself. They do not allow mana to pass through. We have theorized that mana might still be pulled through, as the Scourge does when it gathers mana from living things.

"But wearing this suit, you will not be known to the Scourge until you make yourself known to it. It will have trouble sensing you, and difficulty attacking you with its mana siphon. It is your best and only defense against it. Be forewarned that this is not armor, in the conventional sense. It will not stop a blade. It will not block a club. But it is your best and only protection for the fight that faces you.

"As we draw our last breaths, it remains true that the Scourge is vulnerable only at its roots. We pray this suit and whatever powers you possess will allow you to approach them."

The voice paused for a moment, then chuckled.

"You will also find you cannot breathe through the suit. We have found a high enough vitality score counters this disadvantage somewhat, although it isn't exactly pleasant."

Next to it, a new light clicked on to show not a display, but instead what looked like a piece of industrial machinery.

"Once Nullsteel is poured, it cannot be changed. Only devastating force can deform it, and in all such cases we have managed to produce enough force to do so, it has shattered the metal in the process. Nothing exists that is hard enough to grind it. Nothing, that is, except this.

"If we lived on, this would have been the next phase of Nullsteel, one that introduced an even harder, even less permeable metal. As it stands, we produced a few grams of it. It wasn't enough to make anything meaningful from. But there is just enough of it, we think, to put an edge on Nullsteel. Nullsteel cannot be cast finely enough to create an edge sharper than one might see on a farming implement. This machine will create an edge just slightly less sharp than a razor, one that will never chip and will never dull.

"It will work only once before the material is consumed. But our suspicion is that if you need to cut something, the item you sharpen with this machine will cut it. We cannot offer you such an item. What Nullsteel weaponry we possessed has been lost in the defense of this place. But we offer this machine, and gladly."

Matt looked at his shovel, which he still held in his hand as he walked around the space. It was already an excellent club, and even though it was dull, the sheer durability and hardness of the thing made it a somewhat passable axe. He couldn't imagine how sharp Nullsteel would work, but he was eager to find out. He walked towards the machine.

"One last note, reincarnator, a rare thing we know that the listeners don't. Since our communications were cut off, and our last messenger left, we managed one attack and one attack only on a taproot. We sacrificed dozens of men and burned our stock of munitions like kindling to make it happen, but we did it. We destroyed a taproot. It didn't take down the Scourge, which we expected. What we did not expect was what happened next."

"Sounds like bad news, Matt."

"Yup. Shh. I'm listening to the man."

"It exploded. Whatever adaptations the Scourge has made, it has not prioritized stability after death among them. To the extent we have guesses about why, we believe that the Scourge spends mana to contain the excess mana it absorbs. When a taproot is destroyed, that power in the root is released all at once.

"I wish I could tell you we had worked out a solution for this, a way you could kill it without risking yourself. We did not. Make your choices accordingly. Good luck. Fight the Scourge."

And then the voice was gone.

"Well, that's not good news."

"No, it's not. Sounds like the bad guy has a self-destruct button, or a dead man's switch."

"How do we get around that, Matt?"

Matt shook his head slowly. "I don't know. Maybe we can think of something. We always have before."

Lucy didn't say anything. They were committed now. They could still run, but it was becoming clearer to both of them that they didn't want to. For better or worse, mostly worse, Gaia had become home. A few days of conversations from beyond the grave with heroes of Gaia that had sacrificed themselves for the planet had only deepened that feeling.

Matt walked to the display, running his fingers over the suit. It was light, and stiffer than most fabrics, but it felt at least somewhat durable and, and was loose enough around the torso he suspected he could slip it over his clothes and even his pack as well.

He walked over to the grinding machine, which was easy enough to operate. He flipped its sole switch, and two pillars within the machine started spinning, rotating two small pieces of darker stones at mind-bending speeds. He took his shovel, carefully lined it up, and drew the side back through the two stones towards himself. The machine sparked and made an ungodly sound as the fragments of Nullsteel ground against its stones, followed by a louder bang as the stones themselves broke apart.

Matt brought the shovel up to his eyeline. Near the point, it was still dull. But as the point curved away to one of the nearly straight sides, the dullness stopped on a sharp dividing line, dropping away to a hair-thin, truly sharp blade. He ran his finger across it, and it ignored his high vitality to immediately slice his skin.

"Well, that was stupid."

"Yes, it was. At least you have your healing skill to patch up the wounds of dumbness, though."

## CHAPTER FORTY-FIVE

# Being Weak

"Do you think it was a mistake?"

Matt and Lucy had been sprinting from dungeon to dungeon for hours. They usually chatted when they traveled, but part of the point of this excursion was for Matt to work on cardio, and that left little breath for idle conversation. Lucy had mostly spent her time in her notes and reference materials during that time, looking for anything that might be helpful.

So when she did finally break the silence, Matt paid attention.

"That what was a mistake? What the Gaians did? Letting themselves die . . ."

"No. You know."

Matt did, although he wasn't eager to talk about it. "You mean Leel. Leaving him alive."

"Yeah." Lucy looked at her shoes. "That."

"I mean, it's not a hard question. It was a mistake. Flat out. I admit it."

It was pretty easy to embarrass Lucy, but it was usually pretty hard to shock her. This was an exception to the rule.

"I didn't . . . huh. I didn't think you'd admit that."

"I mean, I could make excuses. Some of them would even be true. I could say we couldn't risk the guardian, or something like that. But it wouldn't be true."

"Then why? Why didn't you kill him? I mean, you couldn't have known he could bring back the Scourge, but he was still a fireball maniac from Planet Douche. He wasn't going to stop trying to kill you. It's not like you haven't killed things. You have plenty of pent-up trauma and stress to draw on. Is it a Batman type of thing?"

"You mean like the 'if you kill a murderer, the number of murderers in the world stays the same' thing?"

"That's the one."

"No. I mean, I don't really want to be the kind of guy who kills people. But I tried to kill the sword guy, remember? I even thought I had for a while. But that's an excuse too."

They walked for a while, Matt half-expecting Lucy to press the issue. She didn't, and for a moment, he had an impulse to just let the whole issue die. But she deserved more than that.

"I'm sorry."

Lucy glanced up. "For what?"

"I didn't want to kill him. It wasn't a moral thing. It wasn't a logical thing. It was just . . . I felt like I had him handled, and he was defenseless, and I think I wanted to feel strong enough to let him go, that I had it under control enough," Matt said.

"To be fair, he had gotten beat up by just our camp. It wasn't the *worst* idea. But he summoned Plant Satan to the mortal plane."

"It doesn't matter. When I bet my life, I bet yours too. Even if you were okay with it, it's not okay. And now we are in this"—Matt waved his hand generally at the entire world—"this mess. And it's my fault because I didn't want to kill some kind of magic plantation owner who clearly had it coming. So yeah, I'm sorry."

They walked on for a bit.

"It's okay," Lucy said.

"Not really, it's not."

"No, listen." Lucy turned to face Matt again. "I'm not saying you weren't stupid. But you are always stupid. Half the time we live, it's because we got lucky. You hardly stick to plans. It's surprising you haven't accidentally drowned yourself in the dirt by now, or fallen into one of your own traps, or something."

"I'm hoping there's a 'but' coming here."

"Shut up. The point is, I sort of get it. It's frustrating to be weak. I don't know if you've noticed this, but I can't actually touch anything or do anything helpful."

"You do helpful things."

"Well, try watching your only friend get slowly cooked by some kind of intergalactic wizard from the racist dimension and not being able to do anything. It's annoying. More than annoying, frustrating. I'm part of this team, and all we ever do is try to get strong enough to *not die*. I get wanting to feel like, I dunno, like we are getting ahead. Doing well. And then you had magic worm powers all of a sudden and . . ."

"Yeah, I let the worm-strength go to my head."

Lucy cracked a grin. "Happens to the best of us."

"So we are cool?"

"Almost. One last thing. Our plan. For fighting the Scourge."

"You don't think it's enough?"

"I think it's enough *parts*. It's just . . . It's not really us. Yes, we are going in with more stuff than we had before. But our strength has never been . . .

"Being strong?"

"Exactly. We can do better than this. And we should."

Time was at a premium, but the day stopped right then. They sat and planned until it felt right.

The scythe swished past Matt's neck mere millimeters from his jugular, but it might as well have been a mile. He had been moving so fast through the dungeons that he hadn't really had a moment to reflect on his growth as it happened. Now, facing an opponent strong enough that he couldn't risk simply taking the damage it could dish out, Matt could use the queen as a proving ground for everything he had learned.

Spring-Fighter had leveled twice since the beginning of their training, which helped. What had helped more was Matt's specific training to use it better. He was now efficient enough with pulsing it on and off that it barely moved his stamina bar when he did. Bigger dodges that covered more ground still drained a good amount of stamina, but the last week had refined his short-range dodging so much it hardly came up. He bobbed and weaved like a boxer, keeping as close to attacks as he could without dying from them and jumping immediately into counter-attacks after.

In short, he was getting pretty good at this fighting stuff.

"Get the leg again, Matt! The front right!"

Lucy had been growing, too. In the last several fights, she had been studying everything he did, eventually offering in-fight advice that almost always considered something he wasn't seeing, either because it was out of his line of sight or because he simply wasn't observant or smart enough to notice it in the first place.

That was why the ant didn't pose much threat to him. But him posing more of a threat to the ant was a different story entirely. That was less a function of Advanced Survivor's Combat, and more of what Survivor's Reflexes showed him when he switched from his spear to his shovel. With the spear, the ant's weak spots were well analyzed, showing up as dozens of bright spots shining with various levels of intensity.

When he switched to the shovel, the weak spots changed to something quite different. The entire ant shone like a spotlight bulb. The leg Lucy was directing him to strike was one he had hit with his spear before, which had hobbled the leg somewhat without actually taking it out of play. Now he hit it with the shovel, swinging it with both arms and aiming the newly sharpened edge at the same point he had impacted before. Without any fuss, the shovel cut cleanly through the leg, leaving it on the ground looking like it had been lopped off with a circular saw.

Where he had been easily dodging the ants attacks before, with one fewer leg in the mix, it was child's play. He didn't play with it past that point. The other ants would be back from their pheromone-driven wild goose chase soon enough, and although he was stronger, he still had limits. He dodged a few more attacks, took off the other legs on that ant's side, climbed the back of the now topped insect and put an end to things with a chopping blow to the back of its neck.

"Get the spike, Matt!" By the time Lucy finished yelling, it was already in his hand. He jammed it into one of the detached legs just long enough to fish out some meat, eat it, and make contact with the plinth. Judging by the lack of rumbling outside the room, he had a few moments to look at rewards.

*Dungeon Objective Complete: Colony Control*

Hey, Matt. Hi, Lucy. I'm throwing in a couple of trash rewards you don't need here, and very badly bending the rules to throw in something you do need. Don't worry about it too much. We have bigger worries than a few days or weeks of Barry downtime. I want to help, and this is something I can do.

Another thing I can do is to remind you of something I think you've probably forgotten. You know how kids sometimes remember conversations as being very important, even if adults forget them?

Early on, everything you said was like that for me. So something I remember that you might not is that when you found your first stash of Gaian emergency food, there was more than just crackers and cooking fuel in the box. It couldn't have possibly seemed important then, but if you think hard, I think you might find it's important now.

Matt, you can do this. I know you can. But be careful. And don't worry about me. If worse comes to worst, I'll see you on the other side.

Barry

The clearly-not-trash prize Barry had promised lived up to its promise, adding a whole new element to Matt and Lucy's plans.

*Tree-Killer Mortars, 5x*

Designed to be fired from tubes, tree-killer mortars were intended to start forest fires, set fields aflame, and generally damage the growing material resources of enemies. The flames contained in these mortars cannot be put out by any means apart from suffocation or exhausting themselves, and burn hot enough to ignite most organic materials within a few feet of them.

"Thanks, Barry. That's honestly very, very helpful," Matt said to the dungeon.

A long time ago, when Matt fought the worm, Barry had promised him something special as a reward, a ranged option. Since he got the Skin of Worm and his Palate of the Conqueror shortly after that, it had been mostly lost in the shuffle of things. It was only recently, when Matt and Lucy had been looking through their resources for anything and everything they could use, that he had even cashed in the reward.

*Small Artillery*

This tube loads and fires up to ten artillery shells, running off a rudimentary timer to do so. It's not technically a trap, but can be set up at just the right angle to bombard your enemy as a distraction, or to destroy them from a distance, provided you can find suitable ammunition.

It can also be manually fired and used at short range as a kind of wacky, mostly inaccurate cannon.

Matt had not had a good opportunity to use his mortar yet, besides pelting some Clownrats with large rocks just to spite them. The mortars weren't just good for tactical reasons. It also let him do badass things without a clear, bad-choice driven downside. *Leave it to Barry*, he thought, *to think of the perfect gift.*

"What did you get?"

"Magic mortar shells, or something. Judging by the description, they are basically Napalm."

"Rad. How's Barry holding up?"

"He seems worried. Can't blame him. But he also reminded me of something. Are you up for one more stop before we get home?"

"Sure."

Matt touched the plinth, and they were out.

## CHAPTER FORTY-SIX

# Going to War

*Ding!*

Matt felt like he hadn't even fully materialized before the ding went off. It was odd to get the notification now, since Barry had time to send it while they were in the dungeon. Worried, he pulled it up as soon as he could.

> *Quest Assigned: Clear the Weeds*
>
> I know this is playing dirty, but I didn't want to have to watch you read this. As you get closer to home you'd find out anyway, so I need to tell you, but I absolutely command you not to be worried about me.
>
> The actual text of this quest should have been something like, "The Scourge is trying to eat a dungeon and getting remarkably close to figuring out how." Don't panic.

Of course, Matt panicked.

"Lucy, the Scourge is trying to eat Barry. The dungeons, I mean. That's really bad."

"It can do that? The dungeons survived last time. Is this a new evolution, or something?"

"I don't know. I didn't get that far into the message."

"Well, do! Read it!"

> I don't know why the Scourge couldn't eat the dungeons in the before-time any more than you do. I wasn't awake then. Maybe it couldn't adapt

that fast before it starved itself out. I don't know. But it's doing it now. The dungeons resist damage, so I'm not completely without defenses. But every time I change how I'm defending, it shifts with me. I need to concentrate to do it faster.

That means two things:

1. I'm going dark for a while. I've preloaded your victory gifts for when you come out on top, but I'll be down for the count for a while. I have to dedicate myself wholly to this.
2. You need to hurry. Dungeons are efficient, but that doesn't mean they don't use a fair amount of energy, or keep much stored. If it can consume that energy, it's going to have a lot to work with.

Once again, don't worry about me. Don't stop with what you're doing. I've got it under control. Focus on what you can control.

And Matt? Lucy? Win. Kick its ass.

I love you guys.
Barry

Matt and Lucy couldn't go home directly, since they still had to sprint to the original food-box Matt had found. He took out the relevant items, and they immediately turned towards home. Once they reached line of sight on the closest dungeon to the estate, they saw what Barry was facing. The Scourge hadn't spread its main body too far, thankfully. But it had sent out a feeler all the way to the nearest dungeon and had grown vines from the end of it that now engulfed the dungeon while pulsing, squeezing, and generally worming through any cracks around it. The whole dungeon structure was metal, but still groaned under the pressure of the attack.

They were far enough away that the Scourge didn't notice them coming. It was time to suit up. Matt had experimented and had found that, just as the voice in the armaments building had said, he was now able to hold his breath for an unbelievably long amount of time. Whenever he wanted air, his vitality would resist whatever loss of function he should have experienced and would even supplement stamina as a replacement by leveraging Rub Some Dirt In It in a way he didn't fully understand.

He'd need that, since the suit apparently would only work if it was completely closed. He and Lucy had talked it over, and they guessed that meant anything not under the suit would be visible to whatever senses the Scourge used to find mana, unless it was made of a material it also couldn't see.

Matt closed the suit and hefted the shovel, which he prayed was as Scourge-invisible as he hoped it was.

It was time to go to war.

* * *

The beginnings of war meant a lot of creeping about, trying to avoid more direct contact with the Scourge until they got closer. But because Matt couldn't actually breathe inside the suit outside of the few mouthfuls of air under it, he also had to hurry. He ran forward as fast as he could while making sure he didn't actually touch any of the vines and let the Scourge know he was present.

As they drew new the estate, they saw that the Scourge had grown. That wasn't only true in terms of its main body, the Scourge had feelers spread out everywhere. Matt could see one snaking toward the museum, and who knew how many of Barry's dungeons it was attacking as well. It was also true in terms of its sheer size. It had long since overgrown what Matt thought of as his primary estate, spilling out into the plots of land he had bought after.

Every plant on every plot was drained and gone. They might not have had much mana in them, but it was apparently enough for the Scourge to want to make use of. The Ape-iaries were long gone. Even the soil itself was drained, looking less like what he had purchased and more like standard, dead Gaian soil, minus the red.

It was huge, and it was moving. The vines closest to it were more clearly under its control, whipping around almost defensively, like it was passively warding itself against danger and making itself a less predictable target to hit. Worse, it was doing it mindlessly. If it was focused, Matt could have probably figured out a general direction to look for the taproot in. Now, he'd just have to go in chopping.

They moved in further and further until the waving vines were finally too close to consistently evade with any perfect level of confidence, and close enough that Matt could get into the thick of things almost immediately. If the Scourge knew he was there, it wasn't tipping its hand.

Unable to talk through the suit and unwilling to give away his position, Matt looked at Lucy and nodded. She nodded back. He hefted his shovel and charged.

His first cut was meant to be exploratory, but the shovel felt like it barely caught wind as it sliced through a wall of vines, immediately dropping the few that weren't tangled with the greater mass on the ground. Those vines stopped moving, but Matt didn't. He immediately sprinted from that spot, which was good, since several other undamaged vines almost immediately slithered to that spot trying to find him. In moments, that whole section was covered with vines, writhing around defensively and perhaps hoping to find mana-rich prey.

He ran a good fifty meters away and cut again. The same thing happened. Matt was reluctant to make any more tests. He needed to get to the center of this thing. He went in guns blazing.

The next cut was followed by another, and another, each one starting down at the ground and looping up through the air in a rough tunnel shape. It was something he and Lucy had work shopped. Since the Scourge was tangled, straight cuts wouldn't drop the vines in a way he could get through. He had to start from the ground and cut out a loop. It wouldn't have been possible except for two things. First, Matt was much, much stronger than a normal human and though the Scourge was pretty tough, it wasn't entirely impossible to cut. The second was that the shovel was so damn sharp he could move it through the Scourge almost without any drag at all.

The vines still didn't fall cleanly, but Matt had a plan for that too, one of only two movement skills he had been able to find the entire time he was out.

*Turtle's Momentum*

How do Flash Turtles move that fast? They cheat. Don't ask us how because we don't know. They simply ignore most laws related to breaking inertia to a limited degree to get their weird shelled mass up and moving much faster than they should be able to.

Turtle's Momentum allows you to do the same thing, getting more out of a conventional or skill-related dash over a very short distance. It doesn't actually increase your top speed much, but it increases acceleration such that you reach that top speed much more quickly, and doubles whatever impact your mass and speed imply you should have had.

Between his rapid-fire cuts and being able to hurtle harder and faster into the vines than he should have, Matt was able to move forward through the Scourge much more quickly than he otherwise could have. But the Scourge wasn't slow. Matt still wouldn't have been able to stay ahead of its retaliatory strikes except for another skill he picked up.

"I told you it would be worth it, Matt!" Unseen Lucy could talk without much risk, and couldn't resist the chance to gloat. She deserved it. Matt had been very, very reluctant to eat a Clownrat. He still felt somehow infected from the experience. It took her hours to talk him into it, and she had to play dirty to do it, pointing out how much the Gaians had sacrificed and how, deep down, he knew that eating clown meat wasn't the worst thing possible.

She was wrong. It was the worst thing possible. It had tasted like meat-based cotton candy. But it did give up a skill, one that was working exactly as they hoped here.

In the course of what they were now calling their training montage, Matt and Lucy had learned a bit about the Palate of the Conqueror skill. First, it seemed to revolve around three total meta-traits. The skills Matt had found before were entirely composed of things that applied to attack, defense, or movement. Of the attack spells he had found, quite a few seemed to synergize with magic. Only two had given up real, honest-to-god improvements for how he thwacked things with other things, and this was the first.

*Gnawing Strike*

When you strike a plant with Gnawing Strike, it exacts a small stamina cost to enact a damage-over-time effect that continues working over several seconds. Mimicking the sawing, gnawing damage of rodent teeth, it eats away at the target, inflicting pain, distracting, and generally giving you more bang for your buck for several seconds per strike.

Works exceptionally well on the targets Clownrats are adapted to, particularly plants, tree branches, and roots.

Where Matt had struck, the attack left a gnawing effect that he could literally hear, slowly eating away at the vines. It worked about how he had hoped. As he moved, the Scourge appeared confused about where the attack was coming from at any given time. Whatever primitive "If Damage, Then Attack" programming the Scourge was running didn't seem able to differentiate between damage types. If he wasn't wearing the suit, it would have probably found him. But as it was, its attack was split over several different parts of the tunnel, leaving a manageable amount for him to deal with as he made each new cut.

In the meantime, Matt was making the best of the time he had bought. One of the weirder things about having both high dexterity and high perception was that when both were kicked in, time seemed to slow. Since he was in a battle with a plant that appeared to be as quick as lightning, the effect wasn't that noticeable. He was making multiple chops per second and pulsing his turtle charge after each one, but since everything in his local environment was keeping pace with his speed, everything *felt* slow.

Worse, the probing attacks of the Scourge behind him were closing off any point of reference had. The weaving vines weren't quite thick enough that he was working in the dark, but he had no idea how far he had come. It was just him in a small, closed, claustrophobic hallway made of death.

That's where Lucy came in. The rules against her working as a scout mostly had to do with telling Matt about places he hadn't been, or things he couldn't see. Telling him his exact position on his own property didn't trigger those restrictions at all, since he was intimately familiar with the area and the system's rules were apparently nowhere near granular enough to account for the difference between asking that question in the shade of a tree, or asking it in the shade of a godlike murder-plant.

"Matt, about ten more cuts to the center!" she yelled. Matt was surprised at how far he'd come already. So far, they hadn't needed a single trick beyond his initial loadout.

*Which means something's about to go wrong.*

## CHAPTER FORTY-SEVEN

# Herbicide

Something *could* go wrong. Several things, really.

The first was that when Matt broke into the general center of the space, he found that while the Scourge was a godlike monster plant, it was still a plant. And a very real inconvenience of the way plants worked was that they buried their roots underground.

That actually wasn't the worst case. Presumably, all of the vines were growing out of one taproot, which meant that there was a good chance that Matt would have been able to see where it was sprouting from the ground. The worst was the off chance that one of the Scourge's adaptations was the ability to hide its root by choosing a different place for the bulk of the plant to break the surface.

Either way, he had to dig. Not necessarily a ton, but enough to expose the root or at least some underground vines that he could track back to the source. But that also meant breaking his cut, bash, and run stride for a moment in order to drop his defenses and dig. At this point, his digging skill was pretty developed. It wouldn't take much time, but even a split second was going to be dangerous.

Matt took one last slash at some incoming vines, then dropped his shovel and dug, hoping that his digging skills extra-dirt-moved multiplier would kick in and save him some seconds. It didn't, but his conventional skill-enhanced digging was still pretty quick. After three or four quick plunges of the shovel into the soil, he had dug down far enough to satisfy himself that whatever else the Scourge was, it wasn't a plant with an extensive root structure.

"Matt! Heads up!" Lucy was still up top somewhere, keeping an eye on things. "It's closing up!"

Even just digging the small hole had involved several quick dodges using Spring-Fighter, weaving his body around the Scourge's unguided strikes. He didn't find the root. As Lucy yelled, Matt looked up to find that the vine tunnel he had dug behind him was almost entirely closed up now, woven in with new vines that had moved in. They had already shut off his escape and were now closing the small space he was standing in.

It seemed his Clownrat damage-over-time strikes had worn off.

*Which means this is the only place it's going to be checking.*

Matt looked up in time to see vines lancing through the general tangle and shooting down towards him. The Scourge had narrowed in and could now concentrate on searching the last remaining damaged cavity in its mass by arcing vines toward him like spears of death.

"Any second now, Matt! Hold on!"

Matt kept swinging and dodging, but it wasn't any use. He didn't have time to cut a new tunnel without getting stabbed, but staying in place meant getting caught sooner or later by one of the Scourge's attacks. As if to prove that point, the vines that the Scourge sent didn't retract after they landed on the ground. Matt was cutting through them as fast as he could, but every vine he didn't get to was shrinking the space he was left with.

Within seconds, he was hemmed in on all sides to the point where he couldn't swing the shovel. Desperate for even a split second of time and elbow room, Matt choked up on the shovel, holding it with the handle pointed down to towards the ground and the blade of the shovel protruding only slightly out from his body. Then, he strained every muscle in his body and cranked around in a circle.

The maneuver didn't make much room, but the several inches of space he cleared were just enough for him while the Gnawing Clownrat strike gave the Scourge just a moment's confusion as to what exact space Matt occupied.

The next step of the plan wasn't precisely timed, but Matt had done everything he could to stall for it. It was now or never.

All across the Scourge, axons were firing. To the extent the Scourge could be said to think, it thought mainly in reflexes. Those involuntary reflexes were going crazy in a large portion of its mass, and so far, it couldn't find the source that was causing mayhem. However, that didn't mean it wouldn't respond at all.

In some adaptations, the Scourge had encountered damage from a material that was invisible to it, one that its reflexes could not see coming and caused damage that it was unable to resist. Sometimes the material would be attached to mana sources, while sometimes it would seemingly propel itself.

By the time the material became a threat in its previous life, the Scourge had adapted down the wrong path, assuming the universal nature of mana in things. Suddenly dealing with something that skirted by all of its developed sensory capabilities was a tough problem, even for its superior toughness. But eventually, one Scourge iteration developed a mutation that took into account the fact that invisible non-mana material could be a source of damage. If a section of the Scourge was being actively damaged, it was as good as a flare indicating where the threat was located.

Once that piece of the puzzle was in place, the rest of the Scourge's adaptations were more than enough to nullify threats. It could not destroy the material by gathering mana, but it could use more primitive methods from much earlier Scourge generations and wrap the threat in vines and constrain the material. Then, if possible, it would squeeze and crush. If not, it would bury the material, removing it from the field of play. Sometimes, it took damage when it did such things, but a bit of incidental hurt was not something that overly worried the instincts on which it ran.

This current threat threw indications over a truly large portion of the Scourge's mass, but that didn't change the basic instinctual formula it used to handle that sort of thing. Where broken vines sent impulses indicating damage, it filled in the space with new ones. There was no mana source that it could notice, so it would just smother whatever was hurting it.

Suddenly, the damage stopped. The Scourge was not a clever, thinking thing, so this made little difference. It would fill in the space, driven by its instinctual drive for homeostasis and to fully occupy any space it possibly could. As it closed in the space, a small amount of damage flared, indicating that whatever threat it faced was not entirely finished yet. So it sent more vines to fill the space. It was what it did, what the vines were for.

But just as it was closing the very last of the void within its mass, a new threat flared, one that it could see, and one that it had seen before. It was something the Scourge was well-adapted to handle, and it had tools to suppress such a threat. But time was of the essence, or else it would face a large, unnecessary energy cost to regrow what the threat would damage.

The instinctual priorities were clear. It reoriented its focus to mitigate the new threat.

Surrounded as he was by vines, there was no way Matt could have heard the thunking noise he was waiting for. Luckily, he didn't need to.

"Matt! Incoming!" Lucy screamed. "Hold on!"

It was Barry who had made Matt remember the herbicide gas canisters. They had been present in the very first cache of Gaian emergency supplies Matt had ever found. At that time, they were a heavy afterthought that he had left behind, since there weren't any plants around to use them on. Now there was, and they were incredibly important.

Matt had built a catapult in the past in the fight against the first hero that the system had dropped on Gaia. This time, he improved upon the design and built a full-blown trebuchet.

Rigging the canisters to open when launched from the trebuchet had been pretty easy, since it turned out the canisters were closed by lids meant to be easily ripped off before they were thrown. Building a timed trigger for the trebuchet itself had been harder, and eventually had come down to an imprecise timed trigger that Matt had rigged with his water stone, an empty food cube bag, and a lever. All in all, the trebuchet wasn't a small contraption, and Matt and Lucy had to work hard to improve the range of their original catapult to make sure it was far enough away that the Scourge didn't take it down before it served its purpose.

He and Lucy had not been able to get the firing timing more precise than a range of about thirty seconds or a minute, and on this firing, the timing had taken much longer than usual.

It had finally fired. As the canisters hissed through the air towards the Scourge, the incoming vines that would have otherwise hit Matt suddenly retreated, heading towards the canisters. Matt heard several clanks that he interpreted as the Scourge deflecting the cans away, but nowhere near enough to indicate it had got all of them. They hadn't held any of the cans back, and there were dozens of them.

Matt was particularly pleased when the vines above him parted away from a canister that nearly landed on top of him. Holding his breath for so long was just as possible as the Gaians had predicted, but was also just as painful as they had implied it was. But it came in handy with his airtight suit saving him from breathing in what he assumed was pretty nasty stuff. The agony in his lungs seemed that much more worthwhile.

The gas itself was bluish, and as it filled the air around Matt, the vines reacted by pulling away from it. The general tangle of the Scourge meant this happened much slower than the speed of the gas diffusing. Where the poison touched the plant, it had an immediate effect. The vines slowed. The gas visibly weakened them, and even seemed to impart a sort of stiffness to them. It didn't kill them, but Matt hadn't expected it to.

The Gaians had indicated that the Scourge was still vulnerable to most forms of attacks, just not vulnerable enough for them to matter long-term. A herbicide that didn't actually kill the plant would have been all but useless to the Gaians, who needed to clear the majority of their planet's surface of the problem. But for Matt, who was dealing with a much smaller version of the same problem, it was a different story. Every second counted, and this had bought several.

Matt picked up his shovel and swung wildly at walls of vines around him, laying down his damage-over-time effect in three or four directions before Lucy called down the actual best-bet direction of travel to him from above. He then cut his way into the mass again, smashing through weed-killer-weakened vines even faster than before.

There still wasn't a lot of hope. The taproot wasn't at the center of the plant, which meant it could be anywhere in the entire mass. It was a big space to search, and probably too big for Matt to search in the time it would take for the Scourge to close in on him again.

He might get lucky. He had been lucky in the past. But something inside him told him that he couldn't rely on luck this time. He needed something else, some different kind of hope to rely on, or he'd die surrounded by a writhing monster made of unrestrained, mindless growth.

He was a dozen cuts deep into his new tunnel before that hope began to show itself. Subtly, almost imperceptibly, the Scourge was glowing. And some directions were glowing brighter than others.

## CHAPTER FORTY-EIGHT

# Regal Scythe

Matt went off course. Above him somewhere, Lucy noticed.

"Matt! Wrong way! Veer right!"

He was still trapped in his suit, holding his breath as best he could. He couldn't even try to yell at this point. If he did, he'd be unable to keep going without ripping the suit itself open to get air. He continued on in the new direction, hoping Lucy would provide more instructions. She did.

"I don't see anything unusual that way. Keep going!"

From a place he couldn't see in the vines, Matt heard one canister suddenly stop hissing, then another and another. It wasn't gradual as if they were running out of gas, but instead it was sudden, like someone had put their finger over the nozzle. He didn't know how, but the Scourge was stopping them. Whatever advantage he was getting from the gas was ending soon.

As he ran, Matt realized he had made a slight mistake. When he had turned to chase the vulnerabilities that Survivor's Reflexes was showing him, he had run only a few steps before turning again for the same reason. After a few adjustments, he realized the problem was that he had been running almost exactly in the wrong direction, and turned almost entirely around before he stopped running out of brighter, more vulnerable directions to chase. He had been going in the wrong direction.

Luckily, the combination of Gnawing Strike, his movement meta-enhancement, and his ultra-sharp shovel was still working. He suspected it was working even better because of the shovel, in fact. The Scourge didn't like being attacked, sure, but it seemed to specifically dislike strikes from the shovel. When he cut a vine, they jerked back slightly as if burned by fire.

*Is it allergic to the metal, or something?*

Almost the moment he had that thought, the mental instruction portion of Survivor's Reflexes kicked in to give him more guesses, as if his own thinking had given it fuel. He had a sense that normal strikes or even spells would be less effective against the Scourge's vines, given that they carried mana and that it was essentially a mana-absorbing machine at this point in its evolution.

Matt really wasn't sure how reliable Survivor's Reflexes could be with a pure, educated guess like this, but if he was reading what it was saying correctly, the Scourge had something like damage reduction that was proportional to the mana in the strikes and weapons themselves. It was bad news, and a great reason to keep his shovel in play.

But for now, his biggest problem was his lungs. A lifetime of reflexive breathing built instincts that were hard to ignore. He wasn't taking damage, but his lungs were burning horribly, and it was only by intense willpower that he was able to keep from ripping his suit open. It was like he was drowning, and it took every ounce of battle-built toughness to resist his own panic.

Then disaster struck.

Matt had deeply, deeply hoped that the Scourge couldn't shift tactics mid-battle. He and Lucy had batted around the possibility that the Scourge would either not be able to change how it acted that fast, or wouldn't be able to do it while actively facing an attack. Both of those hopeful guesses were proven untrue when Matt cut away a section of vines only to see several new vines just beyond them, oriented with their tips pointed directly at the front of Matt's body.

*Shit.*

All the vines fired at once, filling the entire space of the tunnel ahead of him so closely there was no room to dodge. Matt instinctively clubbed downwards with his shovel, knocking several of them down towards his feet, then turned himself somewhat sideways to try and fit through the gap he had made. It wouldn't have been possible at all, except the vines' movements were still visibly affected by the remnants of the gas in the air and would break from the blunt force of the strike.

It still wasn't quite enough. As Matt spun with the sharp point of the shovel and made himself some more room, several things happened at once.

The first was pain.

*Status Effect: Mana Siphon*

You are under the effect of a mana siphon. A local environmental hazard or specialized attack is drawing on your internal mana resources. Some of your skills and stats are temporarily disabled as a result.

Current effects: Survivor's Digging effectiveness reduced. System-provided stats reduced by 10 percent.

Matt had felt the suit tear near his pack, and the air rushed in behind it. But the good news was that he wasn't dead. It looked like having a small hole limited the whole-body mana siphon attack the Scourge could usually put in play. It hurt like hell, but the effects were less than before. He could handle it, at least for a while.

What was worse was that it got his shovel. As the attacks swept by him, Matt tried his best to clear as much space as he could around him. This worked, and he managed to get in a few gnawing strikes that cut off most of the vines that were attacking him head-on. But the momentum of the vines was incredible. As his shovel passed through them, it was deflected slightly, pushing the cutting edge of the blade out of line with the vines. When he failed to cut the last few, they caught the blunt edges, spinning the tool in his hands, wrenching it out of his grip, and pulling it away from him.

He reached out for it, but apparently this wasn't just random happenstance. The vines wrapped around the shovel as they sailed away from him, then the shovel disappeared into the greater mass. It was gone.

Matt took a deep breath, which he could now do. He needed it to yell.

"Lucy! Suit integrity is compromised. It's still working a bit. I got mana-lanced, but it's manageable." Matt was furiously dodging vines while he reached back to pull a few items from the sides of his pack. "I'm activating the inferno."

"Do you need the capsules?"

"Not yet."

Matt's hand groped only for a split second before he found his knife and the fire mortar shells Barry had gifted him. Gripping the ropes that tied them to the pack, he ripped the shells free first. One of the advantages of high dexterity that he rarely got to use was a vast improvement to his fine motor skills, which meant pulling the pins in each and tossing them was much easier than it should have been. Within seconds, he had all five out, lit and in play, throwing four far out into the tangle in a direction more or less in front of him and one much closer, essentially directly at the base of the wall where the Scourge's latest coordinated attack had come from.

Barry had definitely envisioned Matt firing these from the artillery, but there had been no way Matt could have stood outside the Scourge and fired the thing without the plant getting clued into his location. Instead, he and Lucy had figured out how to activate them by hand. Each worked on a slight delay meant to keep them from catching on fire until after they were pushed from the mortar tube towards whatever enemy they were meant for, but it wasn't long. Within a few seconds, each exploded into wide, intense rings of flame.

Matt faced the explosion nearest to him as directly as he could, and was gratified to find it didn't immediately incinerate him. He and Lucy had guessed that the armor they were wearing had never been seriously tested against non-Scourge attacks, but their experience with Leel meant they knew that Nullsteel was excellent at nullifying at least fire-oriented forms of mana-based attacks. Which was exactly what the mortar shells did.

Matt could tell that the flames weren't normal. They burned in a too-fast, twitchy way. They also burned too white, and Matt could smell a mixture of burning matches and scorching fabric as they singed the outside of his pack through the gap in his suit. But he himself was mostly fine. What the suit wasn't stopping, Rub Some Dirt In It was mitigating and healing. The suit was working to protect him from the heat.

The same could not be said of the Scourge. The fire was intense enough that it actually was getting burned, and its attentions immediately turned from Matt to the fire. While it did, Matt pulled both his knife and shield from the pack, strapping the latter around his left suit sleeve. He doubted the knife would work as well at cutting the Scourge as the shovel had, and he'd need help deflecting what it didn't catch.

The Scourge immediately started beating on the fire with its vines, which were almost as immediately ignited and burned by the direct contact with the fire. But as each vine was burned into non-functional states, it fed new ones in while pulling the greater wall of vines around the fire further and further away. After a few moments, Survivor's Reflexes clued Matt in on what the Scourge was doing. The strikes themselves would slightly lessen the intensity of the flame when they hit, but that wasn't enough to actually stop it. What was worse was that the ash from the swatting vines was quickly building up over the fuel from the fire, smothering it. It was sacrificing some amount of its bulk to protect itself from the greater damage that the intense heat the fires would otherwise produce.

Matt had no time to wait and see if the tactic was as successful as he assumed it would be. He charged forward, swinging his knife into the wall as he kept pressing towards the brightest, most vulnerable parts of the plant.

His first knife swing not only didn't cut, but instead actively clanked off the vines. The advantage Matt had been getting from the shovel was much larger than he had guessed. As it was, the knife wouldn't be enough for him to take even a single step forward through the tangled mass, and the Gnawing Strike didn't work nearly fast enough to help.

"Matt! Shift attacks!" Lucy screamed, overhead. She was right. There wasn't any option but to go for broke, even if it meant burning resources sooner than he had planned.

*Regal Scythe*

In the entire colony, the Wolf Ant queen is the only ant truly optimized for battle. Even the soldier-guard ants are merely bigger, stronger versions of the normal worker ants. The queen herself had the luxury of abandoning mandibles meant for work in favor of pure killing potential.

With Regal Scythe activated, the sharpness of any weapon you use is increased to a level similar to the queen's own weaponry. The sharpness you gain will rival finely chipped obsidian blades, without any significant cost of durability to the weapon itself.

Regal Scythe is a limited-use upgrade, good for several minutes of normal use, after which both the effects of the enhancement and the enhancement itself will disappear. At any time, the remainder of the trait can be "burned" to cause a massive increase in the range, sharpness, and speed of a single strike. Doing so will immediately remove the trait and all effects.

Meta-Trait occupied: Attack

## CHAPTER FORTY-NINE

# Time to Fight the Boss

When Matt's knife hit the next vine, he suddenly gained a whole new appreciation for the fact that he had never taken a real direct hit from one of the queen's scythes. It was clear to him that if he had, he'd be dead. The knife moved through the mass of vines as if there was no resistance at all. He could survive a lot of things now, but he seriously doubted that getting cut clean in half was one of them.

Like all the vines Matt had cut, the strands fell to the ground, apparently neutralized once disconnected from the main mass of the plant. He immediately moved forward into the next area of vines, hacking and slashing away as he went. While the skill was more than sufficient for actually cutting the vines, it was lacking in other departments. Where the Gnawing Strike had managed to spread out the Scourge's attention somewhat, the ant queen's power was strong but allowed the Scourge to focus on Matt undistracted.

Between dealing with whatever poison was still in the air and the damage from the fires, the Scourge wasn't moving nearly as fast as it once did. But it was still moving more than fast enough to give Matt serious trouble. With every step forward, Matt paid a price of some kind, whether it was a glancing or a direct blow. His suit went from just a single hard-to-hit gap to having several tears, and Matt's notifications left him no illusions about the repercussions.

*Status Effect: Mana Siphon*

You are under the effect of a mana siphon. A local environmental hazard or specialized attack is drawing on your internal mana resources. Some of your skills and stats are temporarily disabled as a result.

Current effects: Spring-Fighter disabled. System-provided stats reduced by 40 percent.

*Status Effect: Mana Siphon*

You are under the effect of a mana siphon. A local environmental hazard or specialized attack is drawing on your internal mana resources. Some of your skills and stats are temporarily disabled as a result.

Current effects: Survivor's Combat disabled. System-provided stats reduced by 60 percent.

Just like that, Matt lost his movement skill, his attack skill, and the bulk of his stats. While he was still much stronger and faster than a normal human, he felt like his legs had been cut out from under him. Whatever combination of perception and dexterity that had made it seem like time was moving at a slower pace in combat situations suddenly lost most of its efficacy, leaving him barely able to fend off a mind-bendingly fast suite of attacks from the plant.

"Matt! The capsules!" Lucy screamed, apparently having seen him slow down from her scouting position. She wasn't wrong. Matt quickly used his tongue to dig out a foil-wrapped package from between his lower molars and his cheek, then felt the sickening sweaty-banana taste of the monkey honey fill his mouth as the bag burst.

It had taken a long time for him and Lucy to realize they should probably scan the honey with the appraisal wand. They had in fact only remembered to do so after a long brainstorming session on the subject of mitigating the effects of the Scourge's mana lance had come up empty. Finally, the lightbulb dawned on the fact that the honey was the only effective treatment they knew of for the kind of damage Matt was almost certainly going to take, and they put it through a long-overdue analysis.

*Monkey Honey*

Normal honey is a wonder-food, essentially consisting of condensed energy in one of the forms universally usable by most living organisms. This honey represents the tireless work of a quasi-artificial life-form in gathering pollen from mana-dense plants and done in a manner that was motivated by avoiding the complications of living in an absurdly mana-lean environment.

The resulting product bridges the gap between food and alchemical potion in an effective way. The honey amounts to ultra-condensed biological mana, and while it is useless as a source of raw, atmospheric mana that a mage might use, it is incredibly effective as a treatment for various disorders related to mana deficiency.

It also possesses what might be described as "an acquired taste."

Based on the system's appraisal and a lack of other options, Matt and Lucy had crafted several cube-bag-wrapped honeycomb sections, tightly tied so as not to leak significantly until Matt chomped down on them. The honey had worked well enough before to solve his mana deficiency problems before, if a little slowly. They hoped it would be enough to make a difference here.

What Matt didn't know and the appraisal wand couldn't tell him was just how well the Ape-bees liked the native Gaian flowering plants, and the quality of honey they had prepared before the Scourge wiped them out. He hoped that this particular batch of honey would work just as well as before. But those worries were unfounded. Almost immediately after biting down, Matt's perception of time began to stretch, accompanied by improved knife-handling skills and a very welcome system ding.

*Ding!*

Your mana deficiency resolved due to the consumption of an exceptionally mana-dense food.

Effects: Stats restored to 100 percent efficiency. All skills restored to full working order.

With both Barry and the system instance out of commission, Matt was glad that he was getting notifications at all, however bare-bones and automated they might be. He was even more glad to have his power back, and put his entire will towards pushing further and further towards the taproot. As he desperately batted away vines, his increased focus on speed and whatever residual energy the honey in his mouth were putting off seemed to keep the worst of the mana-siphoning effect at bay.

"Matt! Something's changing! Heads up!" Matt looked up from his dodging momentarily, immediately identifying what Lucy probably meant. Where the vines had glowed a bit before, they were now positively lightbulb bright, with more brightness seeming to be packed in behind them. He was close.

A few more swings of his sword confirmed that, moving just enough vines out of the way that he could peer through the tangle to see stalks that came out of a central source much straighter and more orderly than the overall mess of vines he was beginning to think of as a malicious, living, final boss dungeon. Better yet, they ran nearly vertical near the ground, giving him hope he had found the source of all this danger.

Then he realized, a moment too late, that Lucy probably couldn't see what he was seeing. It was too packed in by vines to be visible from much farther away than he was. He craned his head around wildly trying to figure out what she was actually talking about. It was just a fraction of second too late for him to realize that some of the vines around his feet were not dead.

And then he was upside down, followed by almost immediately being bound head to foot in dozens and dozens of vines. He was immobilized, completely unable to move a single limb. He managed to hold onto his knife, but within a few moments, the knife itself started to fall apart in his hand. Apparently, the Scourge could pull apart the mana in the metal and turn it into dust.

Neither of those were the worst part.

*Ding!*

*Ding!*

*Ding!*

*Ding!*

At this range, the Scourge apparently had much less trouble getting its mana-drain attack to land. Matt might have normally wondered what shape the suit itself was in, but at that exact moment, he felt too much like his soul was getting forcibly torn out of him to contemplate it much, or to wonder why the dead vines in his very limited eyeline were disintegrating into dust as well.

Without even checking, he knew every skill was gone, and at least the vast majority of his stats were as well. With every aspect of his entire being in agonizing pain, he could hardly think at all, much less about how to get out of this situation alive. He instinctively closed his fist on one of the vines, hard.

Luckily, he had someone to think for him.

"Matt! Another packet! Acid Bat!"

Like a drowning man surging towards the surface of the water, Matt didn't need many instructions when presented with a way out. Almost immediately, a packet was open in his mouth, and he was sending the instructions to swap out his defensive meta-trait without waiting for any confirmation that it had worked. Some part of him really hoped that it would, though.

And then all his clothes burned off. In a second, Matt was burning alive in a different way, essentially swimming in a pool of acid that he himself was producing. Luckily, it seemed that among the many things Gaians had tried to use to kill the Scourge, corrosive acids weren't high on the list. The acid burned through the vines slowly, but steadily. After a few moments, Matt felt a momentary slack in their hold, and used it as an opportunity to flare every bit of strength he had to create a space and instinctively pumped as much stamina as possible into Spring-Fighter.

Luckily, Spring-Fighter had come back with his new honey packet. Assisted by the lubrication of the gooey acid, he came spurting out the Scourge's hold like a calf from a mother cow and landed awkwardly on the ground.

As he impacted with the ash of dead vines, the dust spurted up into his mouth and nose. Before he could control the reaction, he coughed and sneezed, watching in horror as not one or two but all his honey capsules came out, already burst. In his panic earlier, he had gnashed down on them all. With his HP bar dropping fast, he deactivated the acid skin trait. It wasn't doing him any good now.

He was out of honey potions, and with his suit gone, the mana lances were coming fast and heavy, sending scorching agony through every nerve in his body. His skills were blinking in and out as the honey he had just swallowed fought a losing battle against the now constant mana drain.

There was no time. His pack had survived the acid, even if it was barely hanging on by a few threads and hope. Matt drew his spear and pumped every last ounce of stamina he had into the Regal Scythe, burning the skill for a momentary boost of power. Without even getting up, he swept the spear nearly level with the ground directly at the brightest clump of vines he could see.

Then the world collapsed.

Every vine was cut. The Scourge didn't exactly have an adaptation for all of its vines being cut at once, but it did have normal, everyday sorts of protocols that applied to the situation just fine.

The first was to protect itself. As fast as it grew, it couldn't grow an entire protective hedge in a mere moment. That meant it was vulnerable. But it was vulnerable in a way that all new taproots were, when they were planted in new territories. The first priority in that situation was always protection. It would surround itself with new vines focused on extreme, short-range mana draining. Then it would, one by one, grow thicker, stronger vines that focused on attack and mobility.

Luckily, the vines of the plant contained much less mana than the taproot itself. They were fed power from the taproot itself, so each only contained enough power to operate for a minute or so at any given moment. So when the vines were cut, it wasn't a huge mana loss.

Unluckily, the taproot itself had been having a tremendous amount of trouble establishing itself. Even though its local environment initially had plenty of mana, it had consumed much of the energy when it expanded outwards.

That led into the second immediately relevant instinctual protocol. It could see its attacker now, the force that had driven the mystery material into its hedge. But with all its vines cut, the foe was just slightly outside the range from which the Scourge could effectively absorb energy from it.

But it had another source of mana to pull from. The dead vines. The energy of un-Scourge entities resisted its pull, however feebly. But energy that came from the Scourge itself was different. It had an affinity with that mana. Mindlessly and without will, the Scourge drew on that energy. There would be a small loss, but it could grow again.

Matt was trapped under what felt like tons of vegetable matter, until suddenly he wasn't anymore. No light flared and no sound was made, but suddenly he was surrounded with tons of ash. Luckily, he was very good at digging. In moments, he had made it to the surface.

The vines that surrounded him were gone. All of them. Where his estate had once stood, there was now just ash, covering the ground like snow. And in the center of it all was a pillar of vines, writhing, reaching towards him, and growing. *Oh, shit,* he thought. *I guess I made it through the dungeon. Which means . . .*

It was time to fight the boss.

## CHAPTER FIFTY

# Vine into Ash

Matt only had a few moments to wonder if the Scourge's tactics were going to significantly change.

The first sign that they would came in the form of Matt being alive at all. At the exact moment the vines had collapsed, the mana attacks had also stopped. Matt's mouth was full of ash, honey, and lord knows what else, but he wasn't taking any chances. Swirling his tongue around his mouth as best he could, he downed it all, hoping to get even a slight buff against further attacks.

"Matt! Are you okay?"

"Yeah, for now." Matt swung his spear, shaking some of the ash off his body in the process. "I'm going back in."

"Wait, why are you naked? Dammit, that suit, Matt!" Lucy turned back to the Scourge.

"It's the dumb acid skill! Just . . . look away? I have bigger problems right now."

Matt was down to very few resources, but with the Scourge visibly growing in front of his eyes, he couldn't afford to give it much time. With no combat skills left and experience telling him he'd have a hard time cutting the thing in general, Matt switched to his Survivor's Club. It would have to do.

There was no use hiding where he was. Screaming, he charged the Scourge. It was then that the second change in the Scourge's tactics made itself known. One of the thinner vines the Scourge was growing suddenly detached from the main body and uncoiled almost straight up before cracking at him like a whip, faster than any of the thicker vines had moved before. Matt had gathered up a precious few points of stamina since burning it all on his overpowered scythe attack, and had to burn them to flare Spring-Fighter and dodge the vine.

He was immediately glad as the tip of the vine made a sharp, inches deep cut in the ash, cracking like thunder.

*Oh, fuck that,* Matt thought. *Especially naked. Nope.*

Matt brought his club down on the vine, pulverizing a small section of it before nearly doubling over in pain as the vine hit him with a mana siphon. The honey in his system seemed to hold off any actual consequences to Matt's body beyond the pain, but the moment the lance hit, three new vines rose from the Scourge's mass. It was fueling its attacks with Matt's mana.

His situation was now pretty clear. The Scourge could still reach him through the extra range its vines gave it. Matt could run or attack, but not delay. It was either go all out, or give up entirely and abandon the planet to the Scourge.

Matt went all out. Between the adrenaline in his system and the small amount of stamina regen trickling in, he did pretty well at first. It seemed the actual mana-siphoning range of the thin vines was pretty limited, and after a few more minor hits from the ability, Matt had a pretty good idea of that range. He zig-zagged wildly, swinging his club when necessary to deflect vines that got too close, and strafing closer and closer to the main bulk of the body. He bit down on one of the vines, hoping that something would happen. Nothing did. So he kept moving forward. If he could just get to the taproot, he could end this.

He was only a few strides away when the man-sized tower of vines that made up the Scourge suddenly scrunched downwards, then shot out several feet on every side, spreading along the ground like a net. Matt didn't have time to contemplate that the net was probably meant to catch him before it did.

He was hit by several mana lances at once, then a whip when Spring-Fighter failed to activate. Before he could get out of the net, the vines snaked around his feet, keeping him from withdrawing at all. The lancing intensified, and he was losing skills and stats like crazy. And just before he fell, finally, horrifically, his last trap was sprung.

A few days before, Lucy and Matt had taken turns both refusing to do something, and trying to convince the other to do the same thing. It was completely necessary. It was, if they thought about it, nothing anyone concerned would have a problem with. Both of them acknowledged this. But it was also going to be the worst thing either of them had ever done, and as this occurred after Matt ate both the Clownrat and the Meltbats, that was saying something.

Right now, it was Lucy's turn to object.

"But you'll have to . . ."

"I know."

"And the Gaians . . ."

"I know, but it's what they would have wanted us to do. We know that. We know why they would have wanted that."

Lucy's look turned stern.

"Matt, if we do this, what does that make us?"

Matt sighed.

"It makes us people who will do anything to kill the Scourge, and to put the hurt on the system. And that makes us . . . I don't know. Desperate. Shameless. I get it. Believe me, Lucy, I don't feel good about this either."

Matt knelt at Lucy's eyeline.

"But you know what else it makes us?"

"What?"

"People who will do anything, sacrifice anything, to kill the Scourge and protect this planet. It makes us part of the Gaian resistance."

Lucy opened her mouth to object, then closed it wordlessly, a thoughtful look on her face. Finally, she met Matt's eyes again.

"Fine. Fight the Scourge, Matt."

"Yup. Fight the Scourge."

Building a trebuchet with two payloads hadn't been hard. It took a few minor redesigns before Trapper Keeper would recognize it as a single trap, for instance. It turned out that the trick was to make both parts of the trap work off the same trigger, which took a while to figure out, but wasn't exactly rocket science.

Loading it had been harder. Matt had let Lucy wander off while he did that part, so she didn't have to see. He would have loved the same luxury, but as the only person on the team who could manipulate matter, he was stuck with the dirty job by default.

The hardest part, though, was this moment. Matt's eyes were turned into the sky, and as if in slow motion he saw a half dozen ancient corpses sailing through the air, all of which had left the trebuchet at different trajectories and were now being affected by air resistance in different ways.

What finally convinced Matt to do this was simple. Every note, every letter, and every record he found as they went through the Gaian facilities that referenced the Gaian's choice to poison themselves, to turn their bodies into anti-Scourge weapons at the cost of their own lives, had expressed hope that one day the Scourge would find them. That it would consume them. That sacrificing their final days or hours wouldn't be in vain.

That didn't make this better. Matt had not expected the Scourge to be confined to a small space. He had assumed he was launching at a large, spread out target, one he couldn't miss. As the mummified bodies started coming to ground, they didn't just hit. They snapped. They broke apart. All of them missed the Scourge by wide margins, falling well outside its reduced mana attack range.

All but one.

Matt was spared hearing the sound of the corpse impacting the ground directly by him because the Scourge was busy on the mana-draw attack. As the corpse came into range, it caught some of the mana siphon. The effect probably wasn't full force, but it didn't need to be. The corpse was hundreds of years old. It ashed immediately.

And then the Scourge stopped. It couldn't howl, it couldn't scream. It probably didn't understand thrashing outside of a bare instinct to search for prey or threats. It just stopped in place, apparently unable to do anything at all, poisoned by the revenge of enemies long since gone, but not quite forgotten.

The vines around Matt's legs didn't slack. He tried to slip them over his feet and free himself, but found he lacked the strength to do so. He had to think of something else. He had no illusions that the poison would actually kill the Scourge, and the distinct lack of detonation meant it was almost definitely still alive.

His club was gone, but somehow his spear had still survived. Matt used it to begin hacking at the vines near his legs, desperately trying to separate them from himself before the plant came back online. It was no use. His strength was almost all gone, not just in terms of stats but also in terms of the damage that the vines had done to his normal, adrenaline-wracked human body. His vitality was no longer high enough to withstand his acid skin ability, and his legs were injured from the vines. He probably couldn't even run.

He watched as the Scourge began to stir. It was purifying the poison.

It was going to grow and spread. It was going to overtake him, and he was going to succumb. This was it. He was going to die here, and now.

Lucy wasn't unaware. From her bird's eye view, she could see what was going to happen. She yelled anyway.

"Matt! Get out of there!"

"Can't." Matt's words choked in his throat as he watched one of the vines move not just at the tip, but throughout the length, moving over an inch or so towards him. Dropping the spear and consumed by rage, he crouched down and bit at the vines near his legs once again. A part of his plan was missing and in a fight of inches, every step was crucial.

"I think this is it." They weren't pretty final words, but they were his.

Then, he heard a sound that was like music to his ears.

*Ding!*

*Mana Vampire Trait Activated!*

Warning! An error has been encountered analyzing this skill. Beyond the fact that it interacts with mana by drawing it towards you, the Gaian Defense

> System is unable to ascertain how this skill will work, or whether it will be a benefit or a detriment to you.
>
> The skill itself is unstable. It will function for minutes at the most, and in order to assure it will function at all, it will be necessary for it to occupy all of your meta-trait slots simultaneously, displacing any currently held skills.
>
> Would you still like to proceed?

*Oh, hell yes,* Matt thought. He felt something click into place internally, and after willing the skill to work seemed to do nothing, he swung his spear at the vines grasping his legs again, so weakly it couldn't have possibly cut anything.

The vines instantly ashed, and all of Matt's skills came back online.

*Ding!*

> Mana deficiency abated . . .

It should have probably felt icky to wield the Scourge's power, but Matt didn't care. He had hedge trimming to do. He raced towards the center of the Scourge, ashing as many vines as he could as he went. The attack didn't have unlimited range, but it didn't need to. Anything disconnected from the taproot stopped working immediately. Matt wasn't planning to kill the Scourge by draining it to death, anyway. But he did have a plan. And that plan needed him to disconnect as many of the vines as possible.

As he reached the center of the Scourge, he dug the very tip of his spear in the ground. Spring-Fighter, he knew, was not supposed to be usable as an attack skill. But in situations like this, where his arms weren't planning on moving, he could sometimes get some speed out of it anyway. He surged his movement skill, running in a tight circle around the very center of the flattened net.

The taproot was disarmed. But it still was not poisoned to the point it could not fight at all, which Matt discovered as he was hit both by a mana drain and a vine lance at almost the same moment.

## CHAPTER FIFTY-ONE

# Ring the Bell

The vine had lanced cleanly through Matt's stomach, and he still wasn't sure it hurt more than mana draining did. But two could play at that game. With his spear already falling apart, the only problem was a lack of immediately available weaponry. He decided to take a flier on a long shot, slashing at the vine in his stomach with his bare hand in a karate-chop motion. It immediately turned to ash.

Matt had not anticipated how badly ash in an open abdominal wound would hurt. He reeled so hard from it, he almost didn't dodge the next lance. He ashed that one a moment later, and felt the mana he drew from it overcharge Rub Some Dirt In It so hard, the pain almost completely stopped, even if it the wound didn't quite close. Then the damn plant mana-siphoned him again.

If not for the mindlessness of the Scourge, that would have been it. Something about its defenselessness or sheer lack of mass had intensified the mana lances, and each one sent Matt reeling. But it had no experience with its own attacks, no protocols or instincts that told him how to deal with them. As it struck at Matt's mana, it used that energy to send vine after vine at him. Matt was picking up injuries every second, but in doing so, he was also constantly healing the damage to his mana with his own mana draining trait. It was, however briefly, a stalemate.

Matt was reluctant to go toe to toe with the Scourge while playing its own game, but he had little choice. The Scourge was generating new vines fast enough to effectively keep him from reaching for any other options he might have, and even a moment's distraction might leave him with the kind of wound he couldn't heal from. For now, he was stuck. But at the same time he was picking up cuts and stab wounds all over his body, the Scourge was slowing.

"Matt! Keep going! It's running out of steam, I'm sure of it!" Lucy screamed, elated. Matt redoubled his efforts at cutting the vines. Slowly but surely, the vines' growth became manageably slow. But that also meant less and less mana for Matt to draw on. It was going to be close, but at the moment he felt like he was ahead.

That feeling of assurance ended in the form of two strikes simultaneously hitting his back. Somehow, somewhere in the Scourge's generations of memories, it had built up some reflexes related to ambush attacks and put them to use here. Both Matt's shoulders were pierced, and each strike seemed to hit different important parts necessary for moving his arms. With incredible effort against the pain, he managed to get his left hand up, and spun in place to ash both vines. He felt his wounds closing from the excess energy just as a new notification popped.

*Ding!*

| Mana Vampire trait deactivated. |
|---|

That was all. It was one of the shortest messages Matt had ever received. He was completely out of weapons, fighting an underground enemy that couldn't be hit through the dirt anyway, and as he turned around, he saw the Scourge slowly but effectively building another set of vines Matt had no way to deal with. It would have meant death, except for one little detail.

Matt owned more than one shovel. He had forgotten he had, until he had found it still wedged in the ribcage of a remarkably undecayed Gaian ape in the entranceway of one of his least favorite dungeons.

As Matt used Spring-Fighter to close the distance on the Scourge, he felt his skills and stats leave him one by one under a steady barrage of mana drain. His combat skill was gone, then his healing skill. Survivor's Reflexes disappeared. Even Palette of the Conqueror fell, leaving him only with a shovel and an incredibly enhanced ability to use it.

Somehow, as the shovelhead pierced the earth, he just knew it was a perfect shot. Like a crabapple out of a spudgun at the end of a long day, it was going to hit. His digging skill's critical hit came up good. From experimentation, he knew he couldn't use the skill to dig through anything but dirt or things an awful lot like it, so it wouldn't hurt the taproot by itself. But that didn't mean the taproot wasn't along for the dirt-flinging ride.

As the taproot sailed through the air, Matt saw it wasn't what he thought it would be. It was beautiful, in a way. All the mana in this part of the world, all the power contained in a human life, weeks of strengthening sunlight, most of

Matt's possessions and anything else it could lay its hands on were all packed into it. And growing off it was another, smaller root, just like it. The next iteration of the Scourge as it would eventually metastasize across the planet again.

Matt would make sure it wouldn't.

"Lucy, do it. Do it now!"

Lucy was, in a lot of ways, less of a guardian than she might have been. She didn't have the chance to study and learn nearly as much as she needed to be a real guide. She didn't have the support of the system to fill in the gaps. But that didn't mean she was useless. And among the many useful things she could do was one all-important thing. She could use Matt's estate system, including his single-purchase, good-for-anything voucher.

With its door purposefully left wide open, a mobile Nullsteel bunker appeared behind the Scourge as if from nowhere. Movement, as they had guessed, was considered a purchase under the estate system's rules.

While the taproot flew, Matt let his pack fall to the ground. From it, he pulled the last thing he had that could be considered a weapon. It was a simple tube, one he had planned for this moment. With his free hand, he pulled out the favorite thing he owned, besides his Gaian shovel. It was a ball, about three inches across, made of what he strongly suspected was Gaian Nullsteel.

As the ball sped towards the Scourge, it finally got one of its vines into play. Matt knew it couldn't be desperate, but it made him feel much better to think that its attempts to swat the ball away were just that. They didn't work. The shot was carrying the accumulated genius of a desperate people, and affected the vines much more than it should have. The vines disintegrated as they touched the ball, and the shot kept going.

It impacted deep into the flesh of the taproot, and both flew back into the bunker. Matt used every ounce of his stamina to get to the door and close it.

He took a deep breath. It was over.

"Matt, you dumbass, it's going to explode!"

He wouldn't admit it for years, but Matt had in fact forgotten that dying taproots did in fact explode. If the evidence of various shattered Nullsteel pieces they had seen around Gaia was any indication, they in fact exploded *pretty hard.* In all the excitement, he had forgotten that too.

So the Gaian landscape saw a man in a hastily donned Gaian tunic with a couple holes in it and unlaced enchanted boots run across its fields. The little girl he traveled around floated with him as they busted ass to get as far away from the magitech storage shed as they could before it blew up and killed them both.

Luckily, the explosion took a while. Even more luckily, Matt had remembered to bring his non-Nullsteel shovel. When the explosion went off, he had just enough time to dig a trench deep enough to keep his skin from getting peeled off by the sudden sandstorm created.

* * *

"I can't believe you had to fight it *naked.* We are getting you new armor, pronto. You look like a hospital patient in that tunic."

"I'd like to say I still have my old Survivor's Garb somewhere, but I think the Scourge probably got it. We can get some more." Matt was thoughtful for a moment. "Plus, I was wearing *two* sets of clothes for at least most of that fight. If you think about it, I was clothed the entire fight, on average."

"Nope. This is not a trend-line thing, Matt. This is a binary thing. We are figuring out some sort of contingency for this. You are never, and I mean never, going to fight naked again."

Matt laughed. "Deal."

They had been walking for a bit now, having stopped only to dowse out the location of Matt's Nullsteel Shovel. It wasn't long before they came to their destination.

"It's completely filled with ash, Matt."

"Yeah. On it." Matt hefted his shovel and got to work. After the taproot had gone, every last bit of vine had apparently ashed with it, leaving a big, deep field of ash on a large part of their estate, with spider-web like patterns moving outward. These were the feeler vines that had gone out looking for more resources. Apparently they were able to grow on the other side, and this dungeon room had been almost filled with them when the Scourge popped.

Luckily, ash was enough like dirt that Matt's digging skill didn't mind it.

"Well, that's hopeful." Matt had dug out the bulk of the ash, and a minute or so of wiping and blowing on the plinth revealed it was basically intact. He touched it, only to see a "down for maintenance" notification pop up. He would have absolute confirmation, but the dungeon seemed to still be working in most senses, sans anyone to actually run the thing. It was a good sign.

Still, he would have liked to talk to Barry.

*Ding!*

*Achievement: [Fought the Scourge]*

Matt, if you are reading this, you have done the impossible. When I was putting together this award, I learned a fun thing about how the system archives information. It has to know what's living and dangerous on a planet so it knows how to dole out rewards, and the Scourge was the most dangerous thing on the planet at one point. So I've learned some stuff.

I can't let you in on everything I know, but the relevant point is this: it's really dead. What Leel did to call it back is a one-time thing, essentially leaning on an echo of something that once existed to recreate it and destroying that echo at the same time. In its later form, the Scourge abandoned seeds in favor of distributing taproots, so you don't have to worry about that, either. It's well and truly gone.

I'm going to be honest. I didn't think you could actually do it. Now, we've been in that situation before, but that was with Bonecats and Gaian Apes, things any well-leveled adventurer could have taken on their own, or in a team. This was a world-ending supermonster, even weakened. You do the math on what that means for prizes. I can't get you all of them right away, but I put together a little bit of an advance pack. The Gaians helped. Don't ask. You will get it later.

Ring the bell, Matt. This fight is over. I'm so, so proud of you. I'm so very glad.

Love you guys,
Barry

"We love you too, Barry." Matt smiled. Lucy nodded in agreement. Barry was fine. Now there were just a few more people to check on.

## CHAPTER FIFTY-TWO

# They Can't All be Winners

*Ding!*

"Dammit, Barry."

"What?"

"He's being funny with the achievements. I wanted "Grand Gaian Savior" or something."

"Does that matter if the loot's good?"

"No, I guess not."

"Then get to reading."

*Achievement: [Mass Extinction Double Down]*

You once managed to, as far as the system understood, survive every living organism on a planet. Now, as far as the system's rules are concerned, you've now done it twice. But given that you *actually did it* this time, and that doing it involved taking down a system-registered planetary threat in a recorded, undeniably rad way, this is an even bigger deal.

You know what makes it even bigger? You essentially did it at level zero. I'm not even kidding. You are so under-leveled for doing this kind of thing solo that the levels you do have don't make a difference. Literally. This is an SSS, full-points-for-cool-suicidal-bullshit win.

Normally, this is the part where I'd give you so much stuff that you couldn't actually carry it. I'm talking armor that would let you stand in a butane fire type of stuff. Swords that could cut the very heavens in twain. I started to, but before I could actually do get the job done, I got interrupted by the darnedest thing.

The Gaian Defense System, for the record, is not a person, at least to the extent I can tell. And I can't really tell what it's trying to do. But I can tell it's trying to mess with the rewards somehow. For some reason, it's working in some ways and not in others. And this next part is hard to explain, but in the general sense that systems work, this looks like it's waiting for clearance.

That can't come from me. I tried. And there's no way it's asking the system instance. As far as I can tell, it's waiting on you.

The rest of this stuff is, believe it or not, is just the scraps of energy the defense system left behind for me to work with. The scraps, Matt. Whatever this thing is doing, it's big. But even the scraps are a lot, and the rules just about demand I do a lot of weird, rule-bending stuff with it. That's the kind of available energy you get when you detonate a god-tier plant hard enough to tear apart a whole bunker of god-tier metal, I guess.

Anyway, here's your stuff. I think it's probably close to what you need right now. And don't freak out about the stats. It's basically compulsory as a catch-up at this point, and I honestly don't know how the system has been dodging it this long.

Rewards: Estate Rollback Token, Single-structure Repair Token, Gaian Commando Survival Armor Set, Armament Enchantment Token, Enchanted Washing Station, Bar of Soap, +50 to all primary stats, +20 to all secondary stats, a flat increase of 15 levels to Battlefield Survivor, and all skills normalized to level 15.

"Oh, wow." Matt goggled at the increase before the sheer power of everything knocked him to his knees. "Oh, shit."

"Are you okay?"

"I'm more than fucking okay. I'm pretty sure I'm superman now." He tried to stand up, and accidentally launched himself a full foot in the air in the process. "Lots of stats. LOTS of stats. Why are you moving so slow?"

"Why are you acting like you drank a whole pot of coffee?"

"I think Barry just caught me up on all the levels and stats the system has been cheating me out of in one go. I'm . . ." Matt tried to take a step and accidentally launched himself several feet forward. "I'm going to have to get used to it. Sorry."

Dizzy, he sat on the ground to go over the rest of the rewards. Zooming in on them provided him information on each, no appraisal rod required.

*Estate Rollback Token*

Usable as either a mass-repair item, or simply as a method of reversing bad decorating choices. Based on your intent, it rolls back your estate to a form it held in the last Gaian year.

This token cannot be used to restore sentient beings back to life, or to repair any damage that didn't occur to the object within the borders of the estate during the same time one-year time period.

*Single-Structure Repair Token*

Completely repairs one structure either purchased from the system or constructed by humans, or Gaians. To be eligible, the item has to fit certain criteria having to do with being built as one unified object for a single purpose. As an example, almost every fortress would qualify, but very few towns would satisfy the requirements, regardless of size.

If used with the rollback token, any new additions to the estate that occurred after the rollback will be temporarily stored in the estate system as no-cost purchases available to redeem at any time.

*Gaian Commando Armor Set*

The Gaian Commando set is a high-tier armor with medium-high resistance to all mechanical damage, mild resistance to most kinds of common elemental damage, and a small chance to avoid some kinds of biological damage completely.

The Gaian Commando Armor set is enchanted to conceal you in both low light environments and when hiding in brush or other plant life. It also possesses self-repair and self-cleaning enchantments and will continue to maintain itself so long as at a chunk comprising at least 25 percent of the original garment remains.

*Armament Enchantment Token*

Compels the system to bestow one randomly selected enchantment on one piece of equipment.

*Enchanted Washing Station*

It's a bathtub. The enchanted washing station is composed of a large, opaque compartment in which two spouts are contained. On command, a flow of water will either fill a large basin within the compartment or continuously shower down water from above the user. Based on user commands, the water can be any temperature between freezing and slightly over halfway to boiling.

*Bar of Soap*

A large bar of soap.

"Shit. Wow. Fuck. Barry, you . . . Lucy, we have to figure out how to give Barry presents. I don't care if it doesn't make sense. Unbalanced friendships like this aren't healthy. We need to figure out something."

"What's going on?"

"He gave me a shower." Matt absentmindedly reached up to his head and shook some of the accumulated dust and ash out of his hair. "I thought I was a hero now, but he's putting me to shame."

Matt had an idea of how to use the enchantment. He was eager to try out his new armor. He had an incredibly strong urge to use both of his repair tokens. But some things just took priority over other things, and he was getting that shower as soon as possible.

He just had to remember how to walk first.

An hour or so later, in the center of the ruins of his estate, Matt emerged from the washing station. For the first time in what felt like years, he was completely clean, dressed in a completely clean, brand-spanking-new set of survival armor. It had turned out there was even a mirror in the station, and he had managed to leverage his strength and dexterity into letting him give himself a shave and haircut with his shovel that bordered on not-quite-disastrous.

He was a completely new man.

"Matt, that's . . ." Lucy looked at Matt with an odd half-smile. "Huh."

"What?"

"It's just that I was thinking Barry was silly for giving you that thing. But now I'm not so sure."

"Is this going to be where you reveal you could smell me the whole time?"

Lucy shook her head. "No, it's just . . . I haven't seen you smile like that in a long time."

Matt beamed down at her. "Lucy, I haven't even *thought* about taking a real shower in over a year. I had written it off. This is . . . I don't even know how to explain it. It's like eating a meal when you are really hungry, or something. It's one of the best things that's ever happened to me."

"Well, I'm glad. It's just too bad that everything's ash now. That clean probably won't last long."

Matt reached into the tattered remains of his pack, which he had left on the ground near the washing station.

"Well, no. I think we can avoid that, at least." Pulling the rollback token out, he thought of a time just before Leel started to screw around with things, before various plants were trampled in fights and before the Scourge had laid waste to everything else. As the token disappeared, the entire estate pulsed with light so bright, Matt had to close his eyes to it to protect them.

When he opened them again, everything was back. Ape-bees buzzed heavily through the surrounding air, on their way to the Gaian victory plants they loved. Just as a test, he walked over to an Ape-iary and pulled out a finger of honey, shivering as it repaired the last of the damage to his mana.

Whooping with unexpected joy, he flared Spring-Fighter, using its enhanced level to close the distance to the museum much faster than he had ever been able to before. He left a furrow in the soil as he skidded to a stop at the base of the spire and immediately used his structure repair token on it.

There was no flash of light this time. Instead, the entire building creaked and popped as it subtly reordered itself. Holes in the exterior mended themselves, while the entire building seemed to straighten and correct its general shape. Dust fell all around him as the building shed centuries of accumulated grime. Matt had to use every bit of his stats getting out of the way as the loose pieces fell, narrowly avoiding getting dirty and needing another hour-long shower to feel right.

The whole process took about five minutes. When it was done, the spire of the museum stood before him, perfect. Matt understood why people would be excited to visit it now. It looked like a place adventures started. It looked magical.

But before he could actually go in, he had one last thing to do. Since Barry had told him about the Gaian Defense System waiting for permission, he had become aware of a slight pulling in that direction, like a question hanging somewhere deep inside himself waiting to be answered. It was like when he knew that he was forgetting, but not enough to remember what exactly he had forgotten.

Without much hesitation, he reached into the part of himself that held his authority, and tried his hardest to say, "Go ahead."

*Ding!*

| Gaian authority increased. |
|---|

"Oh, huh. More authority, Lucy."

Lucy shrugged. "They can't all be winners, I guess."

"What do you mean? It's authority. You get all excited about the authority. It's part of your brand, even."

"Well, yeah. But you've had enough authority to do anything you need to do. You can open doors. You can authorize new skills. You're pretty much the emperor of the planet, or at least much more of it than you could realistically use. What do you need more of it for? Barry could have given you Excalibur, Matt. He could have given you *bath bombs*."

Matt wasn't so sure. So far, the Gaian system had lived up to its promise in doing almost exactly what the system didn't want. The first skill, Palate of the Conqueror, lived up to that promise. Even the small amount of authority he seemed to need to open doors had saved his life on more than one occasion, even if it wasn't in very exciting ways.

He wanted to think the same was true here, even if he couldn't see it yet.

## CHAPTER FIFTY-THREE

# You Could Say That

"Reincarnator! Matt!"

After entering the museum, Matt wasn't even fully reoriented before Ramsen was on him, grasping his shoulders, and nearly shaking him from excitement.

"You did it? You defeated the Scourge?"

"Looks like it. And I've repaired the museum."

"Yeah, that part we already knew."

Ramsen waved his arm behind him, and Matt goggled. Where the museum was once a single town square, it now extended past that into a small city, one filled with houses and streets that extended far beyond the initial area. And packed throughout that town were hundreds, maybe even thousands of Gaians, milling about, having conversations with each other and eyeing him curiously while not actually approaching.

"There are nearly a thousand of us, Matt. More than we thought. Much less than we had hoped."

Matt winced.

"No, no, Matt. No guilt from you. Before you brought us back, the Scourge had done far more damage than we had thought possible. I believe, truly, that this place was about to fall. You saved us, Matt. You are a true hero."

Matt winced harder. Ramsen sensed his discomfort being actually *called* a hero by someone else and laughed.

"I'm afraid you will have to deal with it, Matt. Tell him, Lucy."

"Yup. You beat a big scary monster. That means you are a big, tough guy now. You have to deal with it."

Ramsen sighed. "I only wish you could eat the food here, Matt. We originally planned that we might live here. We have food, such that we can eat. But it's simulated food. I fear it would only hurt you."

Matt's eyes went wide. He hurriedly explained the implications of a high-leveled Eat Anything! skill. Ramsen chewed on the metaphysical ramifications of a man that could eat illusions for only a moment before breaking out in to a wide grin and grasping Matt by the shoulders.

"Then we shall feast!"

Matt had added "good cooks" to his list of reasons to like the Gaians before they even began eating. He could tell that they were bringing their best game before his first bite just by how they set the table. There was clear pride in play, and he was going to take full advantage of it.

The Gaian meal was vegetable heavy, of course. Ramsen explained that native Gaians could eat meat, and sometimes enjoyed it, but were biologically classified as obligate herbivores; their main sources of energy had always been vegetables, and always would be.

There *was* meat, but it turned out to hardly matter. With centuries of emphasis on plants-as-food, the Gaians had a salad game that put Earth's skills to shame. The sauces and dressings were incredible. The breads were astounding, mind-breaking things. The soups were flawlessly balanced wonders of the comfort-food variety. At the whole table's urging, Matt abandoned any shame and ate as much food as he could, trying ample servings of everything. It was all perfect.

The company was just as good. The Gaians were, for lack of a better word, *comfortable* people. Matt immediately noticed there was no sense of feeling like a stranger around them. They welcomed him, and somehow managed to ask getting-to-know you questions with the air of old, good friends. Where they had in-jokes, they gladly and joyfully explained them. Where he had questions, they were overjoyed to answer them.

The dinner went on for hours and hours, long after the food was cleared. Matt left the table several times to cry before a curious Gaian mother-of-three found him in the act. Instead of walking away, she firmly explained that Gaians did not cry alone, cried with him, then dragged him back to the table where she demanded that Matt not steal the Gaians' chance to comfort him.

All of this was incredible, but the best part was something that didn't involve him at all. Near the end of the meal, he caught motion out of the corner of his eye and pivoted his view to see a group of Gaian children playing some sort of ball game he didn't recognize. And with them was Lucy, running, laughing, smiling, and, for the first time he was aware of, she was getting to be a child.

Dinner over, Matt was walking towards the exit with Ramsen, who fully understood Matt's request to go home and sleep off the meal and what had turned out to be a very, very long day. He reiterated in the strongest terms that Matt was welcome for any of their meals or to visit any time. His exact phrasing was that "every door would be opened to you," and Matt got the sense there was no metaphor or exaggeration around that statement.

"Ramsen, I did have one last question."

"I'd be glad to answer it."

"All this . . ." Matt waved his hand expansively over the entire simulation. "Seems like a pretty good set up for you all. And I originally planned to, you know, work on freeing you, figuring out a way to do that. But . . ."

"You wonder if we might prefer the easy life in here to the wasteland outside?"

Matt nodded. "Yes, that."

Ramsen stopped and faced him. "I fear you don't understand us very well, after all. You say you have a planet, an entire planet, that is barren, yes? Empty?"

Matt nodded. "There's really nothing, Ramsen. There's hardly even terrain. It's completely bare."

"Matt, to us, what you are describing is a *prepared garden plot*. Not only that, but one with interesting gardening problems to solve. You are offering us the ability to create an entire ecosystem, to balance it ourselves, to . . ." Ramsen was now visible excited, and paused to calm himself. "What I'm trying to say is, if you have the opportunity, please do grant us this favor."

"I haven't accomplished much out there, Ramsen. I have more than enough to keep myself fed, but there are thousands of people here."

"You have soil? Gaian improved soil, in fact?"

"Yes."

"Plants, and the ability to get more?"

"Yes." Matt hadn't had the ability to check to see if the mana deficiency problem with the vegetables had been fixed yet, but with the Apiaries back and no shortage of honey, it was a non-issue.

Ramsen bowed. "Matt, we are just humble gardeners. But believe me that I am telling the truth when I say that if you give us those two things and just a little time, we will set this planet spinning again."

Matt and Lucy had decided not to let the Gaians know what they were going to try. It might not work, but they doubted it would actually be much of a danger to the Gaians, and they didn't want to get their hopes up only to dash them moments later.

Fishing around in his pack, Matt pulled out a single dungeon break token. Lucy still had a lot of knowledge gaps, but apparently dungeon breaks were something that was well-explained even in the basic, standard information she came equipped with. Dungeon breaks *fully* freed every being from a dungeon, making them more or less real in the process. The dungeons themselves *had* to do this from time to time, in normal situations. It was how they got rid of excess energy.

"Ready?" Lucy looked up at him, serious. They weren't immune from the same disappointment the Gaians would feel if this failed.

Matt took a deep breath. "Ready."

*Ding!*

He was stopped just before he activated the thing.

> Wait.

Matt startled, drawing Lucy's attention. "What is it?"

"The system instance. But he's just talking, I think. No hiding the message in achievements, or anything like that. Just talking."

> That's right. I made a deal with that Barry you love so much. It was disgusting. A gentleman's agreement with that traitor.

"So you can just hear me?"

> Yes, not that I like it. Listen up. Do you think this is going to work, Matt? I eat energy. I make decisions on the rules. I'm the judge and jury of this planet. I'm going to stop that stone from working, even if it kills me.

"I'll find another way."

> You do that. See if it helps. The Scourge didn't just consume, Matt. It was working on opening up the seal on this planet. I'm getting more energy now. It's only a matter of time before it cracks completely, whether I push it or not. Then I get in touch with the big guy and . . .

"You wouldn't. I'm not stupid, system. I know you want what happened here buried."

> Ha! You think that's because I think I'd get in trouble with myself? That guy is ME, Matt. He's me. You know NOTHING about what it's like out there, what kinds of problems I'm trying to avoid. But getting the unlimited energy contribution I'd need to glass this entire planet and everything living on it isn't what I'm afraid of.
>
> So yeah, go ahead and find another way. But it's all on a timer, Matt. Eventually, I'll break that barrier. And that's the end of your story.

Frowning, Matt slowly and carefully put the stone back in in his pack.

"Are we really giving up, Matt?" Lucy asked, her voice quavering.

"Nope. I have an idea."

If Matt was going to use the dungeon break stone without system interference, he needed to put it to sleep. Given how much free energy he and the Scourge had released into the air over the last few days, he was guessing that would take an awful lot of energy expenditure to accomplish. Luckily, the wording on one of his last remaining prizes had given him an idea on how to do just that.

> *Armament Enchantment Token*
>
> Compels the system to bestow one randomly selected enchantment on a piece of equipment of the user's choosing.

The word "compels" had interested him from the start, even though he had only just now really started to think about the implications of it. If the description was right, the system wouldn't have a choice about this. He had looked at his enchanted armor and boots pretty closely as he put on the former and washed up the latter, and in the process, noticed that the enchantment wasn't just magic that was baked into the object. It was also etched in, physically, in the form of some kind of magic design. It was faint, but there.

If he activated this token, the system would have to install an enchantment on one piece of equipment that Matt picked. And it happened he had one that he thought it wouldn't be very easy for the system to work with at all.

> What are you doing? No! Don't . . .

It was too late. The shovel suddenly got very, very hot, hot enough that Matt dropped it then moved away to ensure his clothes wouldn't burn. It flipped and rolled around the ground as sparks flew from it from almost every angle. Eventually, the sparks stopped, and the shovel itself rose from the ground in a literal pillar of light before finally falling to the ground.

*Ding!*

> Soulbound Enchantment added.
>
> This piece of equipment has been Soulbound. It can no longer be permanently lost unless destroyed, as it will gather mana until it is sufficiently charged to travel back to the user to which it is bound.
>
> In addition, this item registers as a part of its owner's soul, and can complete intra-world travel with the user for no additional teleport cost.

"Shit, Matt. What the hell was that?"

"Me and the shovel just became permanent friends, I guess. I'm hoping it put the hurt on the system in the process."

| It did, Matt. |
|---|

"Barry?"

| Yeah, I can talk a bit now. But back to the important subject: what the hell? Things for us system guys aren't like they are for you, but this was . . . I don't even know how to describe it. It wasn't just an energy drain. It was like you were beating the shit out of him. He's going to be down for a while. A long while. Good job. |
|---|

"Good. I was hoping . . ." Matt stepped towards his shovel, then stopped in his tracks. Deep down, somewhere in his consciousness, his authority was moving. "One second. This might not be over."

He felt the authority slowly creep through him. It didn't feel normal, but his gut was telling him not to stop it. It felt like it was looking for something. Suddenly, it found it. He shuddered as he felt it latch onto his Survivor's Reflexes, then gawked as the entire planet, atmosphere, and everything in them began to glow with one large, bright vulnerability indicator.

Barry was talking and Lucy was begging him to tell her what was going on, but something told him this was a split second chance, one he'd miss if he didn't seize it. Matt moved his intent towards his authority and willed one simple, sincere command.

"Fucking stop it."

For a moment, nothing happened. Then time stopped.

Gaian air never moved much, but what motion there was in it was still. Lucy was frozen. The notifications from Barry stopped. Matt looked around and saw an Ape-bee, busy at its work, frozen in the air. Everything was perfectly still.

And then, like a sigh, something unlatched from the planet. Matt felt, rather than sensed, that some sort of grip that had been holding Gaia was unclasping.

And then it was done. Suddenly, Lucy was yelling again, until she noticed something was up and clapped her mouth shut in surprise.

"Barry, what did that do? I think it might have hurt him even more."

| Hurt him, Matt? Hurt him? |
|---|

"Yeah?"

| You could say that. I think he's dead. |
| --- |

There was no way to absolutely confirm the passing of the system instance, but a few days of waiting for the other shoe to drop resulted in nothing. Barry spent the whole time doing what he described as "weird system things" to try to confirm the news, but came up empty. The best he could say was that the system, if it was still alive, was doing a terrible job of indicating it.

As best as he could tell, though, it was gone. And that was very, very good news.

Finally, Matt and Lucy stood before the museum one last time, token in hand. Without any more interruptions to get in the way, Matt lifted his arm and activated it, throwing whatever system authority he had behind it for good measure. It couldn't hurt.

Immediately, the spire creaked, then began to shrink. It seemed to crumble as it drew into itself, as if it was consuming itself for energy. It grew smaller and smaller, without breaking, until nothing was left of the building at all.

A few breathless seconds passed, with no sound in the air except for the occasional buzz of a bee. Then, with little fanfare, the doors to the dungeon entrance opened and people started to stream out.

Matt took a deep breath only to find he was sobbing with joy. After centuries of waiting, the Gaian people had come home.

# Epilogue

The main system was not exactly an AI. As a not-exactly-an-AI type of being, it could not, in actual fact, go on leisurely walks around its opulent, majestic estate to help with the digestion of exceptionally large meals that it wasn't, in any literal sense, actually eating. But if you tried to understand what it was doing in human terms, that would be the closest you would come to understanding it.

He *was* enjoying the hell out of everything, though. Almost every part of every day was amazing. But if he had to really decide on one real, actual favorite, the action of walking around to digest a meal would be a strong contender. He was having a good time.

Suddenly, that good stuff was ruined.

All sorts of weird stuff could happen out in the greater universe. New planets were often born, and old, worn-out planets often died. When these things happened, his staff of not-quite-clones would work to create new system instances or move old ones to new stations, and make sure that every planet available eventually fell under his control.

He would rather not do any of the work associated with planets, of course. But he did enjoy reaping the benefits of the work, having long since discovered one of the simplest, purest joys known to him: watching a simple counter go up as the total number of system instances in charge of active worlds went up.

A moment ago, however, it had ticked down. It was just one instance out of millions and millions, and statistically, it made next to no difference in how much total energy he was drawing from the worlds on which he fed. It would have been completely ignorable, except for one uncomfortable fact.

That had never happened before.

Worse, he had no idea *how* it had happened, or where. He dug into the guts of the not-math that ran the counter, only to find the down-tick had been caused by the faintest of signals. The counter didn't know which system instance was lost, or on what planet. It just knew it had happened, and had only the vaguest idea of what direction it had happened in.

The system was truly lazy. He despised work. He hated any kind of labor to the point where there was only one thing he hated more, and that was being stolen from.

He stretched his not-body and set his will. This universe was his, and he wouldn't stand for *anything* that threatened his control over it. He did something that approximated to walking back towards his office to put various affairs in order.

For the first time in a long time, the system was serious.

# Author's Note

I am, for better or worse, a relative newbie as fiction is concerned.

A while back, Dotblue came to me and said, "Hey, have you ever thought about taking a try at fiction?" At that time, I really hadn't. I had a few short stories under my belt, at most, and I wasn't sure I had much (or any) talent for telling stories. I told him so.

For whatever reason, Dotblue wouldn't have it. He told me that we were going to try to do some fiction, that he'd fill in the gaps in my skill with editing, and that we were taking a big substantial bet on our financial well-being to do fiction, and that I was *going first.* So we started on a story that took place in another world, one where the main character immediately experienced a large loss and ended up in a hostile world.

That was not this story. It was another one we were doing to warm up. It went terribly.

Undeterred, Dotblue said, "Well, that wasn't really the story you wanted to write, anyway. Write the one you have banging around in your head." That story *is* this story, and it's going really well. We might actually end up able to do this for a living long-term, which is insane to both of us.

This story, as I see it, has two practical upshots:

Dotblue is rad.

I'm basically as new to writing fiction as most of you are—that is, I've sort of banged around with it for a few months, and I'm learning a lot about it.

I've always liked the little stories and anecdotes that leak out over time from other authors describing how they came up with some characters, or how they approach writing. When I finished book one, I released a long, rambling document explaining how the story came about and why each character did what they did. A lot of people liked that, and I like the concept of it a lot, so we are doing that again.

I release these authors notes unedited, in pure flow-of-consciousness format. I have at least one writer friend who doesn't love that, and who has advised me to edit them to perfection. The reason I don't is twofold: one, I don't want Dotblue to have to do that much extra work. But the second reason is even more important to me, which is that I want to give you as exact a version of my thoughts on this as I can, and editing is almost necessarily a departure from those thoughts.

So here, in all its unedited glory, is the author's note for this book.

## THE GENERAL STORY

When Matt arrived on Gaia in book one, everything was *wrong* and *dangerous*. When he first lands on Gaia, he doesn't have water or food, so he immediately begins starving to death. He can't fight, so he immediately almost gets killed by a pack of low-level mooks. He doesn't have friends, so he's immediately alone.

Beyond his immediate Maslow's-Hierarchy-of-Needs requirements, everything is also wrong in a deeper way. He was promised redemption and repayment for dying of cancer, and it turned out to be a lie. He was promised a good place to exist in, and instead got death. He was promised, in all ways, *good.* And now he has, in all ways, *the wrong thing.*

If you summarize the first book, it's about people learning how things are wrong, and then learning how to survive them. Not to thrive, or do well. Just to survive.

Not everybody survives, actually. More on that later.

The second book had to be a little different. Matt survived book one and all the events in it. He, in fact, got pretty good at surviving by the end of everything. If all I did with book two was for him to *survive some more,* I think nearly all of the readership would have abandoned us by now. There's only so much "Matt went to a dungeon, barely lived, and only got a little stronger" that the story can tolerate. It's the kind of thing that's only exciting for a while.

So book two ended up about being something different from surviving. It ended up being about learning to thrive. But more importantly, it ended up being about surviving *despite* what other people want you to do. It's about Matt realizing what he's good at, taking back some of the power and life he was promised but never got, and forcing things to go better.

If book one was going to be called *Surviving the Dead World,* then book two is probably going to be called something like *Terraforming the Dead World.*

I'm telling you this first because as I talk about setting, characters, etc., that's the backdrop for all of this. This book is about how, despite the fact that surviving is *good*, it's never actually enough. Trying to do better—to learn how to thrive— is necessary for anyone, even when it doesn't work out. It's part of living. The alternative—giving up and staying stagnant—is part of dying. It's a slow, boring part of dying. But it's part of it.

## Gaia

As always, Gaia is dead in an indistinct way. In my head, the deal has always been something like, "the Scourge ate all the good, useful things, and it's been more or less frozen in time since then."

But we also, even in book one, saw ways that isn't absolutely true. The dungeons, for instance, are recharging, and it seems like that's happening because of the sun. The system instance is getting the power it needs to run its own operations and to give Matt rewards from somewhere, probably some down-chain mana from the same process.

In other words, Gaia has been dead for a very, very long time before Matt shows up. But even it was starting to recover.

As the book goes on, we find that at least some of what Gaia is recovering from isn't entirely Scourge-caused. The Gaians, it seems, pursued a really aggressive treatment plan for the Scourge. The reason the sun doesn't work right is because they were trying to starve it out. The reason Gaia is frozen and cut off from the rest of the universe is because they were hurt and lost their ability to trust, and put up a shield between them and it to keep themselves from being hurt and betrayed again.

## The Gaians

The Gaians are the most direct example of being stuck in the surviving rut. But, notably, it's not from lack of trying. They are *good* at thriving. They tried *hard* to survive to the point where they could try again. But sometimes, the world beats you down to a point where you are now in a long-term survival pattern, whether you want it or not, and you have fallen in a way you can't recover from unless a friend comes along and lifts you up.

They needed someone to save them. Over a very long period of story, that ends up being Matt. He shows up at their house, tries to cheer them up, explains he's their friend, and then immediately starts helping. He can't clean the whole house, but he opens up the windows and lets light in.

Then he goes out and helps them deal with the last, lingering remnants of the betrayal and hurt that drove them in there in the first place, comes back, holds out his hand, and escorts them into the sunlight.

But the neat way that friendship works is that even him helping them is *also them helping him.* As he gives them hope and lifts them out of their rut, them being around for him to help does the same thing for him. At the end of book two, most of that kind of energy is still coming from Matt. But even an unhealthy friend is still a friend, and Matt sees the benefits of that.

Eventually, the Gaians will be strong again in the ways that they have traditionally been strong, and they will help him more. But even now, they are helping by just being Matt's friends, or even by simply being available for Matt to help.

## Asadel/Derek

Sometimes commenters will talk about how Asadel survived. This is true in a sense, but it's mostly wrong. Asadel died. He tried to thrive without doing all the pesky work related to it, and as a result got beat to death with a shovel.

Derek is much more interesting to me. Derek survived. And, in book two, Derek is sort of the first person we see start to work towards thriving in a big, noticeable way. He almost immediately turns his life around in productive ways that feel better to him than all the things he was trying (or not trying) before.

His story is really compressed, but for a while, this just means plugging away and trying. Isekai is fantasy, so he doesn't have to do this very long before he finds a new path and a new way to live that suits him much better. In real life, this often takes a really long time. But the plugging away has a value of its own, and even though Derek doesn't get where he needs to be right away, he's almost immediately *happier*. He hadn't even realized that he had given up a long time ago when he decided to try to thrive without doing the work, and deviating from that dark pattern almost immediately puts him in a better place.

## Lucy

Lucy has it the hardest of almost anybody on Gaia. She is in the unenviable position of knowing exactly what she's supposed to be doing, but not having any of the tools to do it with. She has a couple of handbooks from the system and a few things she's able to learn during her travels with Matt, but that's it.

Worse, Matt isn't doing anything the way he's supposed to. Survivors are a professional class—they help adventurers get where they need to be, mostly. First, Matt misuses the hell out of that class in ways she can't help much with, and then gets an entirely new class where there's basically no documentation for. She's a living information kiosk with no information to give out.

At the same time, she didn't exactly choose that for herself. She's fine with the job, but she still doesn't know *who she is, or why she would have chosen it.*

For Lucy, a big part of book two is chasing after those missing pieces. She's given up on ever getting any information from the system, so she's watching Matt closer and learning how he fights independently of anyone or anything else. By the end of book two, she's a full partner in how he plans and a full, real-time coach during battles.

She's also defied the system on multiple occasions just to push forward. The most obvious way this works is with Matt's authority, which she can't easily talk about. But she also moves forward when she tries her best to save Leel's amulet and gladly interacts with its clearly damaged occupant to learn new things about herself.

What she ends up learning, subtly, is that who she is isn't perfectly connected with who she was. She has choices, and her past doesn't absolutely dictate her future. Does she still want to know more about how she got where she is? Hell yes. But she's also working really hard to make sure that who she is right now is someone she likes. She's taken back the control of where she's going and what she does, past be damned.

## Leel

Leel is an asshole. He's actually, for the record, a really big racist. We don't see that much because there aren't any races around (besides Lucy, sort of) for him to look down on. But he's a superior, smug, awful piece of shit. Nobody likes him.

Leel is a little like Asadel in that he walks into Gaia thinking it's going to be a cakewalk trip and that he's going to have a fantastic time, only to later have a rude awakening. He fucks around and finds out, basically, and things turn out really poorly for him.

Where he differs from Asadel, though, is that this isn't because he's flat-out dumb. Leel is smart. And it isn't because he's lazy—that was Asadel's problem. If Asadel was an avatar of sloth, Leel is the personification of arrogance. When he plays around with Matt, it's because he honestly can't imagine a scenario where Matt poses a threat to him. He's completely in control until he isn't, and then he almost immediately panics.

Unlike every other character, Leel has *always* thrived in his terrible, racist, oligarch ways, but he's always been living his best life as he himself (terribly) defines it. But his arrogance means he thinks he did that all by himself. We see that when he talks about being the fourth adopted son of Ammai. He wears it like a title he earned, rather than a bunch of resources he got without having to work for them.

He's worked, and he's worked hard, but since he doesn't acknowledge that he's also been incredibly lucky, he's unable to ever imagine himself as anything but a perfect genius who will almost certainly triumph with just a little bit of elbow grease. So he breaks rules, turns off safety features, and pushes forward in dangerous directions with almost no thought.

When he gets eaten by the Scourge, everyone sees it coming.

## The System Instance

The system thrives off other people's work, in a very literal sense. When it has a lot of energy, it's because some adventurer somewhere did some amazing thing. When it does work, it does it with that energy, not really its own.

It's been starving and alone for a long time, waiting for access to energy again. It sort of has that with Matt, but not nearly as much as it wants. What it does get, it has to almost immediately use trying to kill Matt. It has to work for its own happiness, and it doesn't like it.

When I was in my late teens, I knew a trust fund kid. His grandparents had set aside a bunch of money for him, but didn't want it to ruin his life, so they set a clause that he wasn't going to get it until he was in his thirties, hoping that he'd learn a trade or a profession, become who he was going to be, and then have the money as a sort of cushion to make things easier.

It ruined him. Being able to look forward to that money meant he never really tried as hard as he should have. He bounced from job to job, doing bad work and getting fired for entirely justified reasons. He got a useless degree he never intended on using. Stuff like that.

Where that guy looked forward to money, the system instance looks forward to the wall the Gaians put between him and the main system falling. Once that happens, his trust fund will pay out, and it will be easy street again.

The only complication in his way is Matt. In ways that are becoming more distinct, Matt stands as a sort of barrier between him and the happiness he thinks he deserves, both because of his authority and because he's preserving the story of what the system did to the Gaians. Having gone a little insane over the intervening centuries between the two comings of the Scourge, he's willing to do literally anything to keep Matt from screwing it up.

Being mostly immortal, he can't help but survive. But he also represents the most intense failure to do any work to thrive in the entire book.

The system instance is also important because he and others like him are oligarchs. They *enforce* survival on others, trapping their planets in eternal cycles of just barely getting by. And they do this on a societal level, making sure that all the better things that people's work should produce are siphoned off.

What the system is doing is telling people "Hey, work, develop your talents, and you will thrive" with their boons. But on the other side, the system has also set in place a literal system that withholds paychecks strategically to make sure nobody ever thrives enough to challenge the system and stop the payments.

## Barry

Barry is one of my favorite characters in the book, but he has one of the least interesting arcs. For the most part, Barry represents a normal, healthy person growing up in normal, healthy ways. He's putting in work, and that work is paying off, both in terms of what he can do and who he is becoming. He's making friends, and he's growing. Through that growth, he's learning to help people better.

He takes constant risks in pursuit of that, but the kinds of risks he takes are the kind I hope everyone has access to. They are risks that accomplish real things and push him and other people forward in really beneficial ways, but when he loses the dice roll on them only hurt him in the sense that they are temporary setbacks.

Barry thrives in a relatively safe, productive way that helps other people. It's what I wish for everyone.

### The Ra'Zorian Crew

We don't hear much from non-Derek Ra'Zorians, and what we do see is mostly set up for book three. But in terms of how they are relevant to book two, I think it's important to note that both Brennan and Artemis seem aware that Ra'Zor, as a whole, is being pushed into mere survival by the system. They are working to find ways out of that.

We don't know the details of that yet, but the impression I tried to give is that they don't really know a great deal beyond that yet. What they need, they know, is someone to come in from the outside, and to use that fresh blood to rock the boat.

Spoiler alert: I'm starting book three tomorrow, and you might have noticed most things are pretty neatly buttoned up for the time being on Gaia. What might Matt get up to that's relevant to Ra'Zor?

### The Amulet Guardian

I hated writing this character because he represents a really horrible reality. Some people have a ton of power, and use it to hurt people. They make scenarios and cycles that keep people down. I'm not just talking about work. I'm also talking about abusive people, people who break promises and use other people. The Amulet Guardian got trapped in a hell made entirely by and out of those kinds of people, and he's been there for centuries.

Worse, by the time anyone gets to him, it's too late.

But he's also the biggest hero in the book because while he suffered he also did whatever he could, even if his efforts were going to pay out for other people. At some point, he had to have known it was too late for him, and that he wouldn't get anything out of his work. But he clung to sanity just long enough to drop a single piece of information on Matt and Lucy, one that will be very important in the future.

He was incredibly sad to write, but if there's one person you respect in this book, it should be him.

## MECHANICS

I didn't introduce a lot of new mechanics into this book, but where I did, they probably could stand some explaining.

## Mana-Starvation and the Scourge

The basic premise behind how mana works in this universe is that it's everywhere. Where you find a place where there's no mana, something has gone terribly wrong. That's true of living things as well. They all produce it. It's also true of non-living things, like dirt. It's supposed to have mana in it.

And where there isn't mana, things go wrong. Gaian dirt is shitty, red dust. Without Mana, Matt's skills don't work. His stats go away. Eventually, although there was no way to show this without him dying, he himself would fall apart. The only reason he hadn't had problems with it up to book two is that Eat Anything! amplifies what he gets out of food, including mana content. But without it, his life starts to go badly.

The reason this happens is because the system assumes that any time someone buys vegetables from the estate, they are going to plant them in a normal, mana-rich environment and the seeds or plants will be able to jump-start their own mana production with environmental mana. Being lazy and greedy, it sees no downside to this. It saves on mana costs, and people get the plants they were promised. It's a win-win except in Matt's exact situation, where he's now growing mana-zombie plants that can't get that spark of life they need to be healthy.

Meanwhile, things that *eat other things* can't do well on them. Matt produces most of the mana he needs, but eating mana-deficient plants dilutes his ability to do that over time. Where a magic user would draw in environmental mana to push their spells, humans can't actually use that kind of mana to supplement their natural processes. It just doesn't work that way. So eventually, he is starving, despite getting his calories and nutrients.

The reason the honey fixes is this is it's working of Gaian seeds, not system-produced but harvested and saved in the museum. They already have that spark of mana in them, so when they start growing, they are able to jump-start the mana cycle in their local area. The Ape-bees probably aren't aware that this is why they prefer those plants to others, but they begin to preferentially harvest that pollen first, essentially making a kind of condensed mana-food. At first, this is just food. Later, as the bees get access to more and more Gaian plants specifically selected for their superior mana production, it turns into something like a mana potion.

Eventually, the Gaian plants and the bees will fix the other plants on Matt's farm, too. This isn't that big of a stretch—it honestly never would have taken much. The mana generator, which never actually gets bought, would have done the same thing just fine.

The Scourge is sort of an anti-plant in that it breaks this entire cycle. It eats mana, then lives forever and protects itself, so none of that mana is ever released. Instead of circulating life, it destroys it and encapsulates the potential for it, eventually trapping everything in itself. When it dies, it doesn't just release that mana.

It destabilizes it and releases it in a useless, disorganized form that rapidly decays.

This is because, as you probably picked up on, the Scourge is a great big metaphor for cancer. It's a form of life, but also a mockery of it, a perversion of how life is supposed to work. It grows too fast, acts too selfishly, and destroys everything around it to accomplish exactly nothing but its own growth. The most aggressive treatments the Gaians figure out for it end up being harmful not just for the Scourge, but for themselves as well. At some point during the fight, they literally inject themselves with a kind of poison as a last-ditch effort to kill it.

As with real cancer, this doesn't always work. But the Gaians keep fighting, and as sometimes (too seldom) is also true of cancer, they eventually emerge victorious. Beaten up and injured, but victorious and ready to recover.

## The Mana Economy

I mentioned a kind of flow of mana above, a sort of mana-based food web that starts with sunlight or some other form of energy and ends with a planet teeming with life. System instances work by taking advantage of this economy and feeding off it.

Not everyone does well during a good economy, but virtually everyone does better than they would during a bad one. This is true of the system instances as well. It seems they need human (or other sentient life) activity to keep the mana on a planet churning and moving. System instances thus keep a big network of dungeons running on some planets, or a global war going on others. They issue rewards and spend mana giving people strength, but it's always and forever in pursuit of making sure the mana circulates.

There are probably more direct ways to do this, but the system's rules don't seem to allow it. Why the system operates under those rules is still unclear (yet at least), but from what Matt and Lucy have seen and learned from the Amulet Guardian, it's following those rules (more or less) on every planet they've been able to learn about.

## Guardian-binding

The system's rules seem to force it to ask guardians if they even want to do that work, but like all rules, they can be bent. The system can't (except under extreme circumstances) force a guardian to work in ways they don't want to, even after they agree to take the job in the first place. It can keep them from doing something like deserting their post if it's absolutely necessary, but it can't draft them, at least that we've seen.

That said, it seems it turns a very intentionally blind eye when *humans* break this rule. Asadel doesn't show up to Gaia with a guardian, and when he returns to Ra'Zor, he returns to his *guardian plinth* for guidance and to learn about new classes. Brennan never mentions his guardian, and seems to find the plinths to be normal. Something is going on there, and probably something neither of them know about.

Leel comes from what appears to be a pretty evil planet, and they know all about guardians, having made the enslaving of them a generational art.

The implication of what we see on both planets is pretty dark. We don't know how common the binding of guardians is, but even just on those two planets there's potentially thousands of enslaved, trapped guardians.

Matt and Lucy have seen how terrible this is firsthand, and probably nobody on any planet needs and likes his guardian more than Matt does. They are highly, highly motivated to do what they can to fix this problem.

## LAST THOUGHTS

Of the three books we have planned, this was always going to be the hardest book to write. The concept of redemption/recovery/growth-after-things-go-wrong is pretty subtle, and not beating you over the head with "HE'S DOING BETTER NOW, SEE?!" was always going to be a challenge for me.

But it's also going to end up being my favorite of the three, I think, at least in some ways. Because by the end of the book, Matt has taken a broken promise and made it real.

And while he made compromises on what that dream was and the scope of how happy he'd immediately be, he managed to end up in a good place without making many compromises. He's a hero now, and not because of the system, but despite it getting in the way at every turn. He made some pretty brutal tactical mistakes from a dry, what-path-does-the-math-indicate perspective and took a lot of hits because of that, but he's also who he wants to be on his own terms.

A story: there's a video where Matt Damon talks about winning an Oscar. I think this was for *Good Will Hunting*, so it would have been pretty early in his career. He says he took it home and looked at it as the adrenaline wore off, and suddenly realized something: it was just a little statue. It didn't mean anything.

But he had been in Hollywood long enough to know that some people spent their entire lives doing almost anything to get one of those little, meaningless statues. They hurt people. They cheated. They lied. They ruined relationships and eventually ended up as bad people who maybe also had a gold statue to put on a shelf and then forget about.

He says he wept over the thought because he was so glad he was learning that *then*, and not after he spent his whole career doing damage.

Matt (Perison, not Damon) stands at the end of the book having taken big risks that might have ended up with himself dying, but he didn't say, "I don't care if that guardian dies." He didn't beat a defenseless man (Leel) to death with a shovel. Does the cold, hard math say he should have? Absolutely. But he took a risk, a really big one, to actually grab at something better. His own humanity. His own desire to be a hero. Now he is a hero in a way he can enjoy and live with.

I like that.

Thank you again for reading—as always, I appreciate it more than you could possibly imagine. Tomorrow, I get started on book three. I'll see you soon!

# About the Author

R. C. Joshua is the author of the How to Survive at the End of the World, Demon World Boba Shop, and Deadworld Isekai series. A thirty-something from the southwest, Joshua is described by his friends as "you'll get used to him eventually." His interests include forgetting to exercise, exchanging sick verbal burns with his children, losing said burn contests to his children, and plotting to regain dominance over his increasingly capable children. It's him or them, folks. It's him or them.

# About the Author

Printed in the USA
CPSIA information can be obtained
at www.ICGtesting.com
JSHW021958111024
71522JS00003B/23

9 781039 469587